RUBY

RUBY

V. C. Andrews

WHEELER PUBLISHING, INC.

★ AN AMERICAN COMPANY ★

Following the death of Virginia Andrews, the Andrews family worked with a carefully selected writer to organize and complete Virginia Andrews' stories and to create additional novels, of which this is one, inspired by her storytelling genius.

This book is a work of fiction. Names, characters, places and incidents are either products of the author's imagination or are used fictitiously. Any resemblance to actual events or locales or persons, living or dead, is entirely coincidental.

Published in Large Print by arrangement with Pocket Books, a division of Simon & Schuster Inc. in the United States and Canada.

Wheeler Large Print Book Series.

Set in 16 pt. Plantin.

Library of Congress Cataloging-in-Publication Data

Andrews, V. C. (Virginia C.)
    Ruby / V. C. Andrews.
      p. cm.
    ISBN 1-56895-074-8 : $25.95
    1. Family—Louisiana—Fiction. 2. Girls—Louisiana—Fiction.
    3. Large type books. I. Title.
    [PS3551.N454R83 1994]
    813'.54—dc20
                                      94-8055
                                         CIP

Prologue

During the first fifteen years of my life, my birth and the events surrounding it were a mystery; as much a mystery as the number of stars that shone in the night sky over the bayou or where the silvery catfish hid on days when Grandpere couldn't catch one to save his life. I knew my mother only from the stories Grandmere Catherine and Grandpere Jack told me and from the few faded sepia photographs of her that we had in pewter frames. It seemed that for as long as I could remember, I always felt remorseful when I stood at her grave and gazed at the simple tombstone that read:

> Gabrielle Landry
> Born May 1, 1927
> Died October 27, 1947

for my birth date and the date of her death were one and the same. Everyday and every night, I carried in my secret heart the ache of guilt when my birthday came around, despite the great effort Grandmere went through to make it a happy day. I knew it was as hard for her to be joyful as it was for me.

But over and above my mother's sad, sad death when I was born, there were dark questions I could never ask, even if I knew how, because I'd be much too scared it would make my grandmother's face, usually so loving, take on that closed, hooded look I dreaded. Some days she sat silently in her rocker and stared at me for what seemed like hours. Whatever the answers were, the truth had torn my grandparents to pieces; it had sent Grandpere Jack into the swamp to live alone in his shack. And from that day forward, Grandmere Catherine could not think of him without great anger flashing from her eyes and sorrow burning in her heart.

The unknown lingered over our house in the bayou; it hung in the spiderwebs that turned the swamps into a jeweled world on moonlit nights; it was draped over the cypress trees like the Spanish moss that dangled over their branches. I heard it in the whispering warm summer breezes and in the water lapping against the clay. I even felt it in the piercing glance of the marsh hawk, whose yellow-circled eyes followed my every move.

I hid from the answers just as much as I longed to know them. Words that carried enough weight and power to keep two people apart who should love and cherish each other could only fill me with fear.

I would sit by my window and stare into the darkness of the swamp on a warm, spring night, letting the breeze that swept in over the swamps from the Gulf of Mexico cool my face; and I would listen to the owl.

But instead of his unearthly cry of "Who, Who, Who," I would hear him call "Why, Why, Why" and I would embrace myself more tightly to keep the trembling from reaching my pounding heart.

Book
One

1

Grandmere's Powers

A loud and desperate rapping on our screen door echoed through the house and drew both my and Grandmere Catherine's attention from our work. That night we were upstairs in the *grenier,* the loom room, weaving the cotton jaune into blankets we would sell at the stand in front of our house on weekends when the tourists came to the bayou. I held my breath. The knocking came again, louder and more frantic.

"Go down and see who's there, Ruby," Grandmere Catherine whispered loudly. "Quickly. And if it's your Grandpere Jack soaked in that swamp whiskey again, shut the door as fast as you can," she added, but something in the way her dark eyes widened said she knew this was someone else and something far more frightening and unpleasant.

A strong breeze had kicked up behind the thick layers of dark clouds that enclosed us like a shroud, hiding the quarter moon and stars in the April Louisiana sky. This year spring had been more like summer. The days and nights were so hot and humid I found mildew on my shoes in the morning. At noon the sun made the goldenrod glisten and drove the gnats and flies into a frenzy to find cool shade. On clear nights I could see where the swamp's Golden Lady spiders had come

5

out to erect their giant nets for their nightly catch of beetles and mosquitos. We had stretched fabric over our windows that kept out the insects but let in whatever cool breeze came up from the Gulf.

I hurried down the stairs and through the narrow hallway that ran straight from the rear of the house to the front. The sight of Theresa Rodrigues's face with her nose against the screen stopped me in my tracks and turned my feet to lead. She looked as white as a water lily, her coffee black hair wild and her eyes full of terror.

"Where's your grandmere?" she cried frantically.

I called out to my grandmother and then stepped up to the door. Theresa was a short, stout girl three years older than I. At eighteen, she was the oldest of five children. I knew her mother was about to have another. "What's wrong, Theresa?" I asked, joining her on the galerie. "Is it your mother?"

Immediately, she burst into tears, her heavy bosom heaving and falling with the sobs, her face in her hands. I looked back into the house in time to see Grandmere Catherine come down the stairs, take one look at Theresa, and cross herself.

"Speak quickly, child," Grandmere Catherine demanded, rushing up to the door.

"My mama . . . gave birth . . . to a dead baby," Theresa wailed.

"Mon Dieu," Grandmere Catherine said, and crossed herself once more. "I felt it," she muttered, her eyes turned to me. I recalled the moments during our weaving when she had raised her gaze and had seemed to listen to the sounds of

6

the night. The cry of a raccoon had sounded like the cry of a baby.

"My father sent me to fetch you," Theresa moaned through her tears. Grandmere Catherine nodded and squeezed Theresa's hand reassuringly.

"I'm coming right away."

"Thank you, Mrs. Landry. Thank you," Theresa said, and shot off the porch and into the night, leaving me confused and frightened. Grandmere Catherine was already gathering her things and filling a split-oak basket. Quickly, I went back inside.

"What does Mr. Rodrigues want, Grandmere? What can you do for them now?"

When Grandmere was summoned at night, it usually meant someone was very sick or in pain. No matter what it was, my stomach would tingle as if I had swallowed a dozen flies that buzzed around and around inside.

"Get the butane lantern," she ordered instead of answering. I hurried to do so. Unlike the frantic Theresa Rodrigues whose terror had lit her way through the darkness, we would need the lantern to go from the front porch and over the marsh grass to the inky black gravel highway. To Grandmere the overcast night sky carried an ominous meaning, especially tonight. As soon as we stepped out and she looked up, she shook her head and muttered, "Not a good sign."

Behind us and beside us, the swamp seemed to come alive with her dark words. Frogs croaked, night birds cawed, and gators slithered over the cool mud.

7

At fifteen I was already two inches taller than Grandmere Catherine who was barely five-feet-four in her moccasins. Diminutive in size, she was still the strongest woman I knew, for besides her wisdom and her grit, she carried the powers of a *Traiteur*, a treater; she was a spiritual healer, someone unafraid to do battle with evil, no matter how dark or insidious that evil was. Grandmere always seemed to have a solution, always seemed to reach back in her bag of cure-alls and rituals and manage to find the proper course of action. It was something unwritten, something handed down to her, and whatever was not handed down, she magically knew herself.

Grandmere was left-handed, which to all of us Cajuns meant she could have spiritual powers. But I thought her power came from her dark onyx eyes. She was never afraid of anything. Legend had it that one night in the swamp she had come face-to-face with the Grim Reaper himself and she'd stared down Death's gaze until he realized she was no one to tangle with just yet.

People in the bayou came to her to cure their warts and their rheumatism. She had her secret medicines for colds and coughs and was said even to know a way to prevent aging, although she never used it because it would be against the natural order of things. Nature was sacred to Grandmere Catherine. She extracted all of her remedies from the plants and herbs, the trees and animals that lived near or in the swamps.

"Why are we going to the Rodrigues house, Grandmere? Isn't it too late?"

"Couchemal," she muttered, and mumbled a

prayer under her breath. The way she prayed made my spine tingle and, despite the humidity, gave me a chill. I clenched my teeth together as hard as I could, hoping they wouldn't chatter. I was determined to be as fearless as Grandmere, and most of the time I succeeded.

"I guess that you are old enough for me to tell you," she said so quietly I had to strain to hear. "A couchemal is an evil spirit that lurks about when an unbaptized baby dies. If we don't drive it away, it will haunt the family and bring them bad luck," she said. "They should have called me as soon as Mrs. Rodrigues started her birthing. Especially on a night like this," she added darkly.

In front of us, the glow of the butane lantern made the shadows dance and wiggle to what Grandpere Jack called "The Song of the Swamp," a song not only made up of animal sounds, but also the peculiar low whistle that sometimes emerged from the twisted limbs and dangling Spanish moss we Cajuns called Spanish Beard when a breeze traveled through. I tried to stay as close to Grandmere as I could without knocking into her and my feet were moving as quickly as they could to keep up. Grandmere was so fixed on our destination, and on the astonishing task before us that she looked like she could walk through the pitch darkness.

In her split-oak basket, Grandmere carried a half-dozen small totems of the Virgin Mary, as well as a bottle of holy water and some assorted herbs and plants. The prayers and incantations she carried in her head.

"Grandmere," I began. I needed to hear the sound of my own voice. *Qu'est-ce—*"

"English," she corrected quickly. "Speak only in English." Grandmere always insisted we speak English, especially when we left the house, even though our Cajun language was French. "Someday you will leave this bayou," she predicted, "and you will live in a world that maybe looks down on our Cajun language and ways."

"Why would I leave the bayou, Grandmere?" I asked her. "And why would I stay with people who looked down on us?"

"You just will," she replied in her usual cryptic manner. "You just will."

"Grandmere," I began again, "why would a spirit haunt the Rodrigueses anyway? What have they done?"

"They've done nothing. The baby was born dead. It came in the body of the infant, but the spirit was unbaptized and has no place to go, so it will haunt them and bring them bad luck."

I looked back. Night fell like a leaden curtain behind us, pushing us forward. When we made the turn, I was happy to see the lighted windows of the Butes, our closest neighbor. The sight of it allowed me to pretend that everything was normal.

"Have you done this many times before, Grandmere?" I knew my grandmother was called to perform many rituals, from blessing a new house to bringing luck to a shrimp or oyster fisherman. Mothers of young brides unable to bear children called her to do whatever she could to make them fertile. More often than not, they

10

became pregnant. I knew of all these things, but until tonight I had never heard of a couchemal.

"Unfortunately, many times," she replied. "As did Traiteurs before me as far back as our days in the old country."

"And did you always succeed in chasing away the evil spirit?"

"Always," she replied with a tone of such confidence that I suddenly felt safe.

Grandmere Catherine and I lived alone in our toothpick-legged house with its tin roof and recessed galerie. We lived in Houma, Louisiana, which was in Terrebonne Parish. Folks said the parish was only two hours away from New Orleans by car, but I didn't know if that was true since I had never been to New Orleans. I had never left the bayou.

Grandpere Jack had built our house himself more than thirty years ago when he and Grandmere Catherine had first been married. Like most Cajun homes, our house was set on posts to keep us above the crawling animals and give us some protection from the floods and dampness. Its walls were built out of cypress wood and its roof out of corrugated metal. Whenever it rained, the drops would tap our house like a drum. The rare stranger to come to our house was sometimes bothered by it, but we were as accustomed to the drumming as we were to the shrieks of the marsh hawks.

"Where does the spirit go when we drive it away?" I asked.

"Back to limbo where it can do good God-fearing folks no harm," she replied.

11

We Cajuns, who were descendants of the Arcadians driven from Canada in the mid-1700s, believed in a spirituality that commingled Catholicism with pre-Christian folklore. We went to church and prayed to saints like Saint Medad, but we clung to our superstitions and age-old beliefs as firmly. Some, like Grandpere Jack, clung to them more. He was often involved in some activity to ward off bad luck and had an assortment of talismans like alligator teeth and dried deer ears to wear around his neck or carry on his belt at times. Grandmere said no man in the bayou needed them more than he did.

The gravel road stretched and turned ahead, but at the pace we were keeping, the Rodrigueses' cypress wood house now bleached a gray-white patina, soon loomed before us. We heard the wailing coming from within and saw Mr. Rodrigues on the front galerie holding Theresa's four-year-old brother in his arms. He sat in a split-oak rocking chair and stared into the night as though he had already seen the evil spirit. It chilled me even more, but I moved forward as quickly as Grandmere Catherine did. The moment he set eyes on her, his expression of sorrow and fear turned to one of hope. It felt good to see how much Grandmere was respected.

"Thanks for comin' so fast, Mrs. Landry. Thanks for comin'," he said, and rose quickly. "Theresa," he cried, and Theresa emerged from the house to take her little brother from him. He opened the door for my grandmother, and after I set the lantern down, I followed her inside.

Grandmere Catherine had been to the

Rodrigueses' house before and went directly to Mrs. Rodrigues's bedroom. She lay there, her eyes closed, her face ashen, her black hair spread out over the pillow. Grandmere took her hand and Mrs. Rodrigues looked up weakly. Grandmere Catherine fixed her gaze on Mrs. Rodrigues and stared hard as though searching for a sign. Mrs. Rodrigues struggled to raise herself.

"Rest, Delores," Grandmere Catherine said. "I am here to help."

"Yes," Mrs. Rodrigues said in a loud whisper. She clutched Grandmere's wrist. "I felt it, Catherine. I felt its heartbeat start and stop and then I felt the couchemal slip away. I felt it . . ."

"Rest, Delores. I will do what has to be done," Grandmere Catherine promised. She patted her hand and turned to me. She nodded slightly and I followed her out to the galerie, where Theresa and the other Rodrigues children waited wide-eyed.

Grandmere Catherine reached into her split-oak basket and plucked out one of her bottles of holy water. She opened it carefully and turned to me.

"Take the lantern and lead me around the house," she said. "Every cistern, every pot with water in it, needs a drop or two of the holy water, Ruby. Make sure we don't miss a one," she warned. I nodded, my legs trembling, and we began our foray.

In the darkness, an owl hooted, but when we turned the corner of the house, I heard something slither through the grass. My heart was thumping so hard, I thought I'd drop the lantern. Would the evil spirit do something to try to stop us? As if

13

to answer my question, something cool and wet slipped past me in the darkness and just grazed my left cheek. I gasped aloud. Grandmere Catherine turned to reassure me.

"The spirit is hiding in a cistern or a pot. It has to hide in water. Don't be afraid," she coached, and then stopped by a cistern used to gather rainwater from the roof of the Rodrigueses' house. She opened her bottle and tipped it so as to spill only a drop or two into it and then closed her eyes and mumbled a prayer. We did the same thing at every barrel and every pot until we circled the house and returned to the front where Mr. Rodrigues, Theresa, and the other two children waited in anticipation.

"I'm sorry, Mrs. Landry," Mr. Rodrigues said, "but Theresa's just told me the children have an old gumbo pot out back. It's surely got some rainwater in it from the downpour late this afternoon."

"Show me," Grandmere ordered Theresa, who nodded and led the way. She was so nervous, she couldn't find it at first.

"We've got to find it," Grandmere Catherine warned. Theresa began to cry.

"Take your time, Theresa," I told her, and squeezed her arm gently to reassure her. She sucked in a deep breath and nodded. Then she bit down on her lower lip and concentrated until she remembered the exact location and took us to it. Grandmere knelt down and dropped the holy water in, whispering her prayer as she did so.

Perhaps it was my overworked imagination; perhaps not, but I thought I saw something pale gray, something that resembled a baby, fly up and

14

way. I smothered a cry, afraid I would
Theresa even more. Grandmere Catherine
up and we returned to the house to offer ou
condolences. She set a totem of the Virgin
at the front door and told Mr. Rodrigues to
sure it remained there for forty days and for
nights. She gave him another one and told him t
put it at the foot of his and his wife's bed and leave
it there just as long. Then we started back to our
own home.

"Do you think you chased it off, Grandmere?"
I asked when we were sufficiently away from the
house and none of the Rodrigues family would
hear.

"Yes," she said. Then she turned to me and
added, "I wish I had the power to chase away the
evil spirit that dwells in your grandpere as easily.
If I thought it would do any good, I'd bathe him
in holy water. Goodness knows, he could use the
washing anyway."

I smiled, but my eyes soon filled with tears as
well. For as long as I could remember, Grandpere
Jack had lived apart from us, lived in his trapper's
shack in the swamp. Most of the time, Grandmere
Catherine had only bad things to say about him
and refused to set eyes on him whenever he did
come around, but sometimes, her voice got softer,
her eyes warmer, and she would wish he would do
this or that to help himself or change his ways.
She didn't like me to go poling a pirogue through
the swamps to visit him.

"God forbid you turn over that flimsy canoe or
fall out. He'd probably be too soaked with whiskey
to hear your cries for help and then there are the

d gators to contend with, Ruby. He a.
he effort of the journey," she'd mutter,
e never stopped me and even though she
aded not to care or want to know about him,
oticed she always managed to listen when I
scribed one of my visits to Grandpere.

How many nights had I sat by my window and looked up at the moon peeking between two clouds and wished and prayed that somehow we could be a family. I had no mother and no father, but only Grandmere Catherine who had been and still was a mother to me. Grandmere always said Grandpere could barely care for himself, much less substitute as a father for me. Still, I dreamed. If they were together again . . . if we were all together in our house, we would be like a normal family. Perhaps then, Grandpere Jack wouldn't drink and gamble. All of my friends at school had regular families, with brothers and sisters and two parents to come home to and love.

But my mother lay buried in the cemetery a half mile away and my father . . . my father was a blank face with no name, a stranger who had come passing through the bayou and met my mother at a *fais dodo*, a Cajun dance. According to Grandmere Catherine, the love they made so wildly and care-free that night resulted in my birth. What hurt me beside my mother's tragic death was the realization that somewhere out there lived a man who never knew he had a daughter, had me. We would never set eyes on each other, never exchange a word. We wouldn't even see each other's shadows or silhouettes like two fishing boats passing in the night.

When I was a little girl I invented a game: the Daddy Game. I would study myself in the mirror and then try to imagine my facial characteristics on a man. I would sit at my drawing table and sketch his face. Conjuring the rest of him was harder. Sometimes I made him very tall, as tall as Grandpere Jack, and sometimes just an inch or so taller than I was. He was always a well-built, muscular man. I decided long ago that he must have been good-looking and very charming to have won my mother's heart so quickly.

Some of the drawings became watercolor paintings. In one of them, I set my imaginary father in a fais dodo hall, leaning against a wall, smiling because he had first set eyes on my mother. He looked sexy and dangerous, just the way he must have looked to draw my beautiful mother to him. In another painting, I had him walking down a road, but turned to wave good-bye. I always thought there was a promise in his face in that picture, the promise of return.

Most of my paintings had a man in them that in my imagination was my father. He was either on a shrimp boat or poling a pirogue through one of the canals or across one of the ponds. Grandmere Catherine knew why the man was in my pictures. I saw how sad it made her, but I couldn't help myself. Lately, she had urged me to paint swamp animals and birds more often than people.

On weekends, we would put some of my paintings out with our woven blankets, sheets, and towels, our split-oak baskets and palmetto hats. Grandmere would also put out her jars of herbal cures for headaches, insomnia, and coughs. Sometimes, we had a pickled snake or a large bullfrog in a jar because the tourists who drove by and stopped loved to buy them. Many loved to eat Grandmere's gumbo or jambalaya. She would ladle out small bowls of it and they would sit at the benches and tables in front of our house and enjoy a real Cajun lunch.

All in all, I suppose my life in the bayou wasn't as bad as the lives some motherless and fatherless children led. Grandmere Catherine and I didn't have many worldly goods, but we had our small safe home and we were able to get by with our loom work and handicrafts. From time to time, although admittedly not often enough, Grandpere Jack would drop by to give us part of what he made trapping muskrats, which was the main way he earned a living these days. Grandmere Catherine was too proud or too angry at him to accept it gracefully. Either I would take it or Grandpere would just leave it on the kitchen table.

"I don't expect no thanks from her," he would mutter to me, "but at least she could acknowledge I'm here leaving her the damn money. It's hard earned, it is," he would declare in a loud voice on the galerie steps. Grandmere Catherine would say nothing in reply, but usually keep on doing whatever she was doing inside.

"Thank you, Grandpere," I would tell him.

"Ah, I don't want your thanks. It's not your thanks I'm asking for, Ruby. I just want someone to know I ain't dead and buried or swallowed by a gator. Someone to at least have the decency to look at me," he often moaned, still loud enough for Grandmere to hear.

Sometimes, she appeared in the doorway if he said something that got to her.

"Decency," she cried from behind the screen door. "Did I hear you, Jack Landry, talk of decency?"

"Ah . . . " Grandpere Jack waved his long arm in her direction and turned away to return to the swamp.

"Wait, Grandpere," I cried, running after him.

"Wait? For what? You ain't seen stubborn until you've seen a Cajun woman with her mind made up. There's nothin' to wait for," he declared, and walked on, his hip boots sucking through the spongelike grass and earth. Usually, he wore his red coat which was a cross between a vest and a fireman's raincoat, with huge sewn in pockets that circled around behind from two sides. They had slit openings and were called rat pockets, for that was where he put his muskrats.

Whenever he charged off in anger, his long, stark white hair would fly up and around his head and look like white flames. He was a dark-skinned man. The Landrys were said to have Indian blood. But he had emerald green eyes that twinkled with an impish charm when he was sober and in a good mood. Tall and lanky and strong enough to wrestle with a gator, Grandpere Jack was something of a legend in the bayou. Few men lived off the swamp as well as he did.

But Grandmere Catherine was down on the Landrys and often brought me to tears when she cursed the day she'd married Grandpere.

19

"Let it be a lesson to you, Ruby," she told me one day. "A lesson as to how the heart can trick and confuse the mind. The heart wants what the heart wants. But before you give yourself to a man, be sure you have a good idea as to where he's going to take you. Sometimes, the best way to see the future, is to look at the past," Grandmere advised. "I should have listened to what everyone told me about the Landrys. They're so full of bad blood . . . they've been bad since the first Landrys settled here. It wasn't long before signs were posted in these parts saying, No Landrys Allowed. How's that for bad and how's that for listening to your young heart instead of older wisdom?"

"But surely, you must have loved Grandpere once. You must have seen something good in him," I insisted.

"I saw what I wanted to see," she replied. She was stubborn when it came to him, but for reasons I still didn't understand. That day I must have felt a streak of contrariness or bravery, because I tried to probe at the past.

"Grandmere, why did he move away? Was it just because of his drinking, because I think he would stop if he lived with us again?"

Her eyes cut sharply toward me. "No, it's not just because of his drinking." She was quiet a moment. "Although that's good enough a reason."

"Is it because of the way he gambles away his money?"

"Gambling ain't the worse of it," she snapped in a voice that said I should let the matter drop. But for some reason I couldn't.

20

"Then what is, Grandmere? What did he do that was so terrible?"

Her face darkened and then softened a bit. "It's between him and me," she said. "It ain't for you to know. You're too young to understand it all, Ruby. If Grandpere Jack was meant to live with us . . . things would have been different," she insisted and left me as confused and frustrated as ever.

Grandmere Catherine had such wisdom and such power. Why couldn't she do something to make us a family again? Why couldn't she forgive Grandpere and use her power to change him so that he could live with us once more? Why couldn't we be a real family?

No matter what Grandpere Jack told me and other people, no matter how much he swore, ranted, and raved, I knew he had to be a lonely man living by himself in the swamp. Few people visited him and his home was really no more than a shack. It sat six feet off the marsh on pilings. He had a cistern to collect rainwater and butane lanterns for lights. It had a wood heater for burning scrap lumber and driftwood. At night he would sit on his galerie and play mournful tunes on his accordion and drink his rotgut whiskey.

He wasn't really happy and neither was Grandmere Catherine. Here we were returning from the Rodrigues home after chasing off an evil spirit and we couldn't chase off the evil spirits that dwelt in the shadows of our own home. In my heart I thought Grandmere Catherine was like the shoemaker without any shoes. She can do so much

21

good for others, but she seemed incapable of doing the same sort of things for herself.

Was that the destiny of a Traiteur? A price she had to pay to have the power?

Would it be my destiny as well: to help others but be unable to help myself?

The bayou was a world filled with many mysterious things. Every journey into it, revealed something surprising. A secret until that moment not discovered. But the secrets held in our own hearts were the secrets I longed to know the most.

Just before we reached home, Grandmere Catherine said, "There's someone at the house." With a definite note of disapproval, she added, "It's that Tate boy again."

Paul was sitting on the galerie steps playing his harmonica, his motor scooter set against the cypress stump. The moment he set eyes on our lantern, he stopped playing and stood up to greet us.

Paul was the seventeen-year-old son of Octavious Tate, one of the richest men in Houma. The Tates owned a shrimp cannery and lived in a big house. They had a pleasure boat and expensive cars. Paul had two younger sisters, Jeanne, who was in my class at school, and Toby, who was two years younger. Paul and I had known each other all our lives, but just recently had begun to spend more time together. I knew his parents weren't happy about it. Paul's father had more than one run-in with Grandpere Jack and disliked the Landrys.

"Everything all right, Ruby?" Paul asked quickly as we drew closer. He wore a light blue cotton polo shirt, khaki pants, and leather boots laced tightly beneath them. Tonight he looked taller and wider to me, and older, too.

"Grandmere and I went to see the Rodrigues family. Mrs. Rodrigues's baby was born dead," I told him.

"Oh, that's horrible," Paul said softly. Of all the boys I knew at school, Paul seemed the most sincere and the most mature, although, one of the shyest. He was certainly one of the handsomest with his cerulean blue eyes and thick, *chatin* hair, which was what the Cajuns called brown mixed with blond. "Good evening, Mrs. Landry," he said to Grandmere Catherine.

She flashed her gaze on him with that look of suspicion she had ever since the first time Paul had walked me home from school. Now that he was coming around more often, she was scrutinizing him even more closely, which was something I found embarrassing. Paul seemed a little amused, but a little afraid of her as well. Most folks believed in Grandmere's prophetic and mystical powers.

"Evening," she said slowly. "Might be a downpour yet tonight," she predicted. "You shouldn't be motoring about with that flimsy thing."

"Yes, ma'am," Paul said.

Grandmere Catherine shifted her eyes to me. "We got to finish the weavin' we started," she reminded me.

"Yes, Grandmere. I'll be right along."

She looked at Paul again and then went inside.

"Is your grandmother very upset about losing the Rodrigues baby?" he asked.

"She wasn't called to help deliver it," I replied, and I told him why she had been summoned and what we had done. He listened with interest and then shook his head.

"My father doesn't believe in any of that. He says superstitions and folklore are what keeps the Cajuns backward and makes other folks think we're ignorant. But I don't agree," he added quickly.

"Grandmere Catherine is far from ignorant," I added, not hiding my indignation. "It's ignorant not to take precautions against evil spirits and bad luck."

Paul nodded. "Did you . . . see anything?" he asked.

"I felt it fly by my face," I said, placing my hand on my cheek. "It touched me here. And then I thought I saw it leave."

Paul released a low whistle.

"You must have been very brave," he said.

"Only because I was with Grandmere Catherine," I confessed.

"I wish I had gotten here earlier and been with you . . . to make sure nothing bad happened to you," he added. I felt myself blush at his desire to protect me.

"I'm all right, but I'm glad it's over," I admitted. Paul laughed.

In the dim illumination of our galerie light, his face looked softer, his eyes even warmer. We hadn't done much more than hold hands and kiss a half-dozen times, only twice on the lips, but the memory of those kisses made my heart flutter now when I looked at him and stood so closely to him. The breeze gently brushed aside some strands of hair that had fallen over his forehead. Behind the house, the water from the swamps lapped against the shore and a night bird flapped its wings above us, invisible against the dark sky.

"I was disappointed when I came by and you weren't home," he said. "I was just about to leave when I saw the light of your lantern."

"I'm glad you waited," I replied, and his smile widened. "But I can't invite you in because Grandmere wants us to finish the blankets we'll put up for sale tomorrow. She thinks we'll be busy this weekend and she's usually right. She always remembers which weekends were busier than others the year before. No one has a better memory for those things," I added.

"I got to work in the cannery all day tomorrow, but maybe I can come by tomorrow night after dinner and we can walk to town to get a cup of crushed ice," Paul suggested.

"I'd like that," I said. Paul stepped closer to me and fixed his gaze on my face. We drank each other in for a moment before he worked up enough courage to say what he really had come to say. "What I really want to do is take you to the fais dodo next Saturday night," he declared quickly.

I had never been out on a real date before. Just the thought of it filled me with excitement. Most girls my age would be going to the fais dodo with their families and dance with boys they met there, but to be picked up and escorted and to dance only with Paul all night . . . that sent my mind reeling.

"I'll have to ask Grandmere Catherine," I said, quickly adding, "but I'd like that very much."

"Good. Well," he said, backing up toward his motor scooter, "I guess I better be going before that downpour comes." He didn't take his eyes off me as he stepped away and he caught his heel on a root. It sat him down firmly.

"Are you all right?" I cried, rushing to him. He laughed, embarrassed.

"I'm fine, except for a wet rear end," he added, and laughed. He reached up to take my hand and stand, and when he did, we were only inches apart. Slowly, a millimeter at a time, our lips drew closer and closer until they met. It was a short kiss, but a firmer and more confident one on both our parts. I had gone up on my toes to bring my lips to his and my breasts grazed his chest. The unexpected contact with the electricity of our kiss sent a wave of warm, pleasant excitement down my spine.

"Ruby," he said, bursting with emotion now. "You're the prettiest and nicest girl in the whole bayou."

"Oh, no, I'm not, Paul. I can't be. There are so many prettier girls, girls who have expensive clothes and expensive jewelry and—"

"I don't care if they have the biggest diamonds and dresses from Paris. Nothing could make them prettier than you," he blurted out. I knew he wouldn't have had the courage to say these things if we weren't standing in the shadows and I couldn't see him as clearly. I was sure his face was crimson.

"Ruby!" my grandmother called from a window. "I don't want to stay up all night finishing this."

"I'm coming, Grandmere. Good night, Paul," I said, and then I leaned forward to peck him on the lips once more before I turned and left him standing in the dark. I heard him start his motor scooter and drive off and then I hurried up to the *grenier* to help Grandmere Catherine.

For a long moment, she didn't speak. She worked and kept her eyes fixed on the loom. Then she shifted her gaze to me and pursed her lips the way she often did when she was thinking deeply.

"The Tate boy's been coming around to see you a great deal, lately, hasn't he?"

"Yes, Grandmere."

"And what do his parents think of that?" she asked, cutting right to the heart of things as always.

"I don't know, Grandmere," I said, looking down.

"I think you do, Ruby."

"Paul likes me and I like him," I said quickly. "What his parents think isn't important."

"He's grown a great deal this year; he's a man. And you're no longer a little girl, Ruby. You've grown, too. I see the way you two look at each other. I know that look too well and what it can lead to," she added.

"It won't lead to anything bad. Paul's the nicest boy in school," I insisted. She nodded but kept her dark eyes on me. "Stop making me feel naughty, Grandmere. I haven't done anything to make you ashamed of me."

"Not yet," she said, "but you got Landry in you and the blood has a way of corrupting. I seen it in your mother; I don't want to see it in you."

My chin began to quiver.

"I'm not saying these things to hurt you, child. I'm saying them to prevent your being hurt," she said, reaching out to put her hand over mine.

"Can't I love someone purely and nicely, Grandmere? Or am I cursed because of Grandpere Jack's blood in my veins? What about your blood? Won't it give me the wisdom I need to keep myself from getting in trouble?" I demanded. She shook her head and smiled.

"It didn't prevent me from getting in trouble, I'm afraid. I married him and lived with him once," she said, and then sighed. "But you might be right; you might be stronger and wiser in some ways. You're certainly a lot brighter than I was when I was your age, and far more talented. Why your drawings and paintings—"

"Oh, no, Grandmere, I'm—"

"Yes, you are, Ruby. You're talented. Someday someone will see that talent and offer you a lot of money for it," she prophesied. "I just don't want you to do anything to ruin your chance to get out of here, child, to rise above the swamp and the bayou."

"Is it so bad here, Grandmere?"

"It is for you, child."

"But why, Grandmere?"

"It just is," she said, and began her weaving again, again leaving me stranded in a sea of mystery.

"Paul has asked me to go with him to the fais

dodo a week from Saturday. I want to go with him very much, Grandmere," I added.

"Will his parents let him do that?" she asked quickly.

"I don't know. Paul thinks so, I guess. Can we invite him to dinner Sunday night, Grandmere? Can we?"

"I never turned anyone away from my dinner table," Grandmere said, "but don't plan on going to the dance. I know the Tate family and I don't want to see you hurt."

"Oh, I won't be, Grandmere," I said, nearly bouncing in my seat with excitement. "Then Paul can come to dinner?"

"I said I wouldn't throw him out," she replied.

"Oh, Grandmere, thank you. Thank you." I threw my arms around her. She shook her head.

"If we go on like this, we'll be working all night, Ruby," she said, but kissed my cheek. "My little Ruby, my darling girl, growing into a woman so quickly I better not blink or I'll miss it," she said. We hugged again and then went back to work, my hands moving with a new energy, my heart filled with a new joy, despite Grandmere Catherine's ominous warnings.

2

No Landrys Allowed

A blend of wonderful aromas rose from the kitchen and seeped into my room to snap my eyes open and start my stomach churning in anticipation. I could smell the rich, black Cajun coffee percolating on the stove and the mixture of shrimp and chicken gumbo Grandmere Catherine was preparing in her black, cast iron cooking pots to sell at our roadside stall. I sat up and inhaled the delicious smells.

Sunlight wove its way through the leaves of the cypress and sycamores around the house and filtered through the cloth over my window to cast a warm, bright glow over my small bedroom which had just enough space for my white painted bed, a small stand for a lamp near the pillow, and a large chest for my clothing. A chorus of rice birds began their ritual symphony, chirping and singing, urging me to get up, get washed, and get dressed so I could join them in the celebration of a new day.

No matter how I tried, I never beat Grandmere Catherine out of bed and into the kitchen. Rarely did I have the opportunity to surprise her with a pot of freshly brewed coffee, hot biscuits, and eggs. She was usually up with the first rays of sunlight that began to push back the blanket of darkness, and she moved so quietly and so gracefully through the house that I didn't hear her footsteps in the hallway or down the stairs, which usually creaked loudly when I descended. Weekend mornings Grandmere Catherine was up especially early so as to prepare everything for our roadside stall.

I hurried down to join her.

"Why didn't you wake me?" I asked.

"I'd wake you when I needed you if you didn't get yourself up, Ruby," she said, answering me the same way she always did. But I knew she would rather take on extra work than shake me out of the arms of sleep.

"I'll fold all the new blankets and get them ready to take out," I said.

"First, you'll have some breakfast. There's time enough for us to get things out. You know the tourists don't come riding by for a good while yet. The only ones who get up this early are the fishermen and they're not interested in anything we have to sell. Go on now, sit down," Grandmere Catherine commanded.

We had a simple table made from the same wide cypress planks from which our house walls were constructed, as were the chairs with their grooved posts. The one piece of furniture Grandmere was most proud of was her oak armoire. Her father had made it. Everything else we had was ordinary and no different from anything every other Cajun family living along the bayou possessed.

"Mr. Rodrigues brought over that basket of fresh eggs this morning," Grandmere Catherine said, nodding toward the basket on the counter by the window. "Very nice of him to think of us during his troubled times."

She never expected much more than a simple thank-you for any of the wonders she worked. She didn't think of her gifts as being hers; she thought of them as belonging to the Cajun people. She believed she was put on this earth to serve and to help those less fortunate, and the joy of helping others was reward enough.

She began to fry me two eggs to go along with her biscuits.

31

"Don't forget to put out your newest pictures today. I love the one with the heron coming out of the water," she said, smiling.

"If you love it, Grandmere, I shouldn't sell it. I should give it to you."

"Nonsense, child. I want everyone to see your pictures, especially people in New Orleans," she declared. She had said that many times before and just as firmly.

"Why? Why are those people so important?" I asked.

"There's dozens and dozens of art galleries there and famous artists, too, who will see your work and spread your name so that all the rich Creoles will want one of your paintings in their homes," she explained.

I shook my head. It wasn't like her to want fame and notoriety brought to our simple bayou home. We put out our handicrafts and wares to sell on weekends because it brought us the necessary income to survive, but I knew Grandmere Catherine wasn't comfortable with all these strangers coming around, even though some of them loved her food and piled compliments at her feet. There was something else, some other reason why Grandmere Catherine was pushing me to exhibit my artwork, some mysterious reason.

The picture of the heron was special to me, too. I had been standing on the shore by the pond behind our house at twilight one day when I saw this grosbeak, a night heron, lift itself from the water so suddenly and so unexpectedly, it did seem to come out of the water. It floated up on its wide, dark purple wings and soared over the

32

cypress. I felt something poetic and beautiful in its movements and couldn't wait to capture some of that in a painting. Later, when Grandmere Catherine set her eyes on the finished work, she was speechless for a moment. Her eyes glistened with tears and she confessed that my mother had favored the blue heron over all the other marsh birds.

"That's more reason for us to keep it," I said.

But Grandmere Catherine disagreed and said, "More reason for us to see it carried off to New Orleans." It was almost as if she were sending some sort of cryptic message to someone in New Orleans through my artwork.

After I ate my breakfast, I began to take out the handicrafts and goods we would try to sell that day, while Grandmere Catherine finished making the roux. It was one of the first things a young Cajun girl learned to make. Roux was simply flour browned in butter, oil, or animal fat and cooked to a nutty brown shade without letting it turn so hot that it burned black. After it was prepared, seafood or chicken, sometimes duck, goose, or guinea hen, and sometimes wild game with sausage or oysters was mixed in to make the gumbo. During Lent Grandmere made a green gumbo that was roux mixed only with vegetables rather than meat.

Grandmere was right. We began to get customers much earlier than we usually did. Some of the people who dropped by were friends of hers or other Cajun folk who had learned about the couchemal and wanted to hear Grandmere tell the story. A few of her older friends sat around and recalled similar tales they had heard from their parents and grandparents.

Just before noon, we were surprised to see a silver gray limousine, fancy and long, going by. Suddenly, it came to an abrupt stop and was then backed up very quickly until it stopped again in front of our stall. The rear door was thrown open and a tall, lanky, olive-skinned man with gray-brown hair stepped out, the laughter of a woman lingering behind him within the limousine.

"Quiet down," he said, then turned and smiled at me.

An attractive blond lady with heavily made-up eyes, thick rouge, and gobs of lipstick, poked her head out the open door. A long pearl necklace dangled from her neck. She wore a blouse of bright pink silk. The first several buttons were not done so I couldn't help but notice that her breasts were quite exposed.

"Hurry up, Dominique. I expect to have dinner at Arnaud's tonight," she cried petulantly.

"Relax. We'll have plenty of time," he said without looking back at her. His attention was fixed on my paintings. "Who did these?" he demanded.

"I did, sir," I said. He was dressed expensively in a white shirt of the snowiest, softest-looking cotton and a beautifully tailored suit in dark charcoal gray.

"Really?"

I nodded and he stepped closer to take the picture of the heron into his hands. He held it at arm's length and nodded. "You have instinct," he said. "Still primitive, but rather remarkable. Did you take any lessons?"

"Just a little at school and what I learned from reading some old art magazines," I replied.

"Remarkable."

"Dominique!"

"Hold your water, will you." He smirked at me again as if to say, "Don't mind her," and then he looked at two more of my paintings. I had five out for sale. "How much are you asking for your paintings?" he asked.

I looked at Grandmere Catherine who was standing with Mrs. Thibodeau, their conversation on hold while the limousine remained. Grandmere Catherine had a strange look in her eyes. She was peering as though she were looking deeply into this handsome, well-to-do stranger, searching for something that would tell her he was more than a simple tourist amusing himself with local color.

"I'm asking five dollars apiece," I said.

"Five dollars!" He laughed. "Firstly, you shouldn't ask the same amount for each," he lectured. "This one, the heron, obviously took more work. It's five times the painting the others are," he declared assuredly, turning to address Grandmere Catherine and Mrs. Thibodeau as if they were his students. He turned back to me. "Why, look at the detail . . . the way you've captured the water and the movement in the heron's wings." His eyes narrowed and he pursed his lips as he looked at the paintings and nodded to himself. "I'll give you fifty dollars for the five of them as a down payment," he announced.

"Fifty dollars, but—"

"What do you mean, as a down payment?" Grandmere Catherine asked, stepping toward us.

"Oh, I'm sorry," the gentleman said. "I should have introduced myself properly. My name is Dominique LeGrand. I own an art gallery in the French Quarter, simply called Dominique's. Here," he said, reaching in and taking a business card from a pocket in his pants. Grandmere took the card and pinched it between her small fingers to look at it.

"And this . . . down payment?"

"I think I can get a good deal more for these paintings. Usually, I just take an artist's work into the gallery without paying anything, but I want to do something to show my appreciation of this young girl's work. Is she your granddaughter?" Dominique inquired.

"Yes," Grandmere Catherine said. "Ruby Landry. Will you be sure her name is shown along with the paintings?" she asked, surprising me.

"Of course," Dominique LeGrand said, smiling. "I see she has her initials on the corner," he said, then turned to me. "But in the future, put your full name there," he instructed. "And I do believe, there is a future for you, Mademoiselle Ruby." He took a wad of money from his pocket and peeled off fifty dollars, more money than I had made selling all my paintings up until now. I looked at Grandmere Catherine who nodded and then I took the money.

"Dominique!" his woman cried again.

"Coming, coming. Philip," he called, and the driver came around to put my paintings in the trunk of the limousine. "Careful," he told him.

36

Then he took down our address. "You will be hearing from me," he said as he got into his limousine again. Grandmere Catherine and I stood beside each other and watched the long car go off until it disappeared around the bend.

"Fifty dollars, Grandmere!" I said, waving the money. Mrs. Thibodeau was quite impressed, but my grandmother looked more thoughtful than happy. I thought she even looked a little sad.

"It's begun," she said in a voice barely above a whisper, her eyes fixed in the direction the limousine had taken.

"What has, Grandmere?"

"The future, your future, Ruby. This fifty dollars is just the beginning. Be sure you say nothing about it if your Grandpere Jack should stumble by," she instructed. Then she returned to Mrs. Thibodeau to continue their discussion about couchemals and other evil spirits that lurk about unsuspecting folks.

But I couldn't contain my excitement. I was terribly impatient with the rest of the day, eager to see it hurry along until Paul was to come. I couldn't wait to tell him, and I laughed to myself thinking I could buy him the crushed ice tonight, instead of him buying it for me. Only, I knew he wouldn't let me pay. He was too proud.

The only thing that kept me from exploding with impatience was the business we did. We sold all our blankets, sheets, and towels and Grandmere sold a half-dozen jars of herbal cures. We even sold a pickled frog. All of Grandmere Catherine's gumbo was eaten. In fact, she had to go in and start to make some more for our own dinner. Finally, the sun dropped below the trees and Grandmere declared our day at the roadside had ended. She was very pleased and sang as she worked on our dinner.

"I want you to have my money, Grandmere," I told her.

"We made enough today. I don't need to take your painting money, Ruby." Then she narrowed her eyes on me. "But give it to me to hide. I know you'll feel sorry for that swamp bum and give him some if not all of it one day. I'll put it in my chest for safekeeping. He wouldn't dare look in there," she said.

Grandmere's oak chest was the most sacred thing in the house. It didn't need to be under lock and key. Grandpere Jack would never dare set his hands on it, no matter how drunk he was when he came here. Even I did not venture to open the lid and sift through the things within, for they were her most precious and personal keepsakes, including things that belonged to my mother when she was a little girl. Grandmere promised that everything in it would some day belong to me.

After we had eaten and had cleaned up, Grandmere sat in her rocking chair on the galerie, and I sat near her on the steps. It wasn't as muggy and hot as the night before because there was a brisk breeze. The sky had only a few scattered clouds so the bayou was well lit by the yellowish white light of the moon. It made the limbs of the trees in the swamp look like bones and the still water glisten like glass. On a night like this, sounds traveled over the bayou quickly and easily. We could hear the happy tunes coming from Mr.

Bute's accordion and the laughter of his wife and children, all gathered on their front galerie. Somewhere, way in the distance down left toward town, a car horn blared, while behind us, the frogs croaked in the swamp. I had not told Grandmere Catherine that Paul was coming, but she sensed it.

"You look like you're sitting on pins and needles tonight, Ruby. Waiting for something?"

Before I could reply, we heard the soft growl of Paul's motor scooter.

"No need to answer," Grandmere said. Moments later, we saw the small light on his motor scooter, and Paul rode into our front yard.

"Good evening, Mrs. Landry," he said, walking up to us. "Hi, Ruby."

"Hello," Grandmere Catherine said, eying him cautiously.

"We have a little relief from the heat and humidity tonight," he said, and she nodded. "How was your day?" he asked me.

"Wonderful! I sold all five of my paintings," I declared quickly.

"All of them? That is wonderful. We'll have to celebrate with two ice cream sodas instead of just crushed ice. If it's all right with you, Mrs. Landry, I'd like to take Ruby to town," he added, turning to Grandmere Catherine. I saw how his request troubled her. Her eyebrows rose and she leaned back in her rocker. Her hesitation made Paul add, "We won't be long."

"I don't want you to take her on that flimsy motor thing," Grandmere said, nodding toward the scooter. Paul laughed.

"I'd rather walk on a night like this anyway, wouldn't you, Ruby?"

"Yes. All right, Grandmere?"

"I suppose. But don't go anywhere but to town and back and don't talk to any strangers," she cautioned.

"Yes, Grandmere."

"Don't worry, I won't let anything happen to her," Paul assured Grandmere. Paul's assurance didn't make her look less anxious, but he and I started toward town, our way well lit by the moon. He didn't take my hand until we were out of sight.

"Your grandmere worries so much about you," Paul said.

"She's seen a lot of sadness and hard times. But we had a good day at the stall."

"And you sold all your paintings. That's great."

"I didn't sell them so much as get them into a New Orleans gallery," I said, and told him everything that had happened and what Dominique LeGrand had said.

Paul was silent for a long moment. Then he turned to me, his face strangely sad. "Someday, you'll be a famous artist and move away from the bayou. You'll live in a big house in New Orleans, I'm sure," he predicted, "and forget all us Cajuns."

"Oh, Paul, how could you say such a horrible thing? I'd like to be a famous artist, of course; but I would never turn my back on my people and . . . and never forget you. Never," I insisted.

"You mean that, Ruby?"

I tossed my hair back over my shoulder and put my hand on my heart. Then, closing my eyes, I said, "I swear on Saint Medad. Besides," I continued, snapping my eyes open, "it will probably be you who leaves the bayou to go to some fancy college and meet wealthy girls."

"Oh, no," he protested. "I don't want to meet other girls. You're the only girl I care about."

"You say that now, Paul Marcus Tate, but time has a way of changing things. Look at my grandparents. They were once in love."

"That's different. My father says no one could live with your grandfather."

"Once, Grandmere did," I said. "And then things changed, things she never expected."

"They won't change with me," Paul boasted. He paused and stepped closer to take my hand again. "Did you ask your grandmother about the fais dodo?"

"Yes," I said. "Can you come to dinner tomorrow night? I think she should have a chance to get to know you better. Could you?"

He was quiet for a long moment.

"Your parents won't let you," I concluded.

"I'll be there," he said. "My parents are just going to have to get used to the idea of you and me," he added, and smiled. Our eyes remained firmly on each other and then he leaned toward me and we kissed in the moonlight. The sound and sight of an automobile set us apart and made us walk faster toward the town and the soda shop.

The street looked busier than usual this evening. Many of the local shrimp fishermen had brought their families in to enjoy the feast at the Cajun Queen, a restaurant that advertised an all-you-can-eat platter of crawfish and potatoes with

41

pitchers of draft beer. In fact, there was a real festive atmosphere with the Cajun Swamp Trio playing their accordion, fiddle, and washboard on the corner near the Cajun Queen. Peddlers were out and folks sat on cypress log benches watching the parade of people go by. Some were eating beignets and drinking from mugs of coffee and some were feasting on sea bob, which was dried shrimp, sometimes called Cajun Peanuts.

Paul and I went to the soda fountain and confectionery store and sat at the counter to have our ice cream sodas. When Paul told the owner, Mr. Clements, why we were celebrating, he put gobs of whip cream and cherries on top of our sodas. I couldn't remember an ice cream soda that had ever tasted as good. We were having such a good time, we almost didn't hear the commotion outside, but other people in the store rushed to the door to see what was happening and we soon followed.

My heart sunk when I saw what it was: Grandpere Jack being thrown out of the Cajun Queen. Even though he had been escorted out, he remained on the steps waving his fist and screaming about injustice.

"I'd better see if I can persuade him to go home and calm down," I muttered, and hurried out. Paul followed. The crowd of onlookers had begun to break up, no longer much interested in a drunken man babbling to himself on the steps. I pulled on the sleeve of his jacket.

"Grandpere, Grandpere . . . "

"Wha . . . who . . . " He spun around, a trickle of whiskey running out of the corner of his mouth and down the grainy surface of his unshaven chin.

For a moment he wobbled on his feet as he tried to focus on me. The strands of his dry, crusty looking hair stood out in every direction. His clothing was stained with mud and bits of food. He brought his eyes closer. "Gabrielle?" he said.

"No, Grandpere. It's Ruby. Ruby. Come along, Grandpere. You have to go home. Come along," I said. It wasn't the first time I had found him in a drunken stupor and had to urge him to go home. And it wasn't the first time he had looked at me with his eyes hazy and called me by my mother's name.

"Wha . . ." He looked from me to Paul and then back at me again. "Ruby?"

"Yes, Grandpere. You must go home and sleep."

"Sleep, sleep? Yeah," he said, turning back toward the Cajun Queen. "Those no good . . . they take your money and then when you voice your opinion about somethin'. . . things ain't what they was around here, that's for sure, that's for damn sure."

"Come on, Grandpere." I tugged his hand and he came off the steps, nearly tripping and falling on his face. Paul rushed to take hold of his other arm.

"My boat," Grandpere muttered. "At the dock." Then he turned and ripped his hand from mine to wave his fist at the Cajun Queen one more time. "You don't know nothin'. None of you remember the swamp the way it was 'fore these damn oil people came. Hear?"

"They heard you, Grandpere. Now it's time to go home."

"Home. I can't go home," he muttered. "She won't let me go home."

I swung my gaze to Paul who looked very upset for me.

"Come along, Grandpere," I urged again, and he stumbled forward as we guided him to the dock.

"He won't be able to navigate this boat himself," Paul declared. "Maybe I should just take him and you should go home, Ruby."

"Oh, no. I'll go along. I know my way through the canals better than you do, Paul," I insisted.

We got Grandpere into his dingy and sat him down. Immediately, he fell over the bench. Paul helped him get comfortable and then he started the motor and we pulled away from the dock, some of the people still watching us and shaking their heads. Grandmere Catherine would hear about this quickly, I thought, and she would just nod and say she wasn't surprised.

Minutes after we pulled away from the dock, Grandpere Jack was snoring. I tried to make him more comfortable by putting a rolled up sack under his head. He moaned and muttered something incoherently before falling asleep and snoring again. Then I joined Paul.

"I'm sorry," I said.

"For what?"

"I'm sure your parents will find out about this tomorrow and be angry."

"It doesn't matter," he assured me, but I remembered how dark Grandmere Catherine's eyes had become when she asked me what his parents thought of his seeing me. Surely they

44

would use this incident to convince him to stay away from the Landrys. What if signs began to appear everywhere saying, "No Landrys Allowed," just like Grandmere Catherine described from the past? Perhaps I really would have to flee from the bayou to find someone to love me and make me his wife. Perhaps this was what Grandmere Catherine meant.

The moon lit our way through the canals, but when we went deeper into the swamp, the sad veils of Spanish moss and the thick, intertwined leaves of the cypress blocked out the bright illumination making the waterway more difficult to navigate. We had to slow down to avoid the stumps. When the moonlight did break through an opening, it made the backs of the gators glitter. One whipped its tail, splashing water in our direction as if to say, you don't belong here. Farther along, we saw the eyes of a marsh deer lit up by the moonbeams. We saw his silhouetted body turn to disappear in the darker shadows.

Finally, Grandpere's shack came into view. His galerie was crowded with nets for oyster fishing, a pile of Spanish moss he had gathered to sell to the furniture manufacturers who used it for stuffing, his rocking chair with the accordion on it, empty beer bottles and a whiskey bottle beside the chair and a crusted gumbo bowl. Some of his muskrat traps dangled from the roof of the galerie and some hides were draped over the railing. His pirogue with the pole he used to gather the Spanish moss was tied to his small dock. Paul gracefully navigated us up beside it and shut off the motor of the dingy. Then we began the difficult task of getting Grandpere out of the boat. He offered little assistance and came close to spilling all three of us into the swamp.

Paul surprised me with his strength. He virtually carried Grandpere over the galerie and into the shack. When I turned on a butane lamp, I wished I hadn't. Clothing was strewn all about and everywhere there were empty and partially empty bottles of cheap whiskey. His cot was unmade, the blanket hanging down with most of it on the floor. His dinner table was covered with dirty dishes and crusted bowls and glasses, as well as stained silverware. From the expression on his face, I saw that Paul was overwhelmed by the filth and the mess.

"He'd be better off sleeping right in the swamp," he muttered. I fixed the cot so he could lower Grandpere Jack onto it. Then we both started to undo his hip boots. "I can do this," Paul said. I nodded and went to the table first to clear it off and put the dishes and bowls into the sink, which I found to be full of other dirty dishes and bowls. While I washed and cleaned, Paul went around the shack and picked up the empty cans and bottles.

"He's getting worse," I moaned, and wiped the tears from my eyes. Paul squeezed my arm gently.

"I'll get some fresh water from the cistern," he said. While he was gone, Grandpere began to moan. I wiped my hands and went to him. His eyes were still closed, but he was muttering under his breath.

"It ain't right to blame me . . . ain't right. She

was in love, wasn't she? What's the difference then? Tell me that. Go on," he said.

"Who was in love, Grandpere?" I asked.

"Go on, tell me what's the difference. You got somethin' against money, do you? Huh? Go on."

"Who was in love, Grandpere? What money?"

He moaned and turned over.

"What is it?" Paul said, returning with the water.

"He's talking in his sleep, but he doesn't make any sense," I said.

"That's easy to believe."

"I think . . . it had something to do with why he and my Grandmere Catherine are so angry at each other all the time."

"I don't think there's much of a mystery to that, Ruby. Look around; look at what he's become. Why should she want to have him in the house?" Paul said.

"No, Paul. It has to be something more. I wish he would tell me," I said, and knelt beside the cot. "Grandpere," I said, shaking his shoulder.

"Damn oil companies," he muttered. "Dredged the swamps and killed the three-cornered grass . . . killing the muskrats . . . nothin' for them to eat."

"Grandpere, who was in love? What money?" I demanded. He moaned and started to snore.

"No sense talking to him when he's like that, Ruby," Paul said.

I shook my head.

"It's the only time he might tell me the truth, Paul." I stood up, still looking down at him.

47

"Neither he nor Grandmere Catherine will talk about it any other time."

Paul came to my side.

"I picked up a bit outside, but it will take a few days to get this place in shape," he commented.

"I know. We'd better start back. We'll dock his boat near my house. He'll pole the pirogue there tomorrow and find it."

"He'll find his head's got a tin drum inside it," Paul said. "That's what he'll find tomorrow."

We left the shack and got into the dingy. Neither of us spoke much on the way back. I sat beside Paul. He put his arm around me and I cradled my head against his shoulder. Owls hooted at us, snakes and gators slithered through the mud and water, frogs croaked, but my mind was fixed on Grandpere Jack's drunken words and I heard or saw nothing else until I felt Paul's lips on my forehead. He had shut off the motor and we were drifting toward the shore.

"Ruby," he whispered. "You feel so good in my arms. I wish I could hold you all the time, or at least have you in my arms whenever I wanted."

"You can, Paul," I replied softly, and turned my face to him so that he could bring his lips down to mine. Our kiss was soft, but long. We felt the boat hit the shore and stop, but neither of us made an attempt to rise. Instead, Paul wrapped his arms tighter around me and slipped down beside me, his lips now moving over my cheeks and gently caressing my closed eyes.

"I go to sleep every night with your kiss on my lips," Paul said.

"So do I, Paul."

His left arm pressed the side of my breast softly. I tingled and waited in excited anticipation. He brought his arm back slowly until his hand gently cupped my breast and his finger slipped over my throbbing, erected nipple beneath the thin cotton blouse and bra to undo the top buttons. I wanted him to touch me; I even longed for it, but the moment he did, my electric excitement was quickly followed by a stream of cold fear, for I felt how strongly I wanted him to do more, go further and kiss me in places so intimate, only I had touched or seen them. Despite his gentleness and his deep expressions of love, I could not get around Grandmere Catherine's dark eyes of warning looming in my memory.

"Wait, Paul," I said reluctantly. "We're going too fast."

"I'm sorry," Paul said quickly, and pulled himself back. "I didn't mean to. I just . . . "

"It's all right. If I don't stop you now, I won't stop you in a few minutes and I don't know what else we will do," I explained. Paul nodded and stood up. He helped me up and I straightened my skirt and blouse, rebuttoning the top two buttons. He helped me out of the boat and then pulled it up so it wouldn't be carried away when the tide from the Gulf raised the level of the water in the bayou. I took his hand and we made our way slowly back to the house. Grandmere Catherine was inside. We could hear her tinkering in the kitchen, finishing up the preparation of the biscuits she would bring to church in the morning.

"I'm sorry our celebration turned out this way,"

I said, and wondered how many more times I would apologize for Grandpere Jack.

"I wouldn't have missed a moment," Paul said. "As long as I was with you, Ruby."

"Is your family going to church in the morning?" He nodded. "Are you still coming to dinner tomorrow night?"

"Of course."

I smiled and we kissed once more before I turned and climbed the steps to the front galerie. Paul waited until I walked in and then he went to his scooter and drove away. The moment Grandmere Catherine turned to greet me, I knew she had heard about Grandpere Jack. One of her good friends couldn't wait to bring her the news first, I was sure.

"Why didn't you just let the police cart him off to jail? That's where he belongs, making a spectacle of himself in front of good folks with all those children in town, too," she said, wagging her head, "What did you and Paul do with him?"

"We took him back to his shack, Grandmere, and if you saw how it was . . . "

"I don't have to see it. I know what a pigsty looks like," she said, returning to her biscuits.

"He called me Gabrielle when he first set eyes on me," I said.

"Doesn't surprise me none. He probably forgot his own name, too."

"At the shack, he mumbled a lot."

"Oh?" She turned back to me.

"He said something about someone being in love and what was the difference about the money. What does all that mean, Grandmere?"

She turned away again. I didn't like the way her eyes skipped guiltily away when I tried to catch them. I knew in my heart she was hiding something.

"I wouldn't know how to begin to untangle the mess of words that drunken mind produces. It would be easier to unravel a spiderweb without tearing it," she said.

"Who was in love, Grandmere? Did he mean my mother?"

She was silent.

"Did he gamble away her money, your money?" I pursued.

"Stop trying to make sense out of something stupid, Ruby. It's late. You should go to bed. We're going to early Mass, and I must tell you, I'm not happy about you and Paul carting that man into the swamp. The swamp is no place for you. It's beautiful from a distance, but it's the devil's lair, too, and wrought with dangers you can't even begin to imagine. I'm disappointed in Paul for taking you there," she concluded.

"Oh, no, Grandmere. Paul didn't want me to go along. He wanted to do it himself, but I insisted."

"Still, he shouldn't have done it," she said, and turned to me, her eyes dark. "You shouldn't be spending all your time with one boy like this. You're too young."

"I'm fifteen, Grandmere. Some fifteen-year-old Cajun girls are already married, some with children."

"Well, that's not going to happen to you. You're going to do better, be better," she said angrily.

51

"Yes, Grandmere. I'm sorry. We didn't mean
. . ."

"All right," she said. "It's over and done with.
Let's not ruin an otherwise special day by talking
about your Grandpere anymore. Go to sleep,
Ruby. Go on," she ordered. "After church, you're
going to help me prepare our Sunday dinner.
We've got a guest, don't we?" she asked, her eyes
full of skepticism.

"Yes, Grandmere. He's coming."

I left her, my mind in a spin. The day had been
filled with so many good things and so many bad.
Maybe Grandmere Catherine was right; maybe it
was better not to try to fathom the dark things.
They had a way of polluting the clear waters,
spoiling the fresh and the wonderful bright things.
It was better to dwell on the happy events.

It was better to think about my paintings
hanging in a New Orleans gallery . . . to
remember the touch of Paul's lips on mine and the
way he made my body sing . . . to dream about a
perfect future with me painting in my own art
studio in our big house on the bayou. Surely the
good things had a way of outweighing the bad,
otherwise we would all be like Grandpere Jack,
lost in a swamp of our own making, not only trying
to forget the past, but trying to forget the future
as well.

3

Wish We Were a Family

In the morning Grandmere Catherine and I put on our Sunday clothes. I brushed my hair and tied it up with a crimson ribbon and she and I set out for church, Grandmere carrying her gift for Father Rush, a box of her homemade biscuits. It was a bright morning with silky white clouds lazily making their way across the nearly turquoise sky. I took a deep breath, inhaling the warm air seasoned with the salt of the Gulf of Mexico. It was the kind of morning that made me feel bright and alive, and aware of every beautiful thing in the bayou.

The moment we walked down the steps of the galerie, I caught sight of the scarlet back of a cardinal as it flew to its safe, high nest. As we strolled down the road, I saw how the buttercups had blossomed in the ditches and how milk white were the small, delicate flowers of the Queen Anne's lace.

Even the sight of a butcher bird's stored food didn't upset me. From early spring, through the summer and early fall, his fresh kills, lizards and tiny snakes, dried upon the thorns of a thorn tree. Grandpere Jack told me the butcher bird ate the cured flesh only during the winter months.

"Butcher birds are the only birds in the bayou that have no visible mates," he told me. "No female naggin' them to death. Smart," he added before spitting out some tobacco juice and swigging a gulp of whiskey in his mouth. What made him so bitter? I wondered again. However, I didn't dwell on it long, for ahead of us the church loomed, its shingled spire lifting a cross high above the congregation. Every stone, every brick, and every beam of the old building had been brought and affectionately placed there by the Cajuns who worshipped in the bayou nearly one hundred and fifty years before. It filled me with a sense of history, a sense of heritage.

But as soon as we rounded the turn and headed toward the church, Grandmere Catherine stiffened and straightened her spine. A group of well-to-do people were gathered in a small circle chatting in front of the church. They all stopped their conversation and looked our way as soon as we came into sight, a distinct expression of disapproval painted on all their faces. That only made Grandmere Catherine hoist her head higher, like a flag of pride.

"I'm sure they're raking over what a fool your grandpere made of himself last night," Grandmere Catherine muttered, "but I will not have my reputation blemished by that man's foolish behavior."

The way she stared back at the gathering told them as much. They looked happy to break up to go inside as the time to enter the church for services drew near. I saw Paul's parents, Octavious and Gladys Tate, standing on the perimeter of the throng. Gladys Tate threw a glance in our direction, her hard as stone eyes on me. Paul, who had been talking with some of his school buddies, spotted me and smiled, but his

54

mother made him join her and his father and sisters as they entered the church.

The Tates, as well as some other wealthy Cajun families, sat up front so Paul and I didn't get a chance to talk to each other before the Mass began. Afterward, as the worshippers filed past Father Rush, Grandmere gave him her box of biscuits and he thanked her and smiled coyly.

"I hear you were at work again, Mrs. Landry," the tall, lean priest said with a gently underlying note of criticism in his voice. "Chasing spirits into the night."

"I do what I must do," Grandmere replied firmly, her lips tight and her eyes fixed on his.

"As long as we don't replace prayer and church with superstition," he warned. Then he smiled. "But I never refuse assistance in the battle against the devil when that assistance comes from the pure at heart."

"I'm glad of that, Father," Grandmere said, and Father Rush laughed. His attention was then quickly drawn to the Tates and some other well-to-do congregants who made sizeable contributions to the church. While they spoke, Paul joined Grandmere and me. I thought he looked so handsome and very mature in his dark blue suit with his hair brushed back neatly. Even Grandmere Catherine seemed impressed.

"What time is supper, Mrs. Landry?" Paul asked. Grandmere Catherine shifted her eyes toward Paul's parents before replying.

"Supper is at six," Grandmere told him, and then went to join her friends for a chat. Paul waited until she was out of earshot.

55

"Everyone was talking about your grandfather this morning," he told me.

"Grandmere and I sensed that when we arrived. Did your parents find out you helped me get him home?"

The look on his face gave me the answer.

"I'm sorry if I caused you trouble."

"It's all right," he said quickly. "I explained everything." He grinned cheerfully. He was the perpetual cockeyed optimist, never gloomy, doubtful, or moody, as I often was.

"Paul," his mother called. With her face frozen in a look of disapproval, her mouth was like a crooked knife slash and her eyes were long and catlike. She held her body stiffly, looking as if she would suddenly shudder and march away.

"Coming," Paul said.

His mother leaned over to whisper something to his father and his father turned to look my way.

Paul got most of his good looks from his father, a tall, distinguished looking man who was always elegantly dressed and well-groomed. He had a strong mouth and jaw with a straight nose, not too long or too narrow.

"We're leaving right this minute," his mother emphasized.

"I've got to go. We have some relatives coming for lunch. See you later," Paul promised, and he darted off to join his parents.

I stepped beside Grandmere Catherine just as she invited Mrs. Livaudis and Mrs. Thibodeau to our house for coffee and blackberry pie. Knowing how slowly they would walk, I hurried ahead, promising to start the coffee. But when I got to our front yard, I saw my grandfather down at the dock, tying his pirogue to the back of the dingy.

"Good morning, Grandpere," I called. He looked up slowly as I approached.

His eyes were half-closed, the lids heavy. His hair was wild, the strands in the back flowing in every direction over his collar. I imagined that the tin drum Paul predicted was banging away in Grandpere's head. He looked grouchy and tired. He hadn't changed out of the clothes he had slept in and the stale odor of last night's rum whiskey lingered on him. Grandmere Catherine always said the best thing that could happen to him was for him to fall into the swamp. "That way, at least he'd get a bath."

"You bring me back to my shack in the swamp last night?" he asked quickly.

"Yes, Grandpere. Me and Paul."

"Paul? Who's Paul?"

"Paul Tate, Grandpere."

"Oh, a rich man's son, eh? Them cannery people ain't much better than the oil riggers, dredging the swamp to make it wider for their damn big boats. You got no business hanging around that sort. There's only one thing they want from the likes of you," he warned.

"Paul's very nice," I said sharply. He grunted and continued to tie his knot.

"Coming from church, are ya?" he asked without looking up.

"Yes."

He paused and looked back toward the road.

"Your grandmere's still gabbin' with those

57

other busybodies, I imagine. That's why they go to church," he claimed, "to nourish gossip."

"It was a very nice service, Grandpere. Why don't you ever go?"

"This here is my church," he declared, and waved his long fingers at the swamp. "I got no priest lookin' over my shoulder, spitting hell and damnation down my back." He stepped into the dingy.

"Would you like a cup of fresh coffee, Grandpere? I'm about to make some. Grandmere has some of her friends coming for blackberry pie and—"

"Hell no. I wouldn't be caught dead with those fishwives." He shifted his eyes to me and softened his gaze. "You look nice in that dress," he said. "Pretty as your mother was."

"Thank you, Grandpere."

"I guess you cleaned up my shack some, too, didn't you?" I nodded. "Well, thanks for that."

He reached for the cord to pull and start his motor.

"Grandpere," I said, approaching. "You were talking about someone who was in love and something about money, last night after we brought you home."

He paused and looked at me hard, his eyes turning to granite very quickly.

"What else did I say?"

"Nothing. But what did you mean, Grandpere? Who was in love?"

He shrugged.

"Probably remembered one of the stories my father told me about his father and grandpere.

58

Our family goes way back to the riverboat gamblers, you know," he said with some pride. "Lots of money traveled through Landry fingers," he said, holding up his muddied hands, "and each of the Landrys cut quite a romantic figure on the river. Lots of women were in love with them. You could line them up from here to New Orleans."

"Is that why you gamble away all your money? Grandmere says it's in the Landry blood," I said.

"Well, she ain't wrong about that. I'm just not as good at it as some of my kinfolk was." He leaned forward, smiling, the gaps in his teeth dark and wide where he had pulled out his own when the aches became too painful to manage. "My great, great-grandpere, Gib Landry, was a sure-thing player. Know what that was?" he asked. I shook my head. "A player who never lost because he had marked cards." He laughed. "They called them 'Vantage tools.' Well, they certainly gave an advantage." He laughed again.

"What happened to him, Grandpere?"

"He was shot to death on the *Delta Queen*. When you live hard and dangerous, you're always gambling," he said, and pulled the cord. The motor sputtered. "Someday, when I got the time, I'll tell you more about your ancestors. Despite what she tells you," he added, nodding toward the house, "you oughta know something about them." He pulled the cord again and this time the motor caught and began to rumble. "I gotta get goin'. I got some oysters to catch."

"I wish you could come to dinner at the house tonight and meet Paul," I said. What I really meant was I wish we were a family.

"What do you mean, meet Paul? Your grandmere invited him to dinner?" he asked skeptically.

"I did. She said it was all right."

He stared at me a long moment and then turned back to his motor.

"Got no time for socializin'. Gotta make me a livin'."

Grandmere Catherine and her friends appeared on the road behind us. I saw Grandpere Jack's eyes linger for a moment and then he sat himself down quickly.

"Grandpere," I cried, but he gunned his motor and turned the dingy to pull away as quickly as he could and head for one of the shallow brackish lakes scattered through the marshes. He didn't look back. In moments, the swamp swallowed him up and only the growl of his motor could be heard as he wound his way through the channels.

"What did he want?" Grandmere Catherine demanded.

"Just to get his dingy."

She kept her eyes fixed on his wake as if she expected he would reappear. She glared and narrowed her eyes into slits as if she were willing the swamp to swallow him up forever. Soon, the sound of his dingy motor died away and Grandmere Catherine straightened herself up again and smiled at her two friends. They quickly returned to their conversation and entered the house, but I lingered a moment and wondered how these two people could have ever been in love enough to marry and have a daughter. How could love or what you thought was love make you so blind to each other's weaknesses?

Later that day, after Grandmere Catherine's friends left, I helped her prepare our supper. I wanted to ask her more about Grandpere Jack, but those questions usually put her in a bad mood. With Paul coming for supper, I dared not risk it.

"We're not doing anything special for supper tonight, Ruby," she told me. "I hope you didn't give the Tate boy that impression."

"Oh, no, Grandmere. Besides, Paul isn't that kind of a boy. You wouldn't even know his family was wealthy. He's so different from his mother and his sisters. Everyone in school says they're stuck-up, but not Paul."

"Maybe, but you don't live the way the Tates live and not get to expect certain things. It's just human nature. The higher you build him up in your mind, Ruby, the harder the fall of disappointment is going to be," she warned.

"I'm not afraid of that, Grandmere," I said with such certainty that she paused to gaze at me.

"You've been a good girl, haven't you, Ruby?"

"Oh, yes, Grandmere."

"Don't ever forget what happened to your mother," she admonished.

For a while I feared Grandmere Catherine would hold this cloud of dread over the house up until and through our dinner, but despite her claim that we weren't having anything special, few things pleased Grandmere Catherine as much as cooking for someone she knew would appreciate it. She set out to make one of her best Cajun

61

dishes: jambalaya. While I helped with that, Grandmere made a custard pie.

"Was my mother a good cook, too, Grandmere?" I asked her.

"Oh, yes," she said, smiling at the memories. "No one picked up recipes as quickly and as well as your mother did. She was cooking gumbo before she was nine years old, and by the time she was twelve, no one could clear out the icebox and make as good a jambalaya."

"When your grandpere Jack was still something of a human being," she continued, "he would take Gabrielle out and show her all the edible things in the swamp. She learned fast, and you know what they say about us Cajuns," Grandmere added, "we'll eat anything that doesn't eat us first."

She laughed and hummed one of her favorite tunes. On Sundays we usually gave the house a good once-over anyway, but this special Sunday, I went at it with more energy and concern, washing down the windows until every speck of dirt was gone, scrubbing the floors until they shone, and dusting and polishing everything in sight.

"You'd think the king of France was coming here tonight," Grandmere teased. "I'm warning you, Ruby, don't let that boy expect more of you than there is."

"I won't, Grandmere," I said, but in my secret put-away heart, I hoped that Paul would be very impressed and brag about us to his parents so much they would drop any opposition they might have to his making me his girlfriend.

By late afternoon, our little home nearly sparkled and was filled with delicious aromas. As the clock ticked closer to six, I grew more and more excited. I hoped that Paul would be early, so I sat outside and waited the last hour with my eyes fixed in the direction he would come. Our table was set and I wore my best dress. Grandmere Catherine had made it herself. It was white with a deep lace hem and a lace panel down the front. The sleeves were soft bells of lace that came to my elbows. I wore a blue sash around my waist.

"I'm glad I let out that bodice some," she said when she saw me. "The way your bosom's blossoming. Turn around," she said, and smoothed out the back of the skirt. "I must say, you're turning out to be a real belle, Ruby. Even more beautiful than your mother was at your age."

"I hope I'm as pretty as you are at your age, Grandmere," I replied. She shook her head and smiled.

"Go on now. I'm enough to scare a marsh hawk to death," she said, and laughed, but for the first time, I got Grandmere Catherine to tell me about some of her old boyfriends and some of the fais dodos she had attended when she was my age.

When the clock struck six, I lifted my eyes in anticipation, expecting Paul's motor scooter to rumble moments later. But it didn't and the road remained quiet and still. After a little while Grandmere came to the door and peered out herself. She gazed sadly at me and then returned to the kitchen to do some final things. My heart began to pound. The breeze became more of a wind; all of the trees waving their branches. Where was he? At about seven, I became very concerned and when Grandmere Catherine appeared in the doorway again, she wore a look of fatal acceptance on her face.

"It's not like him to be late," I said. "I hope nothing has happened to him."

Grandmere Catherine didn't reply; she didn't have to. Her eyes said it all.

"You'd better come in and sit down, Ruby. We made the food and want to enjoy it anyway."

"He's coming, Grandmere. I'm sure he's coming. Something unexpected must have happened," I cried. "Let me wait just a little while longer," I pleaded. She retreated, but at seven-fifteen she came to the door again.

"We can't wait any longer," she declared.

Dejected, all my appetite gone anyway, I rose and went inside. Grandmere Catherine said nothing. She served the meal and sat down.

"This came out as good as it ever has," she declared. Then leaning toward me, she added, "even if I have to say so myself."

"Oh, it's wonderful, Grandmere. I'm just . . . worried about him."

"Well, worry about him on a full stomach," she ordered. I forced myself to eat, and, despite my disappointment, even enjoyed Grandmere Catherine's custard pie. I helped her clean up and then I went back outside and sat on the galerie, waiting and watching and wondering what had happened to ruin what would have been a wonderful evening. Almost an hour later, I heard Paul's motor scooter and saw him coming down the road as fast as he could. He pulled up and dropped his scooter roughly to run up to the house.

"What happened to you?" I cried, standing.

"Oh, Ruby, I'm sorry. My parents . . . they forbad me to come. My father ordered me to my room when I refused to have dinner with them. Finally, I decided to climb out the window and come here anyway. I must apologize to your grandmother."

I sank to the steps of the galerie.

"Why wouldn't they let you come?" I asked. "Because of my grandfather and what happened in town last night?"

"That . . . as well as other things. But I don't care how angry they get at me," he said, stepping up to sit beside me. "They're just being stupid snobs."

I nodded. "Grandmere said this would happen. She knew."

"I'm not going to let them keep me away from you, Ruby. They have no right. They—"

"They're your parents, Paul. You've got to do what they tell you to do. You should go home," I said dryly. My heart felt like it had turned into a glob of swamp mud. It was as if cruel Fate had dropped a sheet of dark gloom over the bayou, and just like Grandmere Catherine often said, Fate was a grim reaper, never kind, with little respect for who was loved and needed.

Paul shook his head. Years seemed to melt from him, and he sat there vulnerable, helpless as a child of six or seven, no more comprehending than I.

"I'm not going to give you up, Ruby. I'm not," he insisted. "They can take away everything they've given me, and I still won't listen to them."

"They'll only hate me more, Paul," I concluded.

"It doesn't matter. What matters is that we care for each other. Please, Ruby," he said, taking my hand. "Say that I'm right."

"I want to, Paul." I looked down. "But I'm afraid."

"Don't be," he told me, reaching out to tilt my head toward him. "I won't let anything happen to you."

I stared at him with huge, wistful eyes. How could I explain? I wasn't worried about myself, I was concerned for him because as Grandmere Catherine always told me, defiance of fate just meant disaster for those you loved. Defying it was as futile as trying to hold back the tide.

"All right?" Paul pursued. "Okay?"

"Oh, Paul."

"It's settled then. Now," he said, standing. "I'm going in to apologize to your grandmother."

I waited for him on the steps. He returned a few minutes later.

"Looks like I missed a real feast. It makes me so angry," he said, gazing out at the road with eyes as furious as Grandpere Jack's could get. I didn't feel comfortable with him hating his parents. At least he had parents, a home, a family. He should hold on to those things and not risk them for the likes of me, I thought. "My parents are unreasonable," he declared firmly.

"They're just trying to do what they think is best for you, Paul," I said.

"You're what's best for me, Ruby," he replied quickly. "They're just going to have to understand that." His blue eyes gleamed with determination. "Well, I'd better go back," he said. "Once again, I'm sorry I ruined your dinner, Ruby."

"It's over now, Paul." I stood up and we gazed at each other for a long moment. What did the Tates fear would happen if Paul loved me? Did they really believe my Landry blood would corrupt him? Or was it merely that they wanted him to know only girls from rich families?

He took my hand into his.

"I swear," he said, "I'll never let them do anything to hurt you again."

"Don't fight with your parents, Paul. Please," I begged.

"I'm not fighting with them; they're fighting with me," he replied. "Good night," he said, and leaned forward to kiss me quickly on the lips. Then he went to his motor scooter and drove into the night. I watched him disappear in the darkness. When I turned around, I saw Grandmere Catherine standing in the doorway.

"He's a nice young man," she said, "but you can't rip a Cajun man away from his mother and father. It will tear his heart in two. Don't put all your heart in this, Ruby. Some things are just not meant to be," she added, and turned around to go back into the house.

I stood there, the tears streaming down my face. For the first time, I understood why Grandpere Jack liked living in the swamp away from people.

Despite what had happened on Sunday, I still had high hopes for the Saturday night fais dodo. But whenever I brought it up with Grandmere, she simply replied, "We'll see." On Friday night, I pressed her harder.

"Paul's got to know if he can come by to pick me up, Grandmere. It's not fair to keep him dangling like bait on a fish line," I said. It was something Grandpere Jack would say, but I was frustrated and anxious enough to risk it.

"I just don't want you to suffer another disappointment, Ruby," she told me. "His parents aren't going to let him take you and they would just be furious if he defied them and did so anyway. They would be angry with me, too."

"Why, Grandmere? How can they blame you?"

"They just would," she said. "Everybody would. I'll take you myself," she said nodding. "Mrs. Bourdeaux is going and she and I can sit together and watch the young people. Besides, it's been a while since I heard good Cajun music."

"Oh, Grandmere," I moaned. "Girls my age are going with boys; some have been on dates for more than a year already. It's not fair; I'm fifteen. I'm not a baby anymore."

"I didn't say you were, Ruby, but—"

"But you're treating me like one," I cried, and ran up to my room to throw myself on my bed.

Maybe I was worse off living with a grandmother who was a spiritual treater, who saw evil spirits and danger in every dark shadow, who was always chanting and lighting candles and putting totems on people's doorways. Maybe the Tates just thought we were a crazy family and that was why they wanted Paul to stay away from me.

Why did my mother have to die so young and why did my real father have to desert me? I had a grandfather who lived like an animal in the middle of the swamp and a grandmother who thought I was a small child. My sadness was mixed suddenly with rage. Here I was, fifteen with other girls my age far less pretty than I enjoying themselves on real dates while I was expected to go trailing along with my grandmere to the fais dodo. Never before did I feel like running away as much as I did now.

I heard Grandmere coming up the stairs, her steps heavier than usual. She tapped gently on my door and looked in. I didn't turn around.

"Ruby," she began. "I'm only trying to protect you."

"I don't want you to protect me," I snapped. "I can protect myself. I'm not a baby," I insisted.

"You don't have to be a baby to need protection," she replied in a tired voice. "Strong grown men often cry for their mothers."

"I don't have a mother!" I shot back, and regretted it as soon as the words left my mouth.

Grandmere's eyes saddened and her shoulders slumped. Suddenly, she looked very old to me. She put her hand on her heart and took a deep breath, nodding.

"I know, child. That's why I try so hard to do what's right for you. I know I can't be your mother, too, but I can do some of what a mother would do. It's not enough; it's never enough, but—"

"I didn't mean to say you don't do enough for me, Grandmere. I'm sorry, but I want to go to the dance with Paul very much. I want to be treated like a young woman and not a child anymore. Didn't you want that when you were my age?" I asked. She stared at me a long moment before sighing.

"All right," she said. "If the Tate boy can take you, you can go with him, but you must promise me you will be home right after the dance."

"I will, Grandmere. I will. Thank you."

She shook her head.

"When you're young," she began, "you don't want to face up to what has to be. Your youth gives you the strength to defy, but defiance doesn't always lead to victory, Ruby. More often than not, it leads to defeat. When you come face-to-face with Fate, don't charge headlong into him. He welcomes that; it feeds him and he's got an insatiable appetite for stubborn, foolish souls."

"I don't understand, Grandmere," I said.

"You will," she told me with that heavy, prophetic tone of hers. "You will." Then she straightened up and sighed again. "I guess I'd better iron your dress," she said.

I wiped the tears from my cheeks and smiled.

"Thank you, Grandmere, but I can do it."

"No, that's all right. I want to keep myself busy," she said, then walked out, her head still hanging lower than usual.

All day Saturday, I debated about my hair. Should I wear it brushed down, tied with a ribbon in the back, or should I wear it up in a French knot? In the end I asked Grandmere to help me put my hair up.

"You have such a pretty face," Grandmere Catherine said. "You should wear your hair back more often. You're going to have a lot of nice boyfriends," she added, more to soothe herself than to please me, I thought. "So remember not to give away your heart too quickly." She took my hand into both of hers and fixed her eyes on me, eyes that looked sad and tired. "Promise?"

"Yes, Grandmere. Grandmere," I said, "are you feeling all right? You've looked very tired all day."

"Just that old ache in the back and my quickened heartbeat now and again. Nothing out of the ordinary," she said.

"I wish you didn't have to work so hard, Grandmere. Grandpere Jack should do more for us instead of drinking up his money or gambling it away," I declared.

"He can't do anything for himself, much less for us. Besides, I don't want anything from him. His money's tainted," she said firmly.

"Why is his money any more tainted than any other trapper's in the bayou, Grandmere?"

"His is," she insisted. "Let's not talk about it. If anything sets my heart beating like a parade drum, that does."

I swallowed my questions, afraid of making her sicker and more tired. Instead, I put on my dress and polished my shoes. Tonight, because the weather was unstable with intermittent showers and stronger winds, Paul was going to use one of his family's cars. He told me his father had said it was all right, but I had the feeling he hadn't told them everything. I was just too frightened to ask and risk not going to the dance. When I heard him drive up, I rushed to the door. Grandmere Catherine followed and stood right behind me.

"He's here," I cried.

"You tell him to drive slowly and be sure you're home right after the dancing," Grandmere said.

Paul rushed up to the *galerie*. The rain had started again, so he held an umbrella open for me.

"Wow, Ruby, you look very pretty tonight," he said, then saw Grandmere Catherine step out from behind me. "Evening, Mrs. Landry."

"You get her home nice and early," she ordered.

"Yes, ma'am."

"And drive very carefully."

"I will."

"Please, Grandmere," I moaned. She bit down on her lip to keep herself silent and I leaned forward to kiss her cheek.

"Have a good time," she muttered. I ran out to slip under Paul's umbrella and we hurried to the car. When I looked back, Grandmere Catherine was still standing in the doorway looking out at us, only she looked so much smaller and older to me. It was as if my growing up meant she was to grow older, faster. In the midst of my excitement, an excitement that made the rainy night seem like a star-studded one, a small cloud of sadness touched my thrilled heart and made it shudder for a second. But the moment Paul started driving away, I smothered the trepidation and saw only happiness and fun ahead.

The fais dodo hall was on the other side of town. All furniture, except for the benches for the older people, was moved out of the large room. In a smaller, adjoining room, large pots of gumbo were placed on tables. We didn't have a stage as such, but platforms were used to provide a place for the musicians, who played the accordion, the fiddle, the triangle, and guitars. There was a singer, too.

People came from all over the bayou, many families bringing their young children as well. The little ones were put in another adjoining room to sleep. In fact, fais dodo was Cajun baby talk for go-to-sleep, meaning put all the small kids to bed so the older folks could dance. Some of the men played a card game called bourré while their wives and older children danced what we called the Two-step.

Paul and I no sooner entered the fais dodo hall than I could hear the whispers and speculations on people's lips—what was Paul Tate doing with one of the poorest young girls in the bayou? Paul didn't seem as aware of the eyes and the whispering as I was, or if he was, he didn't care. As soon as we arrived, we were out on the dance floor. I saw some of my girlfriends gazing at us with green eyes, for just about every one of them would have liked Paul Tate to bring her to a fais dodo.

We danced to one song after another, applauding loudly at the end of each song. Time passed so quickly that we didn't realize we had danced nearly an hour before we decided we were hungry and thirsty. Laughing, feeling as if there were no one else here but the two of us, we headed for refreshments. Both of us were oblivious to the group of boys who followed along, lead by Turner Browne, one of the school bullies. He was a stout, bull-necked seventeen-year-old with a shock of dark brown hair and large facial features. It was said that his family went back to the flatboat polers who had navigated the Mississippi long before the steamboat. The polers were a rough, violent bunch and the Brownes were thought to have inherited those traits. Turner lived up to the family reputation, getting into one brawl after another at school.

"Hey, Tate," Turner Browne said after we had gotten our bowls of gumbo and sat at the corner of a table. "Your mommy know you're out slumming tonight?"

All of Turner's friends laughed. Paul's face turned crimson. Slowly, he stood up.

"I think you'd better take that back, Turner, and apologize."

Turner Browne laughed.

"What'cha gonna do, Tate, tell your daddy on me?"

Again, Turner's friends laughed. I reached up and tugged on Paul's sleeve. He was red-faced and so angry he seemed to give off smoke.

"Ignore him, Paul," I said. "He's too stupid to bother with."

"Shut your mouth," Turner said. "At least I know who my father is."

At that, Paul shot forward and tackled the much larger boy, knocking him to the floor. Instantly, Turner's friends let up a howl and formed a circle, around Paul and Turner, blocking out anyone who might have rushed to put a quick end to it. Turner was able to roll over Paul and pin him down by sitting on his stomach. He delivered a punch to Paul's right cheek. It swelled up almost instantly. Paul was able to block Turner's next punch, just as the older men arrived and pulled him off Paul. When he stood up, Paul's lower lip was bleeding.

"What's going on here?" Mr. Lafourche demanded. He was in charge of the hall.

"He attacked me," Turner accused, pointing at Paul.

"That's not the whole truth," I said. "He—"

"All right, all right," Mr. Lafourche said. "I don't care who did what. This sort of thing doesn't go on in my hall. Now get yourselves out of here. Go on, Browne. Move yourself and your crew before I have you all locked up."

Smiling, Turner Browne turned and led his bunch of cronies away. I brought a wet napkin to Paul and dabbed his lip gently.

"I'm sorry," he said. "I lost my temper."

"You shouldn't have. He's so much bigger."

"I don't care how big he is. I'm not going to allow him to say those things to you," Paul replied bravely. With his cheek scarlet and a little swollen, I could only cry for him. Everything had been going so well; we were having such a good time. Why was there always someone like Turner Browne to spoil things?

"Let's go," I said.

"We can still stay and dance some more."

"No. We'd better get something on your bruises. Grandmere Catherine will have something that will heal you quickly," I said.

"She'll be disappointed in me, angry that I got into a fight while I was with you," Paul moaned. "Damn that Turner Browne."

"No, she won't. She'll be proud of you, proud of the way you came to my defense," I said.

"You think so?"

"Yes," I said, although I wasn't sure how Grandmere would react. "Anyway, if she can fix it so your face doesn't look so bad, your parents won't be as angry, right?"

He nodded and then laughed.

"I look terrible, huh?"

"Not much better than someone who wrestled an alligator, I suppose."

We both laughed and then left the hall. Turner Browne and his friends were already gone, off to guzzle beer and brag to each other, I imagined, so there was no more trouble. It was raining harder when we drove back to the house. Paul pulled as close as he could and then we hurried in under the umbrella. The moment we stepped through the door, Grandmere Catherine looked up from her needlework and nodded.

"It was that bully, Turner Browne, Grandmere. He—"

She lifted her hand, rose from her seat, and went to the counter where she had some of her poultices set out as if she had anticipated our dramatic arrival. It was eerie. Even Paul was speechless.

"Sit down," she told him, pointing to a chair. "After I treat him, you can tell me all about it."

Paul looked at me, his eyes wide, and then moved to the seat to let Grandmere Catherine work her miracles.

4

Learning to Be a Liar

"Here," Grandmere Catherine told Paul, "keep this pressed against your cheek with one hand and this pressed against your lip with the other." She handed him two warm cloths over which she had smeared one of her secret salves. When Paul took the cloths, I saw the knuckles on his right hand were all bruised and scraped as well.

"Look at his hand, too, Grandmere," I cried.

"It's nothing," Paul said. "When I was rolling around on the floor—"

"Rolling around on the floor? At the fais dodo?" Grandmere asked. He nodded and then started to speak.

"We were having some gumbo and—"

"Hold those tight," she ordered. While he was holding the cloth against his lip, he couldn't talk, so I spoke for him, quickly.

"It was Turner Browne. He said one nasty thing after another just to show off in front of his friends," I told her.

"What sort of nasty things?" she demanded.

"You know, Grandmere. Bad things."

She stared at me a moment and then looked at Paul. It wasn't easy to keep anything from Grandmere Catherine. For as long as I could remember, she had a way of seeing right into your heart and soul.

"He made nasty remarks about your mother?"

Grandmere asked. I shifted my eyes away which was as good as saying yes. She took a deep breath, her hand against her heart and nodded. "They won't let it go. They cling to other people's hard times like moss clings to damp wood." She shook her head again and shuffled away, her hand still on her heart.

I looked at Paul. His sad eyes told me how sorry he was he had lost his temper. He started to take the cloth off his lip to say so, but I put my hand over his quickly. Paul smiled at me with his eyes, even though his lips had to be kept in a straight line.

"Just hold it there like Grandmere said," I told him. She looked back at us. I kept my hand over his and smiled. "He was very brave, Grandmere. You know how big Turner Browne is, but Paul didn't care."

"He looks it," she said, and shook her head. "Your Grandpere Jack wasn't much different and still isn't. I wish I had a pretty penny for every time I had to prepare a poultice to treat the injuries he suffered in one of his brawls. One time he came home with his right eye shut tight, and another time, he had a piece of his ear bitten off. You'd think that would make him think twice before getting into any more such conflicts, but not that man. He was at the end of the line when they passed out good sense," she concluded.

The rain that had been pounding on our tin roof subsided until we could hear only a slight *tap, tap, tap*, and the wind had died down considerably. Grandmere opened the batten plank shutters to let the breeze travel through our house again. She took a deep breath.

"I do love the way the bayou smells after a good rain. It makes everything fresh and clean. I wish it would do the same to people," she said, and sighed deeply. Her eyes were still dark and troubled. I never had heard her sound so sad and tired. A kind of paralyzing numbness gripped me and for a moment, I could only sit there and listen to my heart pound. Grandmere suddenly shuddered and embraced herself.

"Are you all right, Grandmere?"

"What? Yes, yes. Okay," she said, moving to Paul. "Let me look at you."

He took the cloths from his lips and cheek and she scrutinized his face. The swelling had subsided, but his cheek was still crimson and his lower lip dark where Turner Browne's fist had split the skin. Grandmere Catherine nodded and then went to the icebox and chipped out a small chunk to wrap in another washcloth.

"Here," she said, returning. "Put this on your cheek until it gets too cold and then put it on your lip. Keep alternating until the ice melts away, understand?"

"Yes, ma'am," Paul said. "Thank you. I'm sorry all this happened. I should have just ignored Turner Browne."

Grandmere Catherine held her eyes on him a moment and then relaxed her expression.

"Sometimes you can't ignore; sometimes the evil won't leave," she said. "But that doesn't mean I expect to see you in any more fights," she warned. He nodded obediently.

"You won't," he promised.

"Hmm," she said. "I wish I had another pretty penny for how many times my husband has made the same promise."

"I keep mine," Paul said proudly. Grandmere liked that and finally smiled.

"We'll see," she said.

"I better get going," Paul declared, standing. "Thanks again, Mrs. Landry."

Grandmere Catherine nodded.

"I'll walk you to the car, Paul," I said. When we stepped out on the galerie, we saw the rain had nearly stopped. The sky was still quite dark, but the glow from the galerie's dangling naked bulb threw a stream of pale white light to Paul's car. Still holding the ice pack against his cheek, he took my hand with his free hand and we walked over the pathway.

"I do feel terrible about ruining the evening," he said.

"You didn't ruin it; Turner Browne ruined it. Besides, we got in plenty of dancing first," I added.

"It was fun, wasn't it?"

"You know," I said. "This was my first real date."

"Really? I used to think you had a stream of boyfriends knocking on your door, and you wouldn't give me the time of day," he confessed. "It took all the courage I could muster, more courage than it took to attack Turner Browne, for me to walk up to you that afternoon at school and ask to carry your books and walk you home."

"I know. I remember how your lips trembled, but I thought that was adorable."

"You did? Well, then I'll just continue to be the shyest young man you ever did see."

"As long as you're not too shy to kiss me now and then," I replied. He smiled and grimaced with the pain it caused to stretch his lip. "Poor Paul," I said, and leaned forward to kiss him ever so gently on that wounded mouth. His eyes were still closed when I pulled back. Then they popped open.

"That's the best poultice, even better than your grandmother's magical medicines. I'm going to have to come around every day and get another treatment," he said.

"It will cost you," I warned.

"How much?"

"Your undying devotion," I replied. His eyes riveted on me.

"You already have that, Ruby," he whispered, "and always will."

Then he leaned forward, disregarding the pain, and kissed me warmly on the lips.

"Funny," he said, opening his car door, "but even with this bruised cheek and split lip, I think this was one of the best nights of my life. Good night, Ruby."

"Good night. Don't forget to keep that ice on your lip like Grandmere told you to," I advised.

"I won't. Thank her again for me. See you tomorrow," he promised, and started his engine. I watched him back away. He waved and then drove into the night. I stood watching until the small red lights on the rear of his car were swallowed by the darkness. Then I turned, embracing myself, and saw Grandmere Catherine standing on the edge of the galerie looking out at me. How long had she been there? I wondered. Why was she waiting like that?

"Grandmere? Are you all right?" I asked when I approached. Her face was so gloomy. She looked pale, forlorn, and as if she had just seen one of the spirits she was employed to chase away. Her eyes stared at me bleakly. Something hard and heavy grew in my chest, making it ache in anticipation.

"Come on inside," she said. "I have something to tell you, something I should have told you long ago."

My legs felt as stiff as tree stumps as I went up the stairs and into the house. My heart, which had been beating with pleasure after Paul's last kiss, beat harder, deeper, thumped deep down into my very soul. I couldn't remember ever seeing such a look of melancholy and sadness on Grandmere Catherine's face. What great burden did she carry? What terrible thing was she about to tell me?

She sat down and stared ahead for a long time as though she'd forgotten I was there. I waited, my hands in my lap, my heart still pounding.

"There was always a wildness in your mother," she began. "Maybe it was the Landry blood, maybe it was the way she grew up, always close to wild things. Unlike most girls her age, she was never afraid of anything in the swamp. She would pick up a baby snake as quickly as she would pick a daisy.

"In the early days, Grandpere Jack took her everywhere he went in the bayou. She fished with him, hunted with him, poled the pirogue when she was just tall enough to stand and push the stick into the mud. I used to think she was going to be a tomboy. However," she said, focusing her eyes on me now, "she was to be anything but a tomboy. Maybe it would have been better if she had been less feminine.

"She grew quickly, blossomed into a flower of womanhood way before her time, and those dark eyes of hers, her long, flowing hair as rich and red as yours, enchanted men and boys alike. I even think she fascinated the birds and animals of the swamp. Often," she said, smiling at her memory, "I would see a marsh hawk peering down with yellow-circled eyes to follow her with his gaze as she walked along the shore of the canal.

"So innocent and so beautiful, she was eager to touch everything, see everything, experience everything. Alas, she was vulnerable to older, shrewder people, and thus, she was tempted to drink from the cup of sinful pleasure.

"By the time she was sixteen, she was very popular and asked to go everywhere by every boy in the bayou. They all pleaded with her for some attention. I saw the way she teased and tormented some who were absolutely in agony over her smile, her laugh, dying for her to say something promising to them whenever they came around.

"She had young boys doing all her chores, even lining up to help Grandpere Jack, who wasn't above taking advantage of the poor souls, I might add. He knew they hoped to court Gabrielle's favor by slaving for him and he had them doing more for him than they did for their own fathers.

It was downright criminal of him, but he wouldn't listen to me.

"Anyway, one night, about seven months after her sixteenth birthday, Gabrielle came to me in this very room. She was sitting right where you're sitting now. When I looked up at her, I didn't need to hear what she was going to say. She was no more than a windowpane, easy to read. My heart did flip-flops; I held my breath.

"'Mama,' she said, her voice cracking, 'I think I'm pregnant.' I closed my eyes and sat back. It was as though the inevitable had occurred, what I had feared and felt might happen, had happened.

"As you know we're Catholics; we don't go to no shack butchers and abort our pregnancies. I asked her who was the father and she just shook her head and ran from me. Later, when Grandpere Jack came home and heard, he went wild. He nearly beat her to death before I stopped him, but he got out of her who the father was," she said, and raised her eyes slowly.

Was that thunder I heard, or was it blood thundering through my veins and roaring in my ears?

"Who was it, Grandmere?" I asked, my voice cracking, my throat choking up quickly.

"It was Octavious Tate who had seduced her," she said, and once again it was as if thunder shook the house, shook the very foundations of our world and shattered the fragile walls of my heart and soul. I could not speak; I could not ask the next question, but Grandmere had decided I was to know it all.

"Grandpere Jack went to him directly. Octavious had been married less than a year and his father was alive then. Your Grandpere Jack was an even bigger gambler in those days. He couldn't pass up a game of bourré even though most times he was the one stuffing the pot. One time he lost his boots and had to walk home barefoot. And another time, he wagered a gold tooth and had to sit and let someone pull it out with a pliers. That's how sick a gambler he was and still is.

"Anyway, he got the Tates to pay him to keep things silent and part of the bargain was that Octavious would take the child and bring it up as his own. What he told his new wife and how they worked it out between them, we never knew, didn't care to know.

"I kept your mother's pregnancy hidden, strapping her up when she started to show in the seventh month. By then it was summer and she didn't have to attend school. We kept her here at the house most of the time. During the final three weeks, she stayed inside mostly and we told everyone that she had gone to visit her cousins in Iberia.

"The baby, a healthy boy, was born and delivered to Octavious Tate. Grandpere Jack got his money and lost it in less than a week, but the secret was kept.

"Up until now, that is," she said, lowering her head. "I had hoped never to have to tell you. You already know what your mother did later on. I didn't want you to think terrible of her and then think terrible of yourself.

"But I never counted on you and Paul . . . becoming more than just friends," she added.

85

"When I saw you two kiss out by his car before, I knew you had to be told," she concluded.

"Then Paul and I are half brother and half sister?" I asked with a gasp. She nodded. "But he doesn't know any of this?"

"As I told you, we didn't know how the Tates dealt with it."

I buried my face in my hands. The tears that burned beneath my lids seemed to be falling inside me as well, making my stomach icy and cold. I shivered and rocked.

"Oh, God, how horrible, oh, God," I moaned.

"You see and understand why I had to tell you, don't you, Ruby dear?" Grandmere Catherine asked. I could feel how troubled she was by making the revelation, how much it bothered her to see me in such pain. I nodded quickly. "You must not let things go any further between the two of you, but it's not your place to tell him what I've told you. It's something his own father must tell him."

"It will destroy him," I said, shaking my head. "It will crack his heart in two, just as it has cracked mine."

"Then don't tell him, Ruby," Grandmere Catherine advised. I looked up at her. "Just let it all end."

"How, Grandmere? We like each other so much. Paul is so gentle and kind and—"

"Let him think you don't care about him anymore like that, Ruby. Let him go and he'll find another girlfriend soon enough. He's a handsome boy. Besides, his parents will only give him more grief if you don't, especially his father, and you will only succeed in breaking the Tates apart."

"His father is a monster, a monster. How could he have done such a thing when he was married for such a short time?" I demanded, my anger overcoming my sadness for the moment.

"I make no excuses for him. He was a grown man and Gabrielle was just an impressionable young girl, but so beautiful, it didn't surprise me that grown men longed for her. The devil, the evil spirit that hovers in the shadows, crept over Octavious Tate day by day, I'm sure, and eventually found entrance into his heart and drove him to seduce your mother."

"Paul would hate him, he would hate his own father if he knew," I said vehemently. Grandmere nodded.

"Do you want to do that, Ruby? Do you want to be the one who puts enmity in his heart and drives him to despise his own father?" she asked softly. "And what will Paul feel about the woman he thinks is his mother? What will you do to that relationship, too?"

"Oh, Grandmere," I cried, and rose off the settee to throw myself at her feet. I embraced her legs and buried my face in her lap. She stroked my hair softly.

"There, there, my baby. You will get over the pain. You're still very young with your whole life ahead of you. You're going to become a great artist and have beautiful things." She put her hand under my chin and lifted my head so she could look into my eyes. "Now do you understand why I dream of you leaving the bayou," she added.

With my tears streaming down my cheeks, I nodded. "Yes," I said. "I do. But I never want to leave you, Grandmere."

"Someday you will have to, Ruby. It's the way of all things, and when that day comes, don't hesitate. Do what you have to do. Promise me you will. Promise," she demanded. She looked so anxious about it, I had to respond.

"I will, Grandmere."

"Good," she said. "Good." She sat back, looking as if she had just aged a year for every minute that passed. I ground the tears from my eyes with my small fists and stood up.

"Do you want something, Grandmere? A glass of lemonade, maybe?"

"Just a glass of cold water," she said, smiling. She patted my hand. "I'm sorry, honey," she said.

I swallowed hard and leaned down to kiss her on the cheek.

"It's not your fault, Grandmere. You have no reason to blame yourself."

She smiled softly at me. Then I got her the glass of water and watched her drink it. It seemed painful for her to do so, but she finished it and rose from her chair.

"I'm very tired, suddenly," she said. "I've got to go to bed."

"Yes, Grandmere. I will soon, too."

After she left, I went to the front door and looked out at where Paul and I had kissed good night.

We didn't know it then, but it was the last time we would ever kiss like that, the last time we would ever feel each other's heart beating and thrill to each other's touch. I closed the door and walked to the stairway, feeling as if someone I knew and loved with all my heart had just died. In a real sense that was true, for the Paul Tate I knew and loved before was gone and the Ruby Landry he had kissed and loved as well was lost. The sin that had given Paul life had reared its ugly head and taken away his love.

I dreaded the days that were now to follow.

That night I tossed and turned and woke from my sleep many times. Each time, my stomach felt as tight as a fist. I wished the whole day and night had just been a bad dream, but there was no denying Grandmere Catherine's dark, sad eyes. The vision of her face lingered behind my eyelids, reminding, reinforcing, confirming that all that had happened and all that I had learned was real and true.

I didn't think Grandmere Catherine had slept any better than I had, even though she had looked so exhausted before going to bed. For the first time in a long time, she was up and about only moments before me. I heard her shuffling past my room and opened the door to watch her make her way to the kitchen.

I hurried to go down to help her with our breakfast. Although the rainstorm of the night before had passed, there were still layers of thin, gray clouds across the Louisiana sky, making the morning look as dreary as I felt. The birds seemed subdued as well, barely singing and calling to each other. It was as if the whole bayou were feeling sorry for me and for Paul.

"Seems a Traiteur should be able to treat her own arthritis," Grandmere muttered. "My joints ache and my recipes for medicine don't seem to help."

Grandmere Catherine was not one to voice complaints about herself. I'd seen her walk miles in the rain to help someone and not utter a single syllable of protest. No matter what infirmity or hard luck she suffered, she always remarked that there were too many who were worse off.

"You don't drop the potato because hills and valleys suddenly appear on your road," she told me, which was a Cajun's way of saying you don't give up. "You bear the brunt; you carry the excess baggage, and you go on." I always felt she was trying to teach me how to live by example, so I knew how much pain she must be suffering to complain about it in my presence this morning.

"Maybe we should take a day off from the road stall, Grandmere," I said. "We've got my painting money and—"

"No," she said. "It's better to keep busy, and besides, we've got to be out there while there are still tourists in the bayou. You know we have enough weeks and months without anyone coming around to buy our things and it's hard enough to scrounge and scrape up a living then."

I didn't say it, because I knew it would only get her angry, but why *didn't* Grandpere Jack do more for us? Why did we let him get away with his lazy, swamp bum life? He was a Cajun man and as such he should bear more responsibility for his family, even if Grandmere was not pleased with him. I made up my mind I would pole out to his shack later and tell him what I thought.

Right after breakfast, I started to set up our roadside stall as usual while Grandmere prepared her gumbo. I saw the strain on her face as she worked and then carried things out, so I ran and got her a chair to sit on as quickly as I could. Despite what she had said, I wished it would rain hard and send us back into the house, so she could rest. But it didn't and just as she had predicted, the tourists began to come around.

About eleven o'clock Paul drove up on his motor scooter. Grandmere Catherine and I exchanged a quick look, but she said nothing more to me as Paul approached.

"Hello, Mrs. Landry," he began. "My cheek is practically all healed and my lip feels fine," he quickly added. The bruise had diminished considerably. There was just a slight pink area on his cheekbone. "Thanks again."

"You're welcome," Grandmere said, "but don't forget your promise to me."

"I won't." He laughed and turned to me. "Hi."

"Hi," I said quickly, and unfolded and folded a blanket so it would rest more neatly on the shelves of the stall. "How come you're not working in the cannery today?" I asked, without looking at him.

He stepped closer so Grandmere wouldn't hear.

"My father and I had it out last night. I'm not working for him anymore and I can't use the car until he says so, which might be never unless—"

"Unless you stop seeing me," I finished for him,

then turned around. The look in his eyes told me I was right.

"I don't care what he says. I don't need the car. I bought the scooter with my own money, so I'll just ride around on it. All I care about doing is getting here to see you as quickly as I can. Nothing else matters," he declared firmly.

"That's not true, Paul. I can't let you do this to your parents and to yourself. Maybe not now, but weeks, months, even years from now, you'll regret driving your parents away from you," I told him sternly. Even I could hear the new, cold tone in my voice. It pained me to be this way, but I had to do it, I had to find a way to stop what could never be.

"What?" He smiled. "You know the only thing I care about is getting to be with you, Ruby. Let them adjust if they don't want to drive us apart. It's all their fault. They're snobby and selfish and—"

"No, they're not, Paul," I said quickly. His face hardened with confusion. "It's only natural for them to want the best for you."

"We've been over this before, Ruby. I told you, you're the best for me," he said. I looked away. I couldn't face him when I spoke these words. We had no customers at the moment, so I walked away from the stall, Paul trailing behind me as closely and as silently as my shadow. I paused at one of our cypress log benches and sat down, facing the swamp.

"What's wrong?" he asked softly.

"I've been thinking it all over," I said. "I'm not sure you're the best for me."

"What?"

Out in the swamp, perched on a big sycamore tree, the old marsh owl stared at us as if he could hear and understand the words we were saying. He was so still, he looked stuffed.

"After you left last night, I gave everything more thought. I know there are many girls my age or slightly older who are already married in the bayou. There are even younger ones, but I don't just want to be married and live happily ever after in the bayou. I want to do more, be more. I want to be an artist."

"So? I would never stop you. I'd do everything I could to—"

"An artist, a true artist, has to experience many things, travel, meet many different kinds of people, expand her vision," I said, turning back to him. He looked smaller, diminished by my words. He shook his head.

"What are you saying?"

"We shouldn't be so serious," I explained.

"But I thought . . . " He shook his head. "This is all because I made a fool of myself last night, isn't it? Your grandmother is really very upset with me."

"No, she's not. Last night just made me think harder, that's all."

"It's my fault," he repeated.

"It isn't anyone's fault. Or, at least it isn't our fault," I added, recalling Grandmere Catherine's revelations last night. "It's just the way things are."

"What do you want me to do?" he asked.

"I want you to . . . to do what I'm going to do . . . see other people, too."

"There's someone else then?" he followed, incredulous. "How could you be the way you were last night with me and the days and nights before that and like someone else?"

"There's not someone else just yet," I muttered.

"There is," he insisted. I looked up at him. His sadness was being replaced with anger rapidly. The softness in his eyes evaporated and a fury took its place. His shoulders rose and his face became as crimson as his bruised cheek. His lips whitened in the corners. He looked like he could exhale fire like a dragon. I hated what I was doing to him. I wished I could just vanish.

"My father told me I was a fool to put my heart and trust in you, in a—"

"In a Landry," I coached sadly.

"Yes. In a Landry. He said the apple doesn't fall far from the tree."

I lowered my head. I thought about my mother letting herself be used by Paul's father for his pleasure and I thought about Grandpere Jack caring more about getting money than what had happened to his daughter.

"He was right."

"I don't believe you," Paul shot back. When I looked at him again, I saw the tears that had washed over his eyes, tears of pain and anger, tears that would poison his mind against me. How I wished I could throw myself into his arms and stop what was happening, but I was thwarted and muzzled by reality. "You don't want to be an artist; you want to be a whore."

"Paul!"

"That's all, a whore. Well, go on, be with as many different men as you like. See if I care. I was crazy to waste my time on a Landry," he added and pivoted quickly, his boots kicking up the grass behind him as he rushed away.

My chin dropped to my chest and my body slumped on the cypress log bench. Where my heart had been, there was now a hollow cavity. I couldn't even cry. It was as if everything in me, every part of me had suddenly locked up, frozen, become as cold as stone. The sound of Paul's motor scooter engine reverberated through my body. The old marsh owl lifted his wings and strutted about nervously on the branch, but he didn't lift off. He remained there, watching me, his eyes filled with accusation now.

After Paul left our house, I got up. My legs were very shaky, but I was able to walk back to the roadside stall just as a carload of tourists pulled up. They were young men and women, loud and full of laughter and fun. The men went wild over the pickled lizards and snakes and bought four jars. The women liked Grandmere's handwoven towels and handkerchiefs. After they had bought everything they wanted and loaded their car, one of the young men paused and approached us with his camera.

"Do you mind if I take your pictures?" he asked. "I'll give you each a dollar," he added.

"You don't have to pay us for our pictures," Grandmere replied.

"Oh, yes, he does," I said. Grandmere Catherine raised her eyebrows in surprise.

"Fine," the young man said and dug into his pocket to produce the two dollars. I took them quickly. "Can you smile?" he asked me. I forced one and he snapped his photos. "Thanks," he said, and got into the car.

"Why did you make him give us two dollars, Ruby? We haven't taken money from tourists in the past." Grandmere asked me.

"Because the world is full of pain and disappointment, Grandmere, and I plan to do all I can from now on to make it less so for us."

She fixed her eyes on me thoughtfully. "I want you to grow up, but I don't want you to grow up with a hard heart, Ruby," she said.

"A soft heart gets pierced and torn more, Grandmere. I'm not going to end up like my mother. I'm not!" I cried and despite my firm and rigid stance, I felt my new wall start to crack.

"What did you say to young Paul Tate?" Grandmere asked. "What did you tell him to make him run off like that?"

"I didn't tell him the truth, but I drove him away, just as you said I should," I moaned through my tears. "Now, he hates me."

"Oh, Ruby, I'm sorry."

"He hates me!" I cried, and turned and ran from her.

"Ruby!"

I didn't stop. I ran hard and fast over the marshland, letting the bramble bushes slap and tear at my dress, my legs, and my arms. I was oblivious to pain; I ignored the ache in my chest and disregarded the puddles and the mud into which I repeatedly stepped. But after a while, the pain in my legs and the needles in my side brought me to a halt, and I could only walk slowly over the long stretch of marshland that ran alongside the canal. My shoulders heaved with my deep sobs. I walked and walked, past the dried domes of grass that were homes to the muskrats and nutrias, avoiding the inlets in which the small green snakes swam. Fatigued and drowning in many emotions, I finally stopped and gasped in air, my hands on my hips, my bosom rising and falling.

After a moment, my eyes focused on a clump of small sycamore trees just ahead. At first, because of its color and size, I didn't see it. But gradually, it formed in my field of vision, seemingly appearing like a vision. I saw a marsh deer watching me with curiosity. It had big, beautiful, but sad looking eyes and it stood as still as a statue.

Suddenly, there was a loud report, the explosion of a high caliber rifle came from the blind, and the deer's knees crumbled. It stumbled a moment in a desperate effort to maintain its stance, but a red circle of blood appeared on its neck and grew larger and larger as the blood emerged. The deer went down quickly after that and I heard the sound of two men cheering. A pirogue shot out from under a wall of Spanish moss and I saw two strangers in the front and Grandpere Jack poling from the rear. He had hired himself out to tourist hunters and brought them to their kill. As the canoe made its way across the pond toward the dead deer, one of the tourists handed the other a bottle of whiskey and they drank to celebrate their

97

kill. Grandpere Jack eyed the bottle and stopped poling so they could give him a swig.

Slowly, I retreated, following my footsteps back. Yes, I thought, the swamp was a beautiful place, filled with wonderful and interesting animal life, with fascinating vegetation, sometimes mysterious and still and sometimes a symphony of nature with its frogs croaking, its birds singing, its gators drumming water with their tails. But it could be a hard, cold place, too, wrought with death and danger, with poisonous snakes and spiders, with quicksand and sticky, sucking mud to draw the unsuspecting intruder down into the darkness beneath. It was a world in which the stronger fed on the weaker and into which men came to enjoy their power over natural things.

Today, I thought, it was like everywhere else on earth, and today, I hated being here.

By the time I returned, the showers had begun and Grandmere Catherine had begun to take in most of our handicraft goods. I hurried to help her with what remained. The rain fell harder and harder, so we had to rush as quickly as we could and we had no time to speak to each other until everything had been safely stored. Then Grandmere got us some towels to wipe our hair and faces. The rain pounded the tin roof and the wind whipped through the bayou. We ran around the house, closing the batten plank shutters.

"It's a real tosser," Grandmere cried. We heard the wind whistle through the cracks in our walls and saw brush and anything else that was loose and light being lifted and driven every which way

98

over the road and lawn. The world outside became very dark. Thunder clapped and lightning scorched the sky. I could hear the cisterns overflowing as sheets of rain came off the roof and collected in the barrels. The drops fell so hard and thick, they bounced when they hit the steps or little walkway in front of the house. For a while it sounded like the tin roof would split. It was as if we had fallen into a drum. Finally, it subsided and just as quickly as it had developed into a heavy downpour, it became a slight drizzle. The sky lightened and moments later, a ray of sunlight threaded itself through the opening in the overcast and dropped a shaft of warm brightness over our home.

Grandmere Catherine took a deep breath of relief and shook her head.

"I never get used to those sudden cloudbursts," she said. "When I was a little girl, I used to crawl under my bed."

I smiled at her.

"I can't imagine you as a little girl, Grandmere," I said.

"Well, I was, honey. I wasn't born this old with bones that creaked when I walked, you know." She pressed her hand against the small of her back and straightened up. "I think I'll make a cup of tea. I'd like something warm in my stomach. How about you?"

"All right, Grandmere," I said. I sat at the kitchen table while she put up the water. "Grandpere Jack is doing some guiding for hunters again. I just saw him in the swamp with two men. They shot a deer."

"He was one of the best at it," she said. "The rich Creoles were always after him when they came here to hunt, and none ever left empty-handed."

"It was a beautiful deer, Grandmere."

She nodded.

"And the thing is, they won't care about the meat; they just want a trophy."

She stared at me a moment. "What did you tell Paul?" she finally asked.

"That we shouldn't just be with each other; that we should see other people. I told him because I was an artist, I wanted to meet other people, but he didn't believe me. I'm not a good liar, Grandmere," I moaned.

"That's not a bad fault, Ruby."

"Yes, it is, Grandmere," I retorted quickly. "This is a world built on lies, lies and deceptions. The stronger and the more successful are good at it."

Grandmere Catherine shook her head sadly.

"It looks that way to you right now, Ruby honey, but don't give into the comfort of hating everything and everyone around you. Those you call stronger and successful might seem so to you, but they're not really happy, for there is a dark place in their hearts that they cannot deny and it makes their souls ache. In the end they are terrified because they know the darkness is what they will face forever."

"You've seen so much evil and so much sickness, Grandmere. How can you still feel hopeful?" I asked.

She smiled and sighed.

"It's when you stop feeling hopeful that the

sickness and the evil wins over you and then what becomes of you? Never lose hope, Ruby. Never stop fighting for hope," she advised. "I know how much you're hurting now and how much poor Paul is suffering, too, but just like this sudden storm, it will end for you and the sun will be out again.

"I always dreamed," she said, coming over to sit beside me and stroke my hair, "that you would have the magical wedding, the one in the Cajun spider legend. Remember? The rich Frenchman imported those spiders from France for his daughter's wedding and released them into the oaks and pines where they wove their canopy of webs. Over them, he sprinkled gold and silver dust and then they had the candlelight wedding procession. The night glittered all around them, promising them a life of love and hope.

"Someday, you will marry a handsome man who could be a prince and you, too, will have a wedding in the stars," Grandmere promised. She kissed me and I threw my arms around her to bury my head in her soft shoulder. I cried and cried and she petted me and soothed me. "Cry honey," she said. "And like the summer rains turn to sunshine so will your tears."

"Oh, Grandmere," I moaned. "I don't know if I can."

"You can," she said. She lifted my chin and looked into my eyes, hers those dark, mesmerizing orbs that had seen evil spirits and visions of the future, "you can and you will," she predicted.

The teapot whistled. Grandmere wiped the tears

from my cheeks and kissed me again, and then got up to pour us our cups.

Later that night, I sat by my window and looked up at the clearing sky and I wondered if Grandmere was right; I wondered if I would have a wedding in the stars. The glitter of gold and silver dust danced under my eyelids when I lay my head on the pillow, but just before I fell asleep, I saw Paul's wounded face once more and then I saw the marsh deer open its mouth to voice an unheard scream as it crumbled to the grass.

5

Who Is the Little Girl If It's Not Me?

The weeks before summer and the end of the school year took ages and ages to pass. I dreaded every day I attended school, for I knew that some time during the day, I would see Paul or he would see me. During the first few days following our terrible talk, he continued to glare at me furiously whenever he saw me. His once beautiful, soft blue eyes that had gazed upon me with love so many times before were now granite cold and full of scorn and contempt. The second time we approached each other in the corridor, I tried to speak to him.

"Paul," I said, "I'd like to talk to you, to just—"

He behaved as if he didn't hear me or he didn't see me and walked past me. I wanted him to know that I wasn't seeing another boy on the side. I felt dreadful and spent most of my school day with a heart that felt more like a lump of lead in my chest.

Time wasn't healing my wounds and the longer we went on not talking to each other, the harder and colder Paul seemed to become. I wished that I could simply rush up to him one day and gush the truth so he would understand why I said the things I had said to him at my house, but every time I decided I would do just that, Grandmere Catherine's heavy words returned: "Do you want to be the one who puts enmity in his heart and drives him to despise his own father?" She was right. In the end he would hate me more, I concluded. And so I kept my lips sealed and the truth buried beneath an ocean of secret tears.

Many times I had found myself furious with Grandmere Catherine or Grandpere Jack for not revealing the secrets in their hearts and keeping my family history a deep mystery, a mystery it should no longer have been for me at my age. Now, I was no better than they had been, keeping the truth from Paul, but there was nothing I could do about it. Worst of all, I had to stand by and watch him fall in love with someone else.

I always knew that Suzzette Daisy, a girl in my class, had a crush on Paul. She didn't wait long to pursue him, but ironically, when Paul first began spending more and more time with Suzzette Daisy, I felt a sense of relief. He would direct more of his energies toward caring for her and less toward hating me, I thought. From across the room, I watched him sit with her and eat his lunch and soon saw them holding hands when they walked through the school corridors. Of course, a part of me was jealous, a part of me raged over the injustice and cried when I saw them laughing and giggling together. Then I heard he had given her his class ring which she wore proudly on a gold chain, and I spent a night drenching my pillow in salty tears.

Most of the girls who had once been envious of Paul's affection for me now gloated. Marianne Bruster actually turned to me in the girls' room one June afternoon and blared, "I guess you don't think you're someone special anymore since you were dumped for Suzzette Daisy."

The other girls smiled and waited for me to respond.

"I never thought I was someone special, Marianne," I said. "But thank you for thinking so," I added.

For a moment she was dumbfounded. Her mouth opened and closed. I started past her, but she spun about, flinging her hair over her face, then tossing it back and whipping around to make it fan out in a circle as she grinned broadly at me.

"Well, that's just like you," she said, her hands on her hips, her head wagging from side to side as she spoke. "Just like you to be smart about it. I don't know where you come off being snotty," she continued, now building on her anger and frustration. "You're certainly no better than the rest of us."

"I never said I was, Marianne."

"If anything, you're worse. You're a bastard child. That's what you are," she accused. The others nodded. Encouraged, she reached out to seize my arm and continue. "Paul Tate finally has

104

shown some sense. He belongs with someone like Suzzette and certainly not a low-class Cajun like a Landry," she concluded.

I pulled away and brushed at my tears as I rushed from the girls' room. It was true—everyone thought Paul belonged with someone like Suzzette Daisy and thought they were the perfect couple. She was a pretty girl with long, light brown hair and stately features, but more important, her father was a rich oil man. I was sure Paul's parents were overjoyed at his choice of a new girlfriend. He'd have no trouble getting the car and going to dances with Suzzette.

Yet despite his apparent happiness with his new girlfriend, I couldn't help but detect a wistful look in his eyes when he saw me occasionally and especially at church. Starting a relationship with Suzzette, and the passage of more time since our split-up, finally began to calm him. I even thought he was close to speaking to me, but every time he seemed to be headed in that direction, something stopped him and turned him away again.

Finally, mercifully, the school year ended, and with it my daily contact with Paul, as slight as it had been. Outside of school he and I truly did live in two different worlds. He no longer had any reason to come my way. Of course, I still saw him at church on Sunday, but in the company of his parents and sisters, he especially wouldn't even look in my direction. Occasionally, I would hear what sounded like his motor scooter's engine and go running to my doorway to look out in anticipation and in the hope that I would see him pull into our drive just as he used to so many times before.

But the sound either turned out to be someone else on a motorcycle or some old car passing by.

These were my days of darkness, days when I was so sad and tired that I had to fight to get out of bed each morning. Making everything seem worse and harder was the intensity with which the heat and the humidity greeted the bayou this particular summer. Everyday temperatures hovered near a hundred with humidity often only a degree or two less. Day after day the swamps were calm, still, not even the tiniest wisp of a breeze weaving its way up from the Gulf to give us any relief.

The heat took a great toll on Grandmere Catherine. More than ever, she was oppressed by the layers and layers of heavy humidity. I hated it when she had to walk somewhere to treat someone for a bad spider bite or a terrible headache. More often than not, she would return exhausted, drained, her dress drenched, her hair sticking to her forehead and her cheeks beet red; but these trips and the work she did resulted in some small income or some gifts of food for us and with the tourist trade dwindling down to practically nothing during the summer months, there wasn't much else.

Grandpere Jack wasn't any help. He stopped even his infrequent assistance. I heard he was hunting alligators with some men from New Orleans who wanted to sell the skins to make pocketbooks and wallets and whatever else city folk made out of the swamp creatures' hides. I didn't see him much, but whenever I did, he was usually floating by in his canoe or drifting in his dingy and guzzling some homemade cider or whiskey, satisfied to turn whatever money he had made from his gator hunting into another bottle or jug.

Late one afternoon, Grandmere Catherine returned from a treater mission more exhausted than ever. She could barely speak. I had to rush out to help her up the stairs. She practically collapsed in her bed.

"Grandmere, your legs are trembling," I cried when I helped her take off her moccasins. Her feet were blistered and swollen, especially her ankles.

"I'll be all right," she chanted. "I'll be all right. Just get me a cold cloth for my forehead, Ruby, honey."

I hurried to do so.

"I'll just lay here a while until my heart slows down," she told me, and forced a smile.

"Oh, Grandmere, you can't make these long trips anymore. It's too hot and you're too old to do it."

She shook her head.

"I must do it," she said. "It's why the good Lord put me here."

I waited until she fell asleep and then I left the house and poled our pirogue out to Grandpere's shack. All of the sadness and days of melancholy I had endured the past month and a half turned into anger and fury directed at Grandpere. He knew how hard it was for us during the summer months. Instead of drinking up his spare money every week, he should think about us and come around more often, I decided. I also decided not to discuss it with Grandmere Catherine, for she wouldn't want to admit I was right and she wouldn't want to ask him for a penny.

The swamp was different in the summer. Besides the waking of the hibernating alligators who had been sleeping with tails fattened with stores, there were dozens and dozens of snakes, clumps of them entwined together or slicing through the water like green and brown threads. Of course, there were clouds of mosquitos and other bugs, choruses of fat bullfrogs with gaping eyes and jiggling throats croaking and families of nutrias and muskrats scurrying about frantically, stopping only to eye me with suspicion. The insects and animals continually changed the swamp, their homes making it bulge in places it hadn't before, their webs linking plants and tree limbs. It made it all seem alive, like the swamp was one big animal itself, forming and reforming with each change of season.

I knew Grandmere Catherine would be upset that I was traveling alone through the swamp this later in the summer day, as well as being upset that I was going to see Grandpere Jack. But my anger had come to a head and sent me rushing out of the house to plod over the marsh and pole the pirogue faster than ever. Before long, I came around a turn and saw Grandpere's shack straight ahead. But as I approached, I slowed down because the racket coming from it was frightening.

I heard pans clanging, furniture cracking, Grandpere's howls and curses. A small chair came flying out the door and splashed in the swamp before it quickly sunk. A pot followed and then another. I stopped my canoe and waited. Moments later, Grandpere appeared on his galerie. He was stark naked, his hair wild, holding a bullwhip. Even at this distance, I could see his eyes were bloodshot. His body was streaked with dirt and mud and there were even long, thin scratches up his legs and down the small of his back.

He cracked the whip at something in the air before him and shouted before cracking it again. I soon understood he was imagining some kind of creature and I realized he was having a drunken fit. Grandmere Catherine had described one of them to me, but I had never seen it before. She said the alcohol soaked his brain so bad it gave him delusions and created nightmares, even in the daytime. On more than one occasion, he had one of these fits in the house and destroyed many of their good things.

"I used to have to run out and wait until he grew exhausted and fell asleep," she told me. "Otherwise, he might very well hurt me without realizing it."

Remembering those words, I backed my canoe into a small inlet so he wouldn't see me watching. He cracked the whip again and again and screamed so hard, the veins in his neck bulged. Then he caught the whip in some of his muskrat traps and got it so entangled, he couldn't pull it out. He interpreted this as the monster grabbing his whip. It put a new hysteria into him and he began to wail, waving his arms about him so quickly, he looked like a cross between a man and a spider from where I was watching. Finally, the exhaustion Grandmere Catherine described set in and he collapsed to the porch floor.

I waited a long moment. All was silent and remained so. Satisfied, he was unconscious, I poled myself up to the galerie and peered over the edge to see him twisted and asleep, oblivious to the mosquitos that feasted on his exposed skin.

I tied up the canoe and stepped onto the galerie. He looked barely alive, his chest heaving and falling with great effort. I knew I couldn't lift him and carry him into the house, so I went inside and found a blanket to put over him.

Then, I pulled in a deep fearful breath and nudged him, but his eyes didn't even flutter. He was already snoring. I went cold inside. All the hopes that had lit up were snuffed out by the sight and the stench rising off him. He smelled like he had taken a bath in his jugs of cheap whiskey.

"So much for coming to you for any help, Grandpere," I said furiously. "You are a disgrace." With him unconscious, I was able to vent my anger unchecked. "What kind of a man are you? How could you let us struggle and strain to keep alive and well? You know how tired Grandmere Catherine is. Don't you have any self-respect?

"I hate having Landry blood in me. I hate it!" I screamed, and pounded my fists against my hips. My voice echoed through the swamp. A heron flew off instantly and a dozen feet away, an alligator lifted its head from the water and gazed in my direction. "Stay here, stay in the swamp and guzzle your rotgut whiskey until you die. I don't care," I cried. The tears streaked down my cheeks, hot tears of anger and frustration. My heart pounded.

I caught my breath and stared at him. He moaned, but he didn't open his eyes. Disgusted, I got back into the pirogue and started to pole myself home, feeling more despondent and defeated than ever.

With the tourist trade nearly nonexistent and school over, I had more time to do my artwork. Grandmere Catherine was the first to notice that my pictures were remarkably different. Usually in a melancholy mood when I began, I tended now to use darker colors and depict the swamp world at either twilight or at night with the pale white light of a half moon or full moon penetrating twisted sycamores and cypress limbs. Animals stared out with luminous eyes and snakes coiled their bodies, poised to strike and kill any intruders. The water was inky, the Spanish moss dangling over it like a net left there to ensnare the unwary traveler. Even the spiderwebs that I used to make sparkle like jewels now appeared more like the traps they were intended to be. The swamp was an eerie, dismal, and depressing place and if I did include my mysterious father in the picture, he had a face masked with shadows.

"I don't think most people would like that picture, Ruby," Grandmere told me one day as she stood behind me and watched me visualize another nightmare. "It's not the kind of picture that will make them feel good, the kind they're going to want to hang up in their living rooms and sitting rooms in New Orleans."

"It's how I feel, what I see right now, Grandmere. I can't help it," I told her.

She shook her head sadly and sighed before retreating to her oak rocker. I found she spent more and more time sitting and falling asleep in it. Even on cloudy days when it was a bit cooler outside, she no longer took her pleasure walks along the canals. She didn't care to go find wild flowers, nor would she visit her friends as much as she used to visit them. Invitations to lunch went unaccepted. She made her excuses, claimed she had to do this or that, but usually ended up falling asleep in a chair or on the sofa.

When she didn't know I was watching, I caught her taking deep breaths and pressing her palm against her bosom. Any exertion, washing clothes or the floors, polishing furniture, and even cooking exhausted her. She had to take frequent rests in between and battle to catch her breath.

But when I asked her about it, she was always ready with an excuse. She was tired from staying up too late the night before; she had a bit of lumbago, she got up too fast, anything and everything but her owning up to the truth—that she hadn't been well for quite some time now.

Finally, on the third Sunday in August, I rose and dressed and went down, surprised I was up and ready before her, especially on a church day. When she finally appeared, she looked pale and very old, as old as Rip van Winkle after his extended sleep. She cringed a bit when she walked and held her hand against her side.

"I don't know what's come over me," she declared. "I haven't overslept like this for years."

"Maybe you can't cure yourself, Grandmere.

Maybe your herbs and potions don't work on you and you should see a town doctor," I suggested.

"Nonsense. I just haven't found the right formula yet, but I'm on the right track. I'll be back to myself in a day or two," she swore, but two days went by and she didn't improve an iota. One minute she would be talking to me and the next, she would be fast asleep in her chair, her mouth wide open, her chest heaving as if it were a struggle to breathe.

Only two events got her up and about with the old energy she used to exhibit. The first was when Grandpere Jack came to the house and actually asked us for money. I was sitting with Grandmere on the galerie after our dinner, grateful for the little coolness the twilight brought to the bayou. Her head grew heavier and heavier on her shoulders until her chin rested on her chest, but the moment Grandpere Jack's footsteps could be heard, her head snapped up. She narrowed her eyes into slits of suspicion.

"What's he coming here for?" she demanded, staring into the darkness out of which he emerged like some ghostly apparition from the swamp: his long hair bouncing on the back of his neck, his face sallow with his grimy gray beard thicker than usual, and his clothes so creased and dirty, he looked like he had been rolling around in them for days. His boots were so thick with mud, it looked caked around his feet and ankles.

"Don't you come any closer," Grandmere snapped. "We just had our dinner and the stink will turn our stomachs."

"Aw, woman," he said, but he stopped about a

half-dozen yards from the galerie. He took off his hat and held it in his hands. Fishhooks dangled from the brim. "I come here on a mission of mercy," he said.

"Mercy? Mercy for who?" Grandmere demanded.

"For me," he replied. That nearly set her laughing. She rocked a bit and shook her head.

"You come here to beg forgiveness?" she asked.

"I came here to borrow some money," he said.

"What?" She stopped rocking, stunned.

"My dingy's motor is shot to hell and Charlie McDermott won't advance me any more credit to buy a new used one from him. I gotta have a motor or I can't earn any money guiding hunters, harvesting oysters, whatnot," he said. "I know you got something put away and I swear—"

"What good is your oath, Jack Landry? You're a cursed man, a doomed man whose soul already has a prime reservation in hell," she told him with more vehemence and energy than I had seen her exert in days. For a moment Grandpere didn't reply.

"If I can earn something, I can pay you back and then some right quickly," he said. Grandmere snorted.

"If I gave you the last pile of pennies we had, you'd turn from here and run as fast as you could to get a bottle of rum and drink yourself into another stupor," she told him. "Besides," she said, "we haven't got anything. You know how times get in the bayou in the summer for us. Not that you showed you cared any," she added.

"I do what I can," he protested.

114

"For yourself and your damnable thirst," she fired back.

I shifted my gaze from Grandmere to Grandpere. He really did look desperate and repentant. Grandmere Catherine knew I had my painting money put away. I could loan it to him if he was really in a fix, I thought, but I was afraid to say.

"You'd let a man die out here in the swamp, starve to death and become food for the buzzards," he moaned.

She stood up slowly, rising to her full five feet four inches of height as if she were really six feet tall, her head up, her shoulders back, and then she lifted her left arm to point her forefinger at him. I saw his eyes bulge with shock and fear as he took a step back.

"You are already dead, Jack Landry," she declared with the authority of a bishop, "and already food for buzzards. Go back to your cemetery and leave us be," she commanded.

"Some Christian you are," he cried, but continued to back up. "Some show of mercy. You're no better than me, Catherine. You're no better," he called, and turned to get swallowed up in the darkness from where he had come as quickly as he had appeared. Grandmere stared after him a few moments even after he was gone and then sat down.

"We could have given him my painting money, Grandmere," I said. She shook her head vehemently.

"That money is not to be touched by him," she said firmly. "You're going to need it someday,

Ruby, and besides," she added, "he'd only do what I said, turn it into cheap whiskey.

"The nerve of him," she continued, more to herself than to me, "Coming around here and asking me to loan him money. The nerve of him . . . ."

I watched her wind herself down until she was slumped in her chair again, and I thought how terrible it was that two people who had once kissed and held each other, who had loved and wanted to be with each other were now like two alley cats, hissing and scratching at each other in the night.

The confrontation with my grandpere drained Grandmere. She was so exhausted, I had to help her to bed. I sat beside her for a while and watched her sleep, her cheeks still red, her forehead beaded with perspiration. Her bosom rose and fell with such effort, I thought her heart would simply burst under the pressure.

That night I went to sleep with great trepidation, afraid that when I woke up, I would find Grandmere Catherine hadn't. But thankfully, her sleep revived her and what woke me the next morning was the sound of her footsteps as she made her way to the kitchen to start breakfast and begin another day of work in the loom room.

Despite the lack of customers, we continued our weaving and handicrafts whenever we could during the summer months, building a stock of goods to put out when the tourist season got back into high swing. Grandmere bartered with cotton growers and farmers who harvested the palmetto leaves with which we made the hats and fans. She traded some of her gumbo for split oak so we could make the baskets. Whenever it appeared we were bone-dry and had nothing to offer in return for craft materials, Grandmere reached deeper into her sacred chest and came up with something of value she had either been given as payment for a treater mission years before, or something she had been saving just for such a time.

Just at one of these hard periods, the second thing occurred to put vim and vigor into her steps and words. The postman delivered a fancy light blue envelope with a lace design on its edges addressed to me. It came from New Orleans, the return address simply Dominique's.

"Grandmere, I've got a letter from the gallery in New Orleans," I shouted running into the house. She nodded, holding her breath, her eyes bright with excitement.

"Go on, open it," she said, slipping into a chair. I sat at the kitchen table while I tore it open and plucked out a cashier's check for two hundred and fifty dollars. There was a note with it.

> Congratulations on the sale of one of your pictures. I have some interest in the others and will be contacting you in the near future to see what else you have done since my visit.
> Sincerely,
> Dominique

Grandmere Catherine and I just looked at each other for a moment and then her face lit up with the brightest, broadest smile I had seen her wear for months. She closed her eyes and offered a

117

quick prayer of thanks. I continued to stare incredulously at the cashier's check.

"Grandmere, can this be true? Two hundred and fifty dollars! For one of my paintings!"

"I told you it would happen. I told you," she said. "I wonder who bought it. He doesn't say?"

I looked again and shook my head.

"It doesn't matter," she said. "Many people will see it now and other well-to-do Creoles will come to Dominique's to look for your work and he will tell them who you are; he will tell them the artist is Ruby Landry," she added, nodding.

"Now you listen to me, Grandmere," I said firmly, "we are going to use this money to live on and not bury in your chest for some future thing for me."

"Maybe just some of it," she accepted, "but most of it has to be put away for you. Some day you will need nicer clothing and shoes and other things, and you will need traveling money, too," she said with certainty.

"Where am I going, Grandmere?" I asked.

"Away from here. Away from here," she muttered. "But for now, let us celebrate. Let's make a shrimp gumbo and a special dessert. I know," she said, "we'll make a Kings Cake." It was one of my favorites: a yeast cake ring with colorful sugar glazes. "I'll invite Mrs. Thibodeau and Mrs. Livaudis for dinner so I can brag about my granddaughter until they burst with envy. But first we'll go to the bank and cash your check," she said.

Grandmere's excitement and happiness filled me with joy I hadn't felt in months. I wished that

118

I had someone special with whom to celebrate and thought about Paul. I had seen him only one other time beside church the whole summer and that was when I was in town shopping for some groceries. When I came out of the store, I caught sight of him sitting in his father's car, waiting for him to come out of the bank. He looked my way and I thought he smiled, but at that moment his father appeared and he snapped his head around to face front. Disappointed, I watched him drive off, not looking back once.

Grandmere and I walked to town to cash my check. On the way we stopped at Mrs. Thibodeau's and Mrs. Livaudis's homes to invite them to our dinner of celebration. Then Grandmere began to cook and bake like she hadn't done for months. I helped her prepare and then set the table. She decided to stack the crisp twenty dollar bills at the center of the table with a rubber band around them just to impress her old friends. When they set eyes on it and heard how I had received it, they were astonished. Some people in the bayou worked a whole month for this much money.

"Well, I'm not surprised," Grandmere said. "I always knew she would become a famous artist someday."

"Oh, Grandmere," I said, embarrassed with all the attention, "I'm far from a famous artist."

"Right now you are, but one day you will be famous. Just wait and see," Grandmere predicted. We served the gumbo and the women got into a discussion about varieties of recipes. There were as many gumbo recipes in the bayou as there were

Cajuns, I thought. Listening to Grandmere Catherine and her friends argue over what combination of ingredients was the best and what accounted for the best roux amused me. Their spirited talk became even more so when Grandmere decided to bring out her homemade wine, something she saved for only very special occasions. One glass of it went right to my head. I felt my face turn crimson, but Grandmere and her two friends poured themselves glass after glass as if it were water.

The good food, the wine, and the laughter reminded me of happier times when Grandmere and I would go to community celebrations and gatherings. One of my favorites had always been Flocking the Bride. Each of the women would bring a chicken to start the flock for a newlywed, and there was always lots to eat and drink, and lots of music and dancing. Grandmere Catherine, being a Traiteur, was always an honored guest.

After we served the cake and cups of rich, thick Cajun coffee, I told Grandmere to take Mrs. Thibodeau and Mrs. Livaudis out to the galerie. I would clear the table and do the dishes.

"We shouldn't leave the one in whose honor we're celebrating with all the work," Mrs. Thibodeau said, but I insisted. After I cleaned up, I realized we still had the stack of money on the table. I went out to ask Grandmere where she thought I should put it.

"Just run up and put it in my chest, Ruby dear," she said. I was surprised. Grandmere Catherine never let me open her chest or rifle through it before. Occasionally, when she opened it, I looked over her shoulder and gazed in at the finely woven linen napkins and handkerchiefs, the silver goblets, and ropes of pearls. I remembered wanting to sift through all the memorabilia, but Grandmere Catherine always kept her chest sacred. I wouldn't dare touch it without her permission.

I hurried away to hide my new fortune. But when I opened the chest, I saw how empty it had become. Gone were the beautiful linens and all but one silver goblet. Grandmere had bartered and pawned much more than I imagined. It broke my heart to see how much of her personal treasure was gone. I knew that every item had had some special value beyond its money value. I knelt down and gazed at what remained: a single string of beads, a bracelet, a few embroidered scarfs, and a pile of documents and pictures, wrapped in rubber bands. The documents included inoculation certificates for me, as well as Grandmere Catherine's grade school diploma, and some old letters with ink so faded they were barely legible.

I sifted through some of the pictures. She still kept pictures of Grandpere Jack as a young man. How handsome he had been when he was a young man in his early twenties, tall and dark with wide shoulders and a narrow waist. A charming smile flashed brightly from the photograph and he stood so straight and proud. It was easy to see why Grandmere Catherine would have fallen in love with such a man. I found the other pictures of her mother and father, sepia colored and old and faded, but enough left for me to see that Grandmere Catherine's mother, my great-grandmother, had been a pretty woman with a sweet, gentle smile and small delicate features. Her father looked dignified and strong, tight-lipped and serious.

I put back the packets of documents and old family photographs, but before I deposited my money in the chest, I saw the edge of another picture sticking out from the pages of Grandmere Catherine's old leather-bound Bible. Slowly, I picked it up, handling the cracked cover carefully and gently opening the crisp pages that wanted to flake at the corners. I gazed at the old photograph.

It was a picture of a very good-looking man standing in front of what looked like a mansion. He was holding the hand of a little girl who looked a lot like me at that age. I studied the picture more closely. The little girl resembled me so much it was like looking at myself at this young age. In fact, the resemblance was so remarkable, I had to go to my room and find a picture of myself as a little girl. I placed the two side by side and studied them again.

It was me, I thought. It really was. But who was this man and where was I when this picture was taken? I would have been old enough to remember a house like this, I thought. I couldn't have been much less than six or seven at the time. I turned the picture over and saw there was scribbling on the back near the bottom.

Dear Gabrielle,
I thought you would like to see her on her seventh birthday. Her hair is very like yours and she's everything I dreamed she would be.
Love,
Pierre

Pierre? Who was Pierre? And this picture, it was sent to my mother? Was this my father? Had I been somewhere with him? But why would he be telling my mother about me? She had already died. Could it be he hadn't known at the time? No, that made no sense, for how could he have gotten me even for a short time and not known my mother was dead? And how could I have been with him and not recalled anything?

The mystery buzzed around inside me like a hive of bees making my stomach tingle. It filled me with a strange sense of foreboding and anxiety. I looked at the little girl again and again compared our faces. The resemblance was undeniable. I had been with this man.

I took a deep breath and tried to calm myself so when I went back downstairs and saw Grandmere and her friends, they wouldn't know something had disturbed me, disturbed my very heart and soul. I knew how hard, if not impossible, it would be for me to hide anything from Grandmere Catherine, but fortunately, she was so involved in an argument over crabmeat ravigote, she didn't notice how disturbed I was.

Finally, her friends grew tired and decided it was time for them to leave. Once again, they offered me their congratulations, kissing and hugging me while Grandmere looked on proudly. We watched them leave and then we went into the house.

"I haven't had a good time like that in ages," Grandmere said, sighing. "And look at what a wonderful job you did cleaning up. My Ruby," she said, turning to me, "I'm so proud of you, dear and . . ."

Her eyes narrowed quickly. She was flushed from the wine and the excitement of all her arguments, but her spiritual powers were not asleep. She quickly sensed something was wrong and stepped toward me.

"What is it, Ruby?" she asked quickly. "What's stirred you up so?"

"Grandmere," I began. "You sent me upstairs to put the money in your chest."

"Yes," she said, and then followed that with a deep gasp. She stepped back, her hand on her heart. "You went looking through my things?"

"I didn't mean to snoop, Grandmere, but I was interested in the old pictures of you and Grandpere Jack, and your parents. Then, I saw something sticking out of your old Bible and I found this," I said, holding the picture out toward her. She looked down at it as if she were looking down at a picture of death and disaster. She took it from me and sat down slowly, nodding as she did so.

"Who is that man, Grandmere? And the little girl—it's me, isn't it?" I asked.

She lifted her head, her eyes swollen with sadness and shook her head.

"No, Ruby," she said. "It's not."

"But it looks just like me, Grandmere. Here," I said, putting the picture of me at about seven years old next to the one of Pierre and the little girl. "See."

Grandmere nodded.

"Yes, it's your face," she said, looking at the two, "but it's not you."

"Then who is it, Grandmere, and who is this man in the picture?"

She hesitated. I tried to wait patiently, but the butterflies in my stomach were flying around my heart, tickling it with their wings. I held my breath.

"I wasn't thinking when I sent you up to put the money in my chest," she began, "but maybe it was Providence's way of letting me know it's time."

"Time for what, Grandmere?"

"For you to know everything," she said, and sat back as if she had been struck, the now all too familiar exhaustion settling into her face again. "To know why I drove your grandpere out and into the swamp to live like the animal he is." She closed her eyes and muttered under her breath, but my patience ran out.

"Who is the little girl if it's not me, Grandmere?" I demanded. Grandmere fixed her eyes on me, the crimson in her cheeks replaced by a paleness the color of oatmeal.

"It's your sister," she said.

"My sister!"

She nodded. She closed her eyes and kept them closed so long, I thought she wouldn't continue.

"And the man holding her hand . . . " she finally added.

She didn't have to say it. The words were already settling in my mind.

". . . is your real father."

6

Room in My Heart

"If you knew who my father was all this time, Grandmere, why didn't you tell me? Where does he live? How did I get a sister? Why did it have to be kept such a secret, and why did this drive Grandpere into the swamp to live?" I fired my questions, one after the other, my voice impatient.

Grandmere Catherine closed her eyes. I knew it was her way to gather strength. It was as if she could reach into a second self and draw out the energy that made her the healer she was to the Cajun people in Terrebonne Parish.

My heart was thumping, a slow, heavy whacking in my chest that made me dizzy. The world around us seemed to grow very still. It was as if every owl, every insect, even the breeze was holding its breath in anticipation. After a moment Grandmere Catherine opened her dark eyes, eyes that were now shadowed and sad, and fixed them on me firmly as she shook her head ever so gently. I thought she released a soft moan before she began.

"I've dreaded this day for so long," Grandmere said, "dreaded it because once you've heard it all, you will know just how deeply into the depths of hell and damnation your grandpere has gone. I've dreaded it because once you've heard it all you will know how much more tragic than you ever dreamed was your mother's short life, and I've dreaded it because once you've heard it all, you will know how much of your life, your family, your history, I have kept hidden from you.

"Please don't blame me for it, Ruby," she pleaded. "I have tried to be more than your grandmere. I have tried to do what I thought was best for you.

"But at the same time," she continued, gazing down at her hands in her lap for a moment, "I must confess I have been somewhat selfish, too, for I wanted to keep you with me, wanted to keep something of my poor lost daughter beside me." She gazed up at me again. "If I have sinned, God forgive me, for my intentions were not evil and I did try to do the best I could for you, even though I admit, you would have had a much richer, much more comfortable life, if I had given you up the day you were born."

She sat back and sighed again as if a great weight had begun to be lifted from her shoulders and off her heart.

"Grandmere, no matter what you've done, no matter what you tell me, I will always love you just as I always have loved you," I assured her.

She smiled softly and then grew thoughtful and serious again.

"The truth is, Ruby, I couldn't have gone on; I would never have had the strength, even the spiritual strength I was born to have, if you hadn't been with me all these years. You have been my salvation and my hope, as you still are. However, now that I'm drawing closer and closer to the end of my days here, you must leave the bayou and go where you belong."

"Where do I belong, Grandmere?"

"In New Orleans."

"Because of my artwork?" I said, nodding in anticipation of her response. She had said it so many times before.

"Not only because of your talent," she replied, and then she sat forward and continued. "After Gabrielle had gotten herself into trouble with Paul Tate's father, she became a very withdrawn and solitary person. She didn't want to attend school anymore no matter how much I begged, so that except for the people who came around here, she saw no one. She became something of a wild thing, a true part of the bayou, a recluse who lived in nature and loved only natural things.

"And Nature accepted her with open arms. The beautiful birds she loved, loved her. I would look out and see how the marsh hawks watched over her, flew from tree to tree to follow her along the canals.

"She would always return with beautiful wild flowers in her hair when she went for a walk that lasted most of the afternoon. Gabrielle could spend hours sitting by the water, dazzled by its ebb and flow, hypnotized by the songs of the birds. I began to think the frogs that gathered around her actually spoke to her.

"Nothing harmed her. Even the alligators maintained a respectful distance, holding their eyes out of the water just enough to gaze at her as she walked along the shores of the marsh. It was as if the swamp and all the wildlife within it saw her as one of their own.

"She would take our pirogue and pole through

those canals better than your Grandpere Jack. She certainly knew the water better, never getting hung up on anything. She went deep into the swamp, went to places rarely visited by human beings. If she had wanted to, she could have been a better swamp guide than your grandpere," Grandmere added, nodding.

"As time went by, Gabrielle became even more beautiful. She seemed to draw on the natural beauty around her. Her face blossomed like a flower, her complexion was as soft as rose petals, her eyes were as bright as the noonday sunlight streaming through the goldenrod. She walked more softly than the marsh deer, who were never afraid to come right up to her. I saw her stroke their heads myself," Grandmere said, smiling warmly, deeply at her vivid memories, memories I longed to share.

"There was nothing sweeter to my ears than the sound of Gabrielle's laughter, no jewel more sparkling than the sparkle of her soft smile.

"When I was a little girl, much younger than you are now, my grandmere told me stories about the so-called swamp fairies, nymphs that dwelled deep in the bayou and would show themselves only to the purest of heart. How I longed to catch sight of one. I never did, but I think I came the closest whenever I looked upon my own daughter, my own Gabrielle," she said and wiped a single fugitive tear from her cheek.

She took a deep breath, sat back, and continued.

"A little more than two years after Gabrielle's involvement with Mr. Tate, a very handsome, young Creole man came from New Orleans with his father to do some duck hunting in the swamp. In town they quickly learned about your grandpere, who was, to give the devil his due," she muttered, "the best swamp guide in this bayou.

"This young man, Pierre Dumas, fell in love with your mother the moment he saw her emerge from the marsh with a baby rice bird on her shoulder. Her hair was long, midway down her back, and it had darkened to a rich, beautiful auburn color. She had my raven black eyes, Grandpere's dark complexion and teeth whiter than the keys of a brand-new accordion. Many a young man who had chanced by and had seen her had lost his heart quickly, but Gabrielle had become wary of men. Whenever one did stop to speak with her, she would simply toss a thin laugh his way and disappear so quickly he probably thought she really was a swamp ghost, one of my grandmere's fairies," Grandmere Catherine said, smiling.

"But for some reason, she did not run from Pierre Dumas. Oh, he was tall and dashing in his elegant clothes, but later, she would tell me that she saw something gentle and loving in his face; she felt no threat. And I never saw a young man smitten as quickly as young Pierre Dumas was smitten. If he could have thrown off his rich clothes that very moment and gone into the swamp to live with Gabrielle then and there, he would have.

"But the truth was he was already married and had been for a little over two years. The Dumas family is one of the oldest and wealthiest families living in New Orleans," Grandmere said. "Those families guard their lineage very closely. Marriages are well thought out and arranged so as to keep up the social standing and protect their blue blood. Pierre's young wife also came from a well-respected, wealthy old Creole family.

"However, to the great chagrin of Pierre's father, Charles Dumas, Pierre's wife had been unable to get pregnant all this time. The prospect of no children was an unacceptable one to Pierre's father, and to Pierre as well. But they were good Catholics and divorce was not an alternative. Neither was adopting a child, for Charles Dumas wanted the Dumas blood to run through the veins of all of his grandchildren.

"Weekend after weekend, Pierre Dumas and his father, more often, just Pierre, would visit Houma and go duck hunting. Pierre began to spend more time with Gabrielle than he did with Grandpere Jack. Naturally, I was very worried. Even if Pierre wasn't already married, his father would not want him to bring back a wild Cajun girl with no rich lineage. I warned Gabrielle about him, but she simply looked at me and smiled as if I were trying to stop the wind.

"'Pierre would never do anything to hurt me,'" she insisted. "Soon, he was coming and not even pretending his purpose was to hire Grandpere Jack to guide him on a hunting trip. He and Gabrielle would pack a lunch and go off in the pirogue, deep into the swamp to places only Gabrielle knew."

Grandmere paused in her tale and stared down at her hands again for a long moment. When she looked up again, her eyes were full of pain.

"This time Gabrielle didn't tell me she was pregnant. She didn't have to. I saw it in her face and soon saw it in her stomach. When I confronted her about it, she simply smiled and said she wanted Pierre's baby, a child she would bring up in the bayou to love the swamp world as much as she did. She made me promise that no matter what happened, I would make sure her child lived here and learned to love the things she loved. God forgive me, I finally gave in and made such a promise, even though it broke my heart to see her with child and to know what it would do to her reputation among our own people.

"We tried to cover up what had happened by telling the story about the stranger at the fais dodo. Some people accepted it, but most didn't care. It was just another reason why they should look down on the Landrys. Even my best friends smiled when they faced me, but whispered behind my back. Many a family I had helped with my healing, contributed to the gossip."

Grandmere took a deep breath before she continued, seeming to draw the strength she needed out of the air.

"Unbeknownst to me, your grandpere and Pierre's father had met to discuss the impending birth. Your grandpere had already had experience selling one of Gabrielle's illegitimate children. His gambling sickness hadn't abated one bit; he still lost every piece of spare change he possessed and then some. He was in debt everywhere.

"A proposal was made some time during the last month and a half of Gabrielle's pregnancy. Charles Dumas offered fifteen thousand dollars for

132

Pierre's child. Grandpere agreed, of course. Back in New Orleans, they were already concocting the fabrications to make it appear the child was really Pierre's wife's. Grandpere Jack told Gabrielle and it broke her heart. I was furious with him, but the worst was yet to come."

She bit down on her lower lip. Her eyes were glazed with tears, tears I was sure were burning under her eyelids, but she wanted desperately to get all of the story told before she collapsed in sorrow. I got up quickly and got her a glass of water.

"Thank you, honey," she said. She drank some and then nodded. "I'm all right." I sat down again, my eyes, my ears, my very soul fixed on her and her every word.

"Poor Gabrielle began to wilt with sorrow. She felt betrayed, but not so much by Grandpere Jack. She had always accepted his bad qualities and weaknesses the same way she accepted some of the uglier and crueler things in nature. For Gabrielle, Grandpere Jack's flaws were just the way things were, the way they were designed to be.

"But Pierre's willingness to go along with the bargain, to do what his father wanted was different. They had made secret promises to each other about the soon-to-be-born child. Pierre was going to send money to help care for the baby. He was going to visit more often. He even said he wanted the child to be brought up in the bayou where he or she would always be part of Gabrielle and her world, a world Pierre professed to love more than his own now that he had met and fallen in love with Gabrielle.

"She was so heartbroken when Grandpere Jack came to her and told her the bargain and how all the parties had agreed, that she did not put up any resistance. Instead, she spent long hours sitting in the shadows of the cypress and sycamore trees gazing out at the swamp as if the world she loved had somehow conspired to betray her as well. She had believed in its magic, worshipped its beauty and she had believed that Pierre had been won over by it as well. Now, she knew there were stronger, harder, crueler truths, the worst one being that Pierre's loyalty to his own world and his own family carried more weight with him than the promises he had made to her.

"She didn't eat well, no matter how I nagged and cajoled. I whipped up whatever herbal drinks I could to substitute for what she was missing and provide the nourishment her body needed, but she either avoided them or her depression overcame whatever value they had. Instead of blossoming in the last weeks of her pregnancy, she grew more sickly. Dark shadows formed around her eyes. She had little energy, became listless and slept most of the day away.

"I saw how big she had gotten, of course, and I knew why, but I never spoke a word of it to Grandpere or to Gabrielle. I was afraid the moment Grandpere knew, he would run out and make a second deal."

"Knew why?" I asked. "What?"

"That Gabrielle was about to give birth to twins."

For a moment my thumping heart stopped. The

realization of what she had said thundered through my mind.

"Twins? I have a twin sister?" The possibility had never even occurred to me, even after I had seen how much I resembled the little girl in the picture with Pierre Dumas.

"Yes. She was the baby, the first to be born and the one I surrendered to Grandpere that night. I shall never forget that night," she said. "Grandpere had informed the Dumas family that Gabrielle was in labor. They drove here in their limousine and waited out there in the night. They had brought along a nurse, but I wouldn't permit her to enter my house. I could see the old man's expensive cigar burning in the limousine window as they all waited impatiently.

"As soon as your sister was born, I cleaned and brought her out to Grandpere, who thought I was being very cooperative. He rushed out with the child and collected his blood money. When he returned to the house, I had you cleaned and wrapped and in your weakened mother's arms.

"As soon as he set eyes on you, Grandpere Jack ranted and raved. Why hadn't I told him what to expect? Didn't I realize that I had thrown away another fifteen thousand dollars!

"He decided there was still time and actually went to take you from Gabrielle and run after the limousine. I struck him squarely on the forehead with a frying pan I had kept at my side just for that purpose and I knocked him unconscious. By the time he awoke, I had packed all of his things in two sacks. Then I chased him from the house, threatening to tell the world what he had done if

135

he didn't leave us be. I threw out all his things and he took them and went to live in his trapper's shack. He's been there ever since," she said, "and good riddance to him."

"What happened to my mother?" I asked softly, so softly, I wasn't sure I had spoken.

Finally, Grandmere's tears escaped. They streamed down her cheeks freely, zigzagging to her chin.

"The double birthing, in her weakened state, was too much for her, but before she closed her eyes for the last time, she looked down at you and smiled. I made my promises quickly to her. I would keep you here in the bayou with me. You would grow up much like she had. You would know our world and our lives and some day, when the time was right, you would be told all that I have told you now.

"Gabrielle's last words to me were 'Thank you, *ma mere, ma belle mere.* '"

Grandmere's head dropped as her shoulders shuddered. I got up quickly and went to embrace her, crying with her for a mother I had never seen, never touched, never heard speak my name. What did I know of her? A snip of a ribbon she had worn in her dark red hair, some of her clothes, the few old faded pictures? To never know the sound of her voice, or the feel of her bosom when she embraced me and comforted me, to never bury my face in her hair and feel her lips on my baby cheeks, to never hear that wonderful, innocent laughter Grandmere had described, to never dream, like so many other girls I knew, that I would be as beautiful as my mother—this was the agony left to me.

How was I now to love, even like the man who was my real father but who had betrayed my mother's trust and love and broke her heart so badly she could only pine away?

Grandmere Catherine wiped away her tears and sat back, smiling at me.

"Can you forgive me for keeping all this a secret until now, Ruby?" she asked.

"Yes, Grandmere. I know you did it out of love for me, to protect me. Did my real father ever learn what had happened to my mother and did he ever learn about me?"

"No," Grandmere said, shaking her head. "That is one reason why I have encouraged you in your artwork, and why I wanted you to have your work shown in galleries in New Orleans. I have been hoping that someday, Pierre Dumas might learn of a Ruby Landry and wonder.

"It has brought me great pain and troubled my conscience that you have never met your father and your sister. Now, I feel in my heart that you should and will soon do so. If anything should happen to me, Ruby, you must promise, you must swear here and now, that you will go to Pierre Dumas and tell him who you are."

"Nothing will happen to you, Grandmere," I insisted.

"Nevertheless, promise me, Ruby. I don't want you to stay here and live with that . . . that scoundrel. Promise," she demanded.

"I promise, Grandmere. Now stop this talk.

You're tired; you need to rest. Tomorrow, you will be as good as new," I told her.

She smiled up at me and stroked my hair.

"My beautiful Ruby, my little Gabrielle. You're all your mother dreamed you would be," she said. I kissed her cheek and helped her to her feet.

Never did Grandmere Catherine look older going up to her bedroom. I followed to be sure she was all right and I helped her get into bed. Then, as she had done for me so many, many times before, I brought the blanket to her chin and knelt down to kiss her good night.

"Ruby," she said, seizing my hand as I turned to leave. "Despite what he did, there must be something very good in your father's heart for your mother to have loved him so. Seek only that goodness in him. Leave room in your own heart to love that good part of him and you will find some peace and joy someday," she predicted.

"All right, Grandmere," I said, although I couldn't imagine feeling anything toward him but hatred. I turned out her light and left her in darkness groping with the ghosts of her past.

I went out to the galerie and sat in a rocker to stare out at the night and digest all that Grandmere Catherine had told me. I had a twin sister. She lived somewhere in New Orleans and at this moment, she could be looking up at the same stars. Only, she didn't know about me. What would it be like for her when she finally found out? Would she be as happy and as excited at the prospect of meeting me as I was about meeting her? She had been brought up a Creole in a rich Creole's world in New Orleans. How different would that make us? I wondered, not without some trepidation.

And what of my father? Just as I had always thought, he did not know I existed. How would he react? Would he look down on me and not want to acknowledge my existence? Would he be ashamed? How could I ever go to him as Grandmere Catherine expected I would someday? My very presence would complicate his life so much it would be impossible. And yet ... I couldn't help but be curious. What was he really like, the man who had captured my beautiful mother's heart? My father, the mysterious dark man of my paintings.

Sighing deeply, I gazed through the darkness at that part of the bayou illuminated by the sliver of a pale white moon. I had always felt the depth of the mystery surrounding my life here; I had always heard whispering in the shadows. Truly it was as if the animals, the birds, especially the marsh hawks, wanted me to know who I really was and what had really happened. The dark spots in my past, the hardships of our lives, the tension and the turmoil between Grandmere Catherine and Grandpere Jack forced me to be more mature than I wanted to be at fifteen.

Sometimes, I wanted so badly to be like other young teenage girls I knew, full of silly laughter about nothing at all, and not always burdened down with responsibilities and worries that made me feel so much older than my years. But the same had been true for my poor mother. How quickly her life had flown by. One moment she was like an innocent child, exploring, discovering, living in what must have seemed to her to be an eternal spring; and then, suddenly, all the dark clouds rolled in and her smiles dimmed, her laughter died somewhere in the swamp, and she faded and aged like a leaf drying in the premature autumn of her short life. How unfair. If there is a heaven or a hell, I thought, it's right here on earth. We don't have to die to enter one or the other.

Exhausted, my mind reeling from the revelations, I rose from the rocker and made my way quickly to bed, putting out all the lights behind me as I went, leaving a trail of darkness and returning the world to the demons that feasted so hungrily and so successfully on our vulnerable hearts.

Poor Grandmere, I thought, and said a little prayer for her. She had been through so much trouble and tragedy and yet she cared so for others and especially for me, instead of becoming bitter and cynical. Never did I go to sleep myself loving her more, nor did I ever believe I could go to sleep crying for my dead mother, a mother I had never known, more than I could cry for myself. But I did.

The next morning Grandmere got herself up with a struggle and made her way down to the kitchen. I heard her slow, ponderous footsteps and decided that I would do all that I could to cheer her up again and get her to return to her old, vibrant self. When I joined her at breakfast, I didn't talk about our discussions the night before, nor did I ask her any more questions about the past. Instead, I rattled on about our work and especially about the new painting I was planning.

"It's a painting of you, Grandmere," I said.

"Me? Oh, no, honey. I ain't fit to be the subject of any painting. I'm old and wrinkled and—"

"You're perfect, Grandmere, and very important. I want you sitting in your rocker on the galerie. I'll try to get as much of the house in, too, but you are the subject. After all, how many portraits are there of Cajun spiritual healers? I'm sure, if I do it well, people in New Orleans will pay dearly for it," I added to persuade her.

"I'm not one to sit around all day and model for pictures," she insisted, but I knew she would. It would make it easier for her to rest and her conscience wouldn't bother her so much about not working on her loom or embroidering tablecloths and napkins.

I began the portrait that afternoon.

"Does this mean I've got to wear the same thing every day until you finish that picture, Ruby?" she asked me.

"No, Grandmere. Once I've painted you in something, I don't need to see you in it constantly. The picture is already locked in here," I said, pointing to my temple.

I worked as hard and as fast as I could on her picture, concentrating on capturing her as accurately as I was able. Every day I worked, she fell asleep in her chair midway through the sitting. I thought there was a peacefulness about her and tried to get that feeling in the picture. One day I decided there should be a rice bird on the railing, and then, it came to me that I would put a face in the window looking out. I didn't tell Grandmere, but the face I drew and then painted was my mother's face. I used the old pictures for inspiration.

Grandmere didn't ask to see the painting while I worked on it. I kept it covered in my room at night, for I wanted to surprise her with it when it was finished. Finally, it was, and that night after dinner, I announced it to her.

"I'm sure you made me look a lot better than I do," she insisted, and sat back in anticipation as I brought it out and uncovered it before her. For a long moment, she said nothing, nor did the expression on her face change. I thought she didn't like it. And then, she turned to me as if she were looking at a ghost.

"It's been passed on to you," she said in a whisper.

"What has, Grandmere?"

"The powers, the spirituality. Not in the form it has been passed on to me, but in another form, in an artistic power, a vision. When you paint, you see beyond what is there for other people to see. You see inside.

"I've often felt the spirit of Gabrielle in this house," she said, looking around. "How many times have I paused outside and looked back at the house and seen her gazing out of a window, smiling at me or looking wistfully at the swamp, at a bird, at a deer? And Ruby, she's always looked something like that to me," she said, nodding at the painting. "When you painted, you saw her, too. She was in your vision," she said. "She was in your eyes. God be praised." She lifted her arms for me to go to her so she could embrace me and kiss me.

"It's a beautiful picture, Ruby. Don't sell it," she said.

"I won't, Grandmere."

She took a deep breath and ground away the tiny tears from the corners of her eyes. Then we went into the living room to decide where I should hang the painting.

Summer drew to an end on the calendar, but not in the bayou. Our temperatures and humidity hung up there as high as they had been in the middle of July. The oppressive heat seemed to undulate through the air, wave after wave weighing us down, making the days longer than they were, making everything we did, harder than it was.

Throughout the fall and early winter, Grandmere Catherine had her usual treater missions, especially ministering her herbal cures and her spiritual powers to the elderly. They saw her as far more sympathetic to their arthritic pains and aches, their stomach and back troubles, their headaches and fatigue than any ordinary physician would be. She understood because she suffered from the same maladies.

One early February day with the sky a hazy blue and the clouds no more than smokelike wisps smeared here and there from one horizon to the other, a pickup truck came bouncing over our drive, the horn blaring. Grandmere and I were in the kitchen, having some lunch.

"Someone's in trouble," she declared, and got up as quickly as she could to go to the front door.

It was Raul Balzac, a shrimp fisherman, who

lived about ten miles down the bayou. Grandmere was very fond of his wife, Bernadine, and had treated her mother for lumbago time after time before she had passed away last year.

"It's my boy, Mrs. Landry," Raul cried from the truck. "My five-year-old. He's burning up something terrible."

"Insect bite?" Grandmere asked quickly.

"Can't find anything on him that says so," Raul replied.

"Be right with you, Raul," she said, and went back to get her basket of medicines and spiritual things.

"Should I come with you, Grandmere?" I asked as she hurried out.

"No, dear. Stay and make us dinner. Prepare one of your good jambalayas," she added, and went to Raul's truck. He helped her in and then quickly drove off, bouncing over the drive as hard as he had when he had arrived. I couldn't blame him for being anxious and frightened, and once again, I was proud of Grandmere Catherine for being the one to whom he came for assistance, the one in whom he placed such trust.

Later in the day, I did what she asked and worked on our dinner while I listened to some of the latest Cajun music on the radio. There was a prediction of another downpour, one that would be full of lightning and thunder. The static on the radio told me the prediction would come true and sure enough, by late afternoon, the sky had turned that purplish dark color that often preceded a violent storm. I was worried about Grandmere Catherine and after I had battened down all the windows, I stood by the door waiting and watching for Raul's pickup. But the rain came before the truck did.

We had hail and then a pounding downpour that sounded like it would drill holes even through the metal roof. Wave after wave of rain was washed over the bayou by the wind that came rushing over the sycamores and cypresses, bending and twisting the branches, tearing leaves and limbs from trees. The distant low, rumbling thunder soon became real boomers, crashing down around the house like boulders and then lighting up the sky with fire. Hawks shrieked, everything that lived struggled to find a hole to crawl in to remain safe and dry. The railings on the porch groaned and the whole house seemed to turn and twist in the wind. I couldn't recall a storm as fierce, nor when I was more frightened by one.

Finally, it began to recede and the heavy drops thinned. The wind slowed down and became less and less severe until it was nothing more than a brisk breeze. Night fell quickly afterward, so I didn't see the resulting damage around the swamp, but the rain trickled on for hours and hours.

I expected Raul was waiting for the storm to stop before bringing Grandmere Catherine home, but as the hours ticked by and the storm dissipated until it was finally nothing more than a sprinkle, the truck still did not appear. I grew more and more nervous and wished that we had a telephone like most of the other people in the bayou, although I imagined the lines would have been down just like they often were after such a storm and the telephone would have been useless.

Our supper was long done. It simmered in the pot. I wasn't all that hungry, being so anxious, but finally, I ate some and then cleaned up. Grandmere had still not returned. I spent the next hour and a half waiting on the galerie, just watching the darkness for the lights of Raul's truck. Occasionally, a vehicle did appear, but it was someone else all the time.

Finally, nearly twelve hours after Raul had come for Grandmere Catherine, his truck turned into the drive. I saw him clearly, and I saw his oldest son, Jean, but I didn't see Grandmere Catherine. I ran down the galerie steps as he came to a stop.

"Where's my grandmere?" I called before he could speak.

"She's in the back," he said. "Resting."

"What?"

I hurried around and saw Grandmere Catherine lying on an old mattress, a blanket over her. The mattress was on a wide sheet of plywood and was used as a makeshift bed for Raul's children when he and his wife went on long journeys.

"Grandmere!" I cried. "What's wrong with her?" I asked as Raul came around.

"She collapsed with exhaustion a few hours ago. We wanted to keep her overnight, but she insisted on us bringing her home and we wanted to do whatever she asked. She broke my boy's fever. He's going to be all right," Raul said, smiling.

"I'm happy about that, Mr. Balzac, but Grandmere Catherine . . . "

146

"We'll help you get her into the house and to bed," he said, and nodded to Jean. They lowered the rear of the truck and the two of them lifted the mattress and board with Grandmere Catherine off the truck. She stirred and opened her eyes.

"Grandmere," I said, taking her hand, "what's wrong?"

"I'm just tired, so tired," she muttered. "I'll be fine," she added, but her eyelids clamped down shut so quickly alarm filled me.

"Quickly," I said, and rushed ahead to open the door for them. They brought her up to her room and eased her off the mattress and into her own bed.

"Is there anything we can do for you, Ruby?" Raul asked.

"No. I'll take care of her. Thank you."

"Thank her for us again," Raul said. "My wife will send something over in the morning and we'll stop by to see how she is."

I nodded and they left. I took off Grandmere's shoes and helped her off with her dress. She was like someone drugged, barely opening her eyes, barely moving her arms and legs. I don't think she realized I had put her to bed.

All that night I sat at her side, waiting for her to awaken. She moaned and groaned a few times, but she never woke up until morning when I felt her nudge my leg. I was asleep in the chair beside the bed.

"Grandmere," I cried. "How are you?"

"I'm all right, Ruby. Just weak and tired. How did I get home and in bed? I don't remember."

"Mr. Balzac and his son Jean brought you in their truck and carried you in."

"And you sat up all night watching over me?" she asked.

"Yes."

"You poor dear." She struggled to smile. "I missed your jambalaya. Was it good?"

"Yes, Grandmere, although I was too worried about you to eat much. What happened to you?"

"The strain of what I had to do, I suppose. That poor little boy was bitten by a cottonmouth, but on the bottom of his foot where it was hard to see. He was running barefoot through the marsh grass and must have disturbed one," she said.

"Grandmere, you've never been this exhausted after a treater mission before."

"I'll be all right, Ruby. Please, just get me some cold water," she said.

I did so. She drank it slowly and then closed her eyes again.

"I'll just rest some more and then get up, dear," she said. "You go on and have something for breakfast. Don't worry. Go on," she said. Reluctantly, I did so. When I returned to look in on her, she was fast asleep again.

Before lunch, she woke up, but her complexion was waxen, her lips blue. She was too weak to sit up by herself. I had to help her and then she asked me to help her get dressed.

"I want to sit on the galerie," she said.

"I must get you something to eat."

"No, no. I just want to sit on the galerie."

She leaned fully on me to stand and walk. I was never so frightened about her. When she sat back in the rocker, she looked as though she had collapsed again, but a moment later, she opened her eyes and gave me a weak smile.

"I'll just have a little warm water and honey, dear."

I got it for her quickly and she sipped it and rocked herself gently.

"I guess I'm more tired than I thought," she said, and then she turned and gazed at me with such a far-off look in her eyes, a small flutter of panic stirred in my chest. "Ruby, I don't want you to be afraid, but I wish you would do something for me now. It would make me feel less . . . less anxious about myself," she said, taking my hand in hers. Her palms felt cold, clammy.

"What is it, Grandmere?" I could feel the tears aching to emerge from my eyes. They stung behind my lids. My throat felt like closing up for good and my heart shrunk until it was barely beating. My blood ran cold, my legs had turned to lead bars.

"I want you to go to the church and fetch Father Rush," she said.

"Father Rush?" The blood drained from my face. "Oh, why, Grandmere? Why?"

"Just in case, dear. I need to make my peace. Please, dear. Be strong," she begged. I nodded and swallowed back my tears quickly. I would not cry in front of her, I thought, and then I kissed her quickly.

Before I turned to leave, she seized my hand again and held me close.

"Ruby, remember your promises to me. Should

something happen to me, you won't stay here. Remember."

"Nothing's happening to you, Grandmere."

"I know, honey, but just in case. Promise again. Promise."

"I promise, Grandmere."

"You'll go to him, go to your real father?"

"Yes, Grandmere."

"Good," she said, closing her eyes. "Good." I gazed at her a moment and then ran down the galerie steps and hurried to town. On the way my tears gushed. I cried so hard, my chest began to ache. I arrived at the church so quickly, I didn't remember the journey.

Father Rush's housekeeper answered the doorbell. Her name was Addie Cochran and she had been with him so long, it was impossible to remember when she wasn't.

"My grandmere Catherine needs Father Rush," I said quickly, an edge of panic in my voice.

"What's wrong?"

"She's . . . she's very . . . she's . . . "

"Oh, dear. He's just at the barber's. I'll go tell him and send him up."

"Thank you," I said, and I turned and ran all the way home, my chest wanting to burst open, the needles in my side poking and sticking me fiercely when I arrived. Grandmere was still on the galerie in her rocker. I didn't realize she wasn't rocking until I reached the steps. She was just sitting still with her eyes half-closed and on her thin white lips was a faint smile. It scared me, that funny, happy smile.

"Grandmere," I whispered fearfully. "Are you all right?"

She didn't reply, nor did she turn my way. I touched her face and realized she was already cold.

Then I fell to my knees on the galerie floor in front of her and embraced her legs. I was still holding on to her and crying when Father Rush finally arrived.

7

The Truth Will Out

Anyone would have thought that the news of Grandmere Catherine's passing must have been caught up in the wind that whipped through the bayou for so many people to have heard about it so quickly; but the loss of a spiritual healer, especially a spiritual healer with Grandmere's reputation, was something special and very important to the Cajun community. Before late morning some of Grandmere Catherine's friends and our neighbors already were arriving. By early afternoon, there were dozens of cars and trucks in front of our house as more and more people stopped by to pay their respects, the women bringing gumbos and jambalaya in big cast iron pots, plus dishes and pans of cake and beignets. Mrs. Thibodeau and Mrs. Livaudis took charge of the wake and Father Rush made the funeral arrangements for me.

Layer after layer of long gray clouds streamed in from the southwest, making for a hazy, peekaboo sun. The heavy air, dark shadows, and the subdued swamp life all seemed appropriate for a day as sad as this one was. The birds barely flitted about; the marsh hawks and herons remained curious but statuelike in their stillness as they watched the gathering that had commenced and continued throughout the day.

No one had seen Grandpere Jack for some time so Thaddeus Bute poled a pirogue out to his shack to give him the dreadful news. He returned without him and mumbled something to the mourners that made people shake their heads and gaze my way with pity. Toward supper Grandpere Jack finally arrived, as usual, resembling someone who had been wallowing in mud. He wore what must have been his best pair of trousers and shirt, but the trousers had holes in the knees and his shirt looked like he had to beat it on a rock in order to soften it enough to slip his arms through the sleeves and button it, wherever there were buttons, that is. Of course, his boots were caked with grime and blades of marsh grass.

He had taken no time to brush down his wild white hair or trim his beard even though he must have known there would be loads of people here. Thick little puffs of hair grew out of his ears and nose. His bushy eyebrows curved up and to the side on his leather tan face, the deeper wrinkles looking like they had a bed of dirt glued there for months. The acrid odors of stale whiskey, swamp earth, fish, and tobacco seemed to arrive at the house long moments before he did. I smiled to myself thinking how Grandmere Catherine would be screaming at him to keep his distance.

But she wasn't going to be screaming at him anymore. She was laid out in the sitting room, her face never so peaceful and still. I sat off to the right of the coffin, my hands folded in my lap, still quite dazed by the reality of what was happening, still disbelieving, hoping it was all a terrible nightmare that would soon end.

The quiet chatter that had begun earlier came to an abrupt pause when Grandpere Jack arrived. As soon as he strode into the house, the people gathered at the doorways parted and stepped back as if they were terrified he might touch them with his polluted hands. None of the men offered theirs to him, nor did he seek any handshakes. Women grimaced after a whiff of him. His eyes shifted quickly from one face to another and then he stepped into the sitting room and froze for a moment at the sight of Grandmere Catherine laid out in her coffin.

He looked at me sharply and then fixed his eyes on Father Rush. For a few moments, it seemed Grandpere Jack didn't trust what his own eyes were telling him or what people were doing here. It looked like the words were on the tip of his tongue and any moment he might ask, "Is she really dead and gone or is this just some scam to get me out of the swamp and cleaned up?" With that skeptical glint in his eyes, he approached Grandmere Catherine's coffin slowly, hat in hand. About a foot or so away, he stopped and gazed down at her, waiting. When she didn't sit up and start screaming at him, he relaxed and turned back to me.

"How you doin', Ruby?" he asked.

"I'm all right, Grandpere," I said. My eyes were bloodshot but dry, for I had exhausted a reservoir of tears. He nodded and then he spun around and glared back at some of the women who were gazing at him with a veil of disgust visibly drawn over their faces.

"Well, what are you all lookin' at? Can't a man mourn his dead wife without you busybodies gaping at him and whispering behind his back? Go on with ya and give me some privacy," he cried.

Outraged and stunned, Grandmere Catherine's friends spun around and, with their heads bobbing, hurried out like a flock of frightened hens to gather on the galerie. Only Mrs. Thibodeau, Mrs. Livaudis, and Father Rush remained in the sitting room with Grandpere Jack and me.

"What happened to her?" Grandpere demanded, his green eyes still lit with fury.

"Her heart just gave out," Father Rush said, gazing warmly at Grandmere. He shook his head gently. "She spent all her energy on helping others, comforting and tending to the sick and the troubled. It finally took its toll on her, God bless her," he added.

"Well, I told her a hundred times if I told her once, to stop parading up and down the bayou to tend to everybody's needs but our own, but she wasn't one to listen. Stubborn to the day she died," Grandpere declared. "Just like most Cajun women," he added, staring at Mrs. Thibodeau and Mrs. Livaudis. They pulled back their shoulders and stiffened their necks like two peacocks.

"Oh, no," Father Rush said, smiling angelically, "you can't keep a soul as great as Mrs. Landry's soul from doing what she can to help the needy. Charity and compassion were her constant companions," he added.

Grandpere grunted. "Charity begins at home I told her, but she never listened to me. Well, I'm sorry she's gone. Don't know who's goin' to send fire and damnation my way. Don't know who's goin' to nag me and chastise me for doin' this or that," Grandpere declared, shaking his head.

"Oh, I expect someone will always be around to chastise you good, Jack Landry," Mrs. Thibodeau replied, nodding at him with her lips tightly pursed.

"Huh?" Grandpere stared at her a moment, but Mrs. Thibodeau had been around Grandmere Catherine too long not to have learned how to stare him down. He ran the back of his hand over his mouth and then shifted his eyes away and grunted again. "Yeah, I suppose," he said. The aromas from the kitchen caught his interest. "Well, I guess you ladies cooked up somethin', didn't you?" he asked.

"There's a spread in the kitchen, gumbo on the stove, and a pot of hot coffee brewing," Mrs. Livaudis said with visible reluctance.

"I'll get you something to eat, Grandpere," I said, rising. I had to do something, keep moving, keep busy.

"Why, thank you, Ruby. That's my only grandchild, you know," he told Father Rush. I snapped my head around sharply and glared at Grandpere. For a moment his eyes twinkled with that impish

155

look and then he smiled and looked away, either not sensing or seeing what I knew or not caring about it. "She's all I got now," he continued. "Only family left. I got to look after her."

"And how do you expect to do that?" Mrs. Livaudis demanded. "You barely look after yourself, Jack Landry."

"I know what I do and I don't. A man can change, can't he? If something tragic like this occurs, a man can change. Can't he, Father? Ain't that so?"

"If it's truly in his heart to repent, anyone can," Father Rush replied, closing his eyes and pressing his hands together as if he were about to offer up a prayer to that effect.

"Hear that and that's a priest talking, not some gossip mouth," Grandpere said, nodding and poking the air between him and Mrs. Livaudis with his thick, long and dirty finger. "I got responsibilities now ... a place to keep up, a granddaughter to see after, and I'm one to do what I say I'm goin' to do, when I say it."

"If you remember you've said it," Mrs. Thibodeau snapped. She was giving him no ground.

Grandpere smirked.

"Yeah, well, I'll remember. I'll remember," he repeated. He threw another look Grandmere Catherine's way, again as if he wanted to be sure she wasn't going to start screaming at him, and then he followed me out to the kitchen to get something to eat. He plopped his long, lanky body into a kitchen chair and dropped his hat on the floor. Then he looked around as I stirred up the gumbo and ladled a bowl for him.

"Ain't been in this house so long, it's like a strange place to me," he said. "And I built it myself!" I poured him a cup of coffee and then stepped back, folding my arms under my bosom and watching him go at the gumbo, shoving mouthful after mouthful in and swallowing with hardly a chew, the rice and roux running down his chin.

"When was the last time you ate something, Grandpere?" I asked. He paused for a moment and thought.

"I don't know . . . two days ago, I had some shrimp. Or was it some oysters?" He shrugged and continued to gulp his food. "But things are going to change for me now," he said, nodding between swallows. "I'm going to clean myself up, move back into my home, and have my grand-daughter take care of me right and proper, and I'm going to do the same for her," he vowed.

"I can't believe Grandmere is actually dead and gone, Grandpere," I said, the tears choking my throat. He gulped some food and nodded.

"Me neither. I would have sworn on a stack of wild deuces that I'd go before she did. I thought that woman would outlive most of the world; she had that much grit in her. She was like some old tree root, just clinging to the things she believed in. I couldn't move her with a herd of elephants, not an inch off her ways."

"Nor could she move you, Grandpere," I quickly replied. He shrugged.

"Well, I'm just a stupid old Cajun trapper, too

dumb to know right from wrong, yet I manage to survive. But I meant what I said out there, Ruby. I'm goin' to change somethin' awful and make things right for you. I swear it," he said, holding up his right palm, blotched with grime, the finger ends stained with tobacco. His deeply serious expression dissolved into a smile. "Could you give me another bowl of this. Ain't ate somethin' this good for ages. Beats the hell out of my swamp guk," he said, and chuckled to himself, a slight whistle coming through the gaps in his teeth as his shoulders shook.

I gave him some more and then I excused myself and went back to sit beside the coffin. I didn't like being away from Grandmere Catherine's side too long. Toward evening, some of Grandpere Jack's swamp cronies arrived supposedly to offer comfort and sympathy, but they were soon all going around behind the house to drink some whiskey and smoke their rolled, dark brown cigarettes.

Father Rush, Mrs. Thibodeau, and Mrs. Livaudis remained as long as they could and then promised to return early in the morning.

"You try to get yourself some rest, Ruby dear," Mrs. Thibodeau advised. "You're going to need your strength for the difficult days ahead."

"Your grandmere would be right proud of you, Ruby," Mrs. Livaudis added, squeezing my hand gently. "Now look after yourself."

Mrs. Thibodeau raised her eyes and gazed toward the rear of the house where the laughter was growing louder by the minute.

"If you need us, you just holler," she said.

"You're always welcome at my house," Mrs. Livaudis added before leaving.

Grandmere Catherine's friends and some of the neighbors had cleaned up and had put everything away before they had left. There was nothing for me to do but kiss Grandmere Catherine good night and go to sleep myself. I heard Grandpere Jack and his trapper friends howl and laugh long into the night. In a way I was grateful for the noise. I lay awake for hours, wondering if there was anything else I could have done to have helped Grandmere Catherine, but then I thought, if she couldn't help herself, what could I do?

Finally, my eyelids became so heavy, I had to let them close. Someone was laughing in the darkness. I heard what sounded like Grandpere's howl and then all was still; and sleep, like one of Grandmere Catherine's miracle medicines, brought me some hours of relief and eased the pain in my heart. In fact, when I awoke early the next morning, I felt so relieved from my deep repose, that for a few moments, I actually believed all that had happened had been some terrible nightmare. In moments, I expected to hear Grandmere Catherine's footsteps as she made her way down to the kitchen to start our breakfast.

But I heard nothing but the soft, sweet sounds of the morning birds. Slowly, the reality of what had occurred settled in again and I sat up, wondering where Grandpere Jack had slept when he had finally stopped cavorting with his trapper friends. When I discovered he wasn't in Grandmere Catherine's room, I thought he might have gone back into the swamp; but when I went down, I found him sprawled out on the galerie, one leg dangling over the edge of the porch floor, his head on his rolled up jacket, an empty bottle of cheap whiskey still clutched in his right hand.

"Grandpere," I said, nudging him. "Grandpere, wake up."

"Huh?" His eyes flickered open and then shut. I shook him harder.

"Grandpere, wake up. People will be arriving here any moment. Grandpere."

"What? What's that?" He kept his eyes open long enough to focus on me and then groaned and folded his body into a sitting position. "What the . . . " He looked around, saw the expression of disappointment on my face and then shook his head. "Must have just passed out with grief," he said quickly. "It can do that to you, Ruby. You think you can handle it, but it seeps into your heart and it just takes you over. That's what happened to me," he said, nodding, trying to convince himself as well as me. "I just couldn't handle the tragedy. Sorry," he said, rubbing his cheeks. "I'll go out back and wash myself with the cistern water and then come in for some breakfast."

"Good, Grandpere," I said. "Did you bring any of your other clothes?"

"Clothes? No."

I remembered there were some old things of his in a box upstairs in Grandmere's room.

"You have some clothes still here that might fit," I said. "I'll find them for you."

"Well, that's right nice of you, honey. Right nice. I can see where we're going to make out just fine. You tending after the house and me, and me trappin' and huntin' and guidin' rich city folks through the swamp. I'll make us more money than I ever did. I'll fix up everything that's broke. I'll make this house look as fresh and as new as it did the day I built it. Why, in no time, I'll change . . . "

"Meanwhile, Grandpere, you'd better go and wash like you said you would." If anything, the stench rising from his clothes and hair had grown doubly worse. "It's getting close to the time people will be coming," I said.

"Right, right." He stood up and looked with surprise at the empty whiskey bottle on the floor of the galerie. "I don't know how I got that. Must have been Teddy Turner or someone who laid it on me for a stupid joke."

"I'll throw it away for you, Grandpere," I said, picking it up quickly.

"Thank you, honey. Thank you." He stuck his right forefinger in the air and thought for a moment until it came back to him. "Wash up, that's first," he said, and stumbled off the galerie and around to the back of the house. I went upstairs and found the old carton of clothes. There were a pair of pants and a few shirts, as well as some socks buried under an old blanket. I took everything out, pressed the pants and shirt, and laid the clothes on Grandmere's bed for him.

"I think I'll do just what Catherine would tell me to do with these old clothes I'm wearing," Grandpere said after he came in from washing himself. "I'll burn them." He laughed. I told him to go up and put on the clothes I found. By the time he had come down again, I had some breakfast made and Mrs. Livaudis and Mrs. Thibodeau arrived to help set up the food for our mourners. They ignored Grandpere even though he did look like a new man washed up and in his fresh clothes.

"I got to trim my beard and hair some, Ruby," Grandpere said. "You think if I sit on a rolled over rain barrel out back you could do it for me?"

"Yes, Grandpere," I said. "I'll do it right after you finish your breakfast."

"I thank you," he said. "We're going to do just fine," he added, more for the benefit of Mrs. Thibodeau and Mrs. Livaudis than for me, I thought. "Just fine. Long as people lets us be," he added pointedly.

After he had finished eating, I took the sewing shears and chopped off as much of his long, ratty hair as I could. Much of it was matted and there were lice, so I had to shampoo him with some of Grandmere Catherine's mixture specially made to get rid of lice as well as crabs and other tiny insects, too. He sat obediently, his eyes closed, a grateful smile on his lips as I worked. I trimmed the beard and cut the excess hair out of his ears and nose. Then I trimmed his eyebrows. When I was finished and I stepped back to look at him, I was surprised and proud of how well I had done. It was possible to look at him now and see why Grandmere Catherine or any woman might have been attracted to him when he was young. His eyes still had a youthful, mirthful glint and his strong cheekbones and jaw gave his face a classic, handsome shape. He gazed at his reflection in a piece of broken glass.

"Well, I'll be. Lookee here now. Who is this?

162

Bet you didn't know your grandpere was a movie star," he said. "Thank you, Ruby." He slapped his hands together. "Well, I'd better go out front and greet some of the mourners, right and proper like," he decided, and went around to take a seat in one of the rockers on the galerie and play the part of a bereaved husband, even though most everyone knew he and Grandmere Catherine hadn't lived together for years.

However, I was beginning to wonder if I couldn't help him change. Sometimes, dramatic events like this made people think harder about their own lives. I could just hear Grandmere Catherine say, "You'd have a better chance of changing a bullfrog into a handsome prince." But maybe all Grandpere Jack needed was another chance. After all, I thought as I cleaned up the gobs of matted hair that had fallen around the barrel, he's the only Cajun family I have left, like it or not.

We had just as many mourners if not more than we had the day before. A steady stream of Cajun folks came from miles and miles away to pay their last respects to Grandmere Catherine, whose reputation had spread much farther through Terrebonne Parish and the surrounding area than I had ever imagined. And so many of the people who arrived had wonderful stories to tell about Grandmere, stories about her earthy wisdom, her miraculous touch, her wonderful remedies, and her strong and always hopeful faith.

"Why, when your grandmother walked into a room of frightened, anxious people concerned over one of their loved ones, it was as if someone lit a candle in the darkness, Ruby honey," Mrs. Allard from Lafayette told me. "We're gonna miss her something terrible."

The people around her nodded and extended their condolences. I thanked them for their kind words and finally got myself up to get something to drink and nibble on some food. It never occurred to me that simply sitting by the coffin and greeting mourners would be so exhausting, but the constant emotional strain took a greater toll than I had imagined it could.

Grandpere Jack, although he wasn't drinking, was holding court vociferously on the front galerie. Every once in a while, he would give out with a shout and rant and rave about one of his pet subjects. "Those damn oil derricks poking their heads above the swamps, changing the landscape from the way it's looked for more than one hundred years, and for what? Just to make some fat Creole oil man wealthy in New Orleans. I say we burn 'em all out. I say—"

I went out back and closed the door behind me. It was nice that all these people came to show their respect and comfort us, but it was beginning to get overwhelming for me. Every time someone came over to squeeze my hand and kiss my cheek, she or he would start up the tears behind my eyes and close my throat until it ached worse than any sore throat ever made it ache. Every muscle in my body was still rope tight from the shock of Grandmere's passing. I took a short walk toward the canal and then felt my head begin to spin.

"Oh," I moaned, bringing my hand to my forehead. But before I could fall backward, a strong pair of arms caught me and held me upright and steady.

"Easy," a familiar voice said. I let myself rest against his shoulder for a moment and then I opened my eyes and looked up at Paul. "You'd better sit down, here, by this rock," he said, guiding me to it. He and I had often sat together on that same rock and thrown little stones into the water to count the ripples.

"Thank you," I said, and let him guide me to it. He sat beside me quickly and put a blade of marsh grass in his mouth.

"Sorry I didn't come yesterday, but I thought there would be so many people around you . . ." He smiled. "Not that there aren't today. Your grandmother was a very famous and beloved woman in the bayou."

"I know. I never fully appreciated how much until now," I said.

"That's usually the way it is. We don't realize how important someone is to us until he or she is gone," Paul replied, the underlying meaning of his words telegraphed through his soft eyes.

"Oh, Paul, she's gone. My grandmere Catherine is gone," I cried, falling into his arms and really beginning to cry. He stroked my hair back and there were tears in his eyes when I looked, as if my pain were his.

"I wish I had been here when it happened," he said. "I wish I had been right beside you."

I had to swallow twice before I could speak again. "I never wanted to send you away from me, Paul. It broke my heart to say the things I said."

165

"Then why did you?" he asked softly. There was so much hurt in his eyes. I could feel what it must have been like for him and I could see the tears that had emerged. It wasn't fair. Why should the two of us suffer so horribly for the sins of our parents? I thought.

"Why did you, Ruby, why?" he asked again; he begged for the answer. I could understand his turmoil. My words, words spoken right near here, were so unexpected and so abrupt, they had to have made him question reality. Anger was the only way in which he could have dealt with such a surprise, such an unreasonable surprise.

I turned away from him and bit down on my lower lip. My mouth wanted to run away with the words and exonerate me from all blame.

"It's not that I didn't love you, Paul," I began slowly. Then I turned back to him. The memories of our short-lived kisses and words of promise flitted like doomed moths to the candle of my burning despair. "And not that I still don't," I added softly.

"Then what could it have been? What could it be?" he asked quickly.

My heart, so torn by sorrow and so tired of sadness, began to thump like an oil drum, heavy, ponderous, as slowly as the dreadful drums in a funeral procession. What was more important now, I questioned: that there be truth between Paul and me, truth between two people who care for each other with such a rare love, a love that demanded honesty, or that I maintain a lie that kept Paul from knowing the sins of his father and therefore kept peace in his family?

"What was it?" he asked again.

"Let me think a moment, Paul," I said and looked away. He waited impatiently beside me. I was sure his heart was beating as quickly as mine was now. I wanted to tell Paul the truth, but what if Grandmere Catherine had been right? What if, in the long run, Paul would hate me more for being the messenger of such devastating news?

Oh, Grandmere, I thought, isn't there a time when the truth must be revealed, when lies and deceptions must be exposed? I know that when we are little, we can be left to dwell in a world of fantasy and fabrication. Maybe, it's even necessary, for if we were told some of the ugly truths about life then, we would be destroyed before we had a chance to develop the hard crusts we needed to shield us from the arrows of hardship, of sadness, of tragedy, and, alas, the arrows that carried the final dark truths: grandmothers and grandfathers, mommies and daddies die, and so do we. We have to understand that the world isn't filled only with sweet sounding bells, soft, wonderful things, delightful aromas, pretty music, and endless promises. It is also filled with storms and hard, painful realities, and promises that are never kept.

Surely, Paul and I were old enough now, I thought. Surely, we could face truth if we could face deception and live on.

"Something happened here a long time ago," I began, "that forced me to say the words I said to you that day."

"Here?"

"In our bayou, our little Cajun world," I said,

nodding. "The truth about it was quickly smothered because it would have brought great pain to many people, but sometimes, perhaps always, when the truth is buried this way, it has a way of coming out, of forcing itself upward into the sunlight again.

"You and I," I said, looking into his confused eyes, "are the truths that were once buried, we are in the sunlight."

"I don't understand, Ruby. What lies? What truths?"

"No one back then when the truth was buried ever dreamed you and I would come to love each other in a romantic sense," I said.

"I still don't understand, Ruby. How could anyone have known years ago about us anyway? And why would it matter then if they had?" he asked, his eyes squinting with confusion.

It was so hard to come right out and say it simply. Somehow, I felt that if Paul came to the understandings himself, if the words were formed in his mind and spoken by him instead of formed in my mind and coming from my lips, it would be less painful.

"The day I lost my mother, you lost yours, too," I finally said. The words felt like tiny, hot embers falling from my lips. The moment I uttered them, that feeling was followed by a chill so cold it was as if someone had poured ice water down the back of my neck.

Paul's eyes rushed over my face, searching for a clearer comprehension.

"My mother . . . died, too?"

His eyes lifted and he took on a far-off look as

his mind raced from point A to point B. Then his face turned crimson and he gazed at me again, this time, his eyes more demanding, more frantic.

"What are you saying . . . that you and I . . . that we're . . . related? That we're brother and sister?" he asked, the corners of his mouth pulled up into his cheeks. I nodded.

"Grandmere Catherine decided to tell me only when she saw what was happening between us," I said. He shook his head, still skeptical. "It was very painful for her to do so. Now that I think back, it wasn't long afterward that age began to creep into her steps and into her voice and heart. Old pains that are revived sting sharper than when they first strike."

"This has got to be a mistake, an old Cajun folktale, some stupid rumor conjured up in a room filled with busybodies," Paul said, wagging his head and smiling.

"Grandmere Catherine never spread gossip, never fanned the flames of idle talk and rumors. You know she hated that sort of thing; she was someone who despised lies and more often than not made people face the truth. She made me do it even though she knew it would break my heart; it was something she had to do, even though it hurt her so much, too.

"But I can't stand your not liking me, your hating me and thinking I wanted to hurt you anymore, Paul. I die every time you look at me furiously at school. Still, almost every night, I go to sleep crying over you. Of course, we can't be in love, but I can't stand our being enemies."

"I never thought of you as an enemy. I just . . . "

"Hated me. Go on, you can say it now. It doesn't hurt for me to hear it now, now that I have suffered through it," I said and smiled through my tears.

"Ruby," Paul said, shaking his head, "I can't believe what you're telling me; I can't believe that my father . . . that your mother . . . "

"You're old enough now to know the truth, Paul. Maybe I'm being selfish by telling it to you. Grandmere Catherine warned me not to, warned me that you would eventually hate me for causing any rift in your family, but I can't stand the lies between us anymore, and especially now, on top of my losing her and my realization that I'm all alone."

Paul stared at me a moment and then he got up and walked down to the edge of the water. I watched him just stand there, kicking some stones into the water, thinking, realizing, coming to terms with what I had told him. I knew that the same sort of tumult that was going on in his heart had gone on in mine, and the same sort of confusion was whirling around in his head. He shook his head again, more vigorously this time, and turned back to me.

"We have all these photographs, pictures of my mother when she was pregnant with me, pictures of me right after I was born, and—"

"Lies," I said. "All pretend, deceptions to hide the sinful acts."

"No, you're wrong. It's all a terrible, stupid mistake, don't you see?" he said, folding his hands into fists. "And we're being made to suffer for it.

I'm sure it can't be true." He nodded, convincing himself. "I'm sure," he said, walking back to me.

"Grandmere Catherine wouldn't lie to me, Paul."

"No, your grandmere wouldn't lie to you, but maybe she thought by telling you this story, she could keep you from getting involved with me and that was good because my family would make such a stink and you and I would suffer. Sure, that's it," he said, comfortable with the theory. "I'll prove it to you. I don't know how I will right now, but I will and then . . . then we'll be together just as we dreamed we would."

"Oh, Paul, how I wish you were right," I said.

"I am," he said confidently. "You'll see. I'll get beat up over you at another fais dodo yet," he added, laughing. I smiled but turned away.

"What about Suzzette?" I asked.

"I don't love Suzzette. I never did. I just had to have someone to . . . to . . . "

"To make me jealous?" I asked, turning back quickly.

"Yes," he confessed.

"I don't blame you for doing that, only you did it very convincingly," I said, smiling.

"Well, I'm . . . good at it."

We laughed. Then I grew serious again and reached up for his hand. He helped me stand. We were inches apart, facing each other.

"I don't want you to be hurt, Paul. Don't put too much hope in your disproving the things Grandmere Catherine told me. Promise me that when you find out the truth . . . "

"I won't find out the lie," he insisted.

"Promise me," I pursued, "promise that if you find out that what Grandmere told me is true, you will accept it as I have and go on to love someone else as much. Promise me."

"I can't," he said. "I can't love anyone else as much as I love you, Ruby. It's not possible."

He embraced me and I buried my face in his shoulder for a moment. He drew me closer. Beneath his shirt, I could feel his steady heartbeat. Then I felt his lips on my hair and I closed my eyes and dreamed we were far away, living in a world where there were no lies and deceit, where it was always spring and where the sunshine touched your heart as well as your face and made you forever young.

The screech of a marsh hawk made me lift my head quickly. I saw it seize a smaller bird, one that might have just learned how to fly, and then go off with its prize, unconcerned that it left some mother bird destroyed, too.

"Sometimes I hate it here," I said quickly. "Sometimes, I feel like I don't belong."

Paul looked at me with surprise.

"Of course you belong here," he said. It was on the tip of my tongue to tell him the rest of it, to tell him about my twin sister and my real father who lived in a big house somewhere in New Orleans, but I shut the lid on the truth. Enough had been revealed for one day.

"I'd better get back inside and continue to greet the people," I said, starting toward the house.

"I'll come with you and stay with you as long as I can," he said. "My parents sent over some food.

I gave it to Mrs. Livaudis. They send their regards. They would have come themselves but . . . "

He stopped in the middle of his explanation and smirked.

"I'm not making any excuses for them. My father doesn't like your grandpere," he said.

I wanted to tell him why; I wanted to go on and on and give him all the details Grandmere Catherine had given me, but I thought enough was enough. Let him discover as much of the truth as he was able to himself, as much of it as he was able to face. For truth was a bright light and just like any bright light, it was hard to look into it.

I nodded. He hurried to join me, to thread his arm through mine, and return to the wake to sit beside me where he didn't fully realize or yet believe he belonged. After all, it was his grandmother, too, who had died.

8

It's Hard to Change

Grandmere Catherine's funeral was one of the biggest ever held in Terrebone Parish, for practically all of the mourners who had come to the wake and then some came to the services in church and at the cemetery. Grandpere Jack was on his best behavior and wearing the best clothes he could get. With his hair brushed, his beard trimmed, and his boots cleaned and polished, he looked more like a responsible member of the community. He told me he hadn't been in church

173

since his mother's funeral, but he sat beside me and sang the hymns and recited the prayers. He stood at my side at the cemetery, too. It seemed like as long as he didn't have any whiskey flowing through his veins, he was quiet and respectful.

Paul's parents came to the church, but not to the cemetery. Paul came to the graveside by himself and stood on the other side of me. We didn't hold hands, but he made his close presence known with a touch or a word.

Father Rush began his prayers and then delivered his last blessing. And then the coffin was lowered. Just when I had thought my sorrow had gone as deeply as it could into my very soul; just when I had thought my heart could be torn no more, I felt the sorrow go deeper and tear more. Somehow, even though she was dead, with her body still in the house, with her face in quiet repose, I had not fully understood how final her death was, but now, with the sight of her coffin going down, I could not remain strong. I could not accept that she would not be there to greet me in the morning and to comfort me before bed. I could not accept that we wouldn't be working side by side, struggling to provide for ourselves; I could not accept that she wouldn't be singing over the stove or marching down the steps to go on one of her treater missions. I didn't have the strength. My legs became sticks of butter and collapsed beneath me. Neither Paul nor Grandpere could get to me before my body hit the earth and my eyes shut out the reality.

I awoke on the front seat of the car that brought us to the cemetery. Someone had gone to a nearby brook and dipped a handkerchief into the water. Now, the cool, refreshing liquid helped me regain consciousness. I saw Mrs. Livaudis leaning over me, stroking my hair, and I saw Paul standing right behind her, a look of deep concern on his face.

"What happened?"

"You just fainted, dear, and we carried you to the car. How are you now?" she asked.

"I'm all right," I said. "Where's Grandpere Jack?" I asked. I tried sitting up, but my head began to spin and I had to fall back against the seat.

"He went off already," Mrs. Livaudis said, smirking, "with his usual swamp bums. You just rest there, dear. We're taking you home now. Just rest," she advised.

"I'll be right behind you," Paul said, leaning in. I tried to smile and then closed my eyes. By the time we reached the house, I felt strong enough to get up and walk to the galerie steps. There were dozens of people waiting to help. Mrs. Thibodeau directed I be taken up to my room. They helped me off with my shoes and I lay back, now feeling more embarrassed than exhausted.

"I'm fine," I insisted. "I'll be all right. I should go downstairs and—"

"You just lie here awhile, dear," Mrs. Livaudis said. "We'll bring you something cool to drink."

"But I should go downstairs . . . the people . . . "

"Everything's taken care of. Just rest a bit more," Mrs. Thibodeau said. I did as they ordered. Mrs. Livaudis returned with some cold lemonade. I felt a lot better after I had drunk it and said so.

"If you're up to it then, the Tate boy wants to see how you are. He's chomping at the bit and pacing up and down at the foot of the stairs like an expectant father," Mrs. Livaudis said, smiling.

"Yes, please, send him in," I said, and Paul was permitted to come upstairs.

"How are you doing?" he asked quickly.

"I'm all right. I'm sorry I was so much trouble," I moaned. "I wanted everything to go smooth and proper for Grandmere."

"Oh, it did. It was the most . . . most impressive funeral I've ever seen. No one could remember more people attending one, and you did fine. Everyone understands."

"Where's Grandpere Jack?" I asked. "Where did he go to so quickly?"

"I don't know, but he just arrived a little while ago. He's downstairs, greeting people on the galerie."

"Was he drinking?"

"A little," Paul lied.

"Paul Tate, you'd better practice more if you're going to try to deceive me," I said. "You're no harder to see through than a clean windowpane."

He laughed.

"He'll be all right. Too many people around him," Paul assured me, but no sooner had he uttered the words than we heard the shouting from below.

"Don't you tell me what to do and what not to do in my own house!" Grandpere raved. "You may run the pants off your men at your homes,

176

but you ain't running off mine. Now just get your butts on outta here and make it quick. Go on, get!"

That was followed by a chorus of uproars and more shouting.

"Help me go down, Paul. I've got to see what he's doing," I said. I got out of bed, slipped into my shoes, and went down to the kitchen where Grandpere had a jug of whiskey in his hands and was already swaying as he glared at the small crowd of mourners in the doorway.

"Whatcha all gapin' at, huh? You never seen a man in mourning? You never seen a man who just buried his wife? Quit your gapin' and go about your business," he cried, took another swig, swayed, and wiped his mouth with the back of his hand. His eyes were blazing. "Go on!" he shouted again, when no one moved.

"Grandpere!" I cried. He gazed at me with those bleary eyes. Then he swung the jug against the sink, smashing it and its contents all over the kitchen. The women shrieked and he howled. He was terrible in his anger, frightening as he whumped around with an energy too great to confine in such a small space.

Paul embraced me and pulled me back up the stairs.

"Wait until he calms down," he said. We heard Grandpere scream again and then we heard the mourners flee the house, the women who had brought their families, grabbing up their children and getting into their trucks and cars with their husbands to hightail it away.

Grandpere ranted and raved awhile longer. Paul

sat beside me on my bed and held my hand. We listened until it grew very quiet downstairs.

"He's settled down," I said. "I'd better go down and start cleaning up."

"I'll help," Paul said.

We found Grandpere collapsed in a rocker on the galerie, snoring. I mopped up the kitchen and cleared away the pieces of broken jug while Paul wiped down our table and straightened up the furniture.

"You'd better go home now, Paul," I said as soon as we were finished. "Your parents are probably wondering where you are so long."

"I hate to leave you here with that . . . that drunk. They ought to lock him up and throw the key away for doing what he did this time. It's not right that Grandmere Catherine's gone and he's still around, and it's not safe for you."

"I'll be all right. You know how he gets after he has his tantrum. He'll just sleep it off and then wake up hungry and sorry for what he did."

Paul smiled, shook his head, and then reached to caress my cheek, his eyes soft and warm.

"My Ruby, always optimistic."

"Not always, Paul," I said sadly. "Not anymore."

"I'll stop by in the morning," he promised. "To see how things are."

I nodded.

"Ruby, I . . . "

"You had better go, Paul," I said. "I don't want any more nasty scenes today."

"All right." He kissed me quickly on the cheek before rising. "I'm going to talk to my father," he promised. "I'm going to get at the truth of things."

I tried to smile, but my face was like dry, brittle china from all the tears and sadness. I was afraid I might simply shatter to pieces right before his eyes.

"I will," Paul pledged at the doorway. Then he was gone.

I sighed deeply, put some of the food away, and walked upstairs to lie down again. I had never felt so tired. I did sleep through a good part of the rest of the day. If anyone came to the house, I didn't hear them. But early in the evening, I heard pots clanking and furniture being shoved around. I sat up, for a moment, very confused. Then, my wits returning, I got out of bed quickly and went downstairs to find Grandpere on his hands and knees tugging at some loose floorboards. Every cabinet door was thrown wide open and all of our pots and pans had been taken out of the cabinets and lay strewn about.

"Grandpere, what are you doing?" I asked. He turned and gazed at me with eyes I hadn't seen before, eyes of accusation and anger.

"I know she's got it hidden somewhere here," he said. "I didn't find it in her room, but I know she's got it somewhere. Where is it, Ruby? I need it," he moaned.

"Need what, Grandpere?"

"Her stash, her money. She always had a pile set aside for a rainy day. Well, my rainy days have come. I need it to get my motor fixed, to get some new equipment." He sat back on his haunches. "I

179

got to work harder to make a go of it for both of us, Ruby. Where is it?"

"There isn't any stash, Grandpere. We were having a hard time of it, too. I once poled out to your shack to see if I could get you to help us get by, but you were collapsed on your galerie," I told him.

He shook his head, his eyes wild.

"Maybe she never told you. She was like that . . . secretive even with her own. There's a stash here somewhere," he declared, shifting his eyes from side to side. "It might take me a while, but I'll find it. If it's not in the house, it's buried somewhere outside, huh? Did you ever see or hear her diggin' out there?"

"There's no stash, Grandpere. You're wasting your time." It was on the tip of my tongue to tell him about my art money, but it was also as if Grandmere Catherine were still there, standing right beside me, forbidding me to mention a word about it. In case he decided to look in her chest for valuables, I made a note to myself to move the money under my mattress.

"Are you hungry?" I asked him.

"No," he said quickly. "I'm going out back before it gets too dark and look some more," he said.

After he left, I put back all the pots and pans and then I warmed some food for myself. I ate mechanically, barely tasting anything. I ate just because I knew I had to in order to keep up my strength. Then, I went back upstairs. I could hear Grandpere's frantic digging in the backyard, his digging and his cursing. I heard him ripping through the smokehouse and even banging around in the outhouse. Finally, he grew exhausted with the searching and came back inside. I heard him get himself something to eat and drink. His frustration was so great, he moaned like a calf that had lost its mother. Soon, he was talking to ghosts.

"Where'd you put the money, Catherine? I got to have the money to take care of our granddaughter, don't I? Where is it?"

Finally, he grew quiet. I tiptoed out and looked over the railing to see him collapsed at the kitchen table, his head on his arms. I returned to my room and I sat by my window and gazed up at the horned moon half hidden by dark clouds and I thought, this is the same moon that rode high over New Orleans, and I tried to imagine my future. Would I be rich and famous and live in a big house some day like Grandmere Catherine predicted?

Or was all that just a dream, too? Just another web, dazzling in the moonlight, a mirage, an illusion of jewels woven in the darkness, waiting, full of promises that were as empty and as light as the web itself?

There was no period in my life when I thought time passed more slowly than it did during the days following Grandmere Catherine's funeral and burial. Every time I looked at the old and tarnished brass clock set in its cherry wood case on the windowsill in the loom room and saw that instead of an hour only ten minutes had passed, I was surprised and disappointed. I tried to fill my every moment, keep my hands and my mind busy so I wouldn't think and remember and mourn, but no matter how much work I did and how hard I worked, there was always time to remember.

One memory that returned with the persistence of a housefly was my recollection of the promise I had made to Grandmere Catherine should anything bad happen to her. She had reminded me of it the day she had died and she had forced me to repeat my vow. I had promised not to stay here, not to live with Grandpere Jack. Grandmere Catherine wanted me to go to New Orleans and find my real father and my sister, but the very thought of leaving the bayou and getting on a bus to go to a city that loomed as far away and as strange to me as a distant planet was terrifying. I was positive I would stand out as clearly as a crawfish in a pot of duck gumbo. Everyone in New Orleans would take one look at me and say to himself, "There's an ignorant Cajun girl traveling on her own." They would laugh at me and mock me for sure.

I had never traveled very far, especially on my own, but it wasn't the fear of the journey, nor even the size of the city and the unfamiliarity with city life that frightened me the most. No, what was even more terrifying was imagining what my real father would do and say as soon as I presented myself. How would he react? What would I do if he shut the door in my face? After having deserted Grandpere Jack and then, after having been rejected by my father, where would I go?

I had read enough about the evils of city life to know about the horrors that went on in the slums, and the terrible fates young girls such as myself suffered. Would I become one of those women I had heard about, women who were taken into bordellos to provide men with sexual pleasures? What other sort of work would I be able to get? Who would hire a young Cajun girl with a limited education and only simple handicraft skills? I envisioned myself ending up sleeping in some gutter, surrounded by other downcast and down-trodden people.

No, it was easier to put off the promise and lock myself upstairs in the *grenier* for most of the day, working on the linens and towels as if Grandmere Catherine were still alive and just downstairs doing one of her kitchen chores before joining me. It was easier to pretend I had to finish something she had started while she was off on one of her treater missions, easier to make believe nothing had changed.

Of course, part of my day involved caring for Grandpere Jack, preparing his meals and cleaning up after him, which was an endless chore. I made him his breakfast every morning before he left to go fishing or harvesting Spanish moss in the swamp. He was still mumbling about finding Grandmere Catherine's stash and he still spent every spare moment digging and searching around the house. The longer he looked and located nothing, the more he believed I was hiding what I knew.

"Catherine wasn't one to let herself go and die and leave something buried without someone knowing where," he declared one night after he had begun to eat his supper. His green eyes darkened as he focused them on me with suspicion. "You didn't dig somethin' up and hide it where

I've already looked, have you, Ruby? Wouldn't surprise me none to learn that Catherine had told you to do just such a thing before she died."

"No, Grandpere. I've told you time after time. There was no stash. We had to spend everything we made. Before Grandmere died, we were depending on what she got from some of her treater missions, too, and you know how much she hated taking anything for helping people." What my eyes must have shown convinced him I was not lying, at least for the time being.

"That's jus' it," he said, chewing thoughtfully, "people gave her things, gave her money, too, I'm sure. I just wonder if she left anything with one of those busybodies, 'specially that Mrs. Thibodeau. One of these nights, I might pay that woman a visit," he declared.

"I wouldn't do that, Grandpere," I warned him.

"Why not? The money don't belong to her; it belongs to me . . . us that is."

"Mrs. Thibodeau would call the police and have you put in jail if you so much as stepped on the floor of her galerie," I advised him. "She's as much as told me so." Once again, his piercing eyes glared my way before he went back to his food.

"All you women are in cahoots," he muttered. "A man does the best he can to keep food on the table, keep the house together. Women take all that for granted. Especially, Cajun women," he mumbled. "They think it's all coming to them. Well it ain't, and a man's got to be treated with more respect, especially in his own home. If I find that money's been hidden on me . . . "

It did no good to argue with him. I saw why Grandmere Catherine made no attempt to change the way he thought, but I did hope that in time, he would give up his frantic search for the nonexistent stash and concentrate on reforming himself the way he had promised and work hard at making a good life for us. Some days he did return from the swamp laden down with a good fish catch or a pair of ducks for our gumbo. But some days, he spent most of his time poling from one brackish pond to the next, mumbling to himself about one of his favorite gripes and then settling down in his pirogue to drink himself into a stupor, having traded his catch for a cheap bottle of gin or rum. Those nights he returned empty-handed and bitter, and I had to make do with what we had and concoct a poor Cajun's jambalaya.

Grandpere repaired some small things around the house, but left most of his other promises of work unfulfilled. He didn't patch the roof where it leaked or replace the cracked floorboards, and despite my not so subtle suggestions, he didn't improve his hygienic habits either. A week would go by before he would take a bar of soap and water to his body, and even then, it was a quick, almost insignificant rinse. Soon, there were lice in his hair again, his beard was scraggly, and his fingernails were caked with grime. I had to look at something else whenever we ate or I would lose my appetite. It was hard enough contending with the variety of sour and rancid odors that reeked from his clothes and body. How someone could let himself go like that and not care or even notice was beyond me. I imagined it had a lot to do with his drinking.

Every time I looked at the portrait I had done of Grandmere Catherine, I thought about returning to my painting, but whenever I set up my easel, I would just stare dumbly at the blank paper, not a creative thought coming to mind. I attempted a few starts, drawing some lines, even trying to paint a simple moss-covered cypress log, but it was as if my artistic talent had died with Grandmere. I knew she would be furious even to hear such a thought, but the truth was that the bayou, the birds, the plants and trees, everything about it in some way made me think of Grandmere and once I did, I couldn't paint. I missed her that much.

Paul came by nearly every day, sometimes just to sit and talk on the galerie, sometimes to sit and watch me work on the loom. Often, he helped with some chore, especially a chore Grandpere should have completed before going out in the swamp for the day.

"What's that Tate boy doin' around here so much?" Grandpere asked me late one afternoon when he returned just as Paul was leaving.

"He's just a good friend, coming around to be sure everything is all right, Grandpere," I said. I didn't have the courage to tell Grandpere I knew all the ugly truths and the terrible things he had done when my mother was pregnant with Paul. I knew how Grandpere's temper could flare, and how such revelations would just send him sucking on a bottle and then ranting and raving.

"Those Tates think they're special just because they make a pile of money," Grandpere muttered. "You watch out for people like that. You watch out," he warned. I ignored him and went in to prepare supper.

Every day, before Paul left, he made a promise to talk to his father about the past, but every day he returned, I could see immediately that he hadn't worked up the courage yet. Finally, one Saturday night, he told me he and his father were going fishing the next day after church.

"It will just be him and me," he said. "One way or the other, I'll get it all discussed," he promised.

That morning I tried to get Grandpere Jack to go to church with me, but I couldn't shake him out of his deep sleep. The harder I shook him, the louder he snored. It would be the first time I had gone to church without Grandmere Catherine and I wasn't sure I could manage it, but I set out anyway. When I arrived, all of Grandmere's lady friends greeted me warmly. Naturally, they were full of questions concerning how I was getting along living in the same house with Grandpere. I tried to make it sound better than it was, but Mrs. Livaudis pursed her lips and shook her head.

"No one should have to live with such a burden, especially a young girl like Ruby," she declared.

"You sit with us, dear," Mrs. Thibodeau said, and I sat in the pew and sang the hymns alongside them.

Paul and his family had arrived late so we didn't talk, and then he and his father wanted to get back as soon as they could and get their boat in the bayou. I couldn't stop thinking about him all day, wondering every other minute whether or not Paul had brought up the past with his father. I expected to see him shortly after dinner, but he didn't come.

I sat on the galerie and rocked and waited. Grandpere was inside listening to some Cajun music on the radio and kicking up his heels from time to time as he swung a jug up to his lips. Anyone walking by would have thought a hoeing bee or a shingling party was going on.

It got late; Grandpere Jack settled down into his usual unconscious state, and I grew tired. Without a moon, the sky was a deep black, making the twinkling stars that much brighter. I tried to keep my eyes from closing, but the lids seemed to have a mind of their own. I even dozed off and woke with a start at the cry of a screech owl. Finally, I gave up and went up to bed.

I had just settled my head on the pillow and closed my eyes again, when I heard the front door open and close and then heard soft footsteps on the stairs. My heart began to thump. Who had come into our house? With Grandpere Jack in a stupor, anyone could enter and do what he wanted. I sat up and waited, barely breathing.

First, a tall silhouette appeared on the walls and then the dark figure stepped into my doorway.

"Paul?"

"I'm sorry to wake you, Ruby. I wasn't going to come tonight, but I just couldn't sleep," he said. "I knocked, but I guess you didn't hear and when I opened the door, I saw your grandfather sprawled out on the settee in the sitting room, his mouth wide open, the snoring so loud, it's making the walls vibrate."

I leaned over and turned on the light. One look at Paul's face told me he had learned the truth.

"What happened, Paul? I waited for you until

I got too tired," I told him, and sat up, holding the blanket against my flimsy nightgown. He came farther into the room and stood at the foot of my bed, his head bowed. "Did you have the discussion with your father?" He nodded and then lifted his head.

"When I got home from fishing, I just ran into the house and up to my room and shut the door. I didn't go down for dinner, but I just couldn't lie there anymore. I wanted to put my pillow over my face and keep it there until I couldn't breathe," he told me. "I even tried twice!"

"Oh, Paul. What did he tell you?" I asked. Paul sat on the bed and gazed at me silently for a moment. His shoulders slumped and he continued.

"My father didn't want to talk about it; he was surprised by my questions and for a long while just sat there, staring at the water, not speaking. I told him I had to know the truth, that it was important to me, more important than anything else. Finally, he turned to me and said he was going to tell me about it someday; he just didn't think the time had come.

"But I told him it had and I repeated my need to know the truth. At first, he was angry I had found out. He thought Grandpere Jack had told me. He said your grandfather . . . I guess I got to get used to it, even though it makes me sick to the stomach . . . our grandfather," he said, pronouncing the words with a grimace that made it look as if he had swallowed castor oil. "Our grandpere Jack had blackmailed him once before and was trying to figure a way to get money out of him again. Then I told him what Grandmere Catherine had told you and why she had told you, and he nodded and said she was right to do so."

"I'm glad, Paul, glad he told you the truth. Now—"

"Only," Paul added quickly, his eyes growing narrow and dark, "my father's version of the story is a lot different from Grandmere Catherine's version."

"How?"

"According to him your mother seduced him, and he didn't take advantage of her. He claims she was a wild young woman and he wasn't the first to be with her. He said she was hounding him, following him everywhere, smiling and teasing him all the time, and one day, when he was out in the bayou fishing by himself, she came upon him, poling a pirogue. She tore off her clothing and dove into the water naked and then climbed into his boat. That's when it happened. That's when I was made," Paul said bitterly.

My silence bothered him, but I couldn't help it. I was speechless. One part of me wanted to laugh and shout and ridicule such a story. No daughter of Grandmere Catherine's could be such a creature; but another part of me, that part of me that had fantasized such things with Paul told me it might be true.

"I don't believe him of course," Paul said quickly. "I think it happened the way your grandmother told it. He came around here and he seduced your mother, otherwise, why would he have owned up to it so quickly when Grandpere

Jack confronted him and why did he pay him any blackmail money?"

I took a deep breath.

"Did you say that to your father?" I asked.

"No. I didn't want to have any arguments about it."

"I don't know how we'll ever know the whole truth about it," I said.

"What's the difference now?" Paul muttered angrily. "The result is the same. Oh, my father complained again and again about how Grandpere Jack came to him and blackmailed him, and how he had to pay him thousands of dollars to keep the matter secret. He said Grandpere was the lowest of the low who belonged with the slimy things in the swamp. He told me how my mother felt sorry for him, especially because of Grandpere Jack, and how she agreed to pretend to be pregnant so my birth would be accepted by the community as the legitimate birth of a Tate. Then he made me promise I wouldn't say anything to my mother. He told me it would break her heart if she knew I discovered she wasn't really my mother."

"I'm sure it would," I said. "He's not wrong about that, Paul. Why hurt her any more than she has been hurt?"

"What about me?" he cried. "What about . . . us?"

"We're young," I said, thinking about Grandmere Catherine's words of wisdom.

"That doesn't mean it hurts any less," he moaned.

"No, it doesn't, but I don't know what else we can do about it, but go on and try to find other people who we can love and care for as strongly as we love and care for each other now."

"I can't; I won't," he said defiantly.

"Paul, what else can we do?"

He fixed his eyes on me, the defiance in his face, the anger and the pain, too.

"We'll just pretend it isn't so," he said, reaching out to take my hand.

I couldn't stop the tingle that had begun around my heart and then shot through my blood to fly through my stomach and my legs and make my breath quicken. Suddenly everything about him, everything about us was forbidden. Just his merely sitting on my bed, holding my hand, gazing at me with such longing was taboo, and just like most anything prohibited, it carried an elevated excitement along with it. It was like teasing fate, testing, exquisitely tormenting our own souls.

"We can't do that, Paul," I said, my voice barely a whisper.

"Why not? Let's ignore that half of ourselves and think only about the other half. It won't be the first time such a thing happened, especially in the bayou," he said. His hand moved up my wrist, the fingers sliding softly over my skin as he lifted himself to sit closer. I shook my head gently.

"You're just upset and angry now, Paul. You're not thinking about what you're saying to me," I told him. My heart was pounding so hard, I thought I would lose my breath.

"Yes, I am. Who knows about us anyway? Just your grandpere Jack and no one would believe anything he would say, and my father and mother who wouldn't want anyone to know the truth. Don't you see? It doesn't matter."

"But we know; it matters to us."

"Not if we don't let it matter," Paul said. He leaned forward to kiss my forehead. Now that we both knew the truth of his origin, his lips felt as hot as a branding iron. I backed away abruptly and shook my head, not only trying to refuse his advances, but refusing the excitement that was building in my own heart.

My blanket fell away and my nightgown dropped so low most of my bosom was visible. Paul's eyes lowered and rose, climbing slowly back to my neck and shoulders and my face.

"Once we do it, once we ignore the ugly past and make love, we will be able to do it easier and easier every time afterward, Ruby," he said. "Don't you see? Why should the other half of ourselves, the better half be denied? We haven't been brought up as brother and sister; we've never thought of ourselves as related.

"If you just close your eyes and forget, if you just let your lips touch mine," he said, drawing close again.

I shook my head, closed my eyes, and sat back as far as I could, but Paul's lips touched mine. I tried to deny him, to slide myself out from under, but he pressed onward, more demanding, his hands finding the bare flesh of my exposed bosom, his fingers turning so the tips would touch my nipples.

"Paul, no," I cried. "Please, don't. We'll be sorry," I said, but I felt myself slipping as the tingle grew into a wave of warm desire. After so much sorrow and so much hardship, my body craved his warm touch, forbidden as it was.

"No, we won't," Paul insisted. His lips grazed my forehead and moved down the side of my face as his hand slipped completely under my nightgown to fully cup my breast. He lifted it to bring his lips to my nipple and I felt myself weaken. I couldn't open my eyes. I couldn't speak. I continued to slide under him and he pressed forward, insistent, driven, unrelenting in his determination to batter down not only my feeble resistance, but all the morals and laws of church and man that not only forbid our erotic touching, but looked down on it with disgust.

"Ruby," he whispered in my ear, sending my mind spinning, my heart racing, "I love you."

"What the hell in tarnation is goin' on here!" we suddenly heard. Paul snapped back and I gasped. Grandpere Jack was standing in the hallway gazing in at us, his hair sticking up and out, his eyes wide and bloodshot, his body swaying as if a wind were tearing through the house.

"Nothing," Paul said, and stood up, quickly straightening his clothes.

"Nothing! You call that nothing?" Grandpere Jack focused his gaze and stepped through the doorway. He was still drunk, but he recognized Paul. "Who the hell . . . you're the Tate boy, ain't you? The one who's always comin' around here?"

Paul looked down at me and then nodded at Grandpere.

"Figures you'd come around here at night and sneak into the house and into my granddaughter's room. It's in the Tate blood," Grandpere said.

"That's a lie," Paul snapped.

"Humph," Grandpere said and combed his long fingers through his disheveled hair. "Yeah, well, you got no business bein' in my granddaughter's bedroom this time of night. My advice to you, boy, is to tuck in your tail and git."

"Go on, Paul," I said. "It's better if you go," I added.

He looked down at me, his eyes swimming in tears.

"Please," I whispered. He bit down on his lower lip and then charged out the door, nearly bowling Grandpere Jack over in the process. Paul pounded his way down the steps and out the door.

"Well now," Grandpere Jack said, turning back to me. "Looks like you're a lot older than I thought. Time we thought about finding you a proper husband."

"I don't need anyone finding me a husband, Grandpere, and I'm not ready to marry anyone anyway. Paul wasn't doing anything. We were just talking and—"

"Just talkin'?" He laughed that silent chuckle that made his shoulders shake. "Out in the swamp that kinda talkin' makes new tadpoles," he added, and shook his head. "No, you're right grow'd; I just didn't take a good look at you before," he said, gazing at my uncovered body. I brought the blanket to my chest quickly. "Don't you worry about it none," he said, winking and then he stumbled out and made his way to Grandmere's room where he now slept, whenever he was able to climb the stairs to go to bed.

I sat back, my heart thumping so hard, I

thought it would crack open my chest. Poor Paul, I thought. He was so mixed up, so confused, his anger pulling him in one direction, his feeling for me pulling him in another. Grandpere Jack's surprise arrival and accusations didn't help matters any, but it might have saved us from doing something we would have regretted later on, I thought.

I put out the light and lay back again. I had to confess to myself that for a moment, when Paul was so insistent, part of me wanted to give in and do just what he had said: be defiant and seize what fate had made off-limits. But how do you bury such a dark secret in your heart, and how do you keep it from infecting and eventually destroying the purity of any love you might possess for each other? It couldn't be; it wasn't meant to be. It mustn't be, I thought. If anything, I knew now that I couldn't let myself get that close to him again. I didn't have the strength of will to resist the passion either.

As I closed my eyes and tried to sleep again, I realized, this was another reason, maybe even a bigger reason, to find the strength and the courage to leave.

Maybe that was why Grandmere Catherine was so insistent about it; maybe she knew what would happen between Paul and me despite what we had learned about ourselves. I fell asleep with her words echoing in my mind and my promises to her on my lips.

9

Hard Lessons

I didn't see Paul for the remainder of the weekend and I was surprised when I went to school on Monday and didn't see him there either. When I asked his sister Jeanne about him, she told me he wasn't feeling well, but she looked put out that I had asked, especially in front of her friends, and wouldn't say another thing.

After I returned home from school, I decided to take a short walk along the canal before preparing dinner. I strolled down the path through our yard which was abloom with hibiscus and blue and pink hydrangeas. Spring was rushing in this year, the colors, the sweet scents, and the heightened sense of life and birth was all around me. It was as if Nature herself were trying to comfort me.

But my confused and troubled thoughts were like bees buzzing around in a jar. I heard so many different voices telling me to do so many different things. Run, Ruby, run, one voice urged. Get as far from the bayou and from Paul and Grandpere Jack as you can.

Forget running, be defiant, another voice told me. You love Paul. You know you do. Surrender to your feelings and forget what you've learned. Do what Paul wants you to do: live like it was all a lie.

Remember your promise to me, Ruby, I heard

Grandmere Catherine urge. Ruby . . . your promise . . . remember.

The warm Gulf breeze lifted strands of my hair and made them dance over my forehead. The same warm breeze combed through the moss on the dead cypress trees in the marsh, making it look like some sprawling green animal, lifting and swaying to catch my attention. On a long sandbar, I saw a cottonmouth coiled over some driftwood soaking up the sun, its triangular head the color of a discolored copper penny. Two ducks and a heron sprung up from the water and flew low over the cattails. And then I heard the distant purr of a motorboat as it sliced through the bayou and wove its way closer and closer until it popped out from around a turn.

It was Paul. The moment he saw me, he waved, sped up, and brought the boat close to the shore, the wakes from the motorboat swelling up through the lily pads and cattails and slapping across the cypress roots along the bank.

"Walk down to the shale there," he called, and pointed. I did and he brought the boat as near as he could before shutting the engine and letting it drift up to me.

"Where were you today? Why didn't you come to school?" I asked. He was obviously not sick.

"I was busy, thinking and planning. Come into my boat. I want to show you something," he said.

I shook my head. "I've got to start on dinner for Grandpere Jack, Paul," I told him, retreating a step.

"You've got plenty of time and you know he'll

either be late or not show up until he's too drunk to care," he replied. "Come on. Please," he begged.

"Paul, I don't want anything to happen like it did the other day," I said.

"Nothing will happen. I won't come near you. I just want to show you something. I'll bring you right back," he promised. He held up his hand to take an oath. "I swear."

"You won't come near me and you'll bring me right back?"

"Absolutely," he said, and leaned forward to take my hand as I hopped over the shale and stepped up and into the motorboat. "Just sit back," he said, starting the engine again. He spun the boat around sharply and accelerated with the confidence of an old Cajun swamp fisherman. Even so, I screamed. The best fisherman often ran into gators or sandbars. Paul laughed and slowed down.

"Where are you taking me, Paul Tate?" He steered us through the shadows cast by an over-hang of willow trees, deeper and deeper into the swamp before heading southwest in the direction of his father's cannery. Off in the distance I could see thunderheads over the Gulf. "I don't want to get caught in any storms," I complained.

"My, you can be a nag," Paul said, smiling. He wove us through a narrow passage and then headed for a field, cutting his engine as we drew closer and closer. Finally, he turned it off to let the boat drift.

"Where are we?"

"My land," he replied. "And I don't mean my father's land. My land," he emphasized.

"Your land?"

"Yep," he said proudly and leaned back against the side of the boat. "All that you see—sixty acres actually. It's mine, my inheritance." He gestured broadly at the field.

"I never knew that," I said, gazing over what looked like prime land in the bayou.

"My grandfather Tate left it to me. It's held in trust, but it will be mine as soon as I turn eighteen, but that isn't the best of it," he said, smiling.

"Well, what is then?" I asked. "Stop grinning like a Cheshire cat and tell me what this is all about, Paul Tate."

"Better than tell you, I'll show you," he said, and took up the oar to paddle the boat softly through some marsh grass and into a dark, shadowy area. I stared ahead and soon saw the bubbles in the water.

"What's that?"

"Gas bubbles," he said in a whisper. "You know what it means?"

I shook my head.

"It means oil is under here. Oil and it's on my land. I'm going to be rich, Ruby, very rich," he said.

"Oh, Paul, that's wonderful."

"Not if you're not with me to share it," he said quickly. "I brought you here because I wanted you to see my dreams. I'm going to build a great house on my land. It will be a great plantation, your plantation, Ruby."

"Paul, how can we even think such a thing? Please," I said. "Stop tormenting yourself and me, too."

"We can think of such a thing, don't you see? The oil is the answer. Money and power will make it all possible. I'll buy Grandpere Jack's blessings and silence. We'll be the most respected, prosperous couple in the bayou, and our family—"

"We can't have children, Paul."

"We'll adopt, maybe even secretly, with your doing the same thing my mother did—pretending the baby is yours, and then—"

"But, Paul, we'll be living the same sort of lies, the same deceits, and they will haunt us forever," I said, shaking my head.

"Not if we don't let them, not if we permit ourselves to love and cherish each other the way we always dreamed we would," he insisted.

I turned away from him and watched a bullfrog jump off a log. It created a small circle of ripples that quickly disappeared. In a corner of the pond, I saw bream feeding on insects among the cattails and lily pads. The wind began to pick up and the Spanish moss swayed along with the twisted limbs of the cypress. A flock of geese passed overhead and disappeared over the tops of trees as if they had flown into the clouds.

"It's beautiful here, Paul. And I wish it could be our home someday, but it can't and it's just cruel to bring me here and tell me these things," I said, chastising him softly.

"But, Ruby—"

"Don't you think I wish it could be, wish it as much as you do?" I said, spinning around on him. My eyes were burning with tears of anger and frustration. "The same feelings that are tearing you apart are tearing me, but we're just prolonging the pain by fantasizing like this."

"It's not a fantasy; it's a plan," he said firmly. "I've been thinking about it all weekend. After I'm eighteen . . . "

I shook my head.

"Take me back, Paul. Please," I said. He stared at me a moment.

"Will you at least think about it?" he pleaded. "Will you?"

"Yes," I said, because I saw it was the key that would open the door and let us out of this room of misery.

"Good." He started the engine and drove us back to the dock at my house.

"I'll see you at school tomorrow," he said after he helped me out of the boat. "We'll talk about this every day, think it out clearly, together, okay?"

"Okay, Paul," I said, confident that one morning he would awaken and realize that his plan was a fantasy not meant to become a reality.

"Ruby," he cried as I started toward the house. I turned. "I can't help loving you," he said. "Don't hate me for it."

I bit down on my lower lip and nodded. My heart was soaked in the tears that had fallen behind my eyes. I watched him drive off and waited until his motorboat disappeared into the bayou. Then I took a deep breath and entered the house.

The roar of Grandpere's laughter greeted me and was immediately followed by the laughter of a stranger. I walked into the kitchen slowly to discover Grandpere Jack sitting at the table. He and a man I recognized as Buster Trahaw, the son of a rich sugar plantation owner, sat hunched over a large bowl of crawfish. There were at least a half-dozen or so empty bottles of beer on the table that they had drawn out of a case on the floor at their feet.

Buster Trahaw was a man in his midthirties, tall and stout with a circle of fat around his stomach and sides that made it look as if he wore an inner tube under his shirt. All of the features of his plain face were distorted by the bloat. He had a thick nose with wide nostrils, heavy jowls, a round chin, and a soft mouth with thick purple lips. His forehead protruded over his cavernous dark eyes and his large earlobes leaned away from his head so that from behind, he looked like a big bat. Right now, his dull brown hair was matted down with sweat, the strands sticking to the top of his forehead.

As soon as I stepped into the room, his smile widened, showing a mouthful of large teeth. Pieces of crawfish were visible between the gaps and his thick pink tongue was covered with the meat as well. He brought the neck of a beer bottle to his lips and drew on it so hard, his cheeks folded in and out like the bellows of an accordion. Grandpere Jack spun around in his chair when he caught Buster's smile.

"Well, where you been, girl?" Grandpere demanded.

"I went for a walk," I said.

"Me and Buster been here waitin' on you," Grandpere said. "Buster's our guest for dinner

203

tonight," he said. I nodded and went to the icebox. "Can't you say hello to him?"

"Hello," I said, and turned back to the icebox. "Did you bring any fish or duck or anything for the gumbo, Grandpere?" I asked without looking at him. I took out some vegetables.

"There's a pile of shrimp in the sink just waitin' to be shelled," he replied. "She's one helluva cook, Buster. I'd match her gumbo, her jambalaya, and *étouffée* with any in the bayou," he bragged.

"Don't say?" Buster replied.

"You'll soon see. Yes, sir, you will. And look how nicely she keeps the house, even with a hog like me livin' in it," Grandpere added.

I turned and gazed at him suspiciously, my eyes no more than dark slits. He sounded like he was doing a lot more than bragging about his granddaughter; he sounded like someone advertising something he wanted to sell. My suspicious gaze didn't shake him. "Buster here knows about you, Ruby," he said. "He told me he's seen you walking along the road or tending to the stall or in town many times. Ain't that right, Buster?"

"Yes, sir, it is. And I always liked what I saw," he said. "You keep yourself nice and pretty, Ruby," he said.

"Thank you," I said, and turned away, my heart beginning to pound.

"I told Buster here that my granddaughter, she's gettin' to the point when she should think of settlin' down and havin' a place of her own, her own kitchen, her own flock to tend," Grandpere Jack continued. I started to shell the shrimp.

"Most women in the bayou end up no better than they were to start, but Buster here, he's got one of the best plantations going."

"One of the biggest and best," Buster added.

"I'm still going to school, Grandpere," I said. I kept my back to him and Buster so neither would see the fear in my face or the tears that were starting to escape my lids and trickle down my cheeks.

"Aw, school ain't important anymore, not at your age. You've already gone longer than I did," Grandpere said. "And I bet longer than you did, huh, Buster?"

"That's for sure," Buster said, then laughed.

"All Buster had to learn was how to count the money comin' in, ain't that right, Buster?"

The two of them laughed.

"Buster's father is a sick man; his days are numbered and Buster's going to inherit the whole thing, ain't you, Buster?"

"That's true and I deserve it, too," Buster said.

"Hear that, Ruby?" Grandpere said. I didn't respond. "I'm talking to you, child."

"I heard you, Grandpere," I said. I wiped my tears away with the back of my hand and turned around. "But I told you, I'm not ready to marry anyone and I'm still in school. I want to be an artist anyway," I said.

"Hell, you can be an artist. Buster here would buy you all the paint and brushes you'd need for a hundred years, wouldn't ya, Buster?"

"Two hundred," he said, and laughed.

"See?"

"Grandpere, don't do this," I pleaded. "You're embarrassing me."

"Huh? You're too old for that kind of thing, Ruby. Besides, I can't be around here watchin' over you all day now, can I? Your grandmere's gone; it's time for you to grow up."

"She sure looks good and grow'd up to me," Buster said and wiped his thick tongue over the side of his mouth to scoop in a piece of crawfish that had attached itself to the grizzle of his unshaven face.

"Hear that, Ruby?"

"I don't want to hear that. I don't want to talk about it. I'm not marrying anyone right now," I cried. I backed away from the sink and from them. "And especially not Buster," I added, and charged out of the kitchen and up the stairs.

"Ruby!" Grandpere called.

I paused at the top of the stairway to catch my breath and heard Buster complain.

"So much for your easy arrangements, Jack. You brought me here, got me to buy you this case of beer and she ain't the obedient little lady you promised."

"She will be," Grandpere Jack told him. "I'll see to that."

"Maybe. You're just lucky I like a girl who has some spirit. It's like breaking a wild horse," Buster said. Grandpere Jack laughed. "Tell you what," Buster said. "I'll up what I was going to give you by another five hundred if I can test the merchandise first."

"What'dya mean?" Grandpere asked.

"I don't got to spell it out, do I, Jack? You're

just playin' dumb to get me to raise the ante. All right, I'll admit she's special. I'll give you one thousand tomorrow for a night alone with her and then the rest on our wedding day. A woman should be broken in first anyway and I might as well break in my wife myself."

"A thousand dollars!"

"You got it. What'dya say?"

I held my breath. Tell him to go straight to hell, Grandpere, I whispered.

"Deal," Grandpere Jack said instead. I could see them shaking hands and then opening another bottle of beer.

I hurried into my room and closed the door. If ever I needed proof that all the stories about Grandpere Jack were true, I just got it, I thought. No matter how drunk he got, no matter how many gambling debts he mounted, he should have some feeling for his own flesh and blood. I was seeing firsthand the sort of ugly and selfish animal Grandpere had become in Grandmere Catherine's eyes. Why didn't I have the courage to obey my promise to her immediately? I thought. Why do I always look for the best in people, even when there's not a hint of any there? All my lessons are to be learned the hard way, I concluded.

Less than an hour or so later, I heard Grandpere come up the stairs. He didn't knock on my door; he shoved it open and stood there glaring in at me. He was fuming so fiercely it looked like smoke might pour out of his red ears.

"Buster's gone," he said. "He lost his appetite over your behavior."

"Good."

"You ain't gonna be like this, Ruby," he said, pointing his finger at me. "Your grandmere Catherine spoiled you, probably fillin' you with all sorts of dreams about your artwork and tellin' you you're goin' to be some sort of fancy city lady, but you're just another Cajun girl, prettier than most, I'll admit; but still a Cajun girl who should thank her lucky stars a man as rich as Buster Trahaw's taken interest in her.

"Now, instead of being grateful, what do you do? You make me look like a fool," he said.

"You are a fool, Grandpere," I retorted. His face turned crimson. I sat up in my bed. "But worse, you're a selfish man who would sell his own flesh and blood just to keep himself in whiskey and gambling."

"You apologize for that, Ruby. You hear."

"I'm not apologizing, Grandpere. It's you who have years of apologizing to do. You're the one who has to apologize for blackmailing Mr. Tate and selling Paul to him."

"What? Who told you that?"

"You're the one who has to apologize for arranging the sale of my sister to some Creoles in New Orleans. You broke my mother's heart and Grandmere Catherine's, too," I accused. He stood there sputtering for a moment.

"That's a lie. All of it, a lie. I did what was necessary to do to save the family name and made a little on the side to help us out," he protested. "Catherine just worked you up against me by telling you otherwise and—"

"Just like you're selling me to Buster Trahaw, making a deal with him to come up here tomorrow night," I said, crying. "You, my grandfather, someone who should be looking after me, protecting me . . . you, you're nothing more than . . . than the swamp animal Grandmere said you were," I shouted.

He seemed to swell up, his shoulders rising so he reached his full height, his crimson face turning darker until his complexion was almost the color of my hair, his eyes so full of anger, they seemed luminous.

"I see these busybodies have filled you with defiance and turned you against me. Well, I'm doin' what's best for you by convincing a man as rich and prosperous as Buster to take interest in you. If I make something on the side, too, you should be happy for me."

"I'm not and I won't marry Buster Trahaw," I cried.

"Yes, you will," Grandpere said. "And you'll thank me for it, too," he predicted. Then he turned and left my room, pounding down the stairs.

A short while later, I heard him turn on the radio and then I heard some beer bottles clank and shatter. He was having one of his tantrums. I decided to wait in my room until he fell into his stupor. Afterward, I would leave.

I started to pack a small bag, being as selective as I could about what I would take because I knew I had to travel light. I had my art money hidden under the mattress, but I decided not to take it out until just before I was ready to leave. Of course, I would take the photographs of my mother and the one photograph of my real father and my sister. As

209

I pondered what else to bring, I heard Grandpere's ranting grow more intense. Something else shattered and a chair was smashed. Shortly afterward, I heard something rattle and then I heard his heavy, unsure steps on the stairs.

I cowered back in my bed, my heart thumping. My door was thrown open again and he stood there, gazing in at me, the flames of anger in his eyes fanned by the whiskey and beer he had consumed. He looked around and saw my little bag in the corner.

"Goin' somewheres, are ya?" he asked, smiling. I shook my head. "Thought you might do that . . . thought you might leave me lookin' the fool."

"Grandpere, please," I began but he stepped forward with surprising agility and seized my left ankle. I screamed as he wrapped what looked like a bicycle chain around it and then ran the chain down and around the leg of the bed. I heard him snap on a lock before he stood up.

"There," he said. "That should help bring you to your senses."

"Grandpere . . . unlock me!"

He turned away.

"You'll be thankin' me," he muttered. "Thankin' me." He stumbled out of the door and left me, terrified, crying hysterically.

"Grandpere!" I screamed. My throat ached with the effort and the tears. When I stopped and listened, it sounded as if he had tripped and fallen down the stairs. I heard him curse and then I heard more banging and more furniture shattering. After a while it grew quiet.

Stunned by what he had done, I could only lie

there and sob until my chest felt as if it were filled with stones. Grandpere was worse than a swamp animal; he was a monster, for swamp animals would never be as cruel to their own kind, I thought. And there was just so much to blame on the whiskey and beer.

Out of exhaustion and fear, I fell asleep, eagerly accepting the slumber as a form of escape from the horror I had never dreamed.

When I awoke, I felt as if I had slept for hours, but not even two had passed. I had no chance to think that what had happened was just a bad nightmare either, for the moment I moved my leg, I heard the chain rattle. I sat up quickly and tried to slide it off my ankle, but the harder I tugged, the deeper and sharper it cut into my skin. I moaned and buried my face in my hands for a moment. If Grandpere left me chained up like this all day . . . if I were like this when Buster Trahaw returned, I would be defenseless, helpless.

A cold, electric chill cut through my heart. I couldn't remember ever feeling such terror. I listened. All was quiet in the house. Even the breeze barely made the walls creak. It was as if time stood still, as if I were trapped in the eye of a great storm that was about to break over my head. I took a deep breath and tried to calm myself down enough to think clearly. Then I studied the chain and followed the line of it to the leg of the bed.

A surge of relief came over me when I realized that Grandpere Jack in his drunken state had merely wound and locked the chain around the leg, forgetting that I could lift the bed and slide the chain down. I twisted my body until I had my other leg off the bed and then lowered myself awkwardly, painfully, until I was far enough to get the leverage I needed. It took all the strength I could muster, but the bed lifted and I began to nudge the chain down until it fell off the bottom of the leg. I worked the chain around until I unraveled it from my ankle, which was plenty red and sore. Carefully, as quietly as I could, I lay the chain on the floor. Then I picked up my little bag of clothes and precious items, dug my money out from under the mattress, and went to the bedroom door. I opened it a crack and listened.

All was quiet. The butane lantern below flickered weakly, casting a dim glow and making the distorted silhouettes dance over the stairs and the walls. Was Grandpere asleep in Grandmere Catherine's room? I decided not to look, but instead, I slipped out of my bedroom and tiptoed to the stairs. No matter how softly I walked, however, the wooden floors creaked. It was as if the house wanted to betray me. I paused, listened, and then continued down the stairs. When I reached the bottom, I waited and listened. Then I went forward and discovered Grandpere Jack sprawled on the floor by the front door. He was snoring loudly.

I didn't want to risk stepping over him and going out the front, so I turned to the back, but I stopped halfway to the kitchen. I had to do one last thing, take one last look at the picture I had painted of Grandmere Catherine that hung on the wall in the parlor. I walked back softly and paused in the doorway. Moonlight pouring through the uncovered window illuminated the portrait, and for a moment it seemed to me that Grandmere was smiling, that her eyes were full of happiness because I was keeping to my promise.

"Good-bye, Grandmere," I whispered. "Someday, I'll return to the bayou and I'll take your picture back with me to wherever I live."

How I wished I could hug her and kiss her one more time. I closed my eyes and tried to remember the last time I had, but Grandpere Jack groaned and turned over on the floor. I didn't move a muscle. His eyes opened and closed. If he had seen me, he must have thought it was a dream, for he didn't wake up. Not wasting another second, I turned away and walked quickly but quietly through the kitchen and out the back door. Then, I hurried around the corner of the house and headed for the front.

When I reached the road, I stopped and looked back. Something sweet and sour was in my throat. Despite all that had happened and all that would, it hurt me to leave this simple house that had known my first steps. Within those plain old walls Grandmere Catherine and I had made many a meal together, sung together, and laughed together. On that galerie, she had rocked and told me story after story about her own youthful days. Upstairs in that bedroom, she had nursed me through my childhood illnesses and told me the bedtime stories that made it easier to close my eyes and sleep contentedly, always feeling safe and secure in the cocoon of promises she wove with her soft voice and soft, loving eyes. Sitting by my bedroom window on hot summer nights, I had fantasized my future, seen my prince come, envisioned my jeweled wedding with the gold dust in the spider-webs and the music.

Oh, it was more than an old swamp house I was leaving. It was my entire past, my years of growing and developing, my feelings of joy and feelings of sadness, my melancholy and my ecstasy, my laughter and my tears. How hard it was even now, even after all this, to turn away from it and let dark night shut the door of blackness behind me.

And what of the swamp itself? Could I really tear myself away from the flowers and the birds, from the fish and even the alligators who peered at me with interest? In the moonlight on a limb of a sycamore, sat a marsh hawk, his silhouette dark and proud against the white glow. He opened his wings and held them as if he were saying good-bye for all the swamp animals and birds and fish. And then he closed his wings and I turned and hurried off, the hawk's silhouette still lingering on the surface of my vision.

On the way into Houma, I passed many of the houses of people I knew, people I thought I might never see again. I almost paused at Mrs. Thibodeau's to say good-bye. She and Mrs. Livaudis were such special friends to me and my grandmere, but I was afraid she would try to talk me out of leaving and try to talk me into staying either with her or Mrs. Livaudis. I pledged to myself that someday, when I was finally settled, I would write to both of them.

Few places were still open in town when I arrived. I went directly to the bus station and bought a one-way ticket to New Orleans. I had nearly an hour to wait and spent most of it on a bench in the shadows, fearful that someone would spot me and either try to stop me or tell Grandpere before I left. Twice, I thought about calling Paul, but I was afraid to talk to him. If I told him what Grandpere Jack had done, he was sure to lose his temper and do something terrible. I decided to write him a good-bye note instead. I bought an envelope and a stamp in the station and dug out a piece of paper from my pocketbook.

Dear Paul,
    It would take too long to explain to you why I am leaving Houma without saying good-bye. I think the main reason though is I know how much it would break my heart to look at you and then leave. It hurts so much even writing this note. Let me just tell you that more things happened in the past than I revealed that day, and these events are taking me away from Houma to find my real father and my other life. There is nothing I would want more than to spend the rest of my life at your side. It seems like such a cruel joke for Nature to let us fall in love the way we did and then surprise us with the ugly truth. But I know now that if I didn't leave, you would not give up and you would make it painful for both of us.
    Remember me as I was before we learned the truth, and I'll remember you the same way. Maybe you're right; maybe we'll never love anyone else as much as we love each

other, but we have to try. I will think of you often, and I will imagine you in your beautiful plantation.

Love always,
Ruby

I posted the letter in the mailbox in front of the bus station and then I sat down and choked back my tears and waited. Finally, the bus arrived. It had come from St. Martinville and had made stops and picked up passengers at New Iberia, Franklin, and Morgan City before arriving at Houma, so the bus was nearly filled when I stepped up and gave the driver my ticket. I made my way toward the rear and saw an empty seat on the right next to a pretty caramel skinned woman with black hair and turquoise eyes. She smiled when I sat down, revealing milk white teeth. She wore a bright pink and blue peasant skirt with black sandals, a pink halter, and she had rings and rings of different bracelets on both her arms. She had her hair tied with a white kerchief, a tignon with seven knots whose points all stuck straight up.

"Hello," she said. "Going to the wet grave, too?"

"Wet grave?" I sat down beside her.

"New Orleans, honey. That's what my grandmere called it because you can't bury anyone in the ground. Too much water."

"Really?"

"That's true. Everyone's buried in tombs, vaults, ovens above the ground. You didn't know that?" she asked, holding her smile. I shook my head. "First time to New Orleans then, huh?"

"Yes, it is."

"You picked the best time to visit, you know," she said. I saw how bright her eyes were, how full of excitement she was.

"Why?"

"Why? Why, honey, it's Mardi Gras."

"Oh . . . no," I said, thinking to myself that it was the worst time to go, not the best. I had read and heard about New Orleans at Mardi Gras. I should have realized that was why she was all dressed up. The whole city would be festive. It wasn't the best time to arrive on my real father's doorstep.

"You act like you just stepped out of the swamp, honey."

I took a deep breath and nodded. She laughed.

"My name's Annie Gray," she said, offering her slim, smooth hand. I took it and shook. She had pretty rings on all her fingers, but one ring, the one on her pinky, looked like it was made out of bone and shaped like a tiny skull.

"I'm Ruby, Ruby Landry."

"Pleased to meet you. You got relatives in New Orleans?" she asked.

"Yes," I said. "But I haven't seen them . . . ever."

"Oh, ain't that somethin'?"

The bus driver closed the door and started the bus away from the station. My heart began to race as I saw us drive by stores and houses I had known all my life. We passed the church and then the school, moving over the road I had walked almost every day of my life. Then we paused at an intersection and the bus turned in the direction of New

217

Orleans. I had seen the road sign many times, and many times dreamt of following it. Now I was. In moments we were flying down the highway and Houma was falling farther and farther behind. I couldn't help but look back.

"Don't look back," Annie Gray said quickly.

"What? Why not?"

"Bad luck," she replied.

I spun around to face forward.

"What?"

"Bad luck. Quick, cross yourself three times," she prescribed. I saw she was serious and so I did it.

"I don't need any more of that," I said. That made her laugh. She leaned forward and picked up her cloth bag. Then she dug into it and came up with something to place in my hand. I stared at it.

"What's this?" I asked.

"Piece of neck bone from a black cat. It's gris-gris," she said. Seeing I was still confused, she added, "a magical charm to bring you good luck. My grandmere gave it to me. Voodoo," she added in a whisper.

"Oh. Well, I don't want to take your good luck piece," I said, handing it back. She shook her head.

"Bad luck for me to take it back now and worse luck for you to give it," she said. "I got plenty more, honey. Don't worry about that. Go on," she said, forcing me to wrap my fingers around the cat bone. "Put it away, but carry it with you all the time."

"Thank you," I said, and slipped it into my bag.

"I bet these relatives of yours are excited about seeing you, huh?"

"No," I said.

She tilted her head and smiled with confusion. "No? Don't they know you're comin'?"

I looked at her for a moment and then I looked forward again, straightening myself up in the seat.

"No," I said. "They don't even know I exist," I added.

The bus shot forward, its headlights slicking through the night, carrying me onward toward the future that awaited, a future just as dark and mysterious and as frightening as the unlit highway.

Book
Two

10

An Unexpected Friend

Annie Gray was so excited about arriving in New Orleans during the Mardi Gras, she talked incessantly during the remainder of the trip. I sat with my knees together, my hands nervously twisting on my lap, but I was grateful for the conversation. Listening to her descriptions of previous Mardi Gras celebrations she had attended, I had little time to feel sorry for myself and worry about what would happen to me the moment I stepped off the bus. For the time being at least, I could ignore the troubled thoughts crowded into the darkest corners of my brain.

Annie came from New Iberia, but she had been to New Orleans at least a half-dozen times to visit her aunt, who she said was a cabaret singer in a famous nightclub in the French Quarter. Annie said she was going to live with her aunt in New Orleans from now on.

"I'm going to be a singer, too," she bragged. "My aunt is getting me my first audition in a nightclub on Bourbon Street. You know about the French Quarter, don'tcha, honey?" she asked.

"I know it's the oldest section of the city and there is a lot of music, and people have parties there all the time," I told her.

"That's right, honey, and it has the best restau-

223

rants and many nice shops and loads and loads of antique and art galleries."

"Art galleries?"

"Uh-huh."

"Did you ever hear of Dominique's?"

She shrugged.

"I wouldn't know one from the other. Why?"

"I have some of my artwork displayed there," I said proudly.

"Really? Well, ain't that somethin'? You're an artist." She looked impressed. "And you say you ain't ever been to New Orleans before?"

I shook my head.

"Oh," she squealed, and squeezed my hand. "You're in for a bundle of fun. You've got to tell me where you'll be and I'll send you an invitation to come hear me sing as soon as I get hired, okay?"

"I don't know where I'll be yet," I had to confess. That slowed down her flood of excitement. She pulled herself back in her seat and scrutinized me with a curious smile on her face.

"What do you mean? I thought you said you're going to visit relatives," she said.

"I am . . . I . . . just don't know their address." I allowed my eyes to meet hers briefly before they fled to stare almost blindly at the passing scenery, which right now was a blur of dark silhouettes and an occasional lit window of a solitary house.

"Well, honey, New Orleans is a bit bigger than downtown Houma," she said, laughing. "You got their phone number at least, don'tcha?"

I turned back and shook my head. Numbness tingled in my fingertips, perhaps because I had my fingers locked so tightly together.

224

Her smile wilted and she narrowed her turquoise eyes suspiciously as her gaze shifted to my small bag and then back to me. Then she nodded to herself and sat forward, convinced she knew it all.

"You're runnin' away from home, ain'tcha?" she asked.

I bit down on my lower lip, but I couldn't stop my eyes from tearing over. I nodded.

"Why?" she asked quickly. "You can tell Annie Gray, honey. Annie Gray can keep a secret better than a bank safe."

I swallowed my tears and vanquished my throat lump so I could tell her about Grandmere Catherine, her death, Grandpere Jack's moving in and his quickly arranging for my marriage to Buster. She listened quietly, her eyes sympathetic until I finished. Then they blazed furiously.

"That old monster," she said. "He be Papa La Bas," she muttered.

"Who?"

"The devil himself," she declared. "You got anything that belongs to him on you?"

"No," I replied. "Why?"

"Fixin'," she said angrily. "I'd cast a spell on him for you. My great-grandmere, she was brought here a slave, but she was a mama, a voodoo queen, and she hand me down lots of secrets," she whispered, her eyes wide, her face close to mine. *"Ya, ye, ye li konin tou, gris-gris,"* she chanted. My heart began to pound.

"What's that mean?"

"Part of a voodoo prayer. If I had a snip of your grandpere's hair, a piece of his clothing, even an

225

old sock . . . he never be bothering you again," she assured me, her head bobbing.

"That's all right. I'll be fine now," I said, my voice no more than a whisper either.

She stared at me a moment. The white part of her eyes looked brighter, almost as if there were two tiny fires behind each orb. Finally, she nodded again, patted my hand reassuringly and sat back.

"You be all right, you just don't lose that black cat bone I gave you," she told me.

"Thank you." I let out a breath. The bus bounced and turned on the highway. Ahead of us, the road became brighter as we approached more lighted and populated areas en route to the city that now loomed before me like a dream.

"I tell you what you do when we arrive," Annie said. "You go right to the telephone booth and look up your relatives in the phone book. Besides their telephone number, their address will be there. What's their name?"

"Dumas," I said.

"Dumas. Oh, honey, there's a hundred Dumas in the book, if there's one. Know any first names?"

"Pierre Dumas."

"Probably at least a dozen or so of them," she said, shaking her head. "He got a middle initial?"

"I don't know," I said.

She thought a moment.

"What else do you know about your relatives, honey?"

"Just that they live in a big house, a mansion," I said. Her eyes brightened again.

"Oh. Maybe the Garden District then. You don't know what he does for a living?"

I shook my head. Her eyes turned suspicious as one of her eyebrows lifted quizzically.

"Who's Pierre Dumas? Your cousin? Your uncle?"

"No. My father," I said. Her mouth gaped open and her eyes widened with surprise.

"Your father? And he never set eyes on you before?"

I shook my head. I didn't want to go through the whole story, and thankfully, she didn't ask for details. She simply crossed herself and muttered something before nodding.

"I'll look in the phone book with you. My grandmere told me, I have a mama's vision and can see my way through the dark and find the light. I'll help you," she added, patting my hand. "Only, one thing must be to make it work," she added.

"What's that?"

"You've got to give me a token, something valuable to open the doors. Oh, it ain't for me," she added quickly. "It's a gift for the saints to thank them for help in the success of your gris-gris. I'll drop it by the church. What'cha got?"

"I don't have anything valuable," I said.

"You got any money on you?" she asked.

"A little money I've earned selling my artwork," I told her.

"Good," she said. "You give me a ten dollar bill at the phone booth and that will give me the power. You lucky you found me, honey. Otherwise, you'd be wanderin' around this city all night and all day. Must be meant to be. Must be I be your good gris-gris."

And with that she laughed again and again began describing how wonderful her new life in New Orleans was going to be once her aunt got her the opportunity to sing.

When I first saw the skyline of the city, I was glad I had found Annie Gray. There were so many buildings and there were so many lights, I felt as if I had fallen into a star laden sky. The traffic and people, the maze of streets was overwhelming and frightening. Everywhere I looked out the bus window, I saw crowds of revelers marching through the streets, all of them dressed in bright costumes, wearing masks and hats with bright feathers and carrying colorful paper umbrellas. Instead of masks, some had their faces made up to look like clowns, even the women. People were playing trumpets and trombones, flutes and drums. The bus driver had to slow down and wait for the crowds to cross at almost every corner before finally pulling into the bus station. As soon as he did so, our bus was surrounded by partygoers and musicians greeting the arriving passengers. Some were given masks, some had ropes of plastic jewels cast over their heads and some were given paper umbrellas. It seemed if you weren't celebrating Mardi Gras, you weren't welcome in New Orleans.

"Hurry," Annie told me as we started down the aisle. As soon as I stepped down, someone grabbed my left hand, shoved a paper umbrella into my right, and pulled me into the parade of brightly dressed people so that I was forced to march around the bus with them. Annie laughed and threw her hands up as she started to dance and swing herself in behind me. We marched around as the bus driver unloaded the luggage. When Annie saw hers, she pulled me out of the line and I followed her into the station. People were dancing everywhere, and everywhere I looked, there were pockets of musicians playing Dixieland Jazz.

"There's a phone booth," she said, pointing. We hurried to it. Annie opened the fat telephone book. I had never realized how many people lived in New Orleans. "Dumas, Dumas," she chanted as she ran her finger down the page. "Okay, here be the list. Quickly," she said, turning back to me. "Fold the ten dollar bill as tightly as you can. Go on."

I did what she asked. She opened her purse and kept her eyes closed.

"Just drop it in here," she said. I did so and she opened her eyes slowly and then turned to the phone book again. She did look like someone who had fallen into a trance. I heard her mumble some gibberish and then she put her long right forefinger on the page and ran it down slowly. Suddenly, she stopped. Her whole body shuddered and she closed and then opened her eyes. "It's him!" she declared. She leaned closer and nodded. "He does live in the Garden District, big house, rich." She tore off a corner of the page and wrote the address on it. It was on St. Charles Avenue.

"Are you sure?" I asked.

"Didn't you see my finger stop on the page? I didn't stop it; it was stopped!" she said, eyes wide. I nodded.

"Thank you," I said.

"You welcome, honey. Okay," she said, picking up her suitcase. "I got to get me going. You be all right now. Annie Gray said so. I'll send for you when I start singing somewhere," she said, backing away.

"Annie don't forget you. Don't forget Annie!" she cried. Then she spun around once with her right hand high, the colorful bracelets clicking together. She threw me a wide smile as she danced her way off, falling in with a small group of revelers who marched out the door and into the street.

I gazed at the street address on the tiny slip of paper in the palm of my hand. Did she really have some kind of prophetic power or was this incorrect, an address that would get me even more lost than I imagined? I looked back at the opened telephone book, thinking maybe I should know where the addresses for any other Pierre Dumas were, and was shocked to discover, there was only one Pierre Dumas. What sort of magic was required for this? I wondered.

I laughed to myself, realizing I had paid for my company and entertainment. But who knew how much of what Annie had told me was true and how much wasn't? I wasn't one to be skeptical about supernatural mysteries, not with a Traiteur for a grandmother.

Slowly, I walked to the station entrance. For a moment, I just stood there gaping out at the city. I looked around and floundered, filled with trepidation. Part of me wanted to march right back to the bus. Maybe I'd be better off in Houma living with Mrs. Thibodeau or Mrs. Livaudis, I thought. But the laughter and music from another group of revelers coming off a different bus interrupted my thoughts. When they reached me, one of them, a tall man wearing a white and black wolf mask paused at my side.

"Are you all alone?" he asked.

I nodded. "I just arrived."

A light sprang into his light blue eyes, the only part of his face not hidden by the mask. He was tall with wide shoulders. He had dark brown hair and a young voice causing me to think he was no more than twenty-five.

"So did I. But this is no night to be all alone," he said. "You're very pretty, but it's Mardi Gras. Don't you have a mask to go with that umbrella?"

"No," I said. "Someone gave me this as soon as I got off the bus. I didn't come for the Mardi Gras. I came—"

"Of course you did," he interrupted. "Here," he said, digging into his bag and coming up with another mask, a black one with plastic diamonds around its edges. "Put on this one and come along with us."

"Thank you, but I've got to find this address," I said. He looked at my slip.

"Oh, I know where this is. We won't be far from it. Come along. Might as well enjoy yourself on the way," he added. "Here, put on the mask. Everyone must wear a mask tonight. Go on," he insisted, resting his sharp gaze on me. I saw a smile form around his eyes and I took the mask.

"Now you look like you belong," he said.

"Do you really know this address?" I asked.

"Of course, I do. Come on," he said, taking my hand. Perhaps Annie Gray's voodoo magic was working, I thought. I found a stranger who could take me right to my father's door. I took the stranger's hand and hurried out with him to catch up with the group. There was music all around us and people hawking food and costumes and other masks as well. The whole city had been turned into a grand fais dodo, I thought. There wasn't a sad face anywhere, or if there was, it was hidden behind a mask. Above us, people were raining down confetti from the scrolled iron balconies. Columns and columns of revelers wound around every corner. Some of the costumes the women wore were scant and very revealing. I feasted visually on everything, turning and spinning at this carnival of life: people kissing anyone who was close enough to embrace, obvious strangers hugging and clinging to each other, jugglers juggling colorful balls, sticks of fire, and even knives!

As we danced down the street, the crowds began to swell in size. My newly found guide spun me around and threw his head back with laughter. Then he bought some sort of punch for us to drink and a poor boy shrimp sandwich for us to share. It was filled with oysters, shrimp, sliced tomatoes, shredded lettuce, and sauce piquante. I thought it was delicious. Despite my nervousness and trepidation on arriving in New Orleans to meet my real family, I was having a good time.

"Thank you. My name's Ruby," I said. I had to shout even though he was next to me. That's how loud the laughter, the music, and the shouts of others around us were. He shook his head and then brought his lips to my ear.

"No names. Tonight, we are all mysterious," he said in a loud whisper. He followed that with a quick kiss on my neck. The feel of his wet lips stunned me for a moment. I heard his cackle and then I stepped back.

"Thank you for the drink and the sandwich, but I've got to find this address," I said. He nodded, swallowing the rest of his drink quickly.

"Don't you want to see the parade first?" he asked.

"I can't. I've got to find this address," I emphasized.

"Okay. This is the way," he told me, and before I could object, he seized my hand again and led me away from the procession of frolickers. We hurried down one street and then another before he told me we had to take a shortcut.

"We'll go right through this alley and save twenty minutes at least. There's a mob ahead of us."

The alley looked long and dark. It had ash cans and discarded furniture strewn through it, and there was the acrid stench of garbage and urine. I didn't move.

"Come on," he urged, and pulled me behind him, ignoring my reluctance. I held my breath, hoping now to get through it quickly. But less than halfway through the alley, he stopped and turned to me.

"What's wrong?" I asked, a chill so cold in my stomach it was as if I had swallowed an ice cube whole.

"Maybe we shouldn't hurry so. We're losing the best of the night. Don't you want to have fun?" he asked, stepping closer. He put his hand on my shoulder. I stepped back quickly.

"I've got to get to my relatives and let them know I've arrived," I said, now feeling foolish for allowing myself to be pulled into a dark alley with a stranger who wouldn't show me his face nor tell me his name. How could I have been so desperate and trusting?

"I'm sure they don't expect you so soon on a Mardi Gras night. Tonight is a magical night. Everything is different," he said. "You're a very pretty girl." He lifted the mask from his face, but I couldn't see him well in the shadows. Before I could flee, he embraced me and pulled me to him.

"Please," I said, struggling. "I must go. I don't want to do this."

"Sure you do. It's Mardi Gras. Let yourself loose, abandon yourself," he told me, and pressed his lips to mine, holding me so tightly, I couldn't pull away. I felt his hands move down my back and begin to scoop up my skirt. I turned and struggled, but his long arms had mine pinned against my sides. I started to scream and he squelched it by pressing his mouth into mine. When I felt his tongue jet out and rub over mine, I gasped. His hands had found my panties and he was tugging them down as he swung me about. I felt myself growing faint. How could he keep his mouth over mine so long? Finally, he pulled his head back and I gulped air. He turned me around, pressing me toward what looked like an old, discarded mattress on the alley floor.

"Stop!" I cried, twisting and turning to break free. "Let me go!"

"It's party time!" he cried, and laughed that dry cackle again. But this time, as he brought his face toward me, I managed to pull my right hand out from under his arm and claw his cheeks and nose. He screamed and threw me back in a rage.

"You bitch!" he cried, wiping his face. I cowered in the dark as he lifted his head and released another sick laugh. Had I fled from Buster Trahaw only to put myself into a worse predicament? Where was Annie Gray's magical protection now? I wondered as the stranger started toward me, a dark, dangerous silhouette, a character who had escaped from my worst nightmares to invade my reality.

Fortunately, just as he reached out for me, a group of street celebrants turned into our alley, their music reverberating off the walls. My attacker saw them coming, lowered his mask over his face, and ran in the opposite direction, disappearing into the darkness as if he had fled back to the world of dark dreams.

I didn't waste a moment. I scooped up my bag and ran toward the revelers, who shouted and laughed, trying to hold me back so I would join them.

"NO!" I cried and broke loose to tear through them and out of the alley. Once onto a street, I ran and ran to get myself as far away from that alley as I could, my feet slapping the pavement so hard, my soles stung. Finally, out of breath, my shoulders heaving, my side aching, I stopped.

When I looked up I was happy to see a policeman on the corner.

"Please," I said, approaching him. "I'm lost. I just arrived and I've got to find this address."

"Some night to come to New Orleans and get lost," he said, shaking his head. He took the slip of paper. "Oh, this is in the Garden District. You can take the streetcar. Follow me," he said. He showed me where to wait.

"Thank you," I told him. Shortly afterward, the streetcar arrived. I gave the driver my address and he told me he would let me know when to get off. I sat down quickly, wiped my sweaty face with my handkerchief, and closed my eyes, hoping my heartbeat would slow down before I stood in my father's doorway. Otherwise, the excitement over what had already happened, and my actually confronting him would cause me to simply faint at his feet.

When the streetcar entered what was known as the Garden District of New Orleans, we passed under a long canopy of spreading oaks and passed yards filled with camellias and magnolia trees. Here there were elegant homes with garden walls that enclosed huge banana trees and dripped with purple bugle vine. Each corner sidewalk was embedded with old ceramic tiles that spelled out the names of the streets. Some of the cobblestone sidewalks had become warped by the roots of old oak trees, but to me this made it even more quaint and special. These streets were quieter, fewer and fewer street revelers in evidence.

"St. Charles Avenue," the streetcar operator

cried. An electric chill surged through my body turning my legs to jelly, and for a moment, I couldn't stand up. I was almost there, face-to-face with my real father. My heart began to pound. I reached for the hand strap and pulled myself into a standing position. The side doors slapped open with an abruptness that made me gasp. Finally, I willed one foot forward and stepped down to the street. The doors closed quickly and the streetcar continued, leaving me on the walk, feeling more stranded and lost than ever, clutching my little cloth bag to my side.

I could hear the sounds of the Mardi Gras floating in from every corner of the city. An automobile sped by with revelers hanging their heads out the windows, blowing trumpets and throwing streamers at me. They waved and cried out, but continued on their merry way while I remained transfixed, as firmly rooted as an old oak tree. It was a warm evening, but here in the city, with the streetlights around me, it was harder to see the stars that had always been such a comfort to me in the bayou. I took a deep breath and finally crossed down St. Charles Avenue toward the address on the slip of paper I now clutched like a rosary in my small hand.

St. Charles Avenue was so quiet in comparison to the festive sounds and wild excitement on the inner city streets. I found it somewhat eerie. To me it was as if I had entered a dream, slipped through some magical doorway between reality and illusion, and found myself in my own land of Oz. Nothing looked real: not the tall palm trees, the pretty streetlights, the cobblestone walks and streets, and especially not the enormous houses that looked more like small palaces, the homes of princes and princesses, queens and kings. These mansions, some of which were walled in, were set in the middle of large tracts of land. There were many beautiful gardens full of swelling masses of shining green foliage and heavy with roses and every other kind of flower one could think of.

I strolled on slowly, drinking in the opulence and wondering how one family could live in each of these grand houses with such beautiful grounds. How could anyone be so rich? I wondered. I was so entranced, so mesmerized by the wealth and the beauty, I almost walked right past the address on my slip of paper. When I stopped and looked up at the Dumas residence, I could only stand and gape stupidly. Its outbuildings, gardens, and stables occupied most of this block. All of it was surrounded by a fence in cornstalk pattern.

This was my real father's home, but the ivory white mansion that loomed before me looked more like a house built for a Greek god. It was a two-story building with tall columns, the tops of which were shaped like inverted bells decorated with leaves. There were two galeries, an enormous one before the main entrance and another above it. Each had a different decorative cast iron railing, the one on the bottom showing flowers and the one above, showing fruits.

I strolled along the walk, circling the house and grounds. I saw the pool and the tennis court and continued to gape in awe. There was something magical here. It seemed as if I had entered my dreamland of eternal spring. Two gray squirrels paused in their foray for food and stared out at me, more curious than afraid. The air smelled of green bamboo and gardenias. Blooming azaleas, yellow and red roses, and hibiscus were everywhere in view. The trellises and the gazebo were covered with trumpet vine and clumps of purple wisteria. Redwood boxes on railings and sills were thick with petunias.

Right now the house was lit up, all of its windows bright. Slowly, I made a full circle and then paused at the front gate; but as I stood there gaping, drinking in the elegance and grandeur, I began to wonder what I could have been thinking to have traveled this far and come to this house. Surely the people who lived within such a mansion were so different from me, I might as well have gone to another country where people spoke a different language. My heart sank. A throbbing pain in my head stabbed sharply. What was I doing here, me, a nobody, an orphan Cajun girl who had deluded herself into believing there was a rainbow just waiting for me at the end of my storm of trouble? I knew now that I would have to find my way back to the bus station and return to Houma.

Dejected, my head lowered, I turned from the house and started to walk away when suddenly, seemingly coming from out of the thin air, a small, fire engine red, convertible sports car squeaked to an abrupt stop right in front of me. The driver hopped over the door. He was a tall young man with a shock of shiny golden hair that now fell wildly over his smooth forehead. Despite his blond strands, he had a dark complexion which only made his cerulean eyes glimmer that much more in the glow of the street lamp. Dressed in a tuxedo, his shoulders back, his torso slim, he appeared before me like a prince—gallant, elegant, strong, for the features of his handsome face did seem carved out of some royal heritage.

He had a strong and perfect mouth and a Roman nose, perfectly straight, to go along with those dazzling blue eyes. The lines of his jaw turned up sharply, enhancing the impression that his face had been etched out to duplicate the face of some movie star idol. I was breathless for a moment, unable to move under the radiance of his warm and attractive smile, which quickly turned into a soft laugh.

"Where do you think you're going?" he asked. "And what sort of costume is this? Are you playing the poor girl or what?" he asked, stepping around me as if judging me in some fashion contest.

"Pardon?"

My question threw him into a fit of hysterics. He clutched his side and leaned back on the hood of his sports car.

"That's great," he said. "I love it. Pardon?" he mimicked.

"I don't think it's so funny," I said indignantly, but that just made him laugh again.

"I'd never expect you to choose anything like this," he said, holding his graceful hand out toward me, palm up. "And where did you get that bag, a thrift shop? What's in it anyway, more rags?"

I pulled my bag against my stomach and straightened up quickly.

"These aren't rags," I retorted. He started to laugh again. It seemed I could do nothing, say nothing, gaze at him in no way without causing him to become hysterical. "What's so funny? These happen to be my sole belongings right now," I emphasized. He shook his head and held his wide smile.

"Really, Gisselle, you're perfect. I swear," he said, holding up his hand to take an oath, "this is the best you've ever come up with, and that indignant attitude to go along with it . . . you're going to win the prize for sure. All of your girlfriends will die with envy. Brilliant. And to surprise me, too. I love it."

"First," I began, "my name is not Gisselle."

"Oh," he said, still holding a grin as if he were humoring a mad woman, "and what name have you chosen?"

"My name is Ruby," I said.

"Ruby? I like that," he said, looking thoughtful. "Ruby . . . a jewel . . . to describe your hair. Well, your hair has always been your most prized possession, aside from your real diamonds and rubies, emeralds, and pearls, that is. And your clothes and your shoes," he cataloged with a laugh. "So," he said, straightening up and changing to a serious face, "I'm to introduce you to everyone as Mademoiselle Ruby, is that it?"

"I don't care what you do," I said. "I certainly don't expect you to introduce me to anyone," I added and started away.

"Huh?" he cried. I started to cross the street when he walked quickly behind me and seized my right elbow. "What are you doing? Where are you going?" he asked, his face now contorted in confusion.

"I'm going home," I said.

"Home? Where's home?"

"I'm returning to Houma, if you must know," I said. "Now, if you will be so kind as to let me go, I—"

"Houma? What?" He stared at me a moment and then, instead of releasing me, he seized my other arm at the elbow and turned me fully around so that I would be in the center of the pool of light created by the street lamp. He studied me for a moment, those soft eyes, now troubled and intense as he swept his gaze over my face. "You do look . . . different," he muttered. "And not in cosmetic ways either. I don't understand, Gisselle."

"I told you," I said. "I'm not anyone named Gisselle. My name is Ruby. I come from Houma."

He continued to stare, but still held me at the elbows. Then he shook his head and smiled again.

"Come on, Gisselle. I'm sorry I'm a little late, but you're carrying this too far. I admit it's a great costume and disguise. What else do you want from me?" he pleaded.

"I'd like you to let go of my arms," I said. He did so and stepped back, his confusion now becoming indignation and anger.

"What's going on here?" he demanded. I took a deep breath and looked back at the house. "If you're not Gisselle, then what were you doing in front of the house? Why are you on this street?"

"I was going to knock on the door and introduce

242

myself to Pierre Dumas, but I've changed my mind," I said.

"Introduce yourself to . . . " He shook his head and stepped toward me again.

"Let me see your left hand," he asked quickly. "Come on," he added, and reached for it. I held out my hand and he gazed at my fingers for a moment. Then, when he looked up at me, his face twisted in shock. "You never take off that ring, never," he said, more to himself than to me. "And your fingers," he said, looking at my hand again, "your whole hand is rougher." He released me quickly, as quickly as he would had my hand been a hot coal. "Who are you?"

"I told you. My name is Ruby."

"But you look just like . . . you're the spitting image of Gisselle," he said.

"Oh. So that's her name," I said more to myself than to him. "Gisselle."

"Who are you?" he asked again, now gazing at me as if I were a ghost. "I mean, what are you to the Dumas family? A cousin? What? I demand that you tell me or I'll call the police," he added firmly.

"I'm Gisselle's sister," I confessed in a breath.

"Gisselle's sister? Gisselle has no sister," he replied, still speaking in a stern voice. Then he paused a moment, obviously impressed with the resemblances. "At least, none I knew about," he said.

"I'm fairly sure Gisselle doesn't know about me either," I said.

"Really? But . . . "

"It's too long of a story to tell you and I don't

know why I should tell you anything anyway," I said.

"But if you're Gisselle's sister, why are you leaving? Why are you going back to . . . where'd you say, Houma?"

"I thought I could do this, introduce myself, but I find I can't."

"You mean, the Dumas don't know you're here yet?" I shook my head. "Well, you can't just leave without telling them you're in New Orleans. Come on," he said, reaching for my hand. "I'll bring you in myself."

I shook my head and stepped back, more terrified than ever.

"Come on," he said. "Look. My name's Beau Andreas. I'm a very good friend of the family. Actually, Gisselle is my girlfriend, but my parents and the Dumas have known each other for ages. I'm like a member of this family. That's why I'm so shocked by what you're saying. Come on," he chanted, and took my hand.

"I've changed my mind," I said, shaking my head. "This isn't as good an idea as I first thought."

"What isn't?"

"Surprising them."

"Mr. and Mrs. Dumas don't know you're coming?" he asked, his confusion building. I shook my head. "This is really bizarre. Gisselle doesn't know she has a twin sister and the Dumas don't know you're here. Well, why did you come all this way if you're only going to turn around and go right back?" he asked, his hands on his hips.

"I . . . "

"You're afraid, aren't you?" he said quickly. "That's it, you're afraid of them. Well, don't be. Pierre Dumas is a very nice man and Daphne . . . she is nice, too. Gisselle," he said, smiling, "is Gisselle. To tell you the truth, I can't wait to see the expression on her face when she comes face-to-face with you."

"I can," I said, and turned away.

"I'll just run in and tell them you were here and you're running away," he threatened. "Someone will come after you and it will all be far more embarrassing."

"You wouldn't," I said.

"Of course I would," he replied, smiling. "So you might as well do it the right way." He held out his hand. I looked back at the house and then at him. His eyes were friendly, although a bit impish. Reluctantly, my heart thumping so hard I thought it would take my breath away and cause me to faint before I reached the front door, I took his hand and let him lead me back to the gate and up the walk to the grand galerie. There was a tile stairway.

"How did you get here?" he asked before we reached the door.

"The bus," I said. He lifted the ball and hammer knocker and let the sound echo through what I imagined, from the sound of the reverberation within, was an enormous entryway. A few moments later, the door was opened and we faced a mulatto man in a butler's uniform. He wasn't short, but he wasn't tall either. He had a round face with large dark eyes and a somewhat pug nose. His dark brown hair was curly and peppered with gray strands. There were dime-size brown spots on his cheeks and forehead and his lips were slightly orange.

"Good evening, Monsieur Andreas," he said, then shifted his gaze to me. The moment he set eyes on me, he dropped his mouth. "But Mademoiselle Gisselle, I just saw you . . . " He turned around and looked behind him. Beau Andreas laughed.

"This isn't Mademoiselle Gisselle, Edgar. Edgar, I'd like you to meet Ruby. Ruby, Edgar Farrar, the Dumas' butler. Are Mr. and Mrs. Dumas in, Edgar?" he asked.

"Oh, no, sir. They left for the ball about an hour ago," he said, his eyes still fixed on me.

"Well then, there's nothing to do but wait for them to return. Until then, you can visit with Gisselle," Beau told me. He guided me into the great house.

The entryway floor was a peach marble and the ceiling, which looked like it rose to at least twelve feet above me, had pictures of nymphs and angels, doves and blue sky painted over it. There were paintings and sculptures everywhere I looked, but the wall to the right was covered by an enormous tapestry depicting a grand French palace and gardens.

"Where is Mademoiselle Gisselle, Edgar?" Beau asked.

"She's still upstairs," Edgar said.

"I knew she would be pampering herself forever. I'm never late when it comes to escorting Gisselle anywhere," Beau told me. "Especially a

Mardi Gras Ball. To Gisselle, being on time means being an hour late. Fashionably late, of course," he added. "Are you hungry, thirsty?"

"No, I had half of a poor boy sandwich not so long ago," I said, and grimaced with the memory of what had nearly happened to me.

"You didn't like it?" Beau asked.

"No, it wasn't that. Someone . . . a stranger I trusted, attacked me in an alley on the way here," I confessed.

"What? Are you all right?" he asked quickly.

"Yes. I got away before anything terrible happened, but it was quite frightening."

"I'll bet. The back streets in New Orleans can be quite dangerous during Mardi Gras. You shouldn't have wandered around by yourself." He turned to Edgar. "Where is Nina, Edgar?" he asked.

"Just finishing up some things in the kitchen."

"Good. Come on," Beau insisted. "I'll take you to the kitchen and Nina will give you something to drink at least. Edgar, would you be so kind as to inform Mademoiselle Gisselle that I've arrived with a surprise guest and we're in the kitchen?"

"Very good, monsieur," Edgar said and headed for the beautiful curved stairway with soft carpeted steps and a shiny mahogany balustrade.

"This way," Beau said. He directed me through the entryway, past one beautiful room after another, each filled with antiques and expensive French furniture and paintings. It looked more like a museum to me than a home.

The kitchen was as large as I expected it would be with long counters and tables, big sinks, and walls of cabinets. Everything gleamed. It looked so immaculate, even the older appliances appeared brand-new. Wrapping leftovers in cellophane was a short, plump black woman in a brown cotton dress with a full white apron. She had her back to us. The strands of her ebony hair were pulled tightly into a thick bun behind her head, but she wore a white kerchief, too. As she worked, she hummed. Beau Andreas knocked on the doorjamb and she spun around quickly.

"I didn't want to frighten you, Nina," he said.

"That'll be the day when you can frighten Nina Jackson, Monsieur Andreas," she said, nodding. She had small dark eyes set close to her nose. Her mouth was small and almost lost in her plump cheeks and above her round jaw, but she had beautifully soft skin that glowed under the kitchen fixtures. Ivory earrings shaped like seashells clung to her small lobes.

"Mademoiselle, you changed again?" she asked incredulously.

Beau laughed. "This isn't Gisselle," he said.

Nina tilted her head.

"Go on with you, monsieur. That t'aint enough of a disguise to fool Nina Jackson."

"No, I'm serious, Nina. This isn't Gisselle," Beau insisted. "Her name is Ruby. Look closely," he told her. "If anyone could tell the difference, it would be you. You practically brought up Gisselle," he said.

She smirked, wiped her hands on her apron, and crossed the kitchen to get closer. I saw she wore a small pouch around her neck on a black shoestring. For a moment she stared into my face.

Her black eyes narrowed, burned into mine, and then widened. She stepped back and seized the small pouch between her right thumb and forefinger so she could hold it out between us.

"Who you be, girl?" she demanded.

"My name is Ruby," I said quickly, and shifted my eyes to Beau, who was still smiling impishly.

"Nina is warding off any evil with the voodoo power in that little sack, aren't you, Nina?"

She looked at him and at me and then dropped the sack to her chest again.

"This here, five finger grass," she said. "It can ward off any evil that five fingers can bring, you hear?"

I nodded.

"Who this be?" she asked Beau.

"It's Gisselle's secret sister," he said. "Obviously, twin sister," he added. Nina stared at me again.

"How do you know that?" she asked, taking another step back. "My grandmere, she told me once about a zombie made to look like a woman. Everyone stuck pins in the zombie and the woman screamed in pain until she died in her bed."

Beau roared.

"I'm not a zombie doll," I said. Still suspicious, Nina stared.

"I daresay if you stick pins in her, Nina, she'll be the one to scream, not Gisselle." His smile faded and he grew serious. "She's traveled here from Houma, Nina, but on the way to the house, she had a bad experience. Someone tried to attack her in an alley."

Nina nodded as if she already knew.

"She's actually quite frightened and upset," Beau said.

"Sit you down, girl," Nina said, pointing to a chair by the table. "I'll get you something to make your stomach sit still. You hungry, too?"

I shook my head.

"Did you know Gisselle had a sister?" Beau asked her as she went to prepare something for me to drink. She didn't respond for a moment. Then she turned.

"I don't know anything I'm not supposed to know," she replied. Beau lifted his eyebrows. I saw Nina mix what looked like a tablespoon of blackstrap molasses into a glass of milk with a raw egg and some kind of powder. She mixed it vigorously and brought it back.

"Drink this in one gulp, no air," she prescribed. I stared at the liquid.

"Nina usually cures everyone of anything around here," Beau said. "Don't be afraid."

"My grandmere could do this, too," I said. "She was a Traiteur."

"Your grandmere, a Traiteur?" Nina asked. I nodded. "Then she was holy," she said, impressed. "Cajun Traiteur woman can blow the fire out of a burn and stop bleeding with the press of her palm," Nina explained to Beau.

"I guess she's not a zombie girl then, huh?" Beau asked with a smile. Nina paused.

"Maybe not," she said, still looking at me with some suspicion. "Drink," she commanded, and I did what she said even though it didn't taste great. I felt it bubble in my stomach for a moment and then I did feel a soothing sensation.

"Thank you," I said. I turned with Beau to look at the doorway when we heard the footsteps coming down the hall. A moment later, Gisselle Dumas appeared, dressed in a beautiful red, bare shoulder satin gown with her long red hair brushed until it shone. It was about as long as mine. She wore dangling diamond earrings and a matching diamond necklace set in gold.

"Beau," she began, "why are you late and what's this about a surprise guest?" she demanded. She whirled to confront me, putting her fists on her hips before she turned in my direction. Even though I knew what to expect, the reality of seeing my face on someone else took my breath away. Gisselle Dumas gasped and brought her hand to her throat.

Fifteen years and some months after the day we were born, we met again.

11

Just Like Cinderella

"Who is she?" Gisselle demanded, her eyes quickly moving from wide orbs of amazement to narrow slits of suspicion.

"Anyone can see she's your twin sister," Beau replied. "Her name is Ruby."

Gisselle grimaced and shook her head.

"What sort of a practical joke are you playing now, Beau Andreas?" she demanded. Then she approached me and we stared into each other's faces.

I imagined she was doing what I was doing—searching for the differences; but they were hard to see at first glance. We were identical twins. Our hair was the same shade, our eyes emerald green, our eyebrows exactly the same. Neither of our faces had any tiny scars, nor dimples, nothing that would quickly distinguish one of us from the other. Her cheeks, her chin, her mouth, all were precisely the same shape as mine. Not only did all of our facial features correspond, but we were just about the same height as well. And our bodies had matured and developed as if we had been cast from one mold.

But on second glance, a more scrutinizing second glance, a perceptive inspector would discern differences in our facial expressions and in our demeanor. Gisselle held herself more aloof, more arrogantly. There seemed to be no timidity in her. She had inherited Grandmere Catherine's steel spine, I thought. Her gaze was unflinching and she had a way of tucking in the right corner of her mouth disdainfully.

"Who are you?" she queried sharply.

"My name is Ruby, Ruby Landry, but it should be Ruby Dumas," I said.

Gisselle, still incredulous, still waiting for some sensible explanation for the confusion her eyes were bringing to her brain, turned to Nina Jackson, who crossed herself quickly.

"I am going to light a black candle," she said, and started away, muttering a voodoo prayer.

"Beau!" Gisselle said, stamping her foot.

He laughed and shrugged with his arms out. "I swear I've never seen her before tonight. I found her standing outside the gate when I drove up. She came from . . . where did you say it was?"

"Houma," I said. "In the bayou."

"She's a Cajun girl."

"I can see that, Beau. I don't understand this," she said, now shaking her head at me, her eyes swimming in tears of frustration.

"I'm sure there's a logical explanation," Beau said. "I think I'd better go fetch your parents."

Gisselle continued to stare at me.

"How can I have a twin sister?" she demanded. I wanted to tell her all of it, but I thought it might be better for our father to explain. "Where are you going, Beau?" she cried when he turned to leave.

"To get your father and mother, like I said."

"But . . ." She looked at me and then at him. "But what about the ball?"

"The ball? How can you go running off to the ball now?" he asked, nodding in my direction.

"But I bought this new dress especially for it and I have a wonderful mask and . . ." She embraced herself and glared at me. "How can this happen!" she cried, the tears now streaming down her cheeks. She clasped her hands into small fists and slapped her arms against her sides. "And tonight of all nights!"

"I'm sorry," I said softly. "I didn't realize it was Mardi Gras when I started for New Orleans today, but—"

"You didn't realize it was Mardi Gras!" she chortled. "Oh, Beau."

"Take it easy, Gisselle," he said, returning to embrace her. She buried her face in his shoulder for a moment. As he stroked her hair, he gazed at me, still smiling. "Take it easy," he soothed.

"I can't take it easy," Gisselle insisted, and stamped her foot again as she pulled back. She glared at me angrily now. "It's just some coincidence, some stupid coincidence someone discovered. She was sent here to . . . to embezzle money out of us. That's it, isn't it?" she accused.

I shook my head.

"This is too much to be a coincidence, Gisselle. I mean, just look at the two of you," Beau insisted.

"There are differences. Her nose is longer and her lips look thinner and . . . and her ears stick out more than mine do."

Beau laughed and shook his head.

"Someone sent you here to steal from us, didn't they? Didn't they?" Gisselle demanded, her fists on her hips again and her legs spread apart.

"No. I came myself. It was a promise I made to Grandmere Catherine."

"Who's Grandmere Catherine?" Gisselle asked, grimacing as if she had swallowed sour milk. "Someone from Storyville?"

"No, someone from Houma," I said.

"And a Traiteur," Beau added. I could see he was enjoying Gisselle's discomfort. He enjoyed teasing her.

"Oh, this is just so ridiculous. I do not intend to miss the best Mardi Gras Ball because some . . . Cajun girl who looks a little like me has arrived and claims to be my twin sister," she snapped.

"Looks a little . . . " Beau shook his head. "When I first saw her, I thought it was you."

"Me? How could you think that . . . that," she

said, gesturing at me, "this . . . this person was me? Look at how she's dressed. Look at her shoes!"

"I thought it was your costume," he explained. I wasn't happy hearing my clothes described as someone's costume.

"Beau, do you think I'd ever put on something as plain as that, even as a costume?"

"What's wrong with what I'm wearing?" I asked, assuming an indignant tone myself.

"It looks homemade," Gisselle said after she condescended to gaze at my skirt and blouse once more.

"It is homemade. Grandmere Catherine made both the skirt and blouse."

"See," she said, turning back to Beau. He nodded and saw how I was fuming.

"I'd better go fetch your parents."

"Beau Andreas, if you leave this house without taking me to the Mardi Gras Ball . . . "

"I promise we'll go after this is straightened out," he said.

"It will never be straightened out. It's a horrible, horrible joke. Why don't you get out of here!" she screamed at me.

"How can you send her away?" Beau demanded.

"Oh, you're a monster, Beau Andreas. A monster to do this to me," she cried, and ran back to the stairway.

"Gisselle!"

"I'm sorry," I said. "I told you I shouldn't have come in. I didn't mean to ruin your evening."

He looked at me a moment and then shook his head.

"How can she blame me? Look," he said, "just go into the living room and make yourself comfortable. I know where Pierre and Daphne are. It won't take but a few minutes and they'll come here to see you. Don't worry about Gisselle," he said, backing up. "Just wait in the living room." He turned and hurried out, leaving me alone, never feeling more like a stranger. Could I ever call this house my home? I wondered as I started toward the living room.

I was afraid to touch anything, afraid even to walk on the expensive looking big Persian oval rug that extended from the living room doorway, under the two large sofas and beyond. The high windows were draped in scarlet velvet with gold ties and the walls were papered in a delicate floral design, the hues matching the colors in the soft cushion high back chairs and the sofas. On the thick mahogany center table were two thick crystal vases. The lamps on the side tables looked very old and valuable. There were paintings on all the walls, some landscapes of plantations and some street scenes from the French Quarter. Above the marble fireplace was the portrait of a distinguished looking old gentleman, his hair and full beard a soft gray. His dark eyes seemed to swing my way and hold.

I lowered myself gently in the corner of the sofa on my right and sat rigidly, clinging to my little bag and gaping about the room, looking at the statues, the figurines in the curio case, and the other pictures on the walls. I was afraid to look at the portrait of the man above the fireplace again. He seemed so accusatory.

A hickory wood grandfather's clock that looked as old as time itself ticked in the corner, its numbers all Roman. Otherwise, the great house was silent. Occasionally, I thought I heard a thumping above me and wondered if that was Gisselle storming back and forth in her room.

My heart, which had been racing and drumming ever since I let Beau Andreas lead me into the house, calmed. I took a deep breath and closed my eyes. Had I done a dreadful thing coming here? Was I about to destroy someone else's life? Why was Grandmere Catherine so sure this was the right thing for me to do? My twin sister obviously resented my very existence? What was to keep my father from doing the same? My heart teetered on the edge of a precipice, ready to plunge and die if he came into this house and rejected me.

Shortly after, I heard the sound of Edgar Farrar's footsteps as he raced down the corridor to open the front door. I heard other voices and people hurrying in.

"In the living room, monsieur," Beau Andreas called, and a moment later my eyes took in my real father's face. How many times had I sat before my mirror and imagined him by transposing my own facial features onto the blank visage I conjured before me? Yes, he had the same soft green eyes and we had the same shaped nose and chin. His face was leaner, firmer, his forehead rolled back gently under the shock of thick chestnut hair brushed back at the sides with just a small pompadour at the front.

He was tall, at least six feet two, and had a slim but firm looking torso with shoulders that sloped gracefully into his arms, the physique of a tennis player, easily discernable in his Mardi Gras costume: a tight fitting silver outfit designed to resemble a suit of armor, such as those worn by medieval knights. He had the helmet in his arms. He fastened his gaze on me and his face went from a look of surprise and astonishment to a smile of happy amazement.

Before a word was spoken, Daphne Dumas came up beside him. She wore a bright blue tunic with long, tight sleeves, the skirt of which had a long train and an embroidered gold fringe. It fit closely down to her hips, but was wider after. It was buttoned in front from top to bottom. Over it, she wore a cloak, low at the neck and fastened with a diamond clasp at the right breast. She looked like a princess from a fairy tale.

She was nearly six feet tall herself and stood as correct as a fashion model. With her beautiful looks, her slim, curvaceous figure, she could have easily been one. Her pale reddish blond hair lay softly over her shoulders, not a strand disobedient. She had big, light blue eyes and a mouth I couldn't have drawn more perfectly. It was she who spoke first after she took a good look at me.

"Is this some sort of joke, Beau, something you and Gisselle concocted for Mardi Gras?"

"No, madame," Beau said.

"It's no joke," my father said, stepping into the room and not swinging his eyes from me for an instant. "This is not Gisselle. Hello," he said.

"Hello." We continued to stare at each other,

neither able to shift his gaze, he appearing as eager to visually devour me as I was to devour him.

"You found her on our doorstep?" Daphne asked Beau.

"Yes, madame," he replied. "She was turning away, losing her courage to knock on the front door and present herself," he revealed. Finally, I swung my eyes to Daphne and saw a look in her face that seemed to suggest she wished I had.

"I'm glad you came along, Beau," Pierre said. "You did the right thing. Thank you."

Beau beamed. My father's appreciation and approval were obviously very important to him.

"You came from Houma?" my father asked. I nodded and Daphne Dumas gasped and brought her hands to her chest. She and my father exchanged a look and then Daphne gestured toward Beau with her head.

"Why don't you see how Gisselle is getting along, Beau?" Pierre asked firmly.

"Yes, sir," Beau said, and quickly marched away. My father moved in closer and then sat on the sofa across from me. Daphne closed the two large doors softly and turned in expectation.

"You told them your last name is Landry?" my father began. I nodded.

Mon Dieu," Daphne said. She swallowed hard and reached for the edge of a high back velvet chair to steady herself.

"Easy," my father said, rising quickly to go to her. He embraced her and guided her into the chair. She sat back, her eyes closed. "Are you all right?" he asked her. She nodded without speaking. Then he turned back to me.

"Your grandfather . . . his name is Jack?"

"Yes."

"He's a swamp trapper, a guide?"

I nodded.

"How could they have done this, Pierre?" Daphne cried softly. "It's ghastly. All these years!"

"I know, I know," my father said. "Let me get at the core of this, Daphne." He turned back to me, his eyes still soft, but now troubled, too. "Ruby. That is your name?" I nodded. "Tell us what you know about all this and why you have presented yourself at this time. Please," he added.

"Grandmere Catherine told me about my mother . . . how she became pregnant and then how Grandpere Jack arranged for my sister's . . ."—I wanted to say "sale," but I thought it sounded too harsh—" . . . my sister's coming to live with you. Grandmere Catherine was not happy about the arrangements. She and Grandpere Jack stopped living together soon afterward."

My father shifted his eyes to Daphne, who closed and opened hers. Then he fixed his gaze on me again.

"Go on," he said.

"Grandmere Catherine kept the fact that my mother was pregnant with twins a secret, even from Grandpere Jack. She decided I was to live with her and my mother, but . . ." Even now, even though I had never set eyes on my mother or heard her voice, just mentioning her death brought tears to my eyes and choked back the words.

260

"But what?" my father begged.

"But my mother died soon after Gisselle and I were born," I revealed. My father's cheeks turned crimson. I saw his breath catch and his own eyes tear over, but he quickly regained his composure, glanced at Daphne again, and then turned back to me.

"I'm sorry to hear that," he uttered, his voice nearly cracking.

"Not long ago, my grandmere Catherine died. She made me promise that if something bad happened to her, I would go to New Orleans and present myself to you rather than live with Grandpere Jack," I said. My father nodded.

"I knew him slightly, but I can understand why your grandmother didn't want you to live with him," he said.

"Don't you have any other relatives . . . aunts, uncles?" Daphne asked quickly.

"No, madame," I said. "Or at least, none that I know of in Houma. My grandfather talked of his relatives who live in other bayous, but Grandmere Catherine never liked us to associate with them."

"How dreadful," Daphne said, shaking her head. I wasn't sure if she meant my family life or the present situation.

"This is amazing. I have two daughters," Pierre said, allowing himself a smile. It was a handsome smile. I felt myself start to relax. Under his warm gaze the tension drained out of me. I couldn't help thinking he was so much the father I'd always wanted, a soft-spoken, kindly man.

But Daphne flashed him a cool, chastising look.

"Double the embarrassment, too," she reminded him.

"What? Oh, yes, of course. I'm glad you've finally revealed yourself," he told me, "but it does present us with a trifle of a problem."

"A trifle of a problem? A trifle!" Daphne cried. Her chin quivered.

"Well, somewhat more serious, I'm afraid." My father sat back, pensive.

"I don't mean to be a burden to anyone," I said, and stood up quickly. "I'll return to Houma. There are friends of my grandmere's . . . "

"That's a fine idea," Daphne said quickly. "We'll arrange for transportation, give you some money. Why, we'll even send her some money from time to time, won't we, Pierre? You can tell your grandmother's friends that—"

"No," Pierre said, his eyes fixed so firmly on me, I felt like his thoughts were traveling through them and into my heart. "I can't send my own daughter away."

"But it's not as if she is your daughter in actuality, Pierre. You haven't known her a day since her birth and neither have I. She's been brought up in an entirely different world," Daphne pleaded. But my father didn't appear to hear her. With his gaze still fixed on me, he spoke.

"I knew your grandmother better than I knew your grandfather. She was a very special woman with special powers," he said.

"Really, Pierre," Daphne interrupted.

"No, Daphne, she was. She was what Cajuns call . . . a Traiteur, right?" he asked me. I nodded. "If she thought it was best for you to

262

come here, she must have had some special reasons, some insights, spiritual guidance," Pierre said.

"You can't be serious, Pierre," Daphne said. "You don't put any validity in those pagan beliefs. Next thing, you'll be telling me you believe in Nina's voodoo."

"I never reject it out of hand, Daphne. There are mysteries that logic, reason, and science can't explain," he told her. She closed her eyes and sighed deeply.

"How do you propose to handle this . . . this situation, Pierre? How do we explain her to our friends, to society?" she asked. I was still standing, afraid to take a step away, yet afraid to sit down again, too. I clung so hard to my little bag of possessions, my knuckles turned white while my father thought.

"Nina wasn't with us when Gisselle was supposedly born," he began.

"So?"

"We had that mulatto woman, Tituba, remember?"

"I remember. I remember hating her. She was too sloppy and too lazy and she frightened me with her silly superstitions," Daphne recalled. "Dropping pinches of salt everywhere, burning clothing in a barrel with chicken droppings . . . at least Nina keeps her beliefs private."

"And so we let Tituba go right after Gisselle was supposedly born, remember? At least, that was what we told the public."

"What are you getting at, Pierre? How does

263

that relate to this trifling problem?" she asked caustically.

"We never told the truth because we were working with private detectives," he said.

"What? What truth?"

"To get back the stolen baby, the twin sister who was taken from the nursery the same day she was born. You know how some people believe that missing children are voodoo sacrifices, and how some voodoo queens were often accused of kidnapping and murdering children?" he said.

"I always suspected something like that, myself," Daphne said.

"Precisely. No one's ever proven anything of the sort, however, but there was always the danger of creating mass hysteria over it and causing vigilantes to go out and abuse people. So," he said, sitting back, "we kept our tragedy and our search private. Until today, that is," he added, pressing his hands together and smiling at me.

"She was kidnapped more than fifteen years ago and has returned?" Daphne said. "Is that what we're to tell people, tell our friends?"

He nodded. "Like the Prodigal Son, only this case, it's the Prodigal Daughter, whose fake grandmother got a pang of conscience on her deathbed and told her the truth. Miracle of miracles, Ruby has found her way home."

"But, Pierre . . . "

"You'll be the talk of the town, Daphne. Everyone will want to know the story. You won't be able to keep up with the invitations," he said. Daphne just stared at him a moment and then looked up at me.

"Isn't it amazing?" my father said. "Look at how identical they are."

"But she's so . . . unschooled," Daphne moaned.

"Which, in the beginning, will make her more of a curiosity. But you can take her under your wing just as you took Gisselle," my father explained, "and teach her nice things, correct things, make her over . . . like Pygmalion and Galatea," he said. "Everyone will admire you for it," he told her.

"I don't know," she said, but it was with much less resistance. She gazed at me more analytically. "Maybe scrubbed up with decent clothes . . . "

"These are decent clothes!" I snapped. I was tired of everyone criticizing my garments. "Grandmere Catherine made them and the things she made were always cherished and sought after in the bayou."

"I'm sure they were," Daphne said, her eyes sharp and cold. "In the bayou. But this is not the bayou, dear. This is New Orleans. You came here because you want to live here . . . be with your father," she said, looking at Pierre before looking back at me. "Right?"

I looked at him, too. "Yes," I said. "I believe in Grandmere Catherine's wishes and prophecies."

"Well, then, you have to blend in." She sat back and thought a moment. "It will be quite a challenge," she said, nodding. "And somewhat of an interesting one."

"Of course it will be," Pierre said.

"Do you think I could ever get her to the point where people really wouldn't know the difference between them?" Daphne asked my father. I wasn't sure I liked her tone. It was still as if I were some uncivilized aborigine, some wild animal that had to be housebroken.

"Of course you could, darling. Look at how well you've done with Gisselle, and we both know there's a wild streak in her, don't we?" he said, smiling.

"Yes. I have managed to harness and subdue that part of her, the Cajun part," Daphne said disdainfully.

"I am not wild, madame," I said, nearly spitting my words back at her. "My grandmere Catherine taught me only good things and we went to church regularly, too."

"It's not something people teach you, per se," she replied. "It's something you can't help, something in your heritage," she insisted. "But Pierre's blue blood and my guidance have been strong enough to conquer that part of Gisselle. If you will help, if you really want to become part of this family, I might be able to do it with you, too.

"Although, she's had years and years of poor breeding, Pierre. You must remember that."

"Of course, Daphne," he said softly. "No one expects miracles overnight. As you said so yourself just a moment ago—it's a challenge." He smiled. "I wouldn't ask you if I didn't think you were capable of making it happen, darling."

Placated, Daphne sat back again. When she thought deeply, she pursed her lips and her eyes glittered. Despite the things she had said, I couldn't help but admire her beauty and her regal manner. Would it be so terrible to look and act like such a woman? I wondered, and become someone else's fairy-tale princess? A part of me that wouldn't be denied cried, *Please, please, cooperate, try,* and the part of me that felt insulted by her remarks sulked somewhere in the dark corners of my mind.

"Well, Beau already knows about her," Daphne said.

"Exactly," my father said. "Of course, I could ask him to keep it all a secret, and I'm sure he would die in a duel before revealing it, but things are revealed accidentally, too, and then what would we do? It could unravel everything we've done up until now."

Daphne nodded.

"What will you tell Gisselle?" she asked him, her voice somewhat mournful now. "She'll know the truth about me, that I'm not really her mother." She dabbed at her eyes with a light blue silk handkerchief.

"Of course you're really her mother. She hasn't known anyone else to be her mother and you've been a wonderful mother to her. We'll tell her the story just as I outlined it. After the initial shock, she'll accept her twin sister and hopefully help you, too. Nothing will change except our lives will be doubly blessed," he said, smiling at me.

Was this where I got my blind optimism? I wondered. Was he a dreamer, too?

"That is," he added after a moment, "if Ruby agrees to go along with it. I don't like asking anyone to lie," he told me, "but in this case, it's a good lie, a lie which will keep anyone from being hurt," he said, shifting his eyes toward Daphne.

I thought a moment. I would have to pretend, at least to Gisselle, that Grandmere Catherine had been part of some kidnapping plot. That bothered me, but then I thought Grandmere Catherine would want me to do everything possible to stay here—far away from Grandpere Jack.

"Yes," I said. "It's all right with me."

Daphne sighed deeply and then quickly regained her composure.

"I'll have Nina arrange one of the guest rooms," she said.

"Oh, no. I want her to have the room that adjoins Gisselle's. They will be sisters right from the beginning," my father emphasized. Daphne nodded.

"I'll have her prepare it right away. For tonight, she can use some of Gisselle's night garments. Fortunately," she said, smiling at me with some warmth for the first time, "you and your sister look to be about the same size." She gazed down at my feet. "Your feet look fairly close as well, I see."

"You'll have to go on a shopping spree tomorrow though, darling. You know how possessive Gisselle is with her clothes," my father warned.

"She should be. A woman should take pride in her wardrobe and not be like some college coed, sharing her garments down to her very panties with some roommate." She rose gracefully from the high back chair and shook her head slightly as she gazed at me. "What a Mardi Gras evening this turned out to be." She turned to Pierre. "You're positive about all this. This is what you want to do?"

"Yes, darling. With your full cooperation and guidance, that is," he said, rising. He kissed her on the cheek. "I guess I'll have to make it all up to you doubly now," he added. She looked into his eyes and gave him a small, tight smile.

"The cash register has been ringing for the last five minutes without a pause," she said, and he laughed. Then he kissed her gently on the lips. From the way he gazed at her, I could see how important it was for him to please her. She appeared to bask in the glow of his devotion. After a moment she turned to leave. At the doorway, she paused.

"You will be telling it all to Gisselle?"

"In a few minutes," he said.

"I'm going to bed. This has all been too shocking and has drained me of most of my energy right now," she complained. "But I want to have the strength for Gisselle in the morning."

"Of course," my father said.

"I'll see to her room," Daphne declared and left us.

"Sit down. Please," my father asked. I took my seat again and he sat down, too. "You want something to drink . . . eat?"

"No, I'm fine. Nina gave me something to drink before."

"One of her magical recipes?" he asked, smiling.

"Yes. And it worked."

"It always does. I meant it when I said I have respect for spiritual and mysterious things. You'll have to tell me more about Grandmere Catherine."

"I'd like that."

He took a deep breath and then let it out slowly, his eyes down. "I'm sorry to hear about Gabrielle. She was a beautiful young woman. I had never and have never met anyone like her. She was so innocent and free, a true pure spirit."

"Grandmere Catherine thought she was a swamp fairy," I said, smiling.

"Yes, yes. She might very well have been. Look," he said, growing very serious very quickly, "I know how disturbing and how troubling this all must be to you. In time, you and I will get to know each other better and I'll try to explain it. I won't be able to justify it or turn the bad things that happened into good things. I won't be able to change the events of the past or make mistakes go away, but I hope I will at least get you to see why it happened the way it did. You have a right to know all that," he said.

"Gisselle knows nothing then?" I asked.

"Oh, no. Not a hint. There was Daphne to consider. I had hurt her enough as it was. I had to protect her, and there was no way to do that without creating the fabrication that Gisselle was her child."

"One lie, one mistake, usually creates the need for another and another, and before you know it, you've spun a cocoon of deception around yourself. As you see, I'm still doing that, still protecting Daphne.

"Actually, I was fortunate and am fortunate to have Daphne. Besides being a beautiful woman, she's a woman capable of great love. She loved my father and I believe, she accepted all this because of her love for him, as much as her love for me. In fact, she accepted some responsibility."

His head bowed down into the cradle of his hands.

"Because she was unable to get pregnant herself?" I asked. He lifted his eyes quickly.

"Yes," he said. "I see you know a lot more than I thought. You seem like a very mature girl, perhaps a lot more mature than Gisselle.

"Anyway," he continued, "throughout it all, Daphne has maintained her dignity and poise. That's why I think she can teach you a great deal and why, in time, I hope you will accept her as your mother.

"Of course," he added, smiling, "first, I have to get you to accept me as your father. Any healthy man can make a baby with a woman; but not every man can be a father," he said.

I saw there were tears in his eyes when he spoke. As he talked, I sensed every molecule of his being was striving to reach out and force me to understand even what he himself must have found inexplicable.

I bit down on my tongue to keep from asking any questions. It was difficult to breathe, not to be drowned by everything that was happening so fast.

"What's in your bag?" he inquired.

"Oh, just some of my things and some pictures."

"Pictures?" His eyebrows rose with interest.

"Yes." I opened the bag and took out one of

the pictures of my mother. He took it slowly and gazed at it for a long moment.

"She does seem like a fairy goddess. My memory of those days is like the memory of a dream, pictures and words that float through my brain on the surface of soap bubbles ready to burst if I try too hard to remember the actual details.

"You and Gisselle look a lot like her, you know. I don't deserve the good fortune of having two of you to remind me of Gabrielle, but I thank whatever Fate has brought you here," he said.

"Grandmere Catherine," I said. "That's who you should thank." He nodded.

"I'll spend as much time with you as I can. I'll show you New Orleans myself and tell you about our family."

"What do you do?" I asked, realizing I didn't even know that much about him. The way I asked, the way my eyes widened at the sight of all these expensive furnishings in this mansion made him laugh.

"Right now I make my money in real estate investments. We own a number of apartment buildings and office buildings and we're involved in a number of developments. I have offices downtown."

"We are a very old and established family, who can actually trace their lineage back to the original Mississippi Trading Company, a French colonial company. My father did a genealogy which I will have to show you some day," he added, smiling. "And he proved that we can trace our lineage back to one of the hundred *Filles a la Casette* or casket girls."

"What were they?" I asked.

"Women back in France who were carefully chosen from among good middle-class families and each given only a small chest containing various articles of clothing, and sent over to become wives for the Frenchmen settling the area. They didn't have all that much more than you're carrying in your small bag," he added.

"However," he continued, "the Dumas family history isn't filled only with reputable and highly prized things. We had ancestors who once owned and operated one of the elegant gambling houses and even made money on the bordellos in Storyville. Daphne's family has the same sort of past, but she isn't as eager to own up to it," he said.

He rubbed his hands together and stood up.

"Well, we'll have plenty of time to talk about all this. I promise. Right now, I imagine you're tired. You'd like a bath and a chance to relax and go to sleep. In the morning, you can begin your new life, one that I hope will be wonderful for you. May I kiss you and welcome you to what will become your new home and family," he asked.

"Yes," I said and closed my eyes as he brought his lips to my cheek.

My father's first kiss . . . how many times had I dreamt about it, had I seen him in my dreams approach my bed and lean down to kiss me good night, the mysterious father of my paintings who stepped off the canvas and pressed his lips to my cheek and stroked my hair and drove away all the demons that hover in the shadows of our hearts . . . the father I had never known.

I opened my eyes and looked up into his and saw the tears. His eyes were filled with sorrow and pain, and it seemed he aged a little as he stared at me with much regret.

"I'm glad I've finally found you," I said. In an instant, that sorrow that washed over his beautiful eyes disappeared and his face beamed.

"You must be very special. I don't know why I should be this fortunate." He took my hand and led me out of the living room, talking about some of the other rooms, the paintings, the artworks as we approached the winding stairway.

Just as we reached the upstairs landing, a door was thrust open down right and Gisselle stepped out with Beau Andreas right beside her.

"What are you doing with her?" she demanded.

"Take it easy, Gisselle," our father said. "I'll be explaining it all to you in a moment."

"You're putting her in the room next to mine?" she asked, grimacing.

"Yes."

"This is horrible, horrible!" she screamed, and stepped back into her room before slamming the door.

Beau Andreas, who had come out, looked embarrassed.

"I think I'd better be going," he said.

"Yes," my father told him.

Beau started away and Gisselle jerked open her door again.

"Beau Andreas, how dare you leave this house without me!" she cried.

"But . . . " He looked at my father. "You and your family have things to discuss, to do and—"

"It can wait until morning. It's Mardi Gras," Gisselle declared, and glared at our father. "I've been waiting all year to attend this ball. All my friends are there already," she moaned.

"Monsieur?" Beau said. My father nodded.

"It can wait until morning," he said.

Gisselle swept back the strands of hair she had shaken over her shoulders in her rage and marched out of her room, glaring at me as she walked by to join Beau Andreas. He looked uncomfortable, but let her take his arm, and then the two of them marched down the stairs, Gisselle pounding each step as she descended.

"She has been so looking forward to this ball," my father explained. I nodded, but my father felt the need to continue to justify her behavior. "It wouldn't do any good to force her to stay. She would be less apt to listen and understand. Daphne does so much better with her when she's like this anyway," he added.

"But I'm sure," he said as we continued toward my new bedroom, "in time she will be overjoyed and excited about getting a sister. She's been an only child too long. She's a bit spoiled. Now," he said, "I have another young lady to spoil, too."

The moment we stepped into my new room, I felt that spoiling had begun. It had a dark pine canopy queen-size bed, the canopy made of fine pearl-colored silk with a fringe border. The pillows were enormous and fluffy looking, the bedspread, pillowcases, and top sheet all in chintz, the flowers full of color and glazed. The wallpaper duplicated the floral pattern in the linens. Above the headboard was a painting of a beautiful young woman in a garden setting feeding a parrot. There was a cute black and white puppy tugging at the hem of her full skirt. On each side of the bed were two nightstands, each with a bell shaped lamp. But beside a matching dresser and armoire, the room had a vanity table with an enormous oval mirror in an ivory frame, the frame covered with hand painted red and yellow roses. And in the corner beside it, an old French birdcage hung.

"I have my own bathroom?" I asked, gazing through the open doorway on my right. The plush bathroom had a large tub, sink, and commode, all with brass fixtures. There were even flowers and birds hand painted on the tub and sink.

"Of course. Twin sister or not, Gisselle is not the sort you share a bathroom with," my father said, smiling. "This door," he added, nodding at the door on my left, "joins the two rooms. I hope the day will soon come when the two of you will move back and forth through it eagerly."

"So do I," I said. I went to the windows and gazed out at the grounds of the estate. I saw that I faced the pool and the tennis court. Through the open window, I could smell the green bamboo, gardenias, and blooming camellias.

"Do you like it?" my father asked.

"Like it? I love it. It's the most wonderful room I've ever seen," I declared. He laughed at my exuberance.

"It will be something fresh to see someone appreciate everything around here again. So often, things are taken for granted," he explained.

"I'll never take anything for granted again," I promised.

"We'll see. Wait until Gisselle works you over. Well, I see you've been brought a nightgown to use and there's a pair of slippers beside the bed." He opened a closet and there was a pink silk robe hanging in it. "Here's a robe, too. You'll find all you need in the bathroom—new toothbrush, soaps, but should you need anything, just ask. I want you to treat this house as your home as soon as you can," he added.

"Thank you."

"Well, get comfortable and have a nice sleep. If you get up before the rest of us do, which is quite possible the morning after Mardi Gras, just go down to the kitchen and Nina will fix you some breakfast."

I nodded and he said good night, closing the door softly behind him as he left.

For a long moment I simply stood there gaping at everything. Was I really here, transported over time and distance into a new world, a world where I would have a real mother and father, and as soon as she could accept it, a real sister, too?

I went into the bathroom and discovered the soaps scented with the fragrance of gardenias and the bottles of bubble bath powder. I drew myself a hot bath and luxuriated in the silky smoothness of the sweet-smelling bubbles. Afterward, I put on Gisselle's scented nightgown and crawled under the soft sheet and down bedspread.

I felt like Cinderella.

But just like Cinderella, I couldn't help feeling trepidation; I couldn't help being frightened by the ticking of the clock that swung its hands around to clasp them finally on the hour of twelve, the bewitching hour.

Would it burst my bubble of happiness and turn my carriage into a pumpkin?

Or would it tick on and on, making my claim to a fairy-tale existence that much more secure with each passing minute?

Oh, Grandmere, I thought as my heavy eyelids began to shut, I'm here. I hope you're resting more comfortably because of it.

12

Blue-Blood Welcome

I awoke to the sweet singing of blue jays and mockingbirds and for the first few moments, forgot where I was. My trip to New Orleans and all that had subsequently followed now seemed more like a dream. It must have rained for a while during the night for although the sun was beaming brightly through my windows, the breeze still smelled of rain and wet leaves as well as the redolent scents of the myriad of flowers and trees that surrounded the great house.

I sat up slowly, drinking in my beautiful new room in the light of day. If anything, it looked even more wonderful. Although the furniture, the fixtures, and everything down to a jewelry box on the vanity table were antique, it all looked brand-new, too. It was almost as if this room had been recently prepared, everything polished and cleaned in anticipation of my arrival. Or that I had gone to sleep for years when all these things were brand-new and woken up without realizing time had stood still.

I rose from bed and went to the windows. The sky was a patchwork quilt of soft vanilla clouds and light blue. Below the grounds people were vigorously at work clipping hedges, weeding flower beds, and mowing lawns. Someone was on the tennis court sweeping off the myrtle leaves and tiny branches that had probably been torn and blown in the rain, and another man was scooping the oak and banana tree leaves out of the pool.

It was a wonderful day to start a new life, I decided. With my heart full of joy, I went to the bathroom, brushed my hair, and got dressed in a gray skirt and blouse I had brought in my little bag. I put all my precious possessions in the nightstand drawer and then slipped on my moccasins and left my room to go down to breakfast.

It was very quiet in the house. All the other bedroom doors were shut tight, but as soon as I reached the top of the stairway, I heard the front door thrust open and slammed closed and saw Gisselle come charging into the house, unconcerned about how much noise she was making or whom she might waken.

She threw off her cloak and a headdress of bright feathers, dropping it all on the table in the entryway, and then started for the stairway. I watched her walk halfway up with her head down. When she lifted it and saw me gazing down at her, she stopped.

"Are you just coming in from the Mardi Gras Ball?" I asked, astounded.

"Oh, I forgot all about you," she said, and followed it with a silly, thin laugh. There was something about the way she wobbled that led me to believe she had been drinking. "That's how good a time I had," she added with a flare. "And Beau was good enough not to mention your shocking appearance all night." Her expression turned sour, indignant as my question to her sunk in. "Of course I'm just coming home. Mardi Gras goes until dawn. It's expected. Don't think you can tell my parents anything they don't know and get me in trouble," she warned.

"I don't want to get you in trouble. I was just . . . surprised. I've never done that."

"Haven't you ever gone to a dance and enjoyed yourself, or don't they have such things in the bayou?" she asked with disdain. "Yes. We call them fais dodos," I told her. "But we don't stay out all night."

"Fais dodos? Sounds like a good old time, two-stepping to the sounds of an accordion and a washboard." She smirked and continued to climb the stairs toward me.

"They're usually nice dances with lots of good things to eat. Was the ball nice?" I asked.

"Nice?" She paused on the step just below me and laughed again. "Nice? *Nice* is a word for a school party or an afternoon tea in the garden, but for a Mardi Gras Ball? It was more than nice; it was spectacular. Everyone was there," she added, stepping up. "And everyone ogled me and Beau with green eyes. We're considered the handsomest young Creole couple these days, you know. I don't know how many of my girlfriends begged me to let them have a dance with Beau, and all of them were dying to know where I had gotten this dress, but I wouldn't tell them."

"It is a very pretty dress," I admitted.

"Well, don't expect I'll let you borrow it now that you've stormed into our lives," she retorted, gathering her wits about her. "I still don't understand how you got here and who you are," she added with ice in her voice.

"Your father . . . our father will explain," I said. She flicked me another of her scornful glances before throwing her hair back.

"I doubt anyone can explain it, but I can't listen now anyway. I'm exhausted. I must sleep and I'm certainly not in the mood to hear about you right now." She started to turn but paused to look me over from foot to head. "Where did you get these clothes? Is everything you have handmade?" she asked contemptuously.

"Not everything. I didn't bring much with me anyway," I said.

"Thank goodness for that." She yawned. "I've got to get some sleep. Beau's coming by late in the afternoon for tea. We like reviewing the night before, tearing everyone to shreds. If you're still here, you can sit and listen and learn."

"Of course I'll still be here," I said. "This is my home now, too."

"Please. I'm getting a headache," she said, pinching her temples with her thumb and forefinger. She turned and held her arm out toward me, her palm up. "No more. Young Creole women have to replenish themselves. We're more . . . feminine, dainty, like flowers that need the

281

kiss of soft rain and the touch of warm sunlight. That's what Beau says." She stopped smiling at her own words and glared at me. "Don't you put on lipstick before you meet people?"

"No. I don't own any lipstick," I said.

"And Beau thinks we're twins."

Unable to hold back, I flared. "We are!"

"In your dreams maybe," she countered, and then sauntered to her bedroom. After she entered and closed her door, I went downstairs, pausing to admire her headdress and cloak. Why did she leave it here? Who picked up after her? I wondered.

As if she heard my thoughts, a maid came out of the living room and marched down the corridor to retrieve Gisselle's things. She was a young black woman with beautiful, large brown eyes. I didn't think she was much older than I.

"Good morning," I said.

"Mornin'. You're the new girl who looks just like Gisselle?" she asked.

"Yes. My name's Ruby."

"I'm Wendy Williams," she said. She scooped up Gisselle's things, her eyes glued to me, and then walked away.

I started down the corridor to the kitchen, but when I reached the dining room, I saw my father already seated at the long table. He was sipping coffee and reading the business section of the newspaper. The moment he saw me, he looked up and smiled.

"Good morning. Come on in and sit down," he called. It was a very big dining room, almost as big as a Cajun meeting hall, I thought. Above the long table hung a shoo-fly, a great, wide fan unfurled at dinnertime and pulled to and fro by a servant to provide a breeze and do what it was named for: shoo away flies . . . I imagined it was there just for decoration. I had seen them before in rich Cajun homes where they had electric fans.

"Here, sit down," my father said, tapping the place on his left. "From now on, this is your seat. Gisselle sits here on my right and Daphne sits at the other end."

"She sits so far away," I remarked, gazing down the length of the rich, cherry wood table, polished so much I could see my face reflected in its surface. My father laughed.

"Yes, but that's the way Daphne likes it. Or should I say, that's the proper seating arrangement. So, how did you sleep?" he asked as I took my seat.

"Wonderfully. It's the most comfortable bed I've ever been in. I felt like I was sleeping on a cloud!"

He smiled.

"Gisselle wants me to buy her a new mattress. She claims hers is too hard, but if I get one any softer, she'll sink to the floor," he added, and we both laughed. I wondered if he had heard her come in and knew she had just returned from the ball. "Hungry?"

"Yes," I said. My stomach was rumbling. He hit a bell and Edgar appeared from the kitchen.

"You've met Edgar, correct?" he asked.

"Oh, yes. Good morning, Edgar," I said. He bowed slightly.

"Good morning, mademoiselle."

"Edgar, have Nina prepare some of her blueberry pancakes for Mademoiselle Ruby, please. You'd like that, I expect?"

"Yes, thank you," I said. My father nodded toward Edgar.

"Very good, sir," Edgar said, and smiled at me.

"Some orange juice? It's freshly squeezed," my father said, reaching for the pitcher.

"Yes, thank you."

"I don't think Daphne needs to worry about your manners. Grandmere Catherine did a fine job," he complimented. I couldn't help but shift my eyes away for a moment at the mention of Grandmere. "I bet you miss her a great deal."

"Yes, I do."

"No one can replace someone you love, but I hope I can fill some of the emptiness I know is in your heart," he said. "Well," he continued, sitting back, "Daphne is going to sleep late this morning, too." He winked. "And we know Gisselle will sleep away most of the day. Daphne says she'll take you shopping midafternoon. So that leaves just the two of us to spend the morning and lunch. How would you like me to show you around the city a bit?"

"I'd love it. Thank you," I said.

After breakfast, we got into his Rolls Royce and drove down the long driveway. I had never been in so luxurious an automobile before and sat gaping stupidly at the wood trim, running the palm of my hand over the soft leather.

"Do you drive?" my father asked me.

"Oh, no. I haven't even ridden in cars all that

much. In the bayou we get around by walking or by poling pirogues."

"Yes, I remember," he said, beaming a broad smile my way. "Gisselle doesn't drive either. She doesn't want to be bothered learning. The truth is she likes being carted around. But if you would like to learn how to drive, I'd be glad to teach you," he said.

"I would. Thank you."

He drove on through the Garden District, past many fine homes with grounds just as beautiful as ours, some with oleander-lined pike fences. There were fewer clouds now which meant the streets and beautiful flowers had fewer shadows looming over them. Sidewalks and tiled patios glittered. Here and there the gutters were full of pink and white camellias from the previous night's rain.

"Some of these houses date back to the eighteen-forties," my father told me and leaned over to point to a house on our right. "Jefferson Davis, President of the Confederacy, died in that house in 1899. There's a lot of history here," he said proudly.

We made a turn and paused as the olive green streetcar rattled past the palm trees on the esplanade. Then we followed St. Charles back toward the inner city.

"I'm glad we had this opportunity to be alone for a while," he said. "Besides my showing you the city, it gives me a chance to get to know you and you a chance to get to know me. It took a great deal of courage for you to come to me," he said. The look on my face confirmed his suspicion. He cleared his throat and continued.

"It will be hard for me to talk about your mother when someone else is around, especially Daphne. I think you understand why."

I nodded.

"I'm sure it's harder for you to understand right now how it all happened. Sometimes," he said, smiling to himself, "when I think about it, it does seem like something I dreamt."

It was as though he were talking in a dream. His eyes were glazed and far away, his voice smooth, easy, relaxed.

"I must tell you about my younger brother, Jean. He was always much different from me, far more outgoing, energetic, a handsome Don Juan if there ever was one," he added, breaking into a soft smile. "I've always been quite shy when it came to members of the genteel sex."

"Jean was athletic, a track star and a wonderful sailor. He could make our sailboat slice through the water on Lake Pontchartrain even if there wasn't enough breeze to nudge the willows on the bank."

"Needless to say, he was my father's favorite, and my mother always thought of him as her baby. But I wasn't jealous," he added quickly. "I've always been more business minded, more comfortable in an office crunching numbers, talking on the telephone, and making deals than I have been on a playing field or in a sailboat surrounded by beautiful young women.

"Jean had all the charm. He didn't have to work at making friends or gaining acquaintances. Women and men alike just wanted to be around him, to walk in his shadow, to be favored with his words and smiles."

"The house was always full of young people back then. I never knew who would be encamped in our living room or eating in our dining room or lounging at our pool."

"How much younger than you was he?" I asked.

"Four years. When I graduated from college, Jean had begun his first year and was a track star in college already, already elected president of his college class, and already a popular fraternity man."

"It was easy to see why our father doted on him so and had such big dreams for him," my father said, and he made a series of turns that took us deeper and deeper into the busier areas of New Orleans. But I wasn't as interested in the traffic, the crowds, and the dozens and dozens of stores as I was in my father's story.

We paused for a traffic light.

"I wasn't married yet. Daphne and I had really just begun to date. In the back of his mind, our father was already planning out Jean's marriage to the daughter of one of his business associates. It was to be a wedding made in Heaven. She was an attractive young lady; her father was rich, too. The wedding ceremony and reception would rival those of royalty."

"How did Jean feel about it?" I asked.

"Jean? He idolized our father and would do anything he wanted. Jean thought of it all as inevitable. You would have liked him a great deal, loved him, I should say. He was never despondent and always saw the rainbow at the end of the storm, no matter what the problem or trouble."

"What happened to him?" I finally asked, dreading the answer.

"A boating accident on Lake Pontchartrain. I rarely went out on the boat with him, but this time I let him talk me into going. He had a habit of trying to get me to be more like him. He was always after me to enjoy life more. To him I was too serious, too responsible. Usually, I didn't pay much attention to his complaints, but this time, he argued that we should be more like brothers. I relented. We both drank too much. A storm came up. I wanted to turn around immediately, but he decided it would be more fun to challenge it and the boat turned over. Jean would have been all right, I'm sure. He was a far better swimmer than I was, but the mast struck him in the temple."

"Oh no," I moaned.

"He was in a coma for a long time. My father spared no expense, hired the best doctors, but none of them could do anything. He was like a vegetable."

"How terrible."

"I thought my parents would never get over it, especially my father. But my mother became even more depressed. Her health declined first. Less than a year after the tragic accident, she suffered her first heart attack. She survived, but she became an invalid."

We continued onward, deeper into the business area. My father made one turn and then another and then slowed down to pull the vehicle into a parking spot, but he didn't shut off the engine. He faced forward and continued his remembrances.

"One day, my father came to me in our offices and closed the door. He had aged so since my brother's accident and my mother's illness. A once proud, strong man, now he walked with his shoulders turned in, his head lowered, his back bent. He was always pale, his eyes empty, his enthusiasm for his business at a very low ebb.

"'Pierre,'" he said, 'I don't think your mother's long for this world, and frankly, I feel my own days are numbered. What we would like most to see is for you to marry and start your family.'

"Daphne and I were planning on getting married anyway, but after his conversation with me, I rushed things along. I wanted to try to have children immediately. She understood. But month after month passed and when she showed no signs of becoming pregnant, we became concerned."

"I sent her to specialists and the conclusion was she was unable to get pregnant. Her body simply didn't produce enough of some hormone. I forget the exact diagnosis.

"The news devastated my father who seemed to live only for the day when he would rest his eyes on his grandchild. Not long after, my mother died."

"How terrible," I said. He nodded and turned off the engine.

"My father went into a deep depression. He rarely came to work, spent long hours simply staring into space, took poorer and poorer care of himself. Daphne looked after him as best she could, but blamed herself somewhat, too. I know she did, even though she denies it to this day.

"Finally, I was able to get my father interested in some hunting trips. We traveled to the bayou to hunt duck and geese and contracted with your grandpere Jack to guide us. That was how I met Gabrielle."

"I know," I said.

"You have to understand how dark and dreary my life seemed to me during those days. My handsome, charming brother's wonderful future had been violently ended, my mother had died, my wife couldn't have children, and my father was slipping away day by day.

"Suddenly . . . I'll never forget that moment . . . I turned while unloading our car by the dock, and I saw Gabrielle strolling along the bank of the canal. The breeze lifted her hair and made it float around her, hair as dark red as yours. She wore this angelic smile. My heart stopped and then my blood pounded so close to the surface, I felt my cheeks turn crimson.

"A rice bird lighted on her shoulder and when she extended her arm, it pranced down to her hand before flying off. I still hear that silver laugh of hers, that childlike, wonderful laugh that was carried in the breeze to my ears.

"'Who is that?' I asked your grandfather.

"'Just my daughter,' he said.

"Just his daughter? I thought, a goddess who seemed to emerge from the bayou. Just his daughter?

"I couldn't help myself, you see. I was never so smitten. Every chance I had to be with her, near her, speak to her, I took. And soon, she was doing the same thing—looking forward to being with me.

"I couldn't hide my feeling from my father, but he didn't stand in my way. In fact, I'm sure he was eager to make more trips to the bayou because of my growing relationship with Gabrielle. I didn't realize then why he was encouraging it. I should have known something when he didn't appear upset the day I told him she was pregnant with my child."

"He went behind your back and made a deal with Grandpere Jack," I said.

"Yes. I didn't want such a thing to happen. I had already made plans to provide for Gabrielle and the child, and she was happy about it, but my father was obsessed with this idea, crazed by it."

He took a deep breath before continuing.

"He even went so far as to tell Daphne everything."

"What did you do?" I asked.

"I didn't deny it. I confessed everything."

"Was she terribly upset?"

"She was upset, but Daphne is a woman of character; she's as they say, a very classy dame," he added with a smile. "She told me she wanted to bring up my child as her own, do what my father had asked. He had made her some promises, you see. But there was still Gabrielle to deal with, her feelings and desires to consider. I told Daphne what Gabrielle wanted and that despite the deal my father was making with your grandfather, Gabrielle would object."

"Grandmere Catherine told me how upset my mother was, but I never could understand why

291

she let Grandpere Jack do it, why she gave up Gisselle."

"It wasn't Grandpere Jack who got her to go along. In the end," he said, "it was Daphne." He paused and turned to me. "I can see from the expression on your face that you didn't know that."

"No," I said.

"Perhaps your grandmere Catherine didn't know either. Well, enough about all that. You know the rest anyway," he said quickly. "Would you like to walk through the French Quarter? There's Bourbon Street just ahead of us," he added, nodding.

"Yes."

We got out and he took my hand to stroll down to the corner. Almost as soon as we made the turn, we heard the sounds of music coming from the various clubs, bars, and restaurants, even this early in the day.

"The French Quarter is really the heart of the city," my father explained. "It never stops beating. It's not really French, you know. It's more Spanish. There were two disastrous fires here, one in 1788 and one in 1794, which destroyed most of the original French structures," he told me. I saw how much he loved talking about New Orleans and I wondered if I would ever come to admire this city as much as he did.

We walked on, past the scrolled colonnades and iron gates of the courtyards. I heard laughter above us and looked up to see men and women leaning over the embroidered iron patios outside their apartments, some calling down to people in the street. In an arched doorway, a black man played a guitar. He seemed to be playing for himself and not even notice the people who stopped by for a moment to listen.

"There is a great deal of history here," my father explained, pointing. "Jean Lafitte, the famous pirate, and his brother Pierre operated a clearinghouse for their contraband right there. Many a swashbuckling adventurer discussed launching an elaborate campaign in these court-yards."

I tried to take in everything: the restaurants, the coffee stalls, the souvenir shops, and antique stores. We walked until we reached Jackson Square and the St. Louis Cathedral.

"This is where early New Orleans welcomed heroes and had public meetings and celebrations," my father said. We paused to look at the bronze statue of Andrew Jackson on his horse before we entered the cathedral. I lit a candle for Grandmere Catherine and said a prayer. Then we left and strolled through the square, around the perimeter where artists sold their fresh works.

"Let's stop and have a cafe au lait and some beignets," my father said. I loved beignets, a donutlike pastry covered with powdered sugar.

While we ate and drank, we watched some of the artists sketching portraits of tourists.

"Do you know an art gallery called Dominique's?" I asked.

"Dominique's? Yes. It's not far from here, just a block or two over to the right. Why do you ask?"

"I have some of my paintings on display there," I said.

"What?" My father sat back, his mouth agape. "Your paintings on display?"

"Yes. One was sold. That's how I got my traveling money."

"I can't believe you," he said. "You're an artist and you've said nothing?"

I told him about my paintings and how Dominique had stopped by one day and had seen my work at Grandmere Catherine's and my roadside stall.

"We must go there immediately," he said. "I've never seen such modesty. Gisselle has something to learn from you."

Even I was overwhelmed when we arrived at the gallery. My picture of the heron rising out of the water was prominently on display in the front window. Dominique wasn't there. A pretty young lady was in charge and when my father explained who I was, she became very excited.

"How much is the picture in the window?" he asked.

"Five hundred and fifty dollars, monsieur," she told him.

Five hundred and fifty dollars! I thought. For something I had done? Without hesitation, he took out his wallet and plucked out the money.

"It's a wonderful picture," he declared, holding it out at arm's length. "But you've got to change the signature to Ruby Dumas. I want my family to claim your talent," he added, smiling. I wondered if he somehow sensed that this was a picture depicting what Grandmere Catherine told me was my mother's favorite swamp bird.

After it was wrapped, my father hurried me out

excitedly. "Wait until Daphne sees this. You must continue with your artwork. I'll get you all the materials and we'll set up a room in the house to serve as your studio. I'll find you the best teacher in New Orleans for private lessons, too," he added. Overwhelmed, I could only trot along, my heart racing with excitement.

We put my picture into the car.

"I want to show you some of the museums, ride past one or two of our famous cemeteries, and then take you to lunch at my favorite restaurant on the dock. After all," he added with a laugh, "this is the deluxe tour."

It was a wonderful trip. We laughed a great deal and the restaurant he'd picked was wonderful. It had a glass dome so we could sit and watch the steamboats and barges arriving and going up the Mississippi.

While we ate, he asked me questions about my life in the bayou. I told him about the handicrafts and linens Grandmere Catherine and I used to make and sell. He asked me questions about school and then he asked me if I had ever had a boyfriend. I started to tell him about Paul and then stopped, for not only did it sadden me to talk about him, but I was ashamed to describe another terrible thing that had happened to my mother and another terrible thing Grandpere Jack had done because of it. My father sensed my sadness.

"I'm sure you'll have many more boyfriends," he said. "Once Gisselle introduces you to everyone at school."

"School?" I had forgotten about that for the moment.

"Of course. You've got to be registered in school first thing this week."

A shivering thought came. Were all the girls at this school like Gisselle? What would be expected of me?

"Now, now," my father said, patting my hand. "Don't get yourself nervous about it. I'm sure it will be fine. Well," he said, looking at his watch, "the ladies must all have risen by now. Let's head back. After all, I still have to explain you to Gisselle," he added.

He made it sound so simple, but as Grandmere Catherine would say, "Weaving a single fabric of falsehoods is more difficult than weaving a whole wardrobe of truth."

Daphne was sitting at an umbrella table on a cushioned iron chair on a patio in the garden where she had been served her late breakfast. Although she was still in her light blue silk robe and slippers, her face was made up and her hair was neatly brushed. It looked honey-colored in the shade. She looked like she belonged on the cover of the copy of *Vogue* she was reading. She put it down and turned as my father and I came out to greet her. He kissed her on the cheek.

"Should I say good morning or good afternoon?" he asked.

"For you two, it looks like it's definitely afternoon," she replied, her eyes on me. "Did you have a good time?"

"A wonderful time," I declared.

"That's nice. I see you bought a new painting, Pierre."

"Not just a new painting, Daphne, a new Ruby Dumas," he said, and gave me a wide, conspiratorial smile. Daphne's eyebrows rose.

"Pardon?"

My father unwrapped the picture and held it up.

"Isn't it pretty?" he asked.

"Yes," she said in a noncommittal tone of voice. "But I still don't understand."

"You won't believe this, Daphne," he began, quickly sitting down across from her. He told her my story. As he related the tale, she gazed from him to me.

"That's quite remarkable," she said after he concluded.

"And you can see from the work and from the way she has been received at the gallery that she has a great deal of artistic talent, talent that must be developed."

"Yes," Daphne said, still sounding very controlled. My father didn't appear disappointed by her measured reaction, however. He seemed used to it. He went on to tell her the other things we had done. She sipped her coffee from a beautifully hand painted china cup and listened, her light blue eyes darkening more and more as his voice rose and fell with excitement.

"Really, Pierre," she said, "I haven't seen you this exuberant about anything for years."

"Well, I have good reason to be," he replied.

"I hate to be the one to insert a dark thought, but you realize you haven't spoken to Gisselle yet and told her your story about Ruby," she said.

297

He seemed to deflate pounds of excitement right before my eyes and then he nodded.

"You're right as always, my dear. It's time to wake the princess and talk to her," he said. He rose and picked up my picture. "Now where should we hang this? In the living room?"

"I think it would be better in your office, Pierre," Daphne said. To me it sounded as though she wanted it where it would be seen the least.

"Yes. Good idea. That way I can get to look at it more," he replied. "Well, here I go. Wish me luck," he said, smiling at me, and then he went into the house to talk to Gisselle. Daphne and I gazed at each other for a moment. Then she put down her coffee cup.

"Well now, you've made quite a beginning with your father, it seems," she said.

"He's very nice," I told her. She stared at me a moment.

"He hasn't been this happy for a while. I should tell you, since you have become an instant member of the family, that Pierre, your father, suffers from periods of melancholia. Do you know what that is?" I shook my head. "He falls into deep depressions from time to time. Without warning," she added.

"Depressions?"

"Yes. He can lock himself away for hours, days even, and not want to see or speak to anyone. You can be speaking to him and suddenly, he'll take on a far-off look and leave you in midsentence. Later, he won't remember doing it," she said. I shook my head. It seemed incredible that this man with whom I had just spent several happy hours could be described as she had described him.

"Sometimes, he'll lock himself in his office and play this dreadfully mournful music. I've had doctors prescribe medications, but he doesn't like taking anything.

"His mother was like that," she continued. "The Dumas family history is clouded with unhappy events."

"I know. He told me about his younger brother," I said. She looked up sharply.

"He told you already? That's what I mean," she said, shaking her head. "He can't wait to go into these dreadful things and depress everyone."

"He didn't depress me although it was a very sad story," I said. Her lips tightened and her eyes narrowed. She didn't like being contradicted.

"I suppose he described it as a boating accident," she said.

"Yes. Wasn't it?"

"I don't want to go into it all now. It *does* depress me," see added, eyes wide. "Anyway, I've tried and I continue to try to do everything in my power to make Pierre happy. The most important thing to remember if you're going to live here is that we must have harmony in our house. Petty arguments, little intrigues and plots, jealousies and betrayals have no place in the House of Dumas.

"Pierre is so happy about your existence and arrival that he is blind to the problems we are about to face," she continued. When she spoke, she spoke with such a firm, regal tone, I couldn't do anything but listen, my eyes fixed on her. "He doesn't understand the immensity of the task ahead. I know how different a world you come from and the sort of things you're used to doing and having."

"What sort of things, madame?" I asked, curious myself.

"Just things," she said firmly, her eyes sharp. "It's not a topic ladies like to discuss."

"I don't want or do anything like that," I protested.

"You don't even realize what you've done, what sort of life you've led up until now. I know Cajuns have a different sense of morality, different codes of behavior."

"That's not so, madame," I replied, but she continued as though I hadn't.

"You won't realize it until you've been . . . been educated and trained and enlightened," she declared.

"Since your arrival is so important to Pierre, I will do my best to teach you and guide you, of course; but I will need your full cooperation and obedience. If you have any problems, and I'm sure you will in the beginning, please come directly to me with them. Don't trouble Pierre.

"All I need," she added, more to herself than to me, "is for something else to depress him. He might just end up like his younger brother."

"I don't understand," I said.

"It's not important just now," she said quickly. Then she pulled back her shoulders and stood up.

"I'm going to get dressed and then I'll take you shopping," she said. "Please be where I can find you in twenty minutes."

"Yes, madame."

"I hope," she said, pausing near me to brush some strands of hair off my forehead, "that in time you will become comfortable addressing me as Mother."

"I hope so, too," I said. I didn't mean it to sound the way it did—almost a threat. She pulled herself back a bit and narrowed her eyes before she flashed a small, tight smile and then left to get ready to take me shopping.

While I waited for her, I continued my tour of the house, stopping to look in on what was my father's office. He had placed my picture against his desk before going up to Gisselle. There was another picture of his father, my grandfather, I supposed, on the wall above and behind his desk chair. In this picture, he looked less severe, although he was dressed formally and was gazing thoughtfully, not even the slightest smile around his lips or eyes.

My father had a walnut writing desk, French cabinets, and ladder-back chairs. There were bookcases on both sides of the office, the floor of which was polished hardwood with a small, tightly knit beige oval rug under the desk and chair. In the far left corner there was a globe. Everything on the desk and in the room was neatly organized and seemingly dust free. It was as if the inhabitants of this house tiptoed about with gloved hands. All the furniture, the immaculate floors and walls, the fixtures and shelves, the antiques and statues made me feel like a bull in a china shop. I was afraid to move quickly, turn abruptly, and especially afraid to touch anything, but I entered the office to glance at the pictures on the desk.

In sterling silver frames, my father had pictures of Daphne and Gisselle. There was a picture of two people I assumed to be his parents, my grandparents. My grandmother, Mrs. Dumas, looked like a small woman, pretty with diminutive features, but an overall sadness in her lips and eyes. Where, I wondered, was there a picture of my father's younger brother, Jean?

I left the office and found there was a separate study, a library with red leather sofas and high back chairs, gold leaf tables, and brass lamps. A curio case in the study was filled with valuable looking red, green, and purple hand blown goblets, and the walls, as were the walls in all the rooms, were covered with oil paintings. I went in and browsed through some of the books on the shelves.

"Here you are," I heard my father say, and I turned to see him and Gisselle standing in the doorway. Gisselle was in a pink silk robe and the softest looking pink slippers. Her hair had been hastily brushed and looked it. Pale and sleepy eyed, she stood with her arms folded under her breasts. "We were looking for you."

"I was just exploring. I hope it's all right," I said.

"Of course it's all right. This is your home. Go where you like. Well now, Gisselle understands what's happened and wants to greet you as if for the first time," he said, and smiled. I looked at Gisselle who sighed and stepped forward.

"I'm sorry for the way I behaved," she began.

"I didn't know the story. No one ever told me anything like this before," she added, shifting her eyes toward our father, who looked sufficiently apologetic. "Anyway, this changes things a lot. Now that I know you really are my sister and you've gone through a terrible time."

"I'm glad," I said. "And you don't have to apologize for anything. I can understand why you'd be upset at me suddenly appearing on your doorstep."

She seemed pleased, flashed a look at father and then turned back to me.

"I want to welcome you to our family. I'm looking forward to getting to know you," she added. It had the resonance of something memorized, but I was happy to hear the words nevertheless. "And don't worry about school. Daddy told me you were concerned, but you don't have to be. No one is going to give my sister a hard time," she declared.

"Gisselle is the class bully," our father said, and smiled.

"I'm not a bully, but I'm not going to let those namby-pambies push us around," she swore. "Anyway, you can come into my room later and talk. We should really get to know each other."

"I'd like that."

"Maybe you want to go along with Ruby and Daphne to shop for Ruby's new wardrobe," our father suggested.

"I can't. Beau's coming over." She flashed a smile at me. "I mean, I'd call him and cancel, but he so looks forward to seeing me, and besides, by the time I get ready, you and Mother could be half

303

finished. Come out to the pool as soon as you get back," she said.

"I will."

"Don't let Mother buy those horribly long skirts, the ones that go all the way down to your ankles. Everyone's wearing shorter skirts these days," she advised, but I couldn't imagine telling Daphne what or what not to buy me. I was grateful for anything. I nodded, but Gisselle saw my hesitation.

"Don't worry about it," Gisselle said. "If you don't get things that are in style, I'll let you borrow something for your first day at school."

"That's very nice," our father said. "Thanks for being so understanding, honey."

"You're welcome, Daddy," she said, and kissed him on the cheek. He beamed and then rubbed his hands together.

"I have a set of twins!" he cried. "Both grown and beautiful. What man could be luckier!"

I hoped he was right. Gisselle excused herself to go up and get dressed and I walked out to the front of the house with my father to wait for Daphne.

"I'm sure you and Gisselle will get along marvelously," he said, "but there's bound to be a few hills and valleys in any relationship, especially an instant sister relationship. If you have any real problems, come see me. Don't bother Daphne about it," he said. "She's been a wonderful mother for Gisselle, despite the unusual circumstances, and I'm sure she will be wonderful for you, too; but I feel I should bear most of the responsibilities.

I'm sure you understand. You seem very mature, more mature than Gisselle," he added, smiling.

What a strange predicament, I thought. Daphne wanted me to come to her and he wanted me to come to him, and each appeared to have good reason. Hopefully, I wouldn't have to trouble either.

I heard Daphne's footsteps on the stairway and gazed up. She wore a flowing black skirt, a white velvet blouse, low black heels and a string of real pearls. Her blue eyes glistened and her smile spread to show even white teeth. She carried herself so elegantly.

"There are few things I like to do better than shop," she declared. She kissed my father on the cheek.

"Nothing makes me happier than seeing you and Gisselle happy, Daphne," he told her. "And now, I can add Ruby."

"Go to work, darling. Earn money. I'm going to show your new daughter how to spend it," she retorted.

"And you won't find a better teacher when it comes to that," he quipped. He opened the door for us and we went out.

I still felt this was all too good to be true and that any moment I would wake up in my little room in the bayou. I pinched myself and was happy to feel the tiny sting that assured me it was all real.

13

I Can't Be You

I felt as if I were caught in a whirlwind because of the way my new stepmother went about taking me shopping. As soon as we were finished in one boutique, Daphne whisked me out the door to go to another or to a department store. Whenever she decided something looked nice on me or looked appropriate, she ordered it packed immediately, sometimes buying two, three, and four of the same blouse, the same skirt, even the same pair of shoes, but in different colors. The trunk and the backseat of the car quickly filled up. Each purchase took my breath away and she didn't seem at all concerned about the prices.

Everywhere we went, the salespeople appeared to know Daphne and respect her. We were treated like royalty, some clerks throwing aside anything they were doing the instant Daphne and I marched into their stores. Most assumed I was Gisselle and Daphne did not bother to explain.

"It's not important what these people do and don't know," she told me when a saleslady called me Gisselle. "When they call you Gisselle, just go along for now. The people who matter will be told everything quickly."

Although Daphne didn't have much respect for the salespeople, I noticed how careful they were when they made suggestions, and how concerned they were that Daphne might not approve. As soon as Daphne settled on a color or a style, all of them nodded and agreed immediately, complimenting her in chorus on the choices she had made for me.

She did seem very informed. She knew the latest styles, the designers by name, and the garments that had been featured in fashion magazines, knowing things about clothes that even the salespeople and store owners didn't know yet themselves. Being chic and up-to-date was obviously a high priority for my stepmother, who became upset if the salesperson brought colors that didn't coordinate perfectly or if a sleeve or hem was wrongly cut. Most of the time between stores and traveling in the car, she lectured to me about style, the importance of appearance, and being sure everything I wore matched and coordinated.

"Every time you go out of the house and into society, you make a statement about yourself," she warned, "and that statement reflects on your family.

"I know that living in the bayou you were used to plain clothes, to practical clothes. Being feminine wasn't as important. Some of the Cajun women I've seen who work side by side with their men are barely distinguishable from them. If it weren't for their bosoms—"

"That's not so, Daphne," I said. "Women in the bayou can dress very pretty when they go to the dances and the parties. They may not have rich jewels, but they love beautiful clothes, too, even though they don't have these expensive stores. But they don't need them," I said, my

Cajun pride unfurling like a flag. "My grandmere Catherine made many a gorgeous dress and—"

"You've got to stop doing that, Ruby, and especially remember not to do it in front of Gisselle," she snapped. A small flutter of panic stirred in my chest.

"Stop doing what?"

"Talking about your grandmere Catherine as if she were some wonderful person," she explained.

"But she was!"

"Not according to what we've told Gisselle and what we are telling our friends and society. As far as everyone is to know, this old lady, Catherine, knew you were kidnapped and sold to her family. It's nice that she had remorse on her deathbed and told you the truth so you could return to your real family, but it would be better if you didn't show how much you loved her," she proclaimed.

"Not show how much I loved Grandmere? But—"

"You would only make us look like fools, especially your father," she said. She smiled. "If you can't say anything bad, don't say anything at all."

I sat back. This was too much of a price to pay, even though I knew Grandmere Catherine would tell me to do it. I bit down on my lower lip to keep from voicing any more protest.

"Lies are not deadly sins, you know," she continued. "Everyone tells little lies, Ruby. I'm sure you've done it before."

Little lies? Is that what she considered this story and all the stories that had to follow as a result? Little lies?

"We all have our illusions, our fantasies," she

said, and threw me a quick glance of devilment. "Men, especially, expect it," she added.

What kind of men was she talking about? I wondered. Men who expected their women to lie, to fantasize? Could men be that different in the city world from what they were in the bayou?

"That's why we dress up and make up our faces to please them. Which reminds me, you have nothing for your vanity table," she said, and decided to take me to her cosmetic store next and buy me whatever she decided was appropriate for a teenager. When I explained I had never worn any makeup, even lipstick, she asked the saleswoman to give me a demonstration, finally revealing to someone that I wasn't Gisselle. Daphne abbreviated the story, relating it as if it were nothing extraordinary. Nevertheless, the tale flew through the large store and everyone fluttered about us.

They sat me before a mirror and showed me how to use the rouge, matched up shades of lipstick to my complexion, and taught me how to pluck my eyebrows.

"Gisselle sneaks on eyeliner," Daphne said. "But I don't think that's necessary."

We went through perfumes next, Daphne actually letting me make the final decision this time. I favored one that reminded me of the scent of the fields in the bayou after a summer rain; although I didn't tell Daphne that was the reason. She approved, bought me some talcum powders, some bubble bath, and fragrant shampoo, besides new hairbrushes and combs, bobby pins, ribbons, nail

309

polish, and files. Then she bought a smart, red leather case for me to put all my toiletries in.

After that, she decided we must get my spring and summer coats, a raincoat, and some hats. I had to model a dozen of each in two different stores before she decided which suited me best. I wondered if she put Gisselle through all this every time she took her shopping. She appeared to anticipate my question when she saw me grimace after she had turned down six coats in a row.

"I'm trying to get you things that are similar but yet distinct enough to draw some differences between you and your twin. Of course, it would be nice for you to have some matching outfits, but I don't think Gisselle would approve."

So Gisselle had some say when it came to her own wardrobe, I concluded. How long would it be before I did, too?

I never thought shopping, especially a shopping spree like this in which everything purchased was purchased for me, would be exhausting; but when we left the last department store in which Daphne had bought me dozens of pairs of undergarments, slips, and a few bras, I was happy to hear her say we were finished for now.

"I'll pick up other things for you from time to time when I go shopping for myself," she promised. I looked back at the pile in the rear of the automobile. It was so high and so thick it was impossible to see through the back window. I couldn't imagine what the total cost had been, but I was sure it was an amount that would be staggering to Grandmere Catherine. Daphne caught me shaking my head.

310

"I hope you're happy with it all," she said.

"Oh, yes," I said. "I feel like . . . like a princess."

She raised her eyebrows and looked at me with a small, tight smile.

"Well, you are your daddy's little princess, Ruby. You had better get used to being spoiled. Many men, especially rich Creole men, find it easier and more convenient to buy the love of the women around them, and many Creole women, especially women like me, make it easy for them to do so," she said smugly.

"But it's not really love if someone pays for it, is it?" I asked.

"Of course it is," she replied. "What do you think love is . . . bells ringing, music in the breeze, a handsome, gallant man sweeping you off your feet with poetic promises he can't possibly keep? I thought you Cajuns were more practical minded," she said with that same tight smile. I felt my face turn red, both from anger and embarrassment. Whenever she had something negative to say, I was a Cajun, but whenever she had something nice to say, I was a Creole blue blood, and she made Cajuns sound like such clods, especially the women.

"Up until now, I bet you've only had poor boyfriends. The most expensive gift they could probably give you was a pound of shrimp. But the boys who will be coming around now will be driving expensive automobiles, wearing expensive clothing, and casually be giving you presents that will make your Cajun eyes bulge," she said, and laughed.

"Look at the rings on my hand!" she exclaimed, lifting her right hand off the steering wheel. Every finger had a ring on it. There seemed to be one for every valuable jewel: diamonds, emeralds, rubies, and sapphires all set in gold and platinum. Her hand looked like a display in a jewelry shop window.

"Why I bet the amount of money I have on this hand would buy the houses and food for a year for ten swamp families."

"They would," I admitted. I wanted to add and that seems unfair, but I didn't.

"Your father wants to buy you some nice bracelets and rings himself, and he noted that you have no watch. With beautiful jewelry, nice clothes, and a little makeup, you will at least look like you've been a Dumas for your whole life. The next thing I'll do is take you through some simple rules of etiquette, show you the proper way to dine and speak."

"What's wrong with how I eat and talk?" I wondered aloud. My father hadn't appeared upset at breakfast or lunch.

"Nothing, if you lived the rest of your life in the swamps, but you're in New Orleans now and part of high society. There will be dinner parties and gala affairs. You want to become a refined, educated, and attractive young woman, don't you?" she asked.

I couldn't help wanting to be like her. She was so elegant and carried herself with such an air of confidence, and yet, every time I agreed to something she said or did something she wanted me to do, it was as if I were looking down upon the

Cajun people, treating them as if they were less important and not as good.

I decided I would do what I had to do to make my father happy and blend into his world, but I wouldn't harbor any feelings of superiority, if I could help it. I was only afraid I would become more like Gisselle than, as my father wished, Gisselle would become more like me.

"You do want to be a Dumas, don't you?" she pursued.

"Yes," I said, but not with much conviction. My hesitation gave her reason to glance at me again, those blue eyes darkening with suspicion.

"I do hope you will make every effort to answer the call of your Creole blood, your real heritage, and quickly block out and forget the Cajun world you were unfairly left to live in. Just think," she said, a little lightness in her voice now, "it was just chance Gisselle was the one given the better life. If you would have emerged first from your mother's womb, Gisselle would have been the poor Cajun girl."

The idea made her laugh.

"I must tell her that she could have been the one kidnapped and forced to live in the swamps," she added. "Just to see the look on her face."

The thought brought a broad smile to hers. How was I to tell her that despite the hardships Grandmere Catherine and I endured and despite the mean things Grandpere Jack had done, my Cajun world had its charm, too?

Apparently, if it wasn't something she could buy in a store, it wasn't significant to her, and despite what she told me, love was something you

313

couldn't buy in a store. In my heart I knew that to be true, and that was one Cajun belief she would never change, elegant, rich life at stake or not.

When we drove up to the house, she called Edgar out to take all the packages up to my room. I wanted to help him, but Daphne snapped at me as soon as I made the suggestion.

"Help him?" she said as if I had proposed burning down the house. "You don't help him. He helps you. That's what servants are for, my dear child. I'll see to it that Wendy hangs everything up that has to be hung up in your closet and puts everything else in your armoire and vanity table. You run along and find your sister and do whatever it is girls your age do on your days off from school."

Having servants do the simplest things for me was one of the hardest things for me to get used to, I thought. Wouldn't it make me lazy? But no one seemed concerned about being lazy here. It was expected of you, almost required.

I remembered that Gisselle said she would be out at the pool, lounging with Beau Andreas. They were there, lying on thick cushioned beige metal framed lounges and sipping from tall glasses of pink lemonade. Beau sat up as soon as he set eyes on me and beamed a warm smile. He was wearing a white and blue terry cloth jacket and shorts and Gisselle was in a two-piece dark blue bathing suit, her sunglasses almost big enough to be called a mask.

"Hi," Beau said immediately. Gisselle looked up, lowering and peering over her sunglasses as if they were reading glasses.

"Did Mother leave anything in the stores for anyone else?" she asked.

"Barely," I said. "I've never been to so many big department stores and seen so much clothing and shoes." Beau laughed at my enthusiasm.

"I'm sure she took you to Diana's and Rudolph Vite's and the Moulin Rouge, didn't she?" Gisselle said.

I shook my head.

"To tell you the truth, we went in and out of so many stores and so quickly, I don't remember the names of half of them," I said with a gasp. Beau laughed again and patted his lounge. He pulled his legs up, embracing them around the knees.

"Sit down. Take a load off," he suggested.

"Thanks." I sat down next to him and smelled the sweet scent of the coconut suntan lotion he and Gisselle had on their faces.

"Gisselle told me your story," he said. "It's fantastic. What were these Cajun people like? Did they turn you into their little slave or something?"

"Oh, no," I said, but quickly checked my enthusiasm. "I had my daily chores, of course."

"Chores," Gisselle moaned.

"I was taught handicrafts and helped make the things we sold at the roadside to the tourists, as well as helping with the cooking and the cleaning," I explained.

"You can cook?" Gisselle asked, peering over her glasses at me again.

"Gisselle couldn't boil water without burning it," Beau teased.

"Well, who cares? I don't intend to cook for anyone . . . ever," she said, pulling her eyeglasses off and flashing heat out of her eyes at him. He just smiled and turned back to me.

"I understand you're an artist, too," he said. "And you actually have paintings in a gallery here in the French Quarter."

"I was more surprised than anyone that a gallery owner wanted to sell them," I told him. His smile warmed, the gray-blue in his eyes becoming softer.

"So far my father is the only one who bought one, right?" Gisselle quipped.

"No. Someone else bought one first. That's how I got the money for my bus trip here," I said. Gisselle seemed disappointed, and when Beau gazed at her, she put her glasses on and dropped herself back on the lounge.

"Where is the picture your father bought?" Beau asked. "I'd love to see it."

"It's in his office."

"Still on the floor," Gisselle interjected. "He'll probably leave it there for months."

"I'd still like to see it," Beau said.

"So go see it," Gisselle said. "It's only a picture of a bird."

"Heron," I said. "In the marsh."

"I've been to the bayou a few times to fish. It can be quite beautiful there," Beau said.

"Swamps, ugh," Gisselle moaned.

"It's very pretty there, especially in the spring and the fall."

"Alligators and snakes and mosquitos, not to mention mud everywhere and on everything. Very beautiful," Gisselle said.

"Don't mind her. She doesn't even like going

in my sailboat on Lake Pontchartrain because the water sprays up and gets her hair wet, and she won't go to the beach because she can't stand sand in her bathing suit and in her hair."

"So? Why should I put up with all that when I can swim here in a clean, filtered pool?" Gisselle proclaimed.

"Don't you just like going places and seeing new things?" I asked.

"Not unless she can strap her vanity table to her back," Beau said. Gisselle sat up so quickly it was as if she had a spring in her back.

"Oh, sure, Beau Andreas, suddenly you're a big naturalist, a fisherman, a sailor, a hiker. You hate doing most of those things almost as much as I do, but you're just putting on an act for my sister," she charged. Beau turned crimson.

"I do too like to fish and sail," he protested.

"When do you do it, twice a year at the most?"

"Depends," he said.

"On what, your social calendar or your hair appointment," Gisselle said sharply. Throughout the exchange, my gaze went from one to the other. Gisselle's eyes blazed with so much anger, it was hard to believe she thought of him as her boyfriend.

"You know he has a woman cut his hair at his house," Gisselle continued. The crimson tint in Beau's cheeks rushed down into his neck. "She's his mother's beautician and she even gives him a manicure every two weeks."

"It's just that my mother likes the way she does her hair," Beau said. "I . . . "

"Your hair is very nice," I said. "I don't think

it's unusual for a woman to cut a man's hair. I used to cut my grandpere's hair once in a while. I mean, the man I called Grandpere."

"You can cut hair, too?" Beau asked, his eyes wide with amazement.

"Do you fish and hunt as well?" Gisselle inquired, not disguising her sarcasm.

"I've fished, helped harvest oysters, but I've never hunted. I can't stand to see birds or deer shot. I even hate seeing the alligators shot," I said.

"Harvested oysters?" Gisselle said, shaking her head. "Meet my sister, the fish lady," she added.

"When did you first learn what had happened to you as a baby?" Beau asked.

"Just before my grandmere Catherine died," I replied.

"You mean the woman you thought was your grandmother," Gisselle reminded me.

"Yes. It's hard to think like that after so many years," I explained, more to Beau, who nodded with understanding.

"And did you have a mother and a father?"

"I was told my mother died when I was born and my father ran off."

"So you lived with these grandparents?"

"Just my grandmother. My grandfather is a trapper and lives in the swamp away from us."

"So just before she died, she told you the truth?" Beau asked. I nodded.

"How terrible of them to keep the secret all these years," Gisselle said. She gazed at me for a reaction.

"Yes."

"Lucky your fake grandmother decided to tell

you or you would never have known your real family. That was nice of her," Beau said, which fired up Gisselle.

"These people she lived with are no better than animals, stealing someone's baby and keeping her! Claudine Montaigne told me about these Cajuns who live in a one-room house, everyone in the family sleeping with everyone else. To them incest is nothing more serious than stealing an apple!"

"That's not so," I said quickly.

"Claudine wouldn't lie," Gisselle insisted.

"There are bad people in the bayou just like there are bad people here," I said. "She might have heard of them, but she shouldn't judge everyone the same. Nothing like that ever happened to me."

"You were just lucky," Gisselle insisted.

"No, really . . . "

"They bought a kidnapped baby, didn't they?" she pursued. "Wasn't that terrible enough?"

I looked at Beau. His eyes were fixed intently on me, waiting for my response. What could I say? Put-away thoughts. The truth was forbidden. The lie had to be upheld.

"Yes," I muttered, and shifted my gaze down to my entwined fingers. Gisselle sat back, contented. There was a moment of silence before Beau spoke.

"You know, you two are going to be the center of attention at school next Monday," he said.

"I know. I can't help being nervous about it," I confessed.

"Don't worry. I'll pick the both of you up in the morning and escort you around all day," he

319

promised. "You'll be a curiosity for a while and then things will settle down."

"I doubt it," Gisselle said. "Especially when everyone learns she's lived like a Cajun all of her life and cooked and fished and made little handicrafts to sell by the road."

"Don't listen to her."

"They'll make fun of her whenever I'm not around to protect her," Gisselle insisted.

"If you won't be around, I will," Beau declared.

"I don't want to be a burden for anyone," I said.

"You won't be," Beau assured me. "Right, Gisselle?" he asked. She was reluctant to answer. "Right?"

"Right, right, right," she said. "I'm tired of talking about this."

"I've got to go anyway," Beau said. "It's getting late. Are we still on for tonight?" he asked her. She hesitated. "Gisselle?"

"Are you bringing Martin?" she countered sharply. He threw a glance my way and then looked at her again.

"Are you sure I should? I mean . . . "

"I'm sure. You'd like to meet one of Beau's friends tonight, wouldn't you, Ruby? I mean, you've fished, harvested oysters, chased alligators . . . I'm sure you had a boyfriend, too, didn't you?"

I looked at Beau. His face had turned troubled and concerned.

"Yes," I said.

"So there's no problem, Beau. She'd like to meet Martin," Gisselle said.

"Who's Martin?" I asked.

"The best looking of Beau's friends. Most of the girls like him. I'm sure you will," she said. "Won't she, Beau?"

He shrugged and stood up.

"You'll like him," Gisselle insisted. "We'll meet you out here at nine-thirty," Gisselle said. "Don't be late."

"Right, boss. Ever see anyone that bossy in the bayou?" he asked me. I looked at Gisselle, who smirked.

"Just an alligator," I said, and Beau roared.

"That's not funny!" Gisselle cried.

"See ya later, alligator," Beau quipped, and winked at me before starting off.

"I'm sorry," I said to Gisselle. "I didn't mean to make fun of you or anything." She pouted for a moment and then broke a small smile.

"You shouldn't encourage him," she advised. "He can be a terrible tease."

"He seems very nice."

"Just another spoiled rich boy," Gisselle insisted. "But, he'll do . . . for now."

"What do you mean, 'for now'?"

"What do you think I mean? Don't tell me you promised to marry every boyfriend you had back in the swamp." Her eyes turned suspicious. "How many boyfriends did you have?" she asked.

"Not that many."

"How many?" she demanded. "If we're going to be sisters, we have to trust each other with the intimate details of our lives. Unless you don't want to be that kind of sister," she added.

"Oh, no. I do."

"So? How many?"

"Really only one," I confessed.

"One?" She stared at me a moment. "Well, it must have been a very hot and heavy romance then. Was it?"

"We cared a great deal for each other," I admitted.

"How much is a great deal?" she pursued.

"As much as we could, I suppose."

"Then you did it with him? Went all the way?"

"What?"

"You know... had sexual intercourse."

"Oh, no," I said. "We never went that far."

Gisselle tilted her head and looked skeptical.

"I thought all Cajun girls lost their virginity before they were thirteen," she said.

"What? Who told you such a stupid thing?" I asked quickly. She pulled back as if I had slapped her.

"It's not so stupid. I heard it from a number of people."

"Well, they're all liars then," I said vehemently. "I'll admit that there are many young marriages. Girls don't go off to work or go to college as much, but—"

"So it's true then. Anyway, don't keep defending them. They bought you when you were only a day or so old, didn't they?" Gisselle flared. I shifted my gaze away so she couldn't see the tears in my eyes. How ironic. It was she who had been bought and by a Creole family, not a Cajun. But I could say nothing. I could only swallow the truth and keep it down, only it kept threatening to

322

bubble up and flow out of my mouth on the back of a flurry of hot words.

"Anyway," Gisselle continued in a calmer tone, "the boys will expect you to be a lot more sophisticated than you apparently are."

I looked at her fearfully.

"What do you mean?"

"What did you do with this one devoted boyfriend? Did you kiss and pet at least?" I nodded. "Did you undress, at least partially?" I shook my head. She grimaced. "Did you ever French kiss . . . you know," she added quickly, "touch tongues?" I couldn't remember if that had ever happened. My hesitation was enough to convince her it hadn't. "Did you let him give you hickeys?"

"No."

"Good. I hate them, too. They suck until they're satisfied and we're the ones who walk around with these ugly spots on our necks and breasts."

"Breasts?"

"Don't worry," she said, getting up. "I'll teach you what to do. For now, if Martin or anyone gets too demanding, just tell him you're having your period, understand? Nothing turns them off as fast as that.

"Come on," she said. "Let's go look at the things Mother bought you. I'll help you decide what to wear tonight."

I followed her back to the house, my footsteps on the patio a lot more unsure, my heart beating with a timid thump. Gisselle and I were so identical we could gaze at each other and think we

323

were looking into mirrors, but on the inside, we were more different than a bird and a cat. I wondered what, if anything, we would find to draw us together so we could become the sisters we were meant to be.

Gisselle was surprised by many of the things Daphne had bought me. Then, after she gave it some thought, her surprise turned to jealousy and anger.

"She never buys me skirts this short unless I throw a tantrum, and these colors are always too bright for her. I love this blouse. It's not fair," she wailed. "Now I want new things, too."

"Daphne told me she wanted to buy things that were different from the things you had. She thought you wouldn't like it if we had identical clothes to go along with our identical faces," I explained.

Still pouting, Gisselle held one of my blouses against her and studied it in the mirror. Then she dropped it on the bed and opened the drawers of the armoire to inspect my new panties.

"When I bought a set of these, she thought they were too sexy," she said, holding up the abbreviated light silks.

"I've never worn anything like it," I confessed.

"Well, I'm borrowing this pair of panties, this skirt, and this blouse for tonight," she informed me firmly.

"I don't mind," I said, "but—"

"But what? Sisters share things with each other, don't they?"

I wanted to remind her of the nasty things she had said on the stairway in the morning when I came upon her returning from the ball, how she would never let me borrow her pretty red dress, but I realized that was before my father had had his conversation with her. It did bring about a change in her attitude toward me. Then I recalled something Daphne had said.

"Daphne disapproves of girls sharing things. Even sisters. She said so," I told her.

"You just let me worry about Mother. There are a lot of things she says and then goes and does the exact opposite," Gisselle replied as she went through the blouses to decide if there were any others she wanted to borrow.

And so for the first dinner we would have together as a family, Gisselle and I wore the same style skirt and blouse. She thought it would be amusing for us to brush and tie our hair into French knots as well. We dressed in my room and sat at my vanity table.

"Here," she said, taking a gold ring off her pinky and handing it to me. "You wear this tonight. I'll wear no jewelry, since you have none."

"Why?" I asked. I saw the impish glint in her eyes.

"Daddy wants you on his left, I imagine, and me, as usual on his right."

"So?"

"I'll sit on his left; you sit on his right. Let's see if he knows the difference," she said.

"Oh, he will. He knew I wasn't you the moment he set eyes on me," I told her.

Gisselle didn't know whether to take this as something good or bad. I saw the confusion in her face for a moment and then the decision.

"We'll see," she said. "I told Beau there were differences between us, differences maybe only I can see. I know what," she said, bouncing in her chair. "We'll tease Beau tonight. You'll pretend you're me and I'll pretend I'm you."

"Oh, I couldn't do that," I said, my heart fluttering with the thought of being Beau's girlfriend, even for a few minutes.

"Of course you can. He thought you were me the first time he set eyes on you, didn't he?"

"That was different. He didn't know I existed," I explained.

"I'll tell you exactly how to act and what to say," she continued, ignoring my point. "Oh, this is going to be fun for a change. I mean, real fun, with it all starting at dinner," she decided.

However, just as I predicted, our father knew instantly that we had taken the wrong seats at the dining room table. Daphne, who raised her eyebrows as soon as she saw the two of us in my new clothes, sat down, for the moment confused. But my father threw his head back and roared with laughter.

"What is so funny, Pierre?" Daphne demanded. She had come to dinner dressed formally in a black dress with diamond teardrop earrings and a matching diamond necklace and bracelet. The dress had a V-neck collar that dipped low enough to show the start of her cleavage. I thought she was so beautiful and elegant.

"Your daughters have dressed alike and conspired to test me at their first meal together," he said. "This is Ruby wearing Gisselle's pinky ring and this is Gisselle in Ruby's seat."

Daphne looked from me to Gisselle and then back to me.

"Ridiculous," she said. "Did you think we wouldn't know the difference? Take your proper seats, please," she commanded.

Gisselle laughed and got up. Father's eyes twinkled with delight at me, but then he turned serious, his expression sober when he gazed across the table at Daphne and saw she wasn't amused.

"I hope this is the beginning and the end of such shenanigans," Daphne declared. She directed herself to Gisselle. "I'm trying to teach your sister the proper way to behave at dinner and in the company of others. It's not going to be easy anyway. The last thing I need is for you to set a bad example, Gisselle."

"I'm sorry," she said, and looked down for a moment. Then her head snapped up. "How come you bought her all these short skirts and carried on so much when I wanted them last month?"

"It's what she liked," Daphne said.

I whipped my head around. What I liked? I never was given a chance to offer an opinion. Why did she say that?

"Well, I want some new clothes then, too," Gisselle moaned.

"You can get a few new things, but there's no reason to throw out your entire wardrobe."

Gisselle sat back and looked at me with a smile of satisfaction.

Our meal service began. We ate on a floral pattern set of porcelain china, which Daphne pointed out was nineteenth century. She made everything, down to the napkin holders, sound so expensive and precious, my fingers trembled when I went to lift my fork. I hesitated when I saw there were two. Daphne explained how I was to use the silverware and even how I should sit and hold it.

I didn't know whether or not the meal was something done especially for the occasion of our first dinner together, but it seemed overwhelming.

We began with an appetizer of crabmeat ravigote served in scallop shells. That was followed with grilled cornish game hens with roasted shallots and browned garlic sauce, and Creole green beans. For dessert we were served vanilla ice cream smothered in hot bourbon whiskey sauce.

I saw how Edgar stood just behind Daphne after he served each course, waiting for her to take her first taste and signal approval. I couldn't imagine anyone not being satisfied with anything on the table. My father asked me to describe some of the meals I had in the bayou and I described the gumbos and the jambalayas, the homemade cakes and pastries.

"It doesn't sound like they starved you," Gisselle remarked. I couldn't help sounding enthusiastic over the meals Grandmere Catherine used to make.

"Gumbo is nothing more than a stew," Daphne said. "The food is plain and simple. It doesn't take much imagination. You can see that yourself, can't you, Ruby?" she asked me firmly. I glanced at my father, who waited for my response.

"Nina Jackson is a wonderful cook. I never had such a meal," I admitted. That pleased Daphne and another little crisis seemed to pass. How hard it was for me to get used to belittling and criticizing my life with Grandmere, but I realized that was the currency I would need to pay for the life I now had.

The conversation at the table moved from my description of foods in the bayou to questions Daphne had for Gisselle about the Mardi Gras Ball. She described the costumes and the music, referring to people they all knew. She and Daphne seemed to share opinions about certain families and their sons and daughters. Tired of hearing the gossip, my father began to talk about my artwork.

"I've already inquired about an instructor. Madam Henreid over at the Gallier House has recommended someone to me, an instructor at Tulane who takes pupils on the side. I've already spoken with him and he's agreed to meet Ruby and consider her work," he said.

"How come I never got my singing instructor," Gisselle whined.

"You never really showed that much interest, Gisselle. Every time I asked you to go to the teacher, you had some excuse not to," he explained.

"Well, she should have been brought here," Gisselle insisted.

"She would have come," he said, looking to Daphne.

"Of course she would have come. Do you want your father to call her again?" she asked.

"No," Gisselle said. "It's too late."

"Why?" he asked.

"It just is," she said, pouting.

When dinner was over, my father decided he would show me the room he had in mind for my art studio. He winked at Daphne and had a tight smile on his lips. Reluctantly, Gisselle tagged along. He took us toward the rear of the house and when he threw open the door, there it was—a full art studio, already in place with easels, paints, brushes, clays, everything I would ever need or dreamt of having. For a moment I was speechless.

"I had this all done while you were out shopping with Daphne," he revealed. "Do you like it?"

"Like it? I love it!" I whirled around the room inspecting everything. There was even a pile of art books, going from the most elementary things to the most elaborate and complicated. "It's . . . wonderful!"

"I thought we should waste no time, not with a talent like yours. What do you think, Gisselle?" I turned to see her smirking in the doorway.

"I hate art class in school," she remarked. Then she focused a conspiratorial look on me and added, "I'm going up to my room. Come up as soon as you can. We have some things to prepare for later."

"Later?" my father asked.

"Just girl talk, Daddy," Gisselle said, and left. He shrugged and joined me at the shelves of supplies.

"I told Emile at the art store to give me everything we would need to have a complete studio," he said. "Are you pleased?"

"Oh, yes. There are things here, materials and supplies I have never seen, much less used."

"That's why we need the instructor as soon as possible, too. I think once he sees this studio, he'll be encouraged to take you on as one of his pupils. Not that he shouldn't by just looking at your painting anyway." He beamed his smile down at me.

"Thank you . . . Daddy," I said. His smile widened.

"I like hearing that," he said. "I hoped you felt welcomed."

"Oh, yes, I do. Overwhelmed."

"And happy?"

"Very happy," I said. I stood on my toes to plant a kiss on his cheek. His eyes brightened even more.

"Well," he said. "Well . . . " His eyes watered. "I guess I'll go see what Daphne is up to. Enjoy your studio and paint wonderful pictures here," he added, and walked off.

I stood there in awe of it all for a few moments. The room had a nice view of the sprawling oak trees and garden. It faced west so I could paint the sun on the final leg of its journey. Twilight was always magnificent for me in the bayou. I had high hopes that it would be just as magnificent here as well, for I believed that the things I carried in my heart and in my soul would be with me no matter where I was, where I lived, and what I looked at through my windows. My pictures were inside me, just waiting to be brought out.

After what I thought was only a short while

later, I left the studio and hurried up to Gisselle's room. I knocked on the door.

"Well, it's about time," she said, pulling me in quickly and closing the door. "We don't have all that much time to plan. The boys will be here in twenty minutes."

"I don't think I can do this, Gisselle," I moaned.

"Of course you can," she said. "We'll be sitting around the table at the pool when they arrive. We'll have bottles of Coke and glasses for everyone, with ice. As soon as they approach, you introduce me to Martin. Just say I want you to meet my sister, Ruby. Then, you'll take this out from under the table and pour globs of it into the Coke," she said, and plucked a bottle of rum out of a straw basket. "Make sure you pour at least this much into every glass," she added, holding up her thumb and forefinger a good two inches apart. "Once Beau sees you do that, he'll be convinced you're me," she quipped.

"Then what?"

"Then . . . whatever happens, happens. What's the matter?" she snapped, pulling herself back. "Don't you want to pretend you're me?"

"It's not that I don't want to," I said.

"So? What is it?"

"I just don't think I can be you," I said.

"Why not?" she demanded, her eyes darkening and her eyelids narrowing into slits of anger.

"I don't know enough," I replied. That pleased her and she relaxed her shoulders.

"Just don't talk much. Drink and whenever Beau says something, nod and smile. I know I can be you," she added. And then in a voice that was supposed to be imitative, she said, "I just can't believe I'm here. The food is sooo good, the house is sooo big and I'm sleepin' in a real bed without mosquitos and mud."

She laughed. Was I really like that in her eyes?

"Stop being so serious," she demanded when I didn't laugh at her mockery of me. She dropped the bottle of rum into the basket "Come on," she said, picking it up and seizing my hand. "Let's go tease some stuck-up Creole boys until they beg for mercy."

Trailing along like a kite on a string, I followed my sister out and down the stairs, my heart thumping, my mind in a turmoil. I had never had a day packed with so much excitement. I couldn't begin to imagine what the night would bring.

14

Someone's Crying

"We'll sit over there," Gisselle said, and pointed to lounges on the far end of the pool, near the cabana. It put us far enough away from the outside lights to keep us draped in soft shadows. It was a warm night, as warm as it would be on the bayou, only tonight without the cool breeze that would come up the canals from the Gulf. The sky was overcast; it even felt like it might rain.

Gisselle put the basket with the bottle of rum on the table and I put down the bucket of ice, the Coke, and the glasses. To bolster our courage for Gisselle's prank, she decided we should mix the rum in our Coke before the boys arrived. She did the pouring and it seemed to me she made each drink more rum than Coke. I tried to warn her about the effects of whiskey. After all, I knew about it from painful experiences.

"The man I called Grandpere is a drunk," I told her. "It's poisoned his brain."

I described the time I had poled our pirogue out to see him in the swamp and how he had gone berserk on his galerie. Then I described some of his ranting and raving in the house, how he wrecked things, dug up floorboards, and ended up sleeping in the muck and grime and not caring.

"I hardly think we'll become like that," Gisselle said. "Besides, you don't believe this is the first time I snuck some of our liquor, do you? All of my friends do it and no one is as bad as that old man you described," she insisted.

When I hesitated to take the glass of rum and Coke from her, she put her fist on her hip and scowled.

"Don't tell me you're going to be an old stick-in-the-mud now and not have fun after I've invited the boys over, especially so you could have a boyfriend."

"I didn't say I wouldn't have some. I just—"

"Just have a drink and relax," she insisted. "Here!" she said, and shoved the drink at me. Reluctantly, I took the glass and sipped, while she took long gulps of hers. I couldn't help grimacing. To me it tasted like one of Grandmere Catherine's herbal medicines.

Gisselle stabbed me with a hard penetrating gaze and then shook her head.

"I guess you didn't have much fun living in the bayou. It sounds like all work and no play, which makes Jack a dull boy," she added, and laughed.

"Jack?"

"It's just an expression. Really," she cried, throwing her hand up dramatically, "you're just like someone from a foreign country. I feel like I've got to do what Mother wants to do: teach you how to talk and walk." She took another gulp of her drink. Even Grandpere didn't swig it down that fast, I thought. I wondered if she was as sophisticated as she was making out to be.

"Hi, there," we heard Beau call, and turned to see two silhouettes come around the corner of the house. My heart began to drum in anticipation.

"Just remember to do what I told you to do and say what I told you to say," Gisselle coached.

"It's not going to work," I insisted in a whisper.

"It better," she threatened.

The two boys stepped onto the pool deck and drew closer. I saw that Martin was a good-looking young man, about an inch or so taller than Beau, with jet black hair. He was leaner, longer-legged, and swaggered more when he walked. They were both dressed in jeans with white cotton shirts with buttoned-down collars. When they stepped into the dim pool of illumination cast by a lantern nearby, I noticed that Martin wore an expensive looking gold watch on his left wrist and a silver ID bracelet on the right. He had dark eyes and a smile that tucked the corner of his mouth into his cheek, creating more of a leer.

Gisselle nudged me with her elbow and then cleared her throat to urge me on.

"Hi," I said. My voice wanted to crack, but I felt Gisselle's hot, whiskey-scented breath on my neck, and I held myself together. "Martin, I'd like you to meet my sister, Ruby," I recited.

I couldn't see how anyone would think I was Gisselle, but Martin looked from me to Gisselle and then to me again with astonishment written on his face and not skepticism.

"Wow, you guys are really identical. I wouldn't know one from the other."

Gisselle laughed stupidly.

"Why, thank you, Martin," she said with a silly twang, "That's a real compliment."

I gazed at Beau and saw a wry smile cocking his lips. Surely, he knew what we were doing, I thought, and yet he said nothing.

"Beau told me your story," Martin said to Gisselle, believing she was me. "I've been to the bayou, even to Houma. I could have seen you."

"That would have been nice," Gisselle said. Martin's smile widened. "We don't have too many good-looking boys out there in the swamps."

Martin beamed.

"This is great," he said, looking from me to her again. "I always thought Beau was real lucky having a girlfriend as pretty as Gisselle, and now there's a second Gisselle."

"Oh, I'm not as pretty as my sister," Gisselle said, batting her eyelashes and twisting her shoulder.

Anger, fanned by the rum that heated my blood, made my heart pound. A terrible fury washed over me as I sat here watching her make fun of me. Unable to hold back, I flared.

"Of course you're as pretty as I am, Ruby. If anything, you're prettier," I countered.

Beau laughed. I shot a furious glance at him and he knitted his eyebrows together with a look of confusion. Then he relaxed, his gaze fixing on the glasses in our hands.

"Looks like the girls have been enjoying themselves some before we got here," he said, turning to Martin and wagging his head toward the straw basket, the ice bucket, and Coke.

"Oh, this," Gisselle said, holding up her glass. "Why this is nothin' compared to what we do in the bayou."

"Oh, yeah," Martin said with interest, "and what did you do in the bayou?"

"I don't want to do anything or say anything that might corrupt you city boys," she quipped. Martin smiled at Beau whose eyes were dancing with amusement.

"I can't think of anything I'd like better than to be corrupted by Gisselle's twin sister," Martin said. Gisselle laughed and extended her arm so Martin could sip from her glass. He sat down quickly and did so. I turned back to Beau. Our eyes met, but he didn't say anything to stop the charade from continuing.

"I'll just mix my own drink. If that's all right with you, Gisselle?" he asked me.

Gisselle fixed a stone stare at me before I could reveal my true identity.

"Of course it is, Beau," I said, and sat back against the lounge. How long did she want to keep this up? Martin turned to me.

"Are your parents going to have the police go to the bayou and get these people?" he asked.

"No," I said. "They're all dead and gone."

"But before they died, they tortured me," Gisselle moaned. Martin's head snapped around so he could face her again.

"What did they do?" he asked.

"Oh, things I can't describe. Especially to a boy," she added.

"They did not!" I cried. Gisselle widened her eyes and shot looks of rage at me.

"Really, Gisselle," she said in her most arrogant, haughty voice, "you don't think I told you everything that happened to me, do you? I wouldn't want to give you nightmares."

"Wow," Martin said. He looked up at Beau who still wore a smart, tight smile on his lips.

"Maybe you shouldn't ask your sister about her previous life," he said, sitting at my feet on the lounge. "You'll only bring up bad memories."

"That's right," Gisselle said. "I'd rather not have bad memories tonight anyway," she added, and ran her hand down Martin's left shoulder and arm. "You've never been with a Cajun girl then, Martin?" she asked coquettishly.

"No, but I've heard about them."

She leaned forward until her lips nearly touched his ear.

"It's all true," she said, and threw her head back to laugh. Martin laughed, too, and took a long gulp from Gisselle's drink, emptying the glass. "Gisselle, can you make us another drink?" she asked me in a voice that dripped with enough sweetness to make my stomach bubble.

It took all my self-control to battle back the urge to throw my own drink into her face and run into the house. But surely, this would end soon, I thought, and Gisselle would be satisfied she had had her little fun, all at my expense. I got up and started to make the drink the way she had instructed. Beau kept his eyes on me. I saw that Gisselle noticed how he was watching me, too.

"I just love that ring you gave my sister, Beau," Gisselle said. "Someday, I hope a handsome young man will think enough of me to give me a ring like that. I'd do just about anything for it," she added.

The bottle slipped out of my hand and hit the table, but didn't break. Beau jumped up.

"Here, let me help you," he said, quickly seizing the neck of the bottle before too much rum spilled.

"Oh, Gisselle, you shouldn't waste good rum like that," Gisselle cried, and laughed again. My hand was still trembling. Beau took it quickly into his and gazed into my eyes.

"You all right?" he asked. I nodded. "Let me finish making the drink," he said, and did so, handing it to Gisselle.

"Thank you, Beau," she said. He smirked at her, but said nothing. "I'm sorry I can't talk about myself, Martin," she said, turning back to him, "but I would love to hear about you."

"Sure," he said.

"Let's take a little walk," she suggested, and rose from the lounge. Martin looked at Beau who simply stared expressionless for a moment. Was he waiting to see how far Gisselle would go?

339

Surely, he didn't believe she was me. Why wasn't he putting an end to it then?

She scooped her arm into Martin's and pulled him close to her, laughing at the same time. Then she fed him some of the rum and Coke like she was feeding a baby. He gulped and gulped, his Adam's apple bouncing with the effort until she pulled the glass from his lips and drank some herself.

"What strong arms you have, Martin," she said. "I thought only Cajun boys had arms like this." She flashed a smile back at me. "And Cajun girls," she added with a laugh. She turned him away and they walked deeper into the shadows, Gisselle's laughter louder and sillier.

"Well," Beau said, sitting on my lounge again. "Your sister has really made herself at home."

"Beau," I began, but he put his fingers on my lips.

"No, don't say anything. I know how hard this has all been for you, Gisselle." He leaned toward me.

"But . . . "

Before I could say anything, he pressed his lips to mine, softly at first and then harder as he wrapped his arm around me and brought me into the nook between his shoulder and chest. He pressed the palm of his other hand against the small of my back, lifting me slightly. His kiss and embrace took my breath away. When our lips parted, I gasped. He kissed the tip of my nose and then brought his cheek to mine and whispered.

"You're right," he said. "We shouldn't wait any longer. I can't keep my hands off you. I've thought of nothing else but touching you and making love to you," he said, and slid the palm of his right hand over my hip and up the side of my body until he reached my breast. He pressed his body against me, driving me back on the lounge.

"Wait . . . Beau . . . "

His lips were over mine again, only this time, he performed the French kiss Gisselle had described. The feel of his tongue on mine sent a mixed chill of excitement and fear down my spine. I struggled, wiggling under him, finally pulling my head back enough to free my mouth from his.

"Stop," I gasped. "I'm not Gisselle. I'm Ruby. It was all a prank."

"What?"

I saw from the look in his eyes and the silly smile on his face that he had known. Pressing my hands against his chest, I pushed him away. He sat back, still pretending a look of amazement and shock.

"You're Ruby?"

"Stop it, Beau. You knew all the time. I know you did. I'm not the kind of girl Gisselle is making me out to be. You shouldn't have done that," I admonished. Chastised, he reddened and fired back.

"You played along with the ruse, didn't you?"

"I know and I shouldn't have let her talk me into doing it, but I didn't think she would let it go this far."

Beau nodded, his body relaxing.

"That's my Gisselle . . . always plotting something outrageous. I should pretend to be fooled even more," he said. "It would teach her a lesson."

"What do you mean?" I looked off left and saw that Gisselle and Martin were out by the gazebo. Beau followed my gaze and we saw them kissing. His eyes narrowed and his chin tightened.

"Sometimes, she goes too far," he said, his voice now sounding angry. "Come on," he said, grabbing my hand and standing.

"Where?" I stood up.

"Into the cabana," he said. "It will teach her a lesson."

"But . . . "

"It's all right. We'll just talk. Let her think otherwise though. It will serve her right," he said and tugged me along. Then he opened the cabana door and pulled me into the small room, slamming the door behind us so Gisselle and Martin would be sure to hear it. There was a cot against the far wall but neither of us moved from the door. Without any light, it was hard to see anything after the door had been closed.

"This will get to her," Beau said. "We've been in here before and she knows why."

"This is going too far, Beau. She'll hate me," I said.

"She's not exactly being nice to you right now anyway," he replied.

Talking like this in the pitch darkness was both strange and easy, easy because without seeing him, without feeling his eyes on me, I could relax and say what I wanted. I thought that might be true for him, too.

"I'm sorry I got angry at you before," I said.

"It really isn't any of your fault. I shouldn't have let her talk me into this."

"You were at a disadvantage. Gisselle loves to take advantage of people whenever she can. It doesn't surprise me. But from now on, don't be anyone but yourself. I haven't known you very long, Ruby, but I think you're a very nice girl who's been through some terrible things and has managed to keep her good nature. Don't let Gisselle ruin it," he warned. A moment later, I felt his hand on my cheek. His touch was soft, but I shuddered with surprise.

"Anyway, you kiss better," he whispered. My heart began to thump again. His hand was on my shoulder and then, I felt his breath on my face and sensed his lips moving closer and closer until they found mine. I didn't resist this time, and when his tongue touched mine, I let my own tongue run over the tip of his. He moaned and then, we heard pounding on the door and parted quickly.

"Beau Andreas, you get yourself out here this minute, you hear. This minute," Gisselle cried. Beau laughed.

"Who is it?" he called through the closed door.

"You know very well who I am," she cried. "Now get out here."

Beau opened the door and Gisselle stepped back. A confused Martin stood beside her. She had her arms folded and she wobbled a bit.

"What do you two think you're doing?" she demanded.

"Ruby," he began, "your sister and I—"

"You know I'm not Ruby and she's not me. You know it, Beau Andreas."

"What?" he said, pretending shock and surprise. He looked at me and stepped back. "I could never have known. This is amazing."

"Just stop it, Beau. It was just a little joke. And you," she said, flicking her bloodshot eyes over me. "You played along real well for someone who said she was scared it wouldn't work."

"What is this?" Martin finally said. "Who's who?"

The three of us turned to him. Beau and Gisselle burst into laughter first and then, feeling light-hearted from the rum and Beau's kisses, I couldn't help but laugh myself.

Gisselle explained the prank to Martin and the four of us began again, this time Martin sitting next to me. Gisselle kept pouring the rum into the Cokes, drinking one almost as quickly as she made it. I drank only a little more, but my head was spinning anyway. Afterward, Gisselle pulled Beau into the cabana, gazing back at me with satisfaction as she closed the door behind them.

I sat back on the lounge, unable to clear my mind of Beau's warm touch and Beau's warm kiss. Was it the effect of the rum that filled me with such warmth?

Martin suddenly embraced me and kissed me and tried to go further, but I pushed him away firmly.

"Hey," he said, his eyes half closed, "what's wrong? I thought we were having fun."

"Despite what you might have heard or believed about girls who come from the bayou, Martin, I'm not like that. I'm sorry," I said.

The rum had definitely gotten to him and he

mumbled some apology before falling back on the lounge. Moments later, he was asleep. I waited beside him, but we didn't have to wait long. Suddenly, Beau and Gisselle emerged from the cabana. She was crying about her stomach and heaving so hard, I thought she threw up her lunch as well as her supper. Martin woke up and he and I stood back and watched. She realized what was happening and sobbed with embarrassment.

"I'll take care of her," I told Beau. "You'd better leave."

"Thanks," he said. "This isn't the first time she's done this," he added, and whispered good night after he first whispered, "Yours was the kiss I'll remember tonight."

I was speechless for a moment, watching them walk off, and then Gisselle wailed.

"Oh, I'm going to die!"

"You won't die, but you'll sure wish you had if I remember the way Grandpere felt sometimes," I told her. She moaned again and heaved up some more.

"I've ruined this new blouse," she cried. "Oh, I feel horrible. My head is pounding."

"You'd better go to sleep, Gisselle," I said.

"I can't. I can't move."

"I'll help you into the house. Come on." I embraced her and started her forward.

"Don't let Mother catch us," she warned. "Wait," she said. "Take the bottle of rum in, too." I hated doing all these sneaky things, but I had no choice. With the bottle in the basket in one hand, I helped her up with the other and guided her back to the house, slipping as silently as we could through the door.

It was quiet within. We started up the stairs, Gisselle sniveling to herself. After we reached the landing and started toward her room, I thought I heard something else though. It sounded like someone weeping.

"What's that?" I asked in a whisper.

"What's what?"

"Someone's crying," I said.

"Just get me to my room and forget about it," she said. "Hurry."

We crossed to her door and I helped her in.

"You should take off your clothes and take a shower," I suggested, but she plopped down on her bed and refused to move.

"Leave me alone," she moaned. "Just leave me alone. Hide the bottle in your closet," were her last words.

I stood back and looked at her. She was a dead-weight now. There wasn't anything I could do. I wasn't feeling all that well either and reprimanded myself for letting Gisselle talk me into so many rum and Cokes.

I left her lying facedown on her bed, fully dressed, even wearing her shoes, and started for my room. Once again, however, I heard sobbing. Curious, I crossed the hallway and listened. It was coming from a room down right. I walked softly over to the door and leaned my head against it. There was definitely someone within, crying. It sounded . . . like a man.

The click of footsteps on the stairway sent me scurrying back to my room. I went in quickly and immediately hid the basket with the rum in my closet. Then I went to the door and cracked it open enough to peer out. Daphne, dressed in a flowing blue silk robe, stepped so softly she seemed to glide down the hallway to the master bedroom. Just before she got there, however, she paused as though to listen for the sobbing herself. I saw her shake her head and then go into the bedroom. After she closed her door, I closed mine.

I thought about going out again and knocking on that door to see who was crying. Could it have been my father? Thinking it might have been, I went out and approached the door. I listened, but heard nothing this time. Even so, I knocked softly and waited.

"Anyone in there?" I whispered through the crack between the door and the jamb. There was no response. I knocked again and waited. Still nothing. I was about to turn away when I felt a hand on my shoulder and spun around with a gasp to look into my father's face.

"Ruby," he said, smiling. "Anything wrong?"

"I . . . I thought I heard someone sobbing in this room so I knocked," I said. He shook his head.

"Just your imagination at work, honey," he said. "There hasn't been anyone in that room for years. Where's Gisselle?"

"She just went to sleep," I said quickly. "But I'm almost certain I heard someone," I insisted. He shook his head.

"No. You couldn't have." He smiled. "Gisselle went to bed this early? Must be your good habits are rubbing off already. Well, I'm heading for

347

sleep myself. I've got a busy day tomorrow. Don't forget," he said, "your art instructor will be stopping by at two. I'll be here to meet him also."

I nodded.

"Good night, dear," he said, and kissed me on the forehead. Then he started for the master bedroom. I looked back at the closed door. Could I have imagined it? Was it something that happened because of all the rum I had drunk?

"Daddy?" I said before I crossed to go to my room. He stopped and turned.

"Yes?"

"Whose room was that?" I asked.

He looked at the room and then rolled his dark, shining eyes my way and I saw why they shone— they were full of tears.

"My brother's," he said. "Jean's."

With a sigh he turned and walked away. As if on the legs of a spider, a chill crept up my spine and made me shudder. Fatigued and drowning in many emotions, I returned to my room and got ready for bed. My mind was cluttered with so many different thoughts, my heart full of different feelings. I was so dizzy and tired, I was eager to lay my head upon the soft pillow. When I closed my eyes, a potpourri of the day's images rolled on the backs of my eyelids taking me up and down like a roller coaster. I saw the New Orleans sights I had seen with my father, the myriad of fashions I had waded through with Daphne, my wonderful new art studio, Gisselle's face as she plotted her silly prank and once again, I felt Beau's electrifying kiss when we were in the cabana.

That kiss had frightened me because I had been

unable to stop myself from wanting to kiss him back. That unexpected touch of his lips, his tongue forcing my lips to open, shot through me with a jolt of excitement that tore down all my resistance. Did that mean I was bad, that I had too much of the evil Landry blood running through my veins?

Or was it just that Beau had touched something tender and lonely in me, his soft voice whispering to me in the darkness, his assurances restoring a calm to my bedazzled and bewildered soul? Would any young man's kiss have done that or was it just Beau's?

I tried to remember Paul's kisses, but all those memories were clouded and polluted by the discovery of our real relationship. It was impossible to think of him now as my first love and not feel guilty about it, even though it was neither of our faults.

What a long, complex, and troubling day this had been, and yet what a wonderful one, too. Was this the way my life would be from now on?

The questions tired me out. I longed for sleep. As the drowsiness took over and my mind settled, I heard the faint sound of the sobbing again. It came from the darkest corners of my mind and before I fell asleep, I wasn't sure if it was my own sobbing or the sobbing of someone I had yet to meet.

I was surprised at how late I had slept into the next morning. When I finally awoke, I was sure everyone had gone down and had breakfast without me. Ashamed, I shot out of bed and hurriedly washed and dressed, tying my hair in a bandanna rather than spend the time to brush it out properly. But when I bounced quickly down the stairs and popped into the dining room, I found it empty. Edgar was just cleaning away some cups and dishes.

"Is breakfast over?" I asked.

"Breakfast over? Oh, no, mademoiselle. Monsieur Dumas has eaten and gone to work, but you're the first of the ladies to appear," he replied. "What would you like this morning? Some of Nina's eggs and grits?"

"Yes, thank you," I said. He smiled warmly and said he would bring me some fresh orange juice and a pot of hot coffee. I sat down and waited, expecting to hear either Daphne's or Gisselle's footsteps in the hallway at any moment, but I was still the only one at the table by the time Edgar brought me my complete breakfast. He looked in on me every once in a while to see if there was anything else I wanted.

When I was finished, he was there immediately to clear away my dishes. How long would it take, I wondered, for me to get used to being waited on and looked after like this? I couldn't help having the urge to pick up my own dirty dishes and take them into the kitchen. Edgar smiled down at me.

"And how are you enjoyin' New Orleans, mademoiselle?" he asked.

"I love it," I said. "Have you lived here all your life, Edgar?"

Oh, yes, mademoiselle. My family's been workin' for the Dumas as far back as the Civil War. Of course, they were slaves then," he added, and started for the kitchen. I got up and followed him in to tell Nina how much I had enjoyed her cooking. She looked up with surprise, but was very pleased. She was happy to tell me she had definitely concluded I was no spirit.

"Otherwise, I would be killing a black cat in the cemetery at midnight," she told me.

"My goodness, why?"

"Why? You've got to once a spirit comes haunting. You kill the cat, remove the guts, and cook it all in hot lard with salt and eggs. You eat it as soon as it's lukewarm," she instructed. My stomach started to churn.

"Ugh," I said. "How horrible."

"Then you return to the cemetery the next Friday night and call the cat." Her eyes widened. "When the cat answers, call out the names of the dead people you know and tell the cat that you believe in the devil. When you've seen a spirit once, you'll be sure to see them all the time, so it's best you get to know them and they get to know you.

"Of course," she added as an aside, "this works best in October."

Her talk of spirits made me think about the sobbing I felt sure I had heard in what had been Jean's room.

"Nina, have you ever heard sobbing upstairs coming from what was once my uncle Jean's room?" I asked.

Her eyes, which I thought had become as wide as possible, grew even wider, only now they were full of terror, too.

"You heard that?" she replied. I nodded and

she crossed herself quickly. Then she reached out and seized my wrist. "Come with Nina," she commanded.

"What?"

I let her pull me through the kitchen and out the back way.

"Where are we going, Nina?"

She hurried us through the hallway to the rear of the house.

"This is my room," she told me, and opened the door. I hesitated, gasping at the sight.

The walls of the small room were cluttered with voodoo paraphernalia: dolls and bones, chunks of what looked like black cat fur, strands of hair tied with leather string, twisted roots, and strips of snakeskin. The shelves were crowded with small bottles of multicolored powders, stacks of yellow, blue, green, and brown candles, jars of snake heads, and a picture of a woman sitting on what looked like a throne. Around her picture were white candles.

"That be Marie Laveau," Nina told me when she saw I was looking at the picture, "Voodoo Queen."

Nina had a small bed, a nightstand, and a rattan dresser.

"Sit," she said, pointing to the one and only chair. I did so, slowly. She went to her shelves, found something she wanted, and turned to me. She put a small ceramic jar in my hands and told me to hold it. I smelled the contents.

"Brimstone," she said when I grimaced. Then she lit a white candle and mumbled a prayer. She fixed her eyes on me and said, "Someone put a spell on you for sure. You need to keep the evil spirits away." She brought the candle to the ceramic jar and dipped the flame toward the contents so the brimstone would burn. A small stream of smoke twisted its way up. The stench was unpleasant, but Nina looked relieved that I held onto the jar anyway.

"Close your eyes and lean over so the smoke touches your face," she prescribed. I did so. After a moment, she said, "Okay, good." Then she took the jar from me and smothered the fire. "Now you'll be fine. It's good you do what I say and don't laugh at me.

"But I remember you said your grandmere was a Traiteur woman, right?"

"Yes."

"That's good for you, but remember," she warned, "the evil spirits look to go into holy folk first. That is more of a victory." I nodded.

"Has anyone else ever heard sobbing upstairs, Nina?" I asked.

"It is no good to talk about it. Speak of the devil and he'll come through your door smiling and smoking a long, thin black cigar.

"Now we go back. Madame will come down soon for her breakfast," she told me.

I followed her out again and sure enough, when I re-entered the dining room, I found Daphne dressed and seated at the table.

"Did you have your breakfast?" she asked.

"Yes."

"Where's Gisselle?"

"I guess she's still upstairs," I said. Daphne grimaced.

"This is ridiculous. Why isn't she up and about like the rest of us?" she said, even though she had just risen herself. "Go up and tell her I want her down here immediately, please."

"Yes, madame," I said and hurried up the stairs. I knocked softly on Gisselle's door and then opened it to find her on her side, still asleep and still dressed in the clothes she had worn last night.

"Gisselle, Daphne wants you to wake up and come down," I said, but she didn't move. "Gisselle." I nudged her shoulder. She moaned and turned over, quickly closing her eyes again. "Gisselle."

"Go away," she cried.

"Daphne wants you to—"

"Leave me alone. I feel horrible. My head is killing me and my stomach feels raw inside."

"I told you this would happen. You drank too much too fast," I said.

"Goody for you," she said, her eyes still shut tight.

"What should I tell Daphne?" She didn't respond. "Gisselle?"

"I don't care. Tell her I died," she said, and pulled the pillow over her head. I stared at her for a moment and saw she wasn't going to budge.

Daphne didn't like my report.

"What do you mean she won't get up?" She slapped the coffee cup down so hard on the saucer, I thought it would shatter. "What did you two do last night?" she demanded, her eyes burning with suspicion.

"We just . . . talked to Beau and his friend Martin," I said. "Out by the pool."

354

"Just talked?"

"Yes, ma'am."

"Call me Mother or call me Daphne, but don't call me ma'am. It makes me sound years older than I am," she snapped.

"I'm sorry . . . Mother."

She stared at me furiously a moment and then got up and marched out of the dining room, leaving me standing there with my heart thumping. I didn't lie exactly, I thought. I just didn't tell the whole truth, but if I had, I would have gotten Gisselle into trouble. Even so, I felt bad about it. I wasn't happy about being sneaky and deceptive. Daphne was so upset she pounded her way upstairs.

I wondered what I should do and decided to go to the library to pick out a book and spend the day reading until my art instructor arrived. I was flipping through the pages of a book when I heard Daphne scream from the top of the stairs.

"Ruby!"

I put the book back and hurried to the doorway.

"RUBY!"

"Yes?"

"Get up here this instant," she demanded.

Oh, no, I thought, she's discovered Gisselle's condition and wants to hear the whole story. What was I going to do? How would I protect Gisselle and not lie? When I reached the top of the stairway, I looked across the hallway and saw that the door to my room was wide open and Daphne was standing in my room and not in Gisselle's. I approached slowly.

"Get in here," she commanded. I stepped

through the doorway. She was standing with her arms folded tightly under her bosom, her back straight, and her shoulders up. The skin around her chin was so taut, it looked like it might tear. "I know why Gisselle can't get up," she said. "You two were just talking last night?"

I didn't reply.

"Humph," she said, and then extended her right arm and pointed at my closet. "What is that in your closet on the floor? What is it?" she shrieked when I didn't respond quickly enough.

"A bottle of rum."

"A bottle of rum," she said, nodding, "that you took from our liquor cabinet."

I looked up quickly and started to shake my head.

"Don't deny it. Gisselle has confessed everything . . . how you talked her into taking the rum outside and showed her how to mix it with Coke."

My mouth gaped open.

"What else went on? What did you do with Martin Fowler?" she demanded.

"Nothing," I said. Her eyes grew smaller and she kept nodding as if she heard a string of sentences in her own mind that confirmed some horrible suspicions.

"I told Pierre last night that you had different values, that you grew up in a world so unlike ours, it would be difficult, if not next to impossible, and I told him you could corrupt Gisselle and influence her more than she would influence you. Don't try to deny anything," she snapped when my lips opened. "I was a young girl once. I know the temptations and how easy it is for someone to influence you and get you to do forbidden things."

She shook her head at me.

"And after we were so nice to you, welcoming you into our home, accepting you, with me devoting so much of my time to setting you up properly . . . why is it you people have no sense of decency, no sense of responsibility? Is it in your blood?"

"That's not true. None of this is true," I wailed.

"Please," she said, closing and opening her eyes. "You're cunning. You've been brought up to be shrewd, just like gypsies. Now take this bottle of rum back down to the liquor cabinet."

"I don't even know where that is," I said.

"I'm not going to waste any more of my time on this. It's upset my breakfast and my day as it is. Do it and don't ever do this again. Your father will hear about this, I assure you," she added, and marched past me.

The tears that were burning behind my eyelids broke free and zigzagged down my cheeks to my chin. I went to the closet and picked up the basket. Then I went next door, barging into Gisselle's room. She was taking a shower and singing. I stomped into the bathroom and screamed at her through the glass door.

"What?" she called back, pretending she couldn't hear me. "What?"

"How could you lie and put the blame on me?"

"Wait a minute," she cried, and rinsed her hair before shutting off the water. "Hand me my towel, please," she said. I put the basket down on the counter and got her her towel. "Now, what is it?"

"You told Daphne I was the one who took the bottle of rum," I said. "How could you?"

"Oh, I had to, Ruby. Please don't be mad. I got into trouble about a month ago when I came home very late with whiskey on my breath. I was almost grounded then. She surely would have grounded me now."

"But you blamed me! Now she thinks terrible things about me!"

"You've just arrived. Daddy is still infatuated with you. You can afford to be blamed a little. They won't do anything to you," she explained. "I'm sorry," she said, scrubbing her hair with the towel. "I couldn't think of anything else to do and it worked. It got her off my back."

I sighed.

"We're sisters," she said, smiling. "We've got to help each other out sometimes."

"Not like this, Gisselle, not by lying," I protested.

"Of course by lying. How else? They're just little lies anyway," she said. I looked up sharply. That was just the way Daphne had put things too, little lies. Was this the foundation upon which the Dumas built their happiness and contentment: little lies?

"Don't worry," she said, "I'll smooth it out with Daddy if he seems too upset with you. I'll make it seem as if I encouraged you to encourage me and he'll just be so confused, he won't do anything to either of us. I've done that sort of thing before," she confessed with an oily and evil smile.

"Relax," she said, wrapping her towel around

358

her nude body. "After you have your art lesson, we'll meet Beau and Martin and go down to the French Quarter. We'll have fun, I promise."

"But . . . what am I to do with this? I don't know where the liquor cabinet is."

"It's in the study. I'll show you," she said. "Come help me pick out something to wear."

I shook my head and sighed.

"What a morning this has been already. I told Nina about the sobbing I heard and she hurried me off into her room to burn brimstone and then this."

"The sobbing?"

"Yes," I said, following her out to her closet. "I thought it came from the room that was Jean's."

"Oh," she said as if it were nothing.

"Have you heard it, too?"

"Of course I have," she said. "What about this skirt?" she asked, plucking one off its hanger and holding it against her. "It's not as short as your skirts, but I like the way it fits my hips. And so does Beau," she added, smiling licentiously.

"It's nice. What do you mean, of course you have heard the sobbing? Why of course?"

"Because it's something Daddy often does."

"What? What does he do?"

"He goes into Uncle Jean's room and cries about him. He's done that for . . . for as long as I can remember. He just can't accept the accident and the way things are."

"But he told me no one was crying in there," I said.

"He doesn't like anyone to know. We all

359

pretend it doesn't happen," she explained. I shook my head sadly.

"It was tragic," I said. "He told me about it. Jean sounded like such a wonderful person, and to die that young with everything ahead of you—"

"Die? What do you mean, die? Did he say Uncle Jean died?"

"What? Well, I just . . . he said he was struck by the mast of the sailboat and . . . " I thought for a moment, recalling the details. "And he became a vegetable, but I just assumed he meant . . . "

"Oh, no," she said. "He's not dead."

"He's not? Well, what happened to him then?"

"He's a vegetable, but he's still quite good-looking. He just walks around without a thought in his head and looks at everyone and everything as though he never saw them or remembered them."

"Where is he?"

"In an institution outside of the city. We only see him once a year, on his birthday. At least, that's all I see him. Daddy might go more often. Mother never goes," she said. "How about this blouse?"

She held it up but I was looking right through it. I waited as she put it on.

"Why aren't there any pictures of Jean around?" I asked.

"Will you stop talking about it? Daddy can't stand it normally. I'm surprised he told you anything. There are no pictures because it's too painful for Daddy," she said. "Now, for the last time, what about this blouse?" She turned to look at herself in the mirror.

"It's very nice," I said.

"Oh, I hate that word," she cried. "Nice. Is it sexy?"

I looked at it seriously this time.

"You forgot to put on your bra," I said.

She smiled. "I didn't forget. A lot of girls are doing that these days."

"They are?"

"Of course. Boy, do you have a lot to learn. Lucky you got out of the swamps," she added.

But right now, I wasn't so sure I was so lucky.

15

A Tour of Storyville

I sat with Gisselle on the patio and ate some lunch while she nibbled at her breakfast, complaining how sore her stomach still was from all the vomiting she had done last night. She blamed everyone but herself.

"Beau should have stopped me from drinking too much. I was so busy making sure everyone else had a good time, 1 didn't notice," she claimed.

"I warned you before we began," I reminded her. She smirked.

"It's never done this to me before," she said, but she grimaced in agony.

She had to wear her wide, thick sunglasses because the tiniest light sent ripples of pain up and down her forehead. She had dabbed gobs of rouge on her cheeks and painted her lips thick with lipstick once she saw how pale and wan her complexion was.

The long gray clouds that had made most of the morning dreary had come apart on the journey from one horizon to the other, and a soft sea of blue appeared to accompany the sunshine that rained down upon us to brighten the blossoms of the magnolias and camellias. The blue jays skittered from branch to branch with more spirit and energy, their songs more melodious.

In such a warm, beautiful setting, it was hard to feel unhappy or discouraged, but I couldn't keep the dark foreboding from inching its way into my thoughts. It moved slowly but surely like the shadow of a cloud. Daphne was very disappointed in me. Soon my father would be too, and Gisselle thought it was good for us to lie to both Daphne and him. I felt like going to Nina to ask her to find me a magical solution, some powder or enchanted bone to erase the bad things that had happened.

"Stop sitting there and pouting," Gisselle ordered. "You worry too much."

"Daphne is furious at me, thanks to you," I replied. "And soon Daddy will be, too."

"Why do you keep calling her Daphne? Don't you want to call her Mother?" she wondered. I shifted my gaze away from her and shrugged.

"Of course I do. It's just . . . hard right now. Both of our parents seem like strangers to me. I haven't been living here all my life," I replied, and looked at her. She chewed on my answer as she chewed on her croissant and jam.

"You just called Daddy, Daddy," she said. "Why should that be easier?"

"I don't know," I said quickly, and dropped my gaze so she couldn't see the dishonesty. I couldn't stand living with all this deception. Somehow, someday, it was bound to make our lives more miserable. I felt certain of that.

Gisselle sipped her coffee but continued to stare at me as she chewed lazily.

"What?" I asked, anticipating some question or suspicion.

"What did you do with Beau in the cabana before I came back and knocked on the door?" she demanded. I couldn't help but flush red. Her voice was filled with accusation.

"Nothing. It was Beau's little joke in response to what you did. We just . . . stood there and talked."

"In the dark, Beau Andreas just stood there and talked?" she asked, a wry smile on her face.

"Yes."

"You're not a good liar, sister dear. I'll have to give you lessons."

"That's not something I want to excel at doing," I responded.

"You will. Especially if you want to live in this house," she said nonchalantly.

Before I could reply, Edgar stepped through the French doors and approached us.

"What is it, Edgar?" Gisselle asked petulantly. Because of her hangover, every little noise, every little interruption annoyed her this morning.

"Monsieur Dumas has arrived. He and Madame

Dumas want to see you both in the study," he said.

"Tell them we'll be there in a moment. I'm just finishing my croissant," she said, and turned her back on him.

Edgar threw a glance my way, his eyes showing his unhappiness at Gisselle's tone of voice. I smiled at him and his expression softened.

"Very good, mademoiselle," he said.

"Edgar is such a stuffed shirt. He creeps around the house as if he owns it and everything in it," Gisselle complained. "If I put a vase on a table, he'll return it to where it was originally. Once, I changed all the pictures around in the living room just to annoy him. The next day, they were all back in their original places. He's memorized where everything belongs, down to a glass ashtray. If you don't believe me, try moving something."

"I'm sure he's just taking pride in things and how well they're kept," I said. She shook her head and gobbled down her last piece of croissant.

"Let's go get this over with," she declared, and stood up. As we approached the study, we could hear Daphne complaining.

"Whenever I ask you to come home for lunch or meet me somewhere for lunch, you always have an excuse. You're always too busy to interrupt your precious workday. But all of a sudden, you have all this time to spare to arrange for an art instructor for your Cajun daughter," she decried.

Gisselle smiled at me and grabbed my arm to pull me back so we would delay our entrance.

"This is good. I love it when they have a spat," she whispered excitedly. Not only didn't I want to be an eavesdropper, but I was afraid they would say something to reveal the whole truth.

"I always try to make myself available for you, Daphne. If I can't, it's because of something that can't be helped. And as for coming home today, I thought in light of the circumstances, I had to do something special for her," my father protested.

"Do something special for her in light of the circumstances? What about my circumstances? Why can't you do something special for me? You used to think I was someone special," Daphne retorted.

"I do," he protested.

"But not as special as your Cajun princess apparently. Well, what do you think now after I told you what happened?"

"I'm disappointed of course," he said. "I'm quite surprised." It broke my heart to hear his voice so full of disillusionment, but Gisselle's smile widened with glee.

"Well, I'm not," Daphne emphasized. "I warned you, didn't I?"

"Gisselle," I whispered. "I've got to tell—"

"Come on," she said quickly, and pulled me forward to enter the study. Daphne and our father turned promptly to face us. I could have burst into tears at the sight of his sad and disappointed face. He sighed deeply.

"Sit down, girls," he said, and nodded toward one of the leather sofas. Gisselle moved instantly and I followed, but sat away from her, practically at the other end. Our father stared at us a moment with his hands behind his back and then glanced at Daphne, who pulled her head up and folded her arms under her bosom expectantly. My father turned to me.

"Daphne has told me what happened here last night and what she found in your room. I don't mind either of you having wine at dinner, but sneaking hard liquor and drinking it with boys . . ."

I flashed a look at Gisselle who looked down at her hands in her lap.

"It's not the way young women of character behave. Gisselle," he said, turning to her. "You shouldn't have permitted this to happen."

She pulled off her sunglasses and started to cry, emitting real tears from her eyes at will as if she had some sort of a reservoir of tears stored just under her eyelids to be dipped into at a moment's notice.

"I didn't want to do it, especially right here at our home, but she insisted and I wanted to do what you said: make her feel wanted and loved as soon as I could. Now I'm in trouble," she wailed.

Shocked by what she said, I tried to meet her eyes and hold them, but she refused to look at me, afraid once she did, she couldn't look away.

Daphne widened her eyes and nodded at my father who shook his head.

"I didn't say you were in trouble. I just said I was disappointed in you two, that's all," he replied. "Ruby," he said, turning back to me. "I know that alcoholic beverages were common in your household."

I started to shake my head.

"But we have a different view of that here. There's a time and a place for imbibing and young girls should never do it on their own. Next thing you know, one of your boyfriends gets drunk and everyone gets into the car with him and . . . I just don't like to think what could happen."

"Or what young girls can be talked into doing after they've consumed alcohol," Daphne added. "Don't forget that aspect," she advised my father. He nodded obediently.

"Your mother is right, girls. It's just not a good idea. Now, I'm willing to forgive everyone, put this bad incident aside, as long as I have your solemn promise, both of your solemn promises, that nothing like this will occur again."

"I promise," Gisselle said quickly. "I didn't want to do it anyway. I had a terrible headache this morning. Some people are used to drinking a lot of alcohol and some are not," she added, throwing a glance at me.

"That's very true," Daphne said, glaring at me. I looked away so that no one would see how much I was fuming inside. The heat that built itself up in my chest felt as if it could burn a hole through me.

"Ruby?" my father asked. I swallowed hard to keep my tears from choking me and forced out the words.

"I promise," I said.

"That's good. Now then," he began, but before he could continue, we heard the door chimes. He looked at his watch. "I expect that is Ruby's art instructor," he said.

"Under the circumstances," Daphne said, "don't you think you should postpone this?"

"Postpone? Well . . . " He looked at me and I

looked down quickly. "We can't just turn the man away. He's giving his time, traveled here—"

"You shouldn't have been so impulsive," Daphne said. "Next time, I would like you to discuss it with me before you give the girls anything or do anything for them. After all," she said firmly, "I am their mother."

My father pressed his lips together as if to shut up any words in his mouth and nodded.

"Of course. It won't happen again," he assured her.

"Excuse me, monsieur," Edgar said, coming to the doorway, "but a Professor Ashbury has arrived. His card," he said, handing the card to my father.

"Show him in, Edgar."

"Very good, monsieur," he said.

"I don't think you need me for this," Daphne said. "I have some phone calls to return. As you predicted, everyone and anyone who knows us wants to hear the story of Ruby's disappearance and arrival. Telling the story repeatedly is proving to be exhausting. We should have it printed and distributed," she added, spun on her heels and marched out of the study.

"I've got to go take a couple of aspirins," Gisselle said, sitting up quickly. "You can tell me about your instructor later, Ruby," she said, smiling at me. I didn't smile back. As she left the study, Edgar brought in Professor Ashbury, so I had no time to tell my father the truth about what had occurred the night before.

"Professor Ashbury, how do you do?" my father said, extending his hand.

Looking like he was in his early fifties, Herbert Ashbury stood about five-feet-nine and wore a gray sports jacket, a light blue shirt, a dark blue tie, and a pair of dark blue jeans. He had a lean face, all of his features sharply cut, his nose angular and a bit long, his mouth thin and smooth like a woman's.

"How do you do, Monsieur Dumas," the professor said in what I thought was a rather soft voice. He extended a long hand with fingers that enveloped my father's hand when they shook. He wore a beautifully hand crafted silver ring set with a turquoise on his pinky.

"Fine, thank you, and thank you for coming and agreeing to consider my daughter. May I present my daughter Ruby," Daddy said proudly, turning toward me.

Because of his narrow cheeks and the way his forehead sloped sharply back into his hairline, Professor Ashbury's eyes appeared larger than they were. Dark brown eyes with specks of gray, they seized onto whatever he was gazing at and held so firmly he looked mesmerized. Right now they fixed so tightly on my face, I couldn't help but be self-conscious.

"Hello," I said quickly.

He combed his long thin fingers through the wild strands of his thin light brown and gray hair, driving the strands off his forehead, and flashed a smile, his eyes flickering for a moment and then growing serious again.

"Where have you had your art instruction up until now, mademoiselle?" he inquired.

"Just a little in public school," I replied.

"Public school?" he said, turning down the corners of his mouth as if I had said "reform school." He turned to my father for an explanation.

"That's why I thought it would be of great benefit to her at this time to have private instruction from a reputable and highly respected teacher," my father said.

"I don't understand, monsieur. I was told your daughter has had some of her works accepted by one of our art galleries. I just assumed . . . "

"That's true," my father replied, smiling. "I will show you one of her pictures. Actually, the only one in my possession at the moment."

"Oh?" Professor Ashbury said, a look of perplexity on his face. "Only one?"

"That's another story, Professor. First things first. Right this way," he instructed, and led the professor to his office where my picture of the blue heron still remained on the floor against his desk.

Professor Ashbury stared at it a moment and then stepped forward to pick it up.

"May I?" he asked Daddy.

"By all means, please."

Professor Ashbury lifted the picture and held it out at arm's length for a moment. Then he nodded and put it down slowly.

"I like that," he said, then turned to me. "You caught a sense of movement. It has a realistic feel and yet . . . there's something mysterious about it. There's an intelligent use of shading. The setting is rather well captured, too. . . . Have you spent time in the bayou?"

"I lived there all of my life," I said.

Professor Ashbury's eyes lit with interest. He shook his head and turned to Daddy. "Forgive me, monsieur," he said, "I don't mean to sound like an interrogator, but I thought you had introduced Ruby as your daughter."

"I did and she is," Daddy said. "She didn't live with me until now."

"I see," he said, gazing at me again. He didn't seem shocked or surprised by the information, but he felt he had to continue to justify his interest in our personal lives. "I like to know something about my students, especially the ones I take on privately. Art, real art, comes from inside," he said, placing the palm of his right hand over his heart. "I can teach her the mechanics, but what she brings to the canvas is something no teacher can create or teach. She brings herself, her life, her experience, her vision," he said. "Do you understand, monsieur?"

"Er . . . yes," Daddy said. "Of course. You can learn all about her if you like. The main question is do you believe as some already have exhibited they do, that she has talent?"

"Absolutely," Professor Ashbury said. He looked at my picture again and then turned back to me. "She might be the best student I've ever had," he added.

My mouth gaped open and my father's face lit with pride. He beamed a broad smile and nodded.

"I thought so, even though I'm no art expert."

"It doesn't take an art expert to see what potential lies here," Professor Ashbury said, looking at my painting once more.

"Let me show you the studio then," my father

371

said, and led Professor Ashbury and me down the corridor. The professor was very impressed, as anyone would be, I imagined.

"It's better than what I have at the college," he whispered as if he didn't want the college trustees to hear.

"When I believe in something or someone, Professor Ashbury, I commit myself fully," my father declared.

"I can see that. Very well, monsieur," he said with some pomposity, "I accept your daughter as one of my students. Provided, of course," he added, shifting his eyes to me, "she is willing to accept my tutelage completely and without question."

"I'm sure she is. Ruby?"

"What? Oh, yes. Thank you," I said quickly. I was still absorbing Professor Ashbury's earlier compliments.

"I will take you through the fundamentals once again," he warned. "I will teach you discipline, and only when I think you are ready, will I turn you loose on your own imaginative powers. Many are born with talent," he declared, "but few have the discipline to develop it properly."

"She does," my father assured him.

"We'll see, monsieur."

"Come to my office, Professor, and we will discuss the financial arrangements," my father said. Professor Ashbury, his eyes still fixed on me, nodded. "When can she have her first lesson with you, Professor?"

"This coming Monday, monsieur," he replied. "Although she has one of the finest home studios in the city, I might ask her to come to mine from time to time," he added.

"That won't be a problem."

"Tres bien," Professor Ashbury said. He nodded at me and left with my father.

My heart was pounding with excitement. Grandmere Catherine had always been so positive about my artistic talent. She had no formal schooling and knew little about art, and yet she was convinced down to her soul that I would be a success. How many times had she assured me of this, and now, an art instructor, a professor at a college, had taken one look at my work and declared me very possibly his best candidate.

Still trembling with joy, I hurried upstairs to tell Gisselle, my heart so full, I had no room for anger anymore. I gushed out all the professor had said. Gisselle, trying on different hats at her vanity table, listened and then turned with a look of puzzlement on her face.

"You really want to spend hours with a teacher after spending most of the day in school?" she asked.

"Of course. This is different. This is . . . what I've always dreamt of doing," I replied.

She shrugged.

"I wouldn't. That's why I never pushed for the singing teacher. We have so little time to have fun. They're always finding things for us to do: teachers pile on the homework, make us study for tests, and then we have to fit our lives to our parents' schedules.

"Once you get to know some of the boys and

make some friends, you won't want to waste your time with art instruction," she declared.

"It's not a waste of my time."

"Please," she sighed. "Here," she said, tossing a dark blue beret at me. "Try this on. We're going to the French Quarter to have some fun. You don't want to tag along looking like someone just born," she added.

We heard the sound of a car horn, a funny *bleep, bleep, bleep.*

"That's Beau and Martin. Come on," she said, jumping up. She grabbed my hand and pulled me along, not showing the slightest regret for the things she had said to our father and Daphne about me only a short while ago. Lies did float about this house as lightly as balloons.

"You're not going to lie to us again about which one of you is which, are you?" Martin asked, smiling as he pulled open the door to Beau's sports car for us.

"Now that you're looking at me in broad daylight," Gisselle retorted, "you surely can tell I'm Gisselle." Martin glanced from me to her and nodded.

"Yes, I can," he said, but he said it in such a way to make it hard to tell if he were complimenting her or complimenting me. Beau laughed. Annoyed, Gisselle declared she and I would sit in the back together.

We squeezed tightly into the small rear seat of Beau's sports car and held our berets on our heads as he shot away from the curve. Speeding down the street, we screamed, Gisselle's voice louder and more filled with pleasure and glee than mine which was driven by a pounding heart as we spun around a turn, tires squealing. I imagined we made quite a sight, twins, their ruby red hair dancing and flicking like flames in the wind. People stopped walking to pause and watch us rush by. Young men whistled and howled.

"Don't you just love it when men do that?" Gisselle screamed in my ear. With the sound of the engine and the wind whistling by us, we had to shout to be heard even sitting next to each other.

I wasn't sure what to say. On occasion in the bayou, walking to town, I recalled men driving by in trucks and cars whistling and calling to me like this. When I was younger, I thought it was funny, but I remembered once being frightened when a man in a dirty brown pickup truck not only called to me, but slowed down and followed me along the road, urging me to get into the truck with him. He claimed he would give me a ride to town, but there was something about the way he leered at me that set my heart thumping. I ended up running back toward home and he drove off. I was afraid to tell Grandmere Catherine because I was sure she would stop letting me walk to town by myself.

And yet, I also knew there were girls my age and older who could parade up and down the street day in and day out and never get a second look. It was flattering and threatening at the same time, but my twin sister seemed to draw satisfaction from this attention and looked surprised that I wasn't having a similar reaction.

Our tour of the French Quarter was quite

different from the one my father had taken me on, for with Beau, Martin, and Gisselle, I was shown things I hadn't seen even though we were walking on the same streets. Maybe it was because we were there at a later part of the day, but the women I saw lingering in the doorways of jazz clubs and bars now were scantily dressed in what at times looked like no more than undergarments to me. Their faces were heavily made up, some using so much rouge and lipstick and eyeliner, they resembled clowns.

Beau and Martin gawked with interest, their faces frozen in licentious smiles. Every once in a while, one would lean over to the other and whisper something that set them both laughing hysterically. Gisselle was always jabbing one or the other with her elbow and then laughing herself.

The courtyards looked darker, the shadows were deeper, the music was louder. Men and in some places, women, hawked from doorways of sparsely lit bars and restaurants entreating the pedestrians to come in and enjoy the best jazz, the best dancing, the best food in New Orleans. We stopped at a stand to buy poor boy sandwiches and Beau managed to get us all bottles of beer even though no one was of age. We sat at a table on the sidewalk and ate and drank, and when two policemen came walking down the other side of the street, my heart thumped in anticipation of all of us being arrested. But they didn't seem to notice or care.

Afterward, we rushed in and out of stores, amusing ourselves with the souvenirs, the toys, and novelties. Then Gisselle directed us into a small store that advertised the most shocking sexual items I had ever seen displayed. You were supposed to be eighteen or over to go into the store, but the salesman didn't chase us out. The boys lingered over magazines and books, smirking and giggling to themselves. Gisselle made me look at a replica of a man's sex organ made of hard rubber. When she asked the salesman if she could see it, I ran out of the store.

They all followed a few moments later, laughing at me.

"I guess Daddy didn't take you in there when he showed you the French Quarter," Gisselle quipped.

"How disgusting," I said. "Why would people buy those things?"

My question made Gisselle and Martin laugh harder, but Beau just smiled.

At the next corner, Martin asked us to wait while he approached a man dressed in a black leather vest with no shirt beneath. He had tattoos on his arms and shoulders. The man listened to Martin and then the both of them walked deeper into the alleyway.

"What's Martin doing?" I asked.

"Getting us something for later," Gisselle said, then looked at Beau, who smiled.

"Getting what?"

"You'll see," she said. Martin emerged, nodding with satisfaction.

"Where do you want to go now?" he asked.

"Let's show her Storyville," Gisselle decided.

"Maybe we should just go down to the nice stores and arcades at the ocean," Beau suggested.

"Oh, it won't hurt her. Besides, she needs an education if she wants to live in New Orleans," Gisselle insisted.

"What is Storyville?" I asked. In my mind I imagined a place where people sold books and items based on famous tales. "What do they sell there?"

My question threw the three of them into another fit of hysterics.

"I don't see why you should laugh at everything I say and ask," I said angrily. "If any of you came into the bayou and went out in the swamp with me, you'd ask a lot of dumb questions, too. And I assure you, you'd be a lot more frightened than I would be," I added. That wiped the smiles and laughter off their faces.

"She's right," Beau said.

"So what. You're in the city now, not the swamp," Gisselle said. "And I, for one, don't have any intention of ever going to the bayou.

"Come on," she added, grabbing my arm roughly, "we'll take you up some streets and you tell us what you think is sold there."

Her challenge restored the smile to Martin's face, but Beau still looked troubled. Unable to cast off my own curiosity now, I let Gisselle take me along until we reached a corner and looked across the street at what seemed to me to be a row of fancy houses.

"Where are the stores?" I asked.

"Just watch over there," Gisselle pointed. She indicated an imposing four-story structure with bay windows on the side and a cupola on the roof. It was painted in a dull white. A luxurious limousine pulled up at the curb and the chauffeur stepped out quickly to open the door for what looked to be a very distinguished older man. He strutted up the short set of steps to the front of the house and rang the bell. A moment later, the large door was pulled open.

We were close enough to hear the music that poured out and see the woman who greeted the gentleman. She was tall and dark olive in complexion. She wore a dress of red brocade with what had to be imitation diamonds on her neck and wrist. They had to be imitation, they were so big; but what was most curious was she wore tall feathers pluming from her head.

Looking past her, I could see a wide entrance hall, crystal chandeliers, gold mirrors, and velvet settees. A black piano player was running his hands over the keys and bouncing on the stool. Just before the door was closed, I caught sight of a girl wearing nothing more than a pair of panties and a bra and carrying a tray filled with what looked like glasses of champagne.

"What is that place?" I asked with a gasp.

"Lulu White's," Beau replied.

"I don't understand. Is it a party?"

"Only for those who pay for it," Gisselle said. "It's a brothel. A whorehouse," she added when I didn't respond quickly.

I gaped back at the big door. A moment later, it was opened again and this time, a gentleman appeared escorting a young woman in a bright green dress with a neckline that practically plummeted to her belly button. For a moment the girl's face was hidden by a fan of white feathers, but when she pulled the fan back, I saw her face and felt my mouth fall open. She brought the man to his waiting car and gave him a big kiss before he stepped into the rear. As the car pulled away, she looked up and saw us.

It was Annie Gray, the quadroon girl who had ridden on the bus with me to New Orleans and used voodoo magic to help me find my father's address. She recognized me immediately, too.

"Ruby!" she called and waved.

"Huh?" Martin said.

"She knows you?" Beau asked.

Gisselle just stepped back, amazed.

"Hello," I called.

"I see you found your way about the city real good, huh?" I nodded, my throat tight. She looked back at the front door. "My aunt works here. I'm just helpin' her out some," she said. "But soon, I'm gettin' a real job. You find your daddy okay?" I nodded. "Hello, boys," she said.

"Hi," Martin said. Beau just nodded.

"I've got to get back inside," Annie said. "You just wait and see. I'll be singin' someplace real soon," she added, and hurried back up the steps. She turned in the doorway and waved and then disappeared within.

"I don't believe it. You know her?" Gisselle declared.

"I met her on the bus," I started to explain.

"You know a real prostitute," she followed. "And you said you didn't know what was here?"

"I didn't," I protested.

"Little miss goody-goody knows a prostitute," Gisselle continued, addressing herself to the boys.

380

They both looked at me as if they had just met me.

"I don't really know her," I insisted, but Gisselle just smiled.

"I don't!"

"Let's go," Gisselle said.

We walked back quickly, no one speaking for quite a while. Every once in a while, Martin would look at me, smile, and shake his head.

"Where should we go to do it?" Beau asked after we all got back into his car.

"My house," Gisselle said. "My mother is probably off at a tea party and Daddy is surely still at work."

"To do what?" I asked.

"Just wait and see," she said. Then she added for the boys, "She probably knows all about it anyway. She knows a prostitute."

"I told you, I don't really know her. I just sat on a bus with her," I insisted.

"She knew you were looking for your daddy. Sounds like you two knew each other real well," Gisselle teased. "You didn't work together someplace, did you?" she asked. Martin spun around, his face full of laughter and curiosity.

"Stop it, Gisselle," I snapped.

Beau pulled away from the curb and shot down the street, leaving her laughter falling behind us.

Edgar greeted us all at the doorway when we returned to the house.

"My mother at home?" Gisselle asked him.

"No, mademoiselle," he replied. She threw a conspiratorial glance at Martin and Beau and then we followed her up the stairway to her room.

"What are we doing?" I asked when she cast off her beret and opened the windows as wide as they would go. Beau flopped on her bed and Martin sat at the vanity table smiling stupidly at me.

"Close the door," she ordered. I did so slowly. Then she nodded at Martin who dug into his pocket and produced what to me looked like the cigarettes Grandpere Jack often rolled for himself.

"Cigarettes?" I said, a bit surprised and even a bit relieved. I knew some kids in the bayou who had started smoking when they were ten or eleven. Some parents didn't even mind, but most did. I never liked the taste nor the feeling that my mouth was turning into an ashtray. I also hated the way some of my school friends' clothing reeked of the smoke.

"Those aren't cigarettes. They're joints," Gisselle said.

"Joints?"

Martin's smile widened. Beau sat up, his eyebrows raised, a look of curiosity about me on his face. I shook my head.

"You never heard of pot, marijuana?" Gisselle asked.

I made a small O with my lips. I had never actually seen it this close up, but I did know of it. There were some small shack bars in the bayou in which such things were supposedly taking place, but Grandmere Catherine had warned me about ever going near them. And some of the kids at school talked about it, with some supposedly smoking it. But no one I had been friendly with did.

"Of course, I've heard of it," I said.

"But you never tried it?" she asked with a smile. I shook my head.

"Should we believe her this time, Beau?" she asked. He shrugged.

"It's the truth," I insisted.

"So this will be your first time," Gisselle said. "Martin." He got up and passed one of the cigarettes to each of us. I hesitated to take mine.

"Go on; it won't bite you," he said, laughing. "You'll love it."

"If you want to hang out with us and the rest of my friends, you can't be a drip," Gisselle said.

I looked at Beau.

"You should try it at least once," he said.

Reluctantly, I took it. Martin lit everyone's and I took a quick puff on mine, blowing the smoke out the moment I felt it touch my tongue.

"No, no, no," Gisselle said. "You don't smoke it like a cigarette. Are you pretending or are you really this dumb?"

"I'm not dumb," I said indignantly. I looked at Beau who had lain back on the bed and inhaled his marijuana cigarette with obvious experience.

"It's not bad," he announced.

"You inhale the smoke and hold it in your mouth for a while," Gisselle instructed. "Go on, do it," she commanded, standing over me with those stone eyes riveted. Reluctantly, I obeyed.

"That's it," Martin said. He was squatting on the floor and puffing on his.

Gisselle put on some music. Everyone's eyes were on me so I continued to puff and inhale, hold the smoke and exhale. I wasn't sure what was supposed to happen, but soon I had a very light-headed feeling. It was as if I could close my eyes and float to the ceiling. I must have had a very funny expression on my face, for the three of them started to laugh again, only this time, without even knowing why, I laughed, too. That made them laugh harder which made me laugh harder. In fact, I was laughing so hard, my stomach started to ache, and no matter how it ached, I couldn't stop laughing. Every time I paused, I looked at one or the other of them and started in again.

Suddenly, my laughing turned to crying. I don't know why it did; it just did. I felt the tears and the expression on my face change. Before I realized it, I was sitting there on the floor, my legs crossed under each other, bawling like a baby.

"Uh-oh," Beau said. He got up quickly and ripped the marijuana cigarette from my fingers. Then he dropped mine and what was left of his own down Gisselle's toilet.

"Hey, that's good stuff," Martin called. "And expensive, too," he added.

"You better do something, Gisselle," Beau said when he saw my crying hadn't ended, but in fact, had gotten worse. My shoulders shook and my chest ached, but I couldn't stop myself. "The stuff was too strong for her."

"What am I supposed to do?" Gisselle cried.

"Calm her down."

"You calm her down," Gisselle said, and sprawled out on her back on the floor. Martin giggled and crawled up beside her.

"Great," Beau said. He approached me and took my arm. "Come on, Ruby. You'd better go lie down in your own room. Come on," he urged.

Still sobbing, I let him help me to my feet and guide me out the door.

"This your room?" he asked, nodding toward the adjacent door. I nodded back and he opened it and led me in. He brought me to my bed and I lay back, my hands over my eyes. Gradually, my sobs grew smaller and wider apart until I was just sniveling. Suddenly, I started to hiccup and I couldn't stop. He went into my bathroom and brought out a glass of water.

"Drink some of this," he said, sitting down beside me and helping me to raise my head. He brought the glass to my lips and I swallowed some water.

"Thank you," I muttered, and then I started to laugh again.

"Oh, no," he said. "Come on, Ruby, get control of yourself. Come on," he urged. I tried to hold my breath, but the air exploded in my mouth, pushing my lips open. Anything and everything I did made me laugh again and again. Finally, I grew too exhausted, swallowed some of the water, closed my eyes, and took deep breaths.

"I'm sorry," I moaned. "I'm sorry."

"It's all right. I've heard of people having a reaction like that, but I haven't seen it before. You feel a little better?"

"I feel all right. Just tired," I added, and let myself fall back to the pillow.

"You're a real mystery, Ruby," he said. "You seem to know a lot more about things than Gisselle does and yet you seem to know a lot less, too."

"I'm not lying," I said.

"What?"

385

"I'm not lying. I just met her on the bus."

"Oh." He sat there for a while. I felt his hand brush my hair and then I sensed him leaning over to kiss me softly on my lips. I didn't open my eyes during the kiss, nor did I open them after, and later, when I thought about it, I wasn't sure if it really had happened or it had been just another part of my reaction to the marijuana.

I was sure I felt him stand up, but I was fast asleep before he reached the door and I didn't wake up again until I felt someone shaking my shoulder so vigorously, the entire bed shook along with it. I opened my eyes and looked up at Gisselle.

"Mother sent me up to get you," she complained.

"What?"

"They're waiting at the dinner table, stupid."

I sat up slowly and ground the sleep out of my eyes so I could gaze at the clock.

"I must have passed out," I said, shocked at the time.

"Yeah, you did, but just don't tell them why or anything about what we did, understand?" she said.

"Of course I won't."

"Good." She stared at me a moment and then her lips softened into a sly smile. "Beau seems to like you a lot," she said. "He was very upset over what happened."

I stared back at her, speechless. It was like waiting for the second shoe to drop and then she dropped it. She shrugged.

"I'm getting bored with him anyway," she said.

"Maybe I'll let you have him. Later on, you can do something nice for me," she added. "Hurry up and come down."

I watched her leave the room and then I shook my head and wondered why any boy would like a girl who treated his affection so lightly she could give it away at a whim and look for someone else.

Or was she pretending to give away something she was already losing? And more important, was it something I wanted?

16

Fitting In

A few days later, the holidays ended and school resumed. Despite everyone's assurances, including Beau's solemn promise to be at my side as much as he could, and Nina's giving me another good luck charm, I couldn't help but be apprehensive and terribly nervous about entering a new high school, especially a city high school.

Beau came by to pick up Gisselle and take her to school, but on this, my first school morning in New Orleans, both Daphne and my father were going to accompany me to registration.

I let Gisselle choose the skirt and blouse I was going to wear, and once again, she decided she would borrow one of my new outfits until she had gotten Daphne to buy her a dozen or so of her own.

"I can't save you a seat near me in any of our classes," she told me before rushing down to meet

Beau. "I'm surrounded by boys, any one of whom would die rather than move. But don't worry. We'll save you a place right next to us in the cafeteria lunch hour," she added breathlessly. She was hurrying because Beau had honked twice and, thanks to her she said, they had been late for school three times this month with a week's detention hovering as punishment on the next tardiness.

"Okay," I called after her. So nervous I felt numb down to my fingertips, I gazed at myself one more time in the mirror, and then went down to wait for my father and Daphne. That was when Nina slipped me my good gris-gris, another section of a black cat's leg bone. Of course, the cat had to have been killed exactly at midnight. I thanked her and stuffed it deep into my pocketbook, alongside the piece of bone Annie Gray had given me. With all this good luck, how could I go wrong? I thought.

A few moments later, Daphne and my father came down the stairs. Daphne looked very chic with her hair brushed back and braided. She wore gold hoop earrings and had chosen to wear an ivory-colored cotton dress that had a belt just under her bosom, long sleeves with frilly cuffs and a high neck. In her high heels and carrying a small parasol that matched her dress, she looked more like a woman dressing for an afternoon lawn party than a mother going to a high school to register her daughter for classes.

My father was full of smiles, but Daphne was very concerned that I begin school in New Orleans with the correct attitude.

"Everyone knows about you by now," she

lectured after we got into the car and drove down the driveway. "You've been the topic of conversation at every bridge game, afternoon tea, and dinner in the Garden District as well as other places. So you can expect the children of these people will be curious about you, too.

"The thing to remember is that now you carry the Dumas name. No matter what happens, no matter what anyone says to you, keep that in the forefront of your thoughts. What you do and what you say reflects on all of us. Do you understand, Ruby?"

"Yes, ma'am. I mean Mother," I said quickly. She had begun to grimace, but my speedy correction pleased her.

"It will be fine," my father said. "You'll get along with everyone and make new friends so quickly your head will spin. I'm sure."

"Just be sure you choose the right friends, Ruby," Daphne warned. "Over the last few years, a different class of people has found their way into this district, some without the breeding or background that Creoles of good standing possess."

A flutter of panic crisscrossed my chest. How would I know how to distinguish a Creole of good breeding from anyone else? Daphne sensed my trepidation.

"If you have any doubts, check with Gisselle first," she added.

Gisselle attended and now I was to attend the Beauregard School, named after a Confederate general about whom few of the students knew or cared to know much. A statue of him standing with his sword drawn and held high had fallen victim to an army of vandals over the years, some of it terribly stained, some of it chipped and cracked. It stood at the center of the square in front of the main entrance.

We arrived just after the first bell announcing the start of the day had rung. To me, the redbrick school looked immense and austere, its looming three floors casting a long dark shadow over the hedges, the flowers, sycamore, oak, and magnolia trees. After we parked and entered the building, we found our way to the principal's office. There was an outer office with an elderly lady serving as secretary. She seemed overwhelmed by the pile of paperwork, the ringing of phones, and the demands of other students who paraded up to her desk with a variety of problems. Her fingers were stained blue from running off multiple copies of messages and announcements on the mimeograph machine. She even had a streak of ink along the right side of her chin. I was sure she had arrived looking prim and proper, but right now strands of her blue-gray hair curled out like broken guitar strings and her glasses perched precariously at the bridge of her nose.

When we entered, she looked up, took in Daphne, turned away from the students and immediately began to primp her hair back until she saw the stains on her fingers. Then she sat down and quickly dropped her hands under her desk.

"Good morning, Madame Dumas," she said. "Monsieur." She nodded at my father who smiled and then she flashed a smile at me. "And this is our new student?"

"Yes," Daphne said. "We have an eight o'clock appointment with Dr. Storm," she added, glancing at the wall clock which had just struck eight.

"Of course, madame. I'll inform him you have arrived," she said, rising. She knocked on the inner office door and then created just enough of an opening to slip herself into the principal's office, closing the door quietly behind her.

The students who had been there retreated from the office, their eyes fixed on me so intently, I felt as if I had a wart on the tip of my nose. After they left, I gazed around at the shelves of pamphlets neatly organized, the posters announcing upcoming sporting and dramatics events, and the posted lists of rules and regulations for fire drills, air-raid drills, and accepted behavior in and out of classes. I noted that smoking was expressly forbidden and that vandalism, despite the condition of the Beauregard statue, was an offense punishable with expulsion.

The secretary reappeared and held the door open for us as she declared, "Dr. Storm will see you now."

Three chairs had been arranged for us in front of the principal's desk. I felt like I had swallowed a dozen live butterflies and envied Daphne for her poise and self-assurance as she led the way. The principal rose to greet us.

Dr. Lawrence P. Storm, as his nameplate read, was a short, stout man with a round face, the jowls of which dipped a half inch or so below his jawline.

He had thick, rubbery lips and bulging dull brown eyes that reminded me of fish. Later, Daphne, who seemed to know everything about anyone in any position of importance, would tell me he suffered from a thyroid condition but she assured me he was the most impressive high school principal in the city with a doctorate in educational philosophy.

Dr. Storm wore his pale yellow hair brushed flat with a part in the center. He extended his puffy small hand and my father took it quickly.

"Monsieur Dumas and Madame Dumas," he said, nodding to Daphne. "You both look well."

"Thank you, Dr. Storm," my father said, but Daphne, who wasn't hiding her discomfort over having this duty, went right to business.

"We're here to register our daughter. I'm sure you know the details by now," she added.

Dr. Storm's bushy eyebrows rose like two caterpillars nudged.

"Yes, madame. Please, have a seat," he said, and we all sat down. Immediately, he began to shuffle papers. "I have had all the paperwork prepared in anticipation of your arrival. I understand your name is Ruby?" he said, looking at me for the first time.

"Yes, monsieur."

"Dr. Storm," Daphne corrected.

"Dr. Storm," I said. He held a tight smile.

"Well now, Ruby," he continued. "Let me welcome you to our school and say that I hope it will be a truly enjoyable and productive experience for you. I have managed to place you in all of your sister's classes so that she can help you catch up.

We will make an attempt to get her transcripts from her previous school," he said, turning to my father, "and any information you can provide to expedite the matter will be appreciated, monsieur."

"Of course," my father said.

"You did attend school this year, did you not, Ruby?" Dr. Storm asked.

"Yes, Dr. Storm. I always attended school," I added pointedly.

"Very good," he said, and then clasped his thick hands together on the desk and leaned forward, his body gliding up into his suit jacket to fill out the shoulders. "But I expect you will find this educational experience somewhat different, my dear. To begin with, the Beauregard School is considered one of the best in the city, one of the most advanced. We have the finest teachers and we have the best results."

He smiled at my father and Daphne and continued.

"Needless to say, you have a rather unique situation here. Your notoriety, the events of your past, have, I am sure, preceded you. You will be the subject of a great deal of curiosity, gossip, etc. In short, you will be the center of attention for some time, which, unfortunately, will make your adjustment that much more difficult.

"But not impossible," he quickly added when he saw the panic written on my face. "I will be available to counsel you and aid you in any way possible. Just come by this office and ask for me whenever you like." His rubbery lips stretched and stretched until they were as thin as pencils and the corners were sharply drawn into his plump cheeks.

"This is your schedule," he said, handing me a sheet of paper. "I have asked one of our honor students, who happens to be in all of your classes, too, to guide you about today." He turned to my father and Daphne.

"It's one of the responsibilities of our honor students. I thought about asking Gisselle, but decided that might just bring more attention to the both of them. I hope you agree."

"Of course, Dr. Storm."

"You understand why we don't have the papers you would ordinarily need for a registration," Daphne said. "This situation has just fallen on us."

"Oh, certainly," Dr. Storm said. "Don't worry about it. I'll take whatever information you have and follow it up like a Sherlock Holmes until we have what we need."

He returned his gaze to me and sat back in his seat.

"Because you are unfamiliar with our rules and regulations and because you will find we do things differently here, I imagine, I have had this pamphlet prepared for you," he said, and held up a packet of stapled papers. "It describes every-thing—our dress codes, behavior codes, grading systems, in short, what is and what is not expected of you.

"I'm sure," he continued, smiling widely again, "that with your home and your family, none of this will prove difficult for you. However," he added, turning firm, "we do have our standards to maintain and we will maintain them. Do you understand?"

"Yes, sir."

"Dr. Storm," he corrected this time himself.

"Dr. Storm."

He smiled again.

"Well then, no sense in keeping her from starting." He rose from his seat and went to the door. "Mrs. Eltz," he said. "Please send for Caroline Higgins." He returned to his desk. "While she is in class, we can go through whatever you have in terms of information about her and I will take it from there. Please be assured," he added, narrowing his eyes, "that whatever you tell me will be held in the strictest confidence."

"I imagine," Daphne said in an icy voice, "that we won't be telling you anything you don't already know."

Daphne's regal posture and aristocratic tone was like water thrown on a budding fire. Dr. Storm appeared to shrink in his chair. His smile was weaker, his retreat from an important administrator to educational bureaucrat well underway. He stuttered, fumbled through some forms and documents, and looked relieved when Mrs. Eltz knocked on the door to announce Caroline Higgins's arrival.

"Good, good," he said, rising again. "Come along then, Ruby. Let's get you started." He escorted me into the outer office, welcoming the distraction and the temporary reprieve from Daphne's demanding gaze.

"This is Ruby Dumas, Caroline," he said, introducing me to a slim, dark haired girl with a pale complexion and a homely face with glasses as thick as goggles that made her eyes seem grotesquely large. Her thin mouth turned downward at the corners, giving her a habitually despondent appearance. She flicked a tiny, nervous smile and extended her slight hand. We shook quickly.

"Caroline already knows what has to be done," Dr. Storm said. "What's first, Caroline?" he asked as if to test her.

"English, Dr. Storm."

"Right. Okay, girls, precede. And remember, Ruby, the door to my office is always open for you."

"Thank you, Dr. Storm," I said, and followed Caroline into the corridor. As soon as we took a half-dozen steps away, she stopped and turned, this time, smiling wider and looking happier.

"Hi. I might as well tell you what everyone calls me so you don't get confused . . . Mookie," she revealed.

"Mookie? Why?"

She shrugged.

"Someone just called me that one day and it stuck like flypaper. If I don't respond when someone calls me that, he or she just doesn't try again," she explained with a tone of resignation. "Anyway, I'm really excited about being your guide. Everyone's been talking about you and Gisselle, and what happened when you were just babies. Mr. Stegman is trying to discuss Edgar Allan Poe, but no one's paying attention. All eyes are on the door and when I was called to come get you, the class started buzzing so much, he had to shout for quiet."

After hearing that preamble, I was terrified of entering the room. But I had to. With my heart pounding so hard that I could feel the thump reverberating down my spine, I followed Mookie, half listening to her description of the school's layout: which corridors were where, where the cafeteria, the gym, and the nurse's office were, and how to get to the ball fields. We paused at the doorway of the English classroom.

"Ready?" she asked.

"No, but I have no choice," I said. She laughed and opened the door.

It was as if a wind had blown into the room and spun everyone's head around. Even the teacher, a tall man with coal black hair and narrow, dark eyes, froze for a moment, his right forefinger up in the air. I searched the sea of curious faces and found Gisselle sitting in the far right corner, a smirk on her face. Just as she had said, she was surrounded by boys, but neither Beau nor Martin were in this class.

"Good morning," Mr. Stegman said, regaining his composure quickly. "Needless to say, we've been expecting you. Please take this seat," he said, indicating the third seat in the row closest to the door. I was surprised there was a desk available that close to the front, but I discovered I was sitting right behind Mookie and imagined it had been prearranged.

"Thank you," I said, and hurried to it, carrying the notebooks, pens, and pencils Daphne had made sure I had.

"My name is Mr. Stegman," he said. "We already know your name, don't we, class?" There was a titter of laughter, all eyes still glued to me. He reached down and picked two textbooks off his desk. "These are yours. I've already copied down the book numbers. This is your grammar book." He held it up. "I suppose I should remind some of you as well. This is the grammar book," he said, and there was more relaxed laughter. "And this is the literature book. We are in the middle of discussing Edgar Allan Poe and his short story, 'The Murders in the Rue Morgue,' a story everyone was supposed to have read over the holidays, I might add," he said, raising his eyes at the class. Some looked very guilty.

He turned back to me.

"For now, you'll just have to listen, but I'd like you to read it tonight."

"Oh, I have read this story, sir," I said.

"What?" He smiled. "You know this story?" I nodded. "And the main character is.

"Dupin, Poe's detective."

"Then you know who the killer is?"

"Yes, sir," I said, smiling.

"And why is this story significant?"

"It's one of the first American detective stories," I said.

"Well, well, well . . . seems our neighbors in the bayou aren't as backward as some of us had anticipated," he said, glaring at the class. "In fact, some of us fit that description more," he said. It seemed to me he was looking at Gisselle. "I sat you across the room from your twin sister because I was afraid I wouldn't be able to tell the difference, but I see I will," he added. There was a lot of laughter this time. I was afraid to look back at Gisselle.

Instead, I looked down, my heart still thumping, as he continued his discussion of the story. Every once in a while, he gazed my way to confirm or reaffirm something he had said, and then he assigned our homework. I turned very slowly and looked at Gisselle. She wore this pained expression, a mixture of surprise and disappointment.

"You made a big hit with Mr. Stegman," Mookie said when the bell rang. "I'm glad you read, too. Everyone makes fun of me for reading so much."

"Why?"

"They just do," Mookie said. Gisselle caught up with us, her flock of girlfriends and boyfriends around her.

"There's no sense introducing you to everyone now," she said. "You'll just forget their names. I'll do it at lunch." Two of her girlfriends groaned and some of the boys looked disappointed. "Oh, all right. Meet Billy, Edward, Charles, and James," she catalogued so quickly I wasn't sure what name belonged to whom. "And this is Claudine and this is Antoinette, my two best friends," she said, indicating a tall brunette and a blonde about our height.

"I can't believe how much you two look alike," Claudine remarked.

"They are twins you know," Antoinette said.

"I know they're twins, but the Gibsons are

twins, too, and Mary and Grace look a lot different."

"That's because they're fraternal twins and not identical," Mookie said somewhat pedantically. "They were born together, but they came from separate eggs."

"Oh, please, give us a break, will you, Miss Know-it-all," Claudine said.

"I'm just trying to be helpful," Mookie pleaded.

"Next time we need a walking encyclopedia, we'll call you," Antoinette said. "Don't you have something to look up in the library?" she added.

"I'm supposed to show Ruby around. Dr. Storm assigned me."

"We're reassigning you. Get lost, Mookie," Gisselle said. "I can take my sister around if I want."

"But—"

"I don't want her to get into any trouble, Gisselle," I said. "It's all right." Mookie looked grateful.

"Suit yourself, but don't bring her with you to our table in the cafeteria. She ruins everyone's appetite," Gisselle said, and the girls laughed.

Beau, coming from another part of the building with Martin, hurried to join us.

"How's it going?" he asked.

"Fine," Gisselle replied. "Don't worry, she's in Mookie's hands. Come on," she said, threading her arm through his before he could reply. She started dragging him away.

"But . . . I'll see you at lunch," he called back.

"We better get going or we'll be late for social studies," Mookie said.

"And we don't want to be late for social studies," the girls and boys who were still around us chorused. Her face turned crimson.

"Show me the way," I said quickly, and we walked off. As we moved down the corridor, student after student stared. Some said a quick hello, some smiled, but most just looked at me and whispered to the person beside him or her. Even some of the teachers stood in their doorways to catch sight of me moving down the corridor.

When, I wondered, would I stop being an object of curiosity, and just blend in with everyone else?

In class after class: social studies, science, and math, I found I wasn't as far behind as everyone had anticipated I would be. A large part of the reason was due to the fact that I did a lot of reading on my own. Grandmere Catherine had always emphasized the importance of education, especially reading, and she encouraged me to bring home library books. Instead of finding my teachers at the Beauregard School intimidating, I found them friendly and eager to be helpful. Like Mr. Stegman, they were impressed with my abilities and with what I already knew. They seemed overjoyed to have someone who took their classes seriously, too.

As the morning went by and my teachers realized what I knew and how vigilantly I did my schoolwork, Gisselle was inevitably compared to me, and reprimanded for not being as serious about her work as I was. Behind their comments and criticism was the thought that her Cajun counterpart was not backward and disadvantaged, but advanced.

I didn't want this to happen. I saw how much it upset her, but there wasn't anything I could do about it. By the time we met at lunch in the cafeteria, she was frustrated and angry, her mood mean and contemptuous of everything and everyone around us.

"I'll see you after lunch," Mookie said, taking one look at Gisselle and then moving to a table of her own.

Beau came up behind me and tickled my ribs before I could object to Mookie's leaving. I squealed and spun around.

"Beau, stop. I'm standing out like crab in a chicken gumbo as it is." He laughed and then beamed his beautiful blue eyes at me softly.

"I hear everyone likes you, especially your teachers," he said. "I knew they would. Come on, let's get some lunch." He escorted me through the line and then we carried our trays to the table at which Gisselle and her friends sat. She was holding court like a queen.

"I was just telling everyone how you had to clean fish and sew little handkerchiefs to sell on the road," she quipped.

There was a titter of laughter.

"Did you also tell them about her artwork and her pictures in the gallery?" Beau asked. Gisselle's smile faded. "In the French Quarter," he added, nodding at Claudine and Antoinette.

"Really?" Claudine said.

"Yes. And she has an instructor from the college

now because he thinks she's very talented," Beau added.

"Beau, please," I pleaded.

"No sense being modest anymore," he said. "You're Gisselle's twin sister, aren't you? Act like it," he added. Everyone laughed, but Gisselle fumed.

The questions followed quickly: When did I start painting? What was it like living in the bayou? What was school really like? Did I see alligators often?

With every question and with every answer, Gisselle grew more and more upset. She tried making jokes about my former life, but no one laughed because everyone was more interested in hearing my stories. Finally, she got up in a huff and declared she was going out for a cigarette.

"Who's coming?" she demanded.

"There's not enough time," Beau said. "And besides, Storm's patrolling the grounds himself these days."

"You were never afraid before, Beau Andreas," she said, flashing her furious eyes at me.

"I'm older and wiser," he quipped. Everyone laughed, but Gisselle pivoted and marched a few steps away before turning around to see who was following. No one had gotten up.

"Suit yourself," she said, and headed for two boys at another table. Their heads lifted in unison when she smiled at them. Then, like bait cast off the fishing boat, she drew them off to follow her outside.

At the end of the day, Beau insisted on taking me home. We waited for Gisselle at his car, but when she didn't show up immediately, Beau decided we would leave without her.

"She's just making me wait for spite," he declared.

"But she'll be so angry, Beau."

"Serves her right. Stop worrying about it," he said, insisting I get in. I looked back when we drove away and thought I saw Gisselle coming out of the doorway. I told Beau, but he only laughed.

"I'll just tell her I thought you were her again," he said, and sped up. With the wind blowing through my hair, the warm sunlight making every leaf, every flower look bright and alive, I couldn't help but feel good. Nina Jackson's cat bone had worked, I thought. My first day at my new school was a big success.

And so too were the days and weeks that followed. I quickly discovered that instead of Gisselle's helping me to catch up, I was helping her, even though she had been the one attending this school and these classes. But this wasn't what she let her friends believe. According to the stories she told each day at lunch, she was spending hours and hours bringing me up-to-date in every subject. One day she giggled and said, "Reviewing everything because of Ruby, I'm starting to do better."

The truth was I ended up doing homework for both of us and as a result, her homework grades did improve. Our teachers wondered aloud about it and gazed at me with knowing glints in their eyes. Gisselle even improved on her test grades because we studied together.

And so my adjustment to the Beauregard School

went along far easier than I had imagined it could. I made friends with a number of students, especially a number of boys, and remained very friendly with Mookie, despite Gisselle's and her friends' attitude toward her. I found Mookie to be a very sensitive and very intelligent person, far more sincere than most, if not all, of Gisselle's friends.

I enjoyed my art lessons with Professor Ashbury, who after only two lessons, declared that I had an artistic eye, "The perception that lets you distinguish what is visually significant and what is not."

Once word of my artistic talents spread, I attracted even more attention at school. Mr. Stegman, who was also the newspaper adviser, talked me into becoming the newspaper's art editor and invited me to produce cartoons to accompany the editorials. Mookie was the editor, so we had more time to spend together. Mr. Divito asked me to join the glee club and the following week, I let myself get talked into auditioning for the school play. That afternoon, Beau appeared too, and to my surprise and secret delight, both he and I were chosen to play opposite each other. The whole school was buzzing about it. Only Gisselle appeared annoyed, especially at lunch the following day when Beau jokingly suggested that she become my understudy.

"That way if something happens, no one will know the difference," he added, but before anyone could laugh, Gisselle exploded.

"It doesn't surprise me that you would say that, Beau Andreas," she said, wagging her head. "You wouldn't know the difference between pretend and the real thing."

Everyone roared. Beau flushed and I felt like crawling under the table.

"The truth is," she snapped, poking her thumb between her breasts, "Ruby has been *my* understudy ever since she came wandering back from the swamp." All of her friends smirked and nodded. Satisfied with her results, she continued. "I had to teach her how to bathe, brush her teeth, and wash the mud out of her ears."

"That's not true, Gisselle," I cried, tears suddenly burning behind my eyelids.

"Don't blame me for telling these things. Blame him!" she said, nodding toward Beau. "You're taking advantage of her, Beau, and you know it," she said, now in a more sisterly tone. Then she pulled herself up and added with a sneer, "Just because she came here thinking it was natural for a boy to put his hands in her clothes."

The gasps around the table drew the attention of everyone in the cafeteria.

"Gisselle, that's a horrible lie!" I cried. I got up, grabbed my books and ran from the cafeteria, my tears streaming down my cheeks. For the remainder of the day, I kept my eyes down and barely spoke a word in class. Every time I looked up, I thought the boys in the room were leering at me and the girls were whispering to each other because of what Gisselle had said. I couldn't wait for the end of the day. I knew Beau would be waiting for me by his car, but I felt horribly self-conscious about being seen with him, so I snuck out another entrance and hurried around the block.

I knew my way around enough not to get lost, but the route I took made the trip back home much longer than I had anticipated, and I felt like running away, even returning to the bayou. I strolled down the wide beautiful streets in the Garden District and paused when I saw two little girls, probably no more than six or seven, playing happily together on their swing set. They looked adorable. I was sure they were sisters; there were so many similarities between them. How wonderful it was to grow up with your sister, to be close and loving, to be sensitive to each other's feelings, to comfort each other in sadness, and to reassure each other when childhood fears invaded your world.

I couldn't help but wonder what sort of sisters Gisselle and I would have been like had we been permitted to grow up together. In my put-away heart of hearts, I was positive now that she would have been a better person growing up with me and Grandmere Catherine. It made me so angry. How unfair it was to rip us apart. Even though he didn't know I existed, my Dumas grandfather had no right to decide Gisselle's future so cavalierly. He'd had no right to play with peoples' lives as if they were no more than cards in a bourré game or checkers on a checkerboard. I couldn't imagine what it was that Daphne had said to my mother to get her to give up Gisselle, but whatever it was, I was sure it was a dreadful lie.

And as far as my father went, I sympathized with him because of the tragedy involving my uncle Jean, and I understood why he would take one look at my mother and fall head over heels in love, but he should have thought more about the consequences and he shouldn't have let my sister be taken away from our mother.

Feeling about as low and miserable as I imagined I could, I finally arrived at our front gate. For a long moment, I gazed up at the great house and wondered if all this wealth and all the advantages it would bring to me was really any better than a simpler life in the bayou. What was it Grandmere Catherine saw in my future? Was it just because she wanted me to get away from Grandpere Jack? Wasn't there a way to live in the bayou and not be under his dirty thumb?

Head down, I walked up the steps and entered the house. It was very quiet, Daddy not yet back from his offices, and Daphne either in the study or up in her suite. I went up the stairs and into my room, quickly closing the door behind me. I threw myself on my bed and buried my face in the pillow. Moments later, I heard a lock opened and turned to see the door adjoining my room and Gisselle's opened for the first time. It had been locked from her side; I had never locked it from mine.

"What do you want?" I said, glaring up at her.

"I'm sorry," she said, looking repentant. It took me by such surprise, I was speechless for a moment. I sat up. "I just lost my temper. I didn't mean to say those terrible things about you, but I lied when I told you I didn't care about Beau anymore and you could have him. All the boys and some of my girlfriends have been teasing me about it."

"I haven't done anything to try and get him to choose me over you," I said.

"I know. It's not your fault and I was stupid to blame you for it. I've already apologized to him for the things I said. He was waiting for you after school."

"I know."

"Where were you?" she asked.

"I just walked around."

She nodded with understanding. "I'm sorry," she repeated. "I'll make sure no one believes the terrible things I said."

Still surprised, but grateful for her change of heart, I smiled. "Thanks."

"Claudine's having a pajama party at her house tomorrow night. Just a bunch of the girls. I'd like you to come with me," she said.

I nodded. "Sure."

"Great. You wanna study for that stupid math test we're having tomorrow?"

"Okay," I said. Was it possible? I wondered. Was there a way for us truly to become the sisters we were meant to be? I hoped so; I hoped so with all my heart.

That night after dinner we did study math. Then we listened to records and Gisselle told me stories about some of the other boys and girls in our so-called group. It was fun gossiping about other kids and talking about music. She promised she would help me memorize my part in the school play, and then she said the nicest thing she had said since I had arrived.

"Now that I've unlocked the door adjoining our two rooms, I want to keep it unlocked. How about you?"

"Sure," I said.

"We don't even have to knock before entering each other's rooms. Except when one of us has some special visitor," she added with a smile.

The next day we both did well on the math test. When the other students saw us walking and talking together, they stopped gazing at me with suspicious smiles. Beau looked very relieved, too, and we had a good play rehearsal after school. He wanted to take me to a movie that night, but I told him I was going to Claudine's pajama party with Gisselle.

"Really?" he said, concerned. "I haven't heard anything about any pajama party. Usually, we boys find out about those things."

I shrugged.

"Maybe it was a spur-of-the-moment idea. Come by the house tomorrow afternoon," I suggested. He still looked troubled, but he nodded.

I didn't know that Gisselle hadn't gotten permission for us to go to Claudine's pajama party until she brought it up at dinner that night. Daphne complained about not enough notice.

"We just decided today," Gisselle lied, shifting her gaze at me quickly to be sure I didn't disagree. I looked down at my food. "Even if we knew, we couldn't tell you or Daddy before anyway," she whined. "You've both been so busy these last few days."

"I don't see any harm in it, Daphne," Daddy

said. "Besides, they deserve some rewards. They've been bringing home some great school grades," he added, winking at me. "I'm very impressed with your improvements, Gisselle," he told her.

"Well," Daphne said, "the Montaigne's are very respectable. I'm glad you've made friends with the right class of people," she told me, and gave us permission.

As soon as dinner was over, we went upstairs to pack our bags. Daddy drove us the three blocks or so to Claudine's home, which was almost as big as ours. Her parents had already gone to some affair outside of the city and wouldn't be back until late. The servants had gone to their quarters so we had the run of the house.

There were two other girls besides Claudine, Gisselle, Antoinette, and I: Theresa Du Pratz and Deborah Tallant. We began by making popcorn and playing records in the enormous family room. Then Claudine suggested we mix vodka and cranberry juice, and I thought, oh, no, here we go again. But all the girls wanted to do it. What was a slumber party without doing something forbidden?

"Don't worry," Gisselle whispered. "I'll mix the drinks and make sure we don't have too much vodka." I watched and saw that she did what she promised, winking at me as she prepared the drinks.

"Did you ever have pajama parties in the bayou?" Deborah asked.

"No. The only parties I attended were parties held in fais dodo halls," I explained, and described them. The girls sat around listening to my descriptions of the food, the music, and the activities.

"What's bourráe?" Theresa asked.

"A card game, sort of a cross between poker and bridge. When you lose a hand, you stuff the pot," I said, smiling. Some of the girls smiled.

"We're not that far away and yet it's like we live in another country," Deborah remarked.

"People aren't really all that different," I said. "They all want the same things—love and happiness."

Everyone was quiet a moment.

"This is getting too serious," Gisselle declared, and looked at Claudine and Antoinette, who nodded.

"Let's go up to the attic and get some of my grandmere Montaigne's things and dress up like we lived in the twenties."

It was obviously something the girls had done before.

"We'll put on the old music, too," Claudine added. Antoinette and Gisselle exchanged conspiratorial glances and then we all marched up the stairway. From the doorway of the attic, Claudine cast out garments, assigning what each would wear. I was given an old-fashioned bathing suit.

"We don't want to see what each other looks like until we all come back downstairs," Claudine said. It was as if there were a prescribed procedure for this sort of fun. "Ruby, you can use my room to change." She opened the door to her very pretty room and gestured for me to enter. Then she assigned Gisselle and Antoinette their rooms and told Theresa and Deborah to go downstairs and find places to use, She would use her parents' room. "Everyone meets in the living room in ten minutes."

I closed the door and went into her room. The old-fashioned bathing suit looked so silly when I held it up before me and gazed in Claudine's vanity mirror. It left little really exposed. I imagined people didn't care so much about getting tans in those days.

Envisioning the fun we would have all parading about in old-time clothes, I hurried to get into the bathing suit. I unfastened my skirt, stepped out of it, and unbuttoned my blouse, quickly slipping it off. I started to get into the bathing suit when there was a knock on the door.

"Who is it?"

Claudine peeked in. "How are you doing?"

"Okay. This is going to be big on me."

"My grandmother was a big lady. Oh, you can't wear your bra and panties under a bathing suit. They didn't do that," she said. "Hurry up. Take everything off, get into the suit, and come downstairs."

"But . . . "

She closed the door again. I shrugged to my image in the mirror and unfastened my bra. Then I lowered my panties. Just as they were down to my knees, I heard muffled laughter. A flutter of panic made my heart skip. I spun around to see the sliding closet door thrown open behind me and three boys emerge, laughing hysterically, Billy, Edward, and Charles. I screamed and scrambled for my garments just as a flashbulb went off. Then I charged out the door, another flash following.

Gisselle, Antoinette, and Claudine emerged from her parents' suite, and Deborah and Theresa came up the stairway, big smiles on all their faces.

"What's going on?" Claudine asked, pretending innocence.

"How could you do this?" I cried. The boys followed me to the doorway of Claudine's room and stared out at me, laughing. They were about to take another picture. Panicking, I gazed around for another place to hide and charged through an opened doorway into another room, slamming the door behind me and shutting away their laughter. As quickly as I could, I put on my clothing. The tears of anger and embarrassment streamed down my cheeks and fell off my chin.

Still trembling, but awash in a terrible anger, I took a deep breath and came out to find no one. I took another deep breath and then walked down the stairs. Voices and laughter came from the family room. I paused at the doorway and looked in to see the boys spread out on the floor, drinking the vodka and cranberry juice and the girls around them on the sofas and chairs. I fixed my gaze on Gisselle hatefully.

"How could you let them do this to me?" I demanded.

"Oh, stop being a spoilsport," she said. "It was just a prank."

"Was it?" I cried. "Then let me see you get up and take off your clothes in front of them while they snap pictures. Go on, do it," I challenged. The boys looked up at her expectantly.

"I'm not that stupid," she said, and everyone laughed.

"No, you're not," I admitted. "Because you're not as trusting. Thanks for the lesson, dear sister," I fumed. Then I pivoted and marched to the front door.

"Where are you going? You can't go home now," she cried, charging after me. I turned at the door.

"I'm not staying here," I said. "Not after this."

"Oh, stop acting so babyish. I'm sure you let boys see you naked in the bayou."

"No, I did not. The truth is people have more morals there than you do here," I spit out. She stopped smiling.

"You going to tell?" she asked.

I just shook my head. "What good would it do?" I replied, and walked out.

I hurried over the cobblestone streets and walks, my heart pounding as I practically jogged through the pools of yellow light cast by the street lanterns. I never noticed another pedestrian; I didn't even notice passing cars. I couldn't wait to get home and march up the stairway.

The first thing I was going to do was lock the door again between Gisselle's room and mine.

17

A Formal Dinner Date

Edgar greeted me at the door, a look of concern on his face when he took one look at mine. I quickly brushed away any lingering tears, but unlike my alligator skinned twin sister, I had a

415

face as thin as cotton. Any mask of deception I tried to wear might as well be made of glass.

"Is everything all right, mademoiselle?" he asked with apprehension.

"Yes, Edgar." I stepped inside. "Is my father downstairs?"

"No, mademoiselle." Something soft and sad in his voice made me turn to meet his eyes. They were dark and full of despair.

"Is something wrong, Edgar?" I asked quickly.

"Monsieur Dumas has retired for the evening," he replied, as if that explained it all.

"And my . . . mother?"

"She, too, has gone to bed, mademoiselle," he said. "Can I get you anything?"

"No, thank you, Edgar," I said. He nodded, then turned and walked away. There was an eerie stillness in the house. Most of the rooms were dark. The teardrop chandeliers above me in the hall were dim and lifeless, making the faces in some of the oil paintings gloomy and ominous. A different sort of panic grew in my chest. It made me feel hollow and terribly alone. A chill shuddered down my spine and sent me to the stairway and the promise of my snug bed waiting upstairs. However, when I reached the landing, I heard it again . . . the sound of sobbing.

Poor Daddy, I thought. How great his sorrow and misery must be to drive him into his brother's room so often and cause him still to cry like a baby after all these years. With pity and compassion in my heart, I approached the door and knocked gently. I wanted to talk to him, not only to comfort him, but to have him comfort me.

"Daddy?"

Just as before, the sobbing stopped, but no one came to the door. I knocked again.

"It's Ruby, Daddy. I came back from the pajama party. I need to talk to you. Please." I listened, my ear to the door. "Daddy?" Hearing nothing, I tried the doorknob and found it would turn. Slowly, I opened the door and peered into the room, a long, dark room with its curtains drawn, but with the light of a dozen candles flickering and casting the shadows of distorted shapes over the bed, the other furniture, and the walls. They performed a ghostly dance, resembling the sort of spirits Grandmere Catherine could drive away with her rituals and prayers. I hesitated, my heart pounding.

"Daddy, are you in here?"

I thought I heard a shuffling to the right and walked farther into the room. I saw no one, but I was drawn to the candles because they were all set up in holders on the dresser and surrounded dozens of pictures in silver and gold frames. All of the pictures were pictures of a handsome young man I could only assume was my uncle Jean. The pictures captured him from boyhood to manhood. My father stood beside him in a few, but most of the pictures were portrait photos, some in color.

He is a very handsome man, I thought, his hair the same sort of blond and brown mixture Paul's is. In every color portrait photo, he had soft bluish-green eyes, a straight nose, not too long or too short, a strong, beautifully drawn mouth that flashed a warm smile full of milk white teeth. From the few full body shots, I saw he had a trim

417

figure, manly and graceful like a bullfighter's with a narrow waist and wide shoulders. In short, my father had not exaggerated when he had described him to me. Uncle Jean was any girl's idea of a dreamboat.

I gazed about the room and even in the dim light saw that nothing had been disturbed or changed since the accident years and years ago. The bed was still made and waiting for someone to sleep in it. It looked dusty and untouched, but everything that had been left on the dressers and nightstands, the desk and armoire was still there. Even a pair of slippers remained at the side of the bed, poised to accept bare feet in the morning.

"Daddy?" I whispered to the darkest corners of the room. "Are you in here?"

"What do you think you're doing?" I heard Daphne demand, and I spun around to see her standing in the doorway, her hands on her hips. "Why are you in there?"

"I . . . thought my father was in here," I said.

"Get out of here this instant," she ordered, and backed away from the door. The moment I stepped out, she reached in and grabbed the door-knob to pull the door shut. "What are you doing home? I thought you and Gisselle were attending a slumber party tonight?"

She scowled at me, then turned her head to look at Gisselle's door. She had a lovely profile, classic, the lines of her face perfect when she burned with anger. I guess I really was an artist at heart. In the midst of this, all I could think of was what it would be like to paint that Grecian visage.

"Is she home, too?" Daphne asked.

418

"No," I said. She spun on me.

"Then why are you home?" she stormed back.

"I . . . didn't feel well, so I came home," I said quickly. Daphne focused her penetrating gaze on me, making me feel as if she were searching my eyes, maybe even my soul. I was forced to shift my eyes guiltily away.

"Are you sure that's the truth? Are you sure you didn't leave the girls to do something else, maybe something with one of the boys?" she asked suspiciously. Really feeling sick now, I still managed to find a voice.

"Oh, no, I came right home. I just want to go to bed," I said.

She continued to stare at me, her eyes riveted to mine, pinning me to her like butterflies were pinned to a board. She folded her arms under her breasts. She was in her silk robe and slippers and had her hair down, but her face was still made up, her lipstick and rough fresh. I bit softly on my lower lip. Panic seized me in a tight grip. I imagined I did look quite sick at this point.

"What's wrong with you?" she demanded.

"My stomach," I said quickly. She smirked, but looked a bit more believing.

"They're not drinking liquor over there, are they?" she asked. I shook my head. "You wouldn't tell me if they were, would you?"

"I . . ."

"You don't have to answer. I know what it's like when a group of teenage girls get together. What surprises me is your letting a mere stomachache stop you from having fun," she said.

"I didn't want to spoil anyone else's," I said. She pulled her head back and nodded softly.

"Okay then, go to bed. If you get any sicker . . . "

"I'll be all right," I said quickly.

"Very good." She started to turn away.

"Why are all those candles lit in there?" I risked asking. Slowly, she turned back to me.

"Actually," she said, suddenly changing her tone of voice to a more reasonable and friendlier one, "I'm glad you saw all that, Ruby. Now you have some idea what I have to put up with from time to time. Your father has turned that room into a . . . into a . . . shrine. What's done is done," she said coldly. "Burning candles, mumbling apologies and prayers won't change things. But he's beyond reason. The whole thing is rather embarrassing, so don't discuss it with anyone and especially don't discuss it in front of the servants. I don't want Nina sprinkling voodoo powders and chanting all over the house.

"Is he in there now?"

She looked at the door.

"Yes," she said.

"I want to talk to him."

"He's not in the talking mood. The fact is, he's not himself. You don't want to talk to him or even see him like this. It would upset him afterward more than it would upset you now. Just go to sleep. You can talk to him in the morning," she said, and narrowed her eyes as a new thought crossed her suspicious mind. "Why is it so important for you to talk to him now anyway? What is it you want to tell him that you can't tell me? Have you done something else that's terrible?"

"No," I replied quickly.

"Then what did you want to say to him?" she pursued.

"I just wanted . . . to comfort him."

"He has his priests and his doctors for that," she said. I was surprised she didn't say he had her, too. "Besides, if your stomach's bothering you so much you had to come home, how can you sit around talking to someone?" she followed quickly like a trial lawyer.

"It feels a little better," I said. She looked skeptical again. "But you're right. I'd better go to sleep," I added. She nodded and I walked to my room. She remained in the hallway watching me until I went inside.

I wanted to tell her the truth. I wanted to describe not only what had happened tonight, but the truth about the night with the rum and all the nasty things Gisselle had said and done at school, but I thought once I had drawn so sharp and clear a battle line between us, Gisselle and I would never be the sisters we were meant to be. She would hate me too much. Despite all that had already happened between us, I still clung to the hope that we would bridge the gap that all these years and different ways of living had created. I knew that right now I wanted that to happen more than Gisselle did, but I still thought she would eventually want it as much. In this hard and cruel world, having a sister or a brother, someone to care for you and love you was not something to throw away nonchalantly. I felt confident that someday, Gisselle would understand that.

I went to bed and lay there listening for my father's footsteps. Some time after midnight, I heard them: slow, ponderous steps outside my door. I heard him pause and then I heard him go on to his own room, exhausted, I was sure, from all the sorrow he had expressed in the room he had turned into a memorial to his brother. Why was his sorrow so long and so deep? I wondered. Did he blame himself?

The questions lingered in the darkness waiting for a chance to leap at the answers, like the old marsh hawk, patiently waiting for its prey.

I closed my eyes and rushed headlong into the darkness within me, the darkness that promised some relief.

The next morning it was my father who woke me, knocking on my bedroom door and poking his head in, his face so bright with smiles I wondered if I had dreamt the events of the night before. How could he move from such deep mental anguish to such a jolly mood? I wondered.

"Good morning," he said when I sat up and ground the sleep out of my eyes with my small fists.

"Hi."

"Daphne told me you came home last night because you didn't feel well. How are you this morning?"

"Much better," I said.

"Good. I'll have Nina prepare something soothing and easy to digest for you to have for breakfast. Just take it easy today. You've made quite a beginning with your art instructor, your schoolteachers . . . you deserve a day off, a day to do nothing but indulge yourself. Take a lesson from Gisselle," he added with a laugh.

"Daddy," I began. I wanted to tell him everything, to confide in him and develop the sort of relationship in which he wouldn't be afraid to confide in me.

"Yes, Ruby?" He took another step into my bedroom.

"We never talked any more about Uncle Jean. I mean, I would like to go see him with you some day," I added. What I really meant to say was I wanted to share the burden of his sorrow and pain. He gave me a tight smile.

"Well, that's very kind of you, Ruby. It would be a blessed thing to do. Of course," he said, widening his smile, "he would think you were Gisselle. It will take some lengthy explanation to get him to even fathom that he has two different nieces."

"Then he can understand things?" I asked.

"I think so. I hope so," he said, his smile fading. "The doctors aren't as convinced of his improvements as I am, but they don't know him as I know him."

"I'll help you, Daddy," I said eagerly. "I'll go there and read to him and talk to him and spend hours and hours with him, if you like," I blurted.

"That's a very nice thought. The next time I go, I will take you along," he said.

"Promise?"

"Of course, I promise. Now let me go downstairs and order your breakfast," he said. "Oh," he said, turning at the doorway, "Gisselle has phoned already to tell us she will be spending the day with the girls, too. She wanted to know how you were doing. I said I would tell you to call them later, and if you were up to it, I'd bring you back."

"I think I'll just do what you suggested, Daddy, and relax here."

"Fine," he said. "About fifteen minutes?"

"Yes. I'm getting up," I said. He smiled and left.

Maybe what I had suggested I would do would be a wonderful thing. Maybe that was the way to get Daddy out of the melancholia Daphne had described and I had witnessed last night. To Daphne, it was all simply too embarrassing. She had no tolerance for it, and Gisselle certainly couldn't care less. Maybe this was one of the reasons Grandmere Catherine sensed I belonged here. If I could help lift the burden of Daddy's sadness, I could give him something a real daughter should.

Buoyed by these thoughts, I rose quickly and dressed to go down to breakfast. As was proving to be more the rule than the exception, Daddy and I had breakfast together while Daphne remained in bed. I asked Daddy why she rarely joined us.

"Daphne likes to wake up slowly. She watches a little television, reads, and then goes through her detailed morning ministrations, preparing to face each day as if she were making a debut in society," he replied, smiling. "It's the price I pay to have such a beautiful and accomplished wife," he added.

And then he did something rare: he talked about my mother, his eyes dreamy, his gaze far-off.

"Now Gabrielle, Gabrielle was different. She woke like a flower opening itself to the morning sunlight. The brightness in her eyes and the rush of warm blood to her cheeks were all the cosmetics she required to face a day in the bayou. Watching her wake up was like watching the sun rise."

He sighed, quickly realized what he was doing and saying, and snapped the newspaper in front of his face.

I wanted him to tell me so much more. I wanted to ask him a million questions about the mother I had never known. I wanted him to describe her voice, her laugh, even her cry. For now it was only through him that I could know her. But every reference he made to her and every thought he had of her was quickly followed by guilt and fear. The memory of my mother was locked away with so many other forbidden things in the closets of the Dumas past.

After breakfast, I did what my father suggested—I curled up on a bench in the gazebo and read a book. Off, over the Gulf, I could see rain clouds, but they were moving in a different direction. Here, sunlight rained down, occasionally interrupted by the slow journey of a thin cloud nudged by the sea breeze. Two mockingbirds found me a curiosity and landed on the gazebo railing, inching their way closer and closer to me, flying off and then returning. My soft greetings made them tilt their heads and flick their wings, but kept them feeling secure, while a gray squirrel paused near the gazebo steps to sniff the air between us.

Every once in a while, I closed my eyes and lay back and imagined I was floating in my pirogue through the canals, the water lapping softly around me. If there was only some way to marry the best of that world with this one, I thought, my life would be perfect. Maybe that was what Daddy had dreamt would happen when he began his love affair with my mother.

"So there you are," I heard a voice cry out, and I opened my eyes to see Beau approaching. "Edgar said he thought he saw you go out here."

"Hi, Beau. I completely forgot that I suggested you come by today," I said, sitting up. He paused at the gazebo steps.

"I've just come from Claudine's," he said. The look on his face told me he already knew more than I anticipated.

"You know what they did to me, don't you?"

"Yes. Billy told me. The girls were all still asleep, but I had a few words with Gisselle," he replied.

"I suppose everyone's laughing about it," I said. His eyes answered before he did. They were full of pity for me.

"A bunch of sharks, that's all they are," he snapped, the blue in his eyes turning steel cold. "They're jealous of you, jealous of the way everyone has taken to you at school, jealous of your accomplishments," he said, and drew closer. I looked away, the tears welling up.

"I'm so embarrassed, I don't know how I'll go to school," I said.

"You'll go with your head high and ignore their sneers and their laughs," he proclaimed.

"I'd like to be able to say I could do that, Beau, but—"

"But nothing. I'll pick you up in the morning and we'll walk in together. But before that . . . "

"What?"

"I came over here to ask you to dinner," he stated with a polite formality, pulling his shoulders back to assume his young Creole gentleman image.

"Dinner?"

"Yes, a formal dinner date," he said. It was on the tip of my tongue to tell him I had never been on a dinner date before, formal or informal, but I kept silent. "I have already taken the liberty of making reservations at Arnaud's," he added with some pride. I assumed from the way he spoke, this was to be a very special evening.

"I'll have to ask my parents," I said.

"Of course." He looked at his watch. "I have a few errands to run, but I'll call you about noon to confirm the time."

"All right," I said breathlessly. A dinner date, a formal date with Beau . . . everyone would hear about this, too. He wasn't just being nice to me in school or just giving me a ride home.

"Good," he said, smiling. "I'll call you." He started away.

"Beau."

"Yes?"

"You're not doing this just to make me feel better after what they did, are you?" I asked.

"What?" He started to laugh and then turned

serious. "Ruby, I just want to be with you and would have asked you for a date whether they pulled that stupid joke on you or not," he declared. "Stop underestimating yourself," he added, turned and walked off leaving me in a whirlpool of mixed emotions that ranged from happiness to terror that I would make an absolute fool of myself and simply add to what had already been done to make me look like I didn't belong.

"What?" Daphne said, looking up sharply from her cup of coffee. "Beau asked *you* to dinner?"

"Yes. He's calling at noon to see if it's all right for me to go," I said. She looked at my father, who had been sitting with her on the patio, having another cup of coffee. He shrugged.

"Why is that so surprising?" he asked.

"Why? Beau has been seeing Gisselle," she replied.

"Daphne, darling, they weren't engaged. They're just teenagers. Besides," he added, beaming a smile at me, "you hoped the time would come when people would accept Ruby as one of us. Apparently, the way you've dressed her, the advice and instruction you have given her on how to carry herself and speak to people, and the good example you set has had remarkable results. You should be proud, not surprised," he added.

Daphne's eyes narrowed as she thought.

"Where is he taking you?" she asked.

"Arnaud's," I said.

"Arnaud's!" She put her coffee cup down sharply. "That's not just any restaurant. You have

428

to wear the proper things. Many of our friends go to that restaurant and we are friendly with the owners."

"So," my father said. "You'll advise her how to dress."

Daphne wiped her lip with the napkin and considered.

"It's time you went to a beautician and had something done with your hair and your nails," she decided.

"What's wrong with my hair?"

"You need your bangs trimmed and I'd like to see it conditioned. I'll make an appointment for this afternoon. They always find time for me at a moment's notice," she said confidently.

"That's very nice," my father said.

"Then you've made a full recovery from your stomach problem?" Daphne asked me pointedly.

"Yes."

"She looks fine," my father said. "I'm very, proud of the way you're adjusting now, Ruby, very proud."

Daphne glared at him.

"You and I haven't been to Arnaud's in months," she remarked.

"Well, I'll make a note of that and we'll go soon. We don't want to go the same night Ruby does. It might make her uncomfortable," he added. She continued to glare.

"I'm glad you're worried about her discomfort, Pierre. Maybe you'll start thinking about mine now," she said, and he reddened.

"I—"

"Go on upstairs, Ruby," she commanded. "I'll be right up to choose your clothes."

"Thank you," I said. I glanced quickly at my father who looked like a little boy who had just been reprimanded, and then I hurriedly left and went up to my room. Why was it that every nice thing that happened to me here always brought along some unpleasantness? I wondered.

Shortly afterward, Daphne came marching into my room.

"You have a two o'clock at the beauty parlor," she said, going to my closet. She threw open the sliding doors and stood back, considering. "I'm glad I thought to buy this," she said, plucking a dress from its hanger, "and the matching shoes." She turned and looked at me. "You're going to need a pair of earrings. I'll let you borrow one of mine and a necklace, too, just so you don't look underdressed."

"Thank you," I said.

"Take special care with them," she warned. She put the dress aside and focused her gaze on me with suspicion again. "Why is Beau taking you to dinner?"

"Why? I don't know. He said he wanted to take me. I didn't ask him to take me, if that's what you mean," I replied.

"No, that's not what I mean. He and Gisselle have been seeing each other for some time now. You come onto the scene and suddenly, he leaves her. What's been going on between you and Beau?" she demanded.

"Going on? I don't know what you mean, Mother."

"Young men, especially young men of Beau's age, are rather sexually driven," she explained. "Their hormones are raging so they look for girls who are more promiscuous, more obliging."

"I'm not one of those girls," I snapped.

"Whether it's true or not," she continued, "Cajun girls have reputations."

"It's not true. The truth is," I fumed, "so-called Creole girls of good breeding are more promiscuous."

"That's ridiculous and I don't want to hear you say such a thing," she replied firmly. I looked down. "I warn you," she continued, "if you did or if you do anything to embarrass me, embarrass the Dumas . . ."

I wrapped my arms around myself and turned away so she couldn't see the tears that clouded my eyes.

"Be ready at one-thirty to go to the beauty parlor," she finally said, and left me trembling with frustration and anger. Was it always going to be this way? Every time I accomplished something or something nice happened to me, she would decide it was because of some indecent reason?

It wasn't until Beau called at noon that I felt better about myself and the promise of the evening. He repeated how much he wanted to take me and was very happy to hear I could go.

"I'll pick you up at seven," he said. "What color is your dress?"

"It's red, like the red dress Gisselle wore to the Mardi Gras Ball."

"Great. See you at seven."

Why he wanted to know the color of my dress

431

didn't occur to me until he came to the door at seven with the corsage of baby white roses. He looked dashing and handsome in his tuxedo. Daphne made a point to appear when Edgar informed me Beau had arrived.

"Good evening, Daphne," he said.

"Beau. You look very handsome," she said.

"Thank you." He turned to me and presented the corsage. "You look great," he said. I saw how nervous he was under Daphne's scrutinizing gaze. His fingers trembled as he opened the box and took out the corsage. "Maybe you'd better put this on her, Daphne. I don't want to stick her."

"You never have trouble doing it for Gisselle," Daphne remarked, but she moved forward and attached the corsage.

"Thank you," I said. She nodded. "Give my regards to the maître d'," she told Beau.

"I will."

I took Beau's arm and eagerly let him lead me out the front door and to his car.

"You look great," he said after we got in.

"So do you."

"Thanks." We pulled away.

"Gisselle didn't come back from Claudine's yet," I told him.

"They're having a party," he said.

"Oh. They called to invite you?"

"Yes." He smiled. "But I told them I had more important things to do," he added, and I laughed, finally feeling as if the heavy cloud of anxiety had begun to move off. It felt good to relax a little and enjoy something for a change.

I couldn't help but be nervous again when we

entered the restaurant. It was filled with many fine and distinguished looking men and women, all of whom gazed up from their plates or turned from their conversations to look us over when we entered and were shown our table. I went through the litany of things Daphne had recited to me on the way to and from the beauty parlor—how to sit up straight and hold my silverware, which fork was for what, putting the napkin on my lap, eating slowly with my mouth closed, letting Beau order our dinners . . .

"And if you should drop something, a knife, a spoon, don't you pick it up. That's what the waiters and busboys are there to do," she said. She kept adding new thoughts. "Don't slurp your soup the way they eat gumbo in the bayou."

She made me feel so self-conscious, I was sure I would do something disgraceful and embarrass Beau and myself. I trembled walking through the restaurant, trembled after we were seated, and trembled when it was time to chose my silverware and begin to eat.

Beau did all he could to make me feel relaxed. He continually complimented me and tried telling jokes about other students we both knew. Whenever something was served, he explained what it was and how it had been prepared.

"The only reason I know all this," he said, "is because my mother is amusing herself by learning how to be a gourmet chef. It's driving everyone in the family crazy."

I laughed and ate, remembering Daphne's final warning: "Don't finish everything and wipe the plate clean. It's more feminine to be full faster and not look like some farmhand feeding her face."

Even though the dinner was sumptuous and it was very elegantly served, I was too nervous to really enjoy it and actually felt relieved when the check came and we rose to leave. I had gotten through this elegant dinner date without doing anything Daphne could criticize, I thought. No matter what happened, I would be a success in her eyes, and for some reason, even though she was often unpleasant to me, her admiration and approval remained important. It was as if I wanted to win the respect of royalty.

"It's early," Beau said when we left the restaurant. "Can we take a little ride?"

"Okay."

I had no idea where we were going, but before I knew it, we had left the busier part of the city behind us. Beau talked about places he had been and places he wanted very much to see. When I asked him what he wanted to do with his life, he said he was thinking very seriously of becoming a doctor.

"That would be wonderful, Beau."

"Of course," he added, smiling, "I'm just blowing air right now. Once I find out what's involved, I'll probably back out. I usually do."

"Don't talk about yourself that way, Beau. If you really want to do something, you will."

"You make it sound easy, Ruby. In fact, you have a way of making the most difficult and troubling things look like nothing. Why just look at the way you've already memorized your part in the play and made some of the other students gain confidence in themselves . . . including me, I might add . . . ” He shook his head. “Gisselle is always putting things down, belittling things I like. She’s so . . . negative sometimes.”

“Maybe she’s not as happy as she pretends to be,” I wondered aloud.

“Yeah, maybe that’s it. But you’ve got every reason to be unhappy and yet, you don’t let other people feel you’re unhappy.”

“My grandmere Catherine taught me that,” I said, smiling. “She taught me to be hopeful, to believe in tomorrow.”

He grimaced with confusion.

“You make her sound so good and yet she was part of the Cajun family that bought you as a stolen baby, right?” he asked.

“Yes, but . . . she didn’t learn about it until years later,” I said, quickly covering up. “And by that time, it was too late.”

“Oh”

“Where are we?” I asked, looking out the window and seeing we were on a highway now that was surrounded by marshlands.

“Just a nice place we go sometimes. There’s a good view up ahead,” he said, and turned down a side road that brought us to an open field, looking back at the lights of New Orleans. “Nice, huh?”

“Yes. It’s beautiful.” I wondered if I would ever get used to the tall buildings and sea of lights. I still felt very much like a stranger.

He turned off his engine, but left the radio playing a soft, romantic song. Although it was mostly cloudy now, stars peeked down through any break in the overcast, twinkling brightly. Beau turned to me and took my hand.

"What sort of dates did you have in the bayou?" he asked.

"I never really went on what you would call a date, I suppose. I went to town for a soda. Once, I went to a fais dodo with a boy. A dance," I added.

"Oh. Oh, yeah."

I couldn't see his face in the darkness and it reminded me of our time in the cabana. Just like then, my heart began to pitter-patter for seemingly no reason. I saw his head and shoulders move toward me until I felt his lips find mine. It was a short kiss, but he followed it with a deep moan and his hands clutched my shoulders and held me tightly.

"Ruby," he whispered. "You look like Gisselle, but you're so much softer, so much lovelier that it's very easy for me to tell the difference between you even with a quick glance." He kissed me again and then kissed the tip of my nose. I had my eyes closed and felt his lips slide softly over my cheeks. He kissed my closed eyes and my forehead and then pulled me closer to him to seal my lips with his in a long, demanding kiss that sent invisible fingers over my breasts and down the small of my stomach, making me tingle to my toes.

"Oh, Ruby, Ruby," he chanted. His lips were on my neck and before I knew it, he brought them to the tops of my breasts, moving quickly to the small valley between them. Whatever resistance was naturally in me, softened. I moaned and let myself sink deeper into the seat as he moved over me, his hands now finding their way over my bosom, his fingers expertly sliding the zipper down until my dress loosened enough for him to bring it lower.

"Oh, Beau, I . . . "

"You're so lovely, lovelier than Gisselle. Your skin is like silk to her sandpaper."

His fingers found the clasp of my bra and almost before I knew it, undid it. Instantly, his mouth moved over my breast, nudging my bra away to expose more and more until he found my nipple, erect, firm, waiting despite the voice within me that tried to keep my body from being so willing. It was truly as though there were two of me: the sensible, quiet, and logical Ruby, and the wild, hungry-for-love-and-affection emotional Ruby.

"I have a blanket in the back," he whispered. "We can spread it out and lie out here under the stars and . . . "

And what? I thought finally. Grope and pet each other until there was no turning back? Suddenly, Daphne's furious face flashed before me and her words resounded: ". . . They look for girls who are more promiscuous, more obliging . . . Whether it is true or not, Cajun girls have reputations."

"No, Beau. We're going too fast and too far. I can't . . . " I cried.

"We'll just sprawl out and be more comfortable," he proposed, keeping his lips close to my ear.

"It would be more than that and you know it, Beau Andreas."

"Come on, Ruby. You've done this before,

haven't you?" he said with a sharpness that cut into my heart.

"Never, Beau. Not like you think," I replied with indignation. My tone made him regret his accusation, but he wasn't easily dissuaded.

"Then let me be the first, Ruby. I want to be your first. Please," he pleaded.

"Beau . . ."

He continued moving his lips over my breasts, urging and encouraging me with his fingers, his touch, his tongue, and hot breath, but I firmed up my resistance, a resistance fueled by the memory of Daphne's accusations and expectations. I would not fit the image of the Cajun girl they wanted me to be. I would not give any of them the satisfaction.

"What's wrong, Ruby? Don't you like me?" Beau moaned when I pulled myself back and held my dress against my bosom.

"I do, Beau. I like you a lot, but I don't want to do this now. I don't want to do what everyone expects I would do . . . even you," I added.

Beau sat back abruptly, his frustration quickly turning into anger.

"You led me to believe you really liked me," he said.

"I do, Beau, but why can't we stop when I ask you to stop? Why can't we just—"

"Just torment each other?" he asked caustically. "Is that what you did with your boyfriends in the bayou?"

"I didn't have boyfriends. Not like you think," I said. He was silent for a moment. Then he took a deep breath.

"I'm sorry. I didn't mean to imply you had dozens of boyfriends."

I put my hand on his shoulder. "Can't we get to know each other a little more, Beau?"

"Yes, of course. That's what I want. But there's no better way than making love," he offered, turning back to me. He sounded so convincing. A part of me wanted to be convinced, but I kept that part under tight wraps, locked behind a door. "You're not going to tell me now you just want to be good friends, are you?" he added with obvious sarcasm when I continued to resist.

"No, Beau. I am attracted to you. I would be a liar to say otherwise," I confessed.

"So?"

"So let's not rush into anything and make me regret it," I added. Those words seemed to stop him cold. He froze in the space between us for a moment and then sat back. I began to fasten my bra.

Suddenly, he laughed.

"What?" I asked.

"The first time I took Gisselle out here, she jumped me and not vice versa," he said, starting the engine. "I guess you two really are very, very different."

"I guess we are," I said.

"As my grandfather would say, *viva la difference,*" he replied, and laughed again, but I wasn't sure if he meant he liked Gisselle's behavior better or he liked mine.

"All right, Ruby," he said, driving us out of the marshlands, "I'll take your advice and believe what you predicted about me."

"Which is?"

"If I really want to do something," he said, "I will. Eventually." In the glow from the light of oncoming cars, I saw him smiling.

He was so handsome; I did like him; I did want him, but I was glad I had resisted and remained true to myself and not to the image others had of me.

When we arrived at the house, he escorted me to the door and then turned me to him to kiss me good night.

"I'll come by tomorrow afternoon and we can rehearse some of our lines, okay?" he said.

"I'd like that. I had a wonderful time, Beau. Thank you."

He laughed.

"Why do you laugh at everything I say?" I demanded.

"I can't help it. I keep thinking of Gisselle. She would expect me to thank her for permitting me to spend a small fortune on dinner. I'm not laughing at you," he added. "I'm just . . . so surprised by everything you do and say."

"Do you like that, Beau?" I met his blue eyes and felt the heat that sprang up from my heart, hoping for the right answer.

"I think I do. I think I really do," he said, as if first realizing it himself, and then he kissed me again before leaving. I watched him for a moment, my heart now full and happy, and then rang the doorbell for Edgar. He opened it so quickly, I thought he had been standing there on the other side, waiting.

"Good evening, mademoiselle," he said.

"Good evening, Edgar," I sang, and started toward the stairway.

"Mademoiselle."

I turned back, still smiling at my last memories of Beau on the steps.

"Yes, Edgar?"

"I was told to tell you to go straight to the study, mademoiselle," he said.

"Pardon?"

"Your father and mother and Mademoiselle Gisselle are waiting for you," he explained.

"Gisselle's home already?" Surprised, but filled with trepidation, I went to the study. Gisselle was sitting on one of the leather sofas and Daphne was in a leather chair. My father was gazing out the window, his back to me. He turned when Daphne said, "Come in and sit down."

Gisselle was glaring at me, hatefully. Did she think I had told on her? Had my father and Daphne somehow heard about what had occurred at the slumber party?

"Did you have a nice time?" Daphne asked. "Behave properly and do everything as I told you to do it in the restaurant?"

"Yes."

My father looked relieved about that, but he still seemed distant, troubled. My eyes went from him, to Gisselle, who looked away quickly, and then back to Daphne, who folded her hands in her lap.

"Apparently, since your arrival, you haven't told us everything about your sordid past," she said. I gazed at Gisselle again. She was sitting

441

back now, her arms folded, her face full of self-satisfaction.

"I don't understand. What haven't I told you?" Daphne smirked.

"You haven't told us about the woman you know in Storyville," she said, and for a moment my heart stopped and then started again, this time driven by a combination of fear and anger and utter frustration. I spun on Gisselle.

"What lies did you tell now?" I demanded. She shrugged.

"I just told how you brought us down to Storyville to meet your friend," she explained, throwing a look of pure innocence at Daddy.

"I? Took you? But—" I sputtered.

"How do you know this . . . this prostitute?" Daphne demanded.

"I don't know her," I cried. "Not like she's telling you."

"She knew your name, didn't she? Didn't she?"

"Yes."

"And she knew you were looking for Pierre and me?" Daphne cross-examined.

"That's true, but—"

"How do you know her?" she demanded firmly. A hot rush of blood heated my face.

"I met her on the bus when I came to New Orleans and I didn't know she was a prostitute," I cried. "She told me her name was Annie Gray, and when we arrived in New Orleans, she helped me find this address."

"She knows this address," Daphne said, nodding at Daddy. He closed his eyes and bit down on his lower lip.

"She told me she was coming here to be a singer," I explained. "She's still trying to find a job. Her aunt promised her and—"

"You want us to believe you thought she was only a nightclub singer?"

"It's the truth!" I turned to Daddy. "It is!"

"All right," he said. "Maybe it is."

"What's the difference?" Daphne remarked. "By now the Andreas family and the Montaignes surely know your . . . our daughter has made the acquaintance of such a person.

"We'll explain it," my father insisted.

"You'll explain it," Daphne retorted. Then she turned back to me. "Did she promise to contact you here and give you an address of where she would be in the future?"

I gazed at Gisselle again. She hadn't left out a detail. Wickedly, she grinned.

"Yes, but—"

"Don't you ever so much as nod at this woman if you should see her someplace, much less accept any letters from her or phone calls, understand?"

"Yes, ma'am." I looked down, the tears so cold they made me shiver on their journey down my cheeks.

"You should have told us about this so we could be prepared should it come up. Are there any other sordid secrets?"

I shook my head quickly.

"Very well." She looked at Gisselle. "Both of you go to bed," she commanded.

I rose slowly and without waiting for Gisselle, started toward the stairway. I walked ponderously up the steps, my head down, my heart feeling so heavy in my chest, it was like I was carrying a chunk of lead up with me.

Gisselle came prancing by, her face molded in a smile of self-satisfaction.

"I hope you and Beau had a good time," she quipped as she passed me.

What possible part of my mother and what possible part of my father combined to create someone so hateful and mean? I wondered.

18

A Curse

Gisselle and I didn't speak to each other very much the next day. I finished breakfast before she came down, and soon after she did, she went off with Martin and two of her girlfriends. Daddy left, saying he had to catch up on some work in his office, and I saw Daphne only for a moment before she hurried out to meet some friends for shopping and lunch. I spent the remainder of the morning in my studio, painting. I was still uncomfortable living in such a big house. Despite the many beautiful antiques and works of art, the expensive French furniture and elaborate tapestries and carpets, for me the house remained as empty and as cold as a museum. It was easy to be lonely here, I thought as I wandered back through the long corridors afterward to have my lunch alone.

And so I was glad when Beau arrived in the early afternoon and we went into my art studio to practice our play lines. First, he looked at the pictures I had drawn and painted under Professor Ashbury's tutelage.

"Well?" I said when he went from one to the other without comment.

"How about doing a picture of me?" he suggested, looking up from a watercolor of a bowl of fruit.

"Of you?" The idea startled me. A slow grin appeared on his handsome face.

"Sure. I hope it would be a lot more interesting than something like this." His grin quickly evaporated. Suddenly, those smiling sapphire eyes looked at me as I had never been looked at before. They darkened so with pure desire. "I'd even pose nude, if you like," he said.

I know my cheeks turned crimson.

"Nude! Beau!"

"It's only for the sake of art, right?" he followed quickly. "And an artist has to practice drawing and painting the human body, doesn't she? Even I know that much," he said. "I'm sure your teacher will be taking you to his studio soon and have you do nudes. I hear there are college guys and girls who do it for the money. Or have you already drawn and painted someone in the nude?" he asked with a wry smile.

"Of course not. I'm not ready for that sort of work yet, Beau," I said, my voice nearly failing. He took a few steps toward me.

"You don't think I'm good-looking enough? You think the college guys will look better?"

"No, I don't. It's not that. It's just . . . "

"Just what?"

"I'd be too embarrassed to draw you. Now stop.

We came in here to memorize play lines," I said, opening my script. He continued to gaze at me with that look of pure longing on his face, his cerulean eyes darkening. I had to fix my eyes on the pages so he couldn't see the excitement he had stirred in my breast. My heart pitter-pattered when the image of him sprawled nude on a chaise flashed before me. I couldn't help but tremble. I hoped he didn't see the way my fingers fumbled with the pages of my script.

"Are you sure?" he questioned. "You never know about something until you try." I took a deep breath, put the script down, and looked up at him sharply.

"I'm sure, Beau. Besides, all I need is for Daphne to believe one more bad thing about me. She has Daddy nearly convinced that I'm some sort of wicked Cajun girl, thanks to Gisselle."

"What do you mean?" Beau asked, quickly sitting beside me. Breathlessly, I gushed forth, describing how I had been interrogated about Annie Gray.

"Gisselle told on you?" He shook his head. "I guess she's just jealous," he said. "Well, she has reason to be," he added, his eyes continuing to grow warmer. "I'm too fond of you now to turn back. She's going to have to get used to it and behave herself."

We stared into each other's eyes for a moment. Outside, the morning overcast had darkened into rain clouds and a hard downpour began, the drops tapping on the windows and streaking down like tears on someone's cheeks.

Gradually, Beau leaned toward me. I didn't

move away and he kissed me softly on the lips. I felt my small wall of resistance start to crumble. Surprising myself, as well as him, I returned his kiss the moment his ended. Neither of us said anything, but we both knew the memorization session was destined to fail. Neither he nor I could concentrate on the play. As soon as I lifted my eyes from the words and met his, my mind stumbled and fumbled.

Finally, he took the play script from my hand and put it aside with his. Then he turned to me.

"Paint me, Ruby," he whispered in a voice as tempting as the serpent's must have been in Paradise. "Draw me and paint me. Let's lock the door and do it," he challenged.

"Beau, I couldn't . . . I just couldn't."

"Why not? You paint animals without clothes," he teased. "And naked fruit, don't you?"

"Stop, Beau."

"It's nothing," he said, growing serious again. "We'll keep it a secret between us," he added. "Why don't we do it right now? There's no one here to disturb us," he said, and began to unbutton his shirt.

"Beau . . . "

With his eyes fixed on me, he stripped off his shirt and then stood up to unfasten his pants.

"Go lock the door," he said, nodding.

"Beau, don't . . . "

"If you don't lock it and someone does walk in . . . "

"Beau Andreas!"

He stepped out of his pants and folded them

neatly over the back of the lounge. He stood only in his briefs, his hands on his hips, waiting.

"How should I pose? Sitting? Knees up? On my stomach?"

"Beau, I said I can't . . . "

"The door," he replied, nodding toward it more emphatically. To move me faster, he tucked his thumbs into the elastic of his briefs and began lowering them over his hips. I jumped out of the chair and rushed to the door. The moment I heard the lock click, I knew I had let it go too far. Was it only because I didn't know how to stop him, or did I permit it to happen, want it to happen? I turned and saw him standing with his shorts in his hand, holding them in front of himself.

"How should I pose?" he asked.

"Put your clothes back on this instant, Beau Andreas," I ordered.

"It's done already. It's too late to turn back. Just start."

He sat down on the lounge, still keeping his briefs over his private parts. Then he nonchalantly brought up his feet and sprawled out, facing me. With a quick gesture, he raised his briefs and draped them over the back of the lounge. My mouth gaped.

"Should I lean on my hand like this? This is good, isn't it?"

I shook my head, turned away from him, and sat down quickly in the nearest chair because my pounding heart had turned my legs to marshmallow.

"Do it, Ruby. Draw me," he ordered. "This is a challenge to see if you can really be an artist and

448

look at someone and see only an object to draw and paint, like a doctor separating himself from his patient so he could do what has to be done."

"I can't, Beau. Please. I'm not a doctor and you're not my patient," I insisted, still without looking at him.

"Our secret, Ruby," he whispered. "It will be our secret," he chanted. "Go on. Look at me. You can do it. Look at me," he commanded.

Slowly, like one hypnotized by his words, I turned my head and gazed at him, at his sleek, muscular torso, at the way the lines of his body turned into each other. Could I do what he asked? Could I look at him and detach myself enough to see him only as something to draw?

The artist in me demanded to know, wanted to know. I rose and went to my easel and flipped over the page to work on a blank one. Then I took the drawing pencil in hand and looked at him, drinking him in with long, visual gulps and then turning what I saw into something on the page. My fingers, trembling badly at first, became stronger, firmer as the lines took shape. I took the most time with his face, capturing him as I saw him in my own mind as well as how he looked to others. I drew him with a deep, strong look in his eyes. Satisfied, I moved to his body and soon I had the outline of his shoulders, his sides, his hips, and his legs. I concentrated on his chest and his neck, capturing the strong muscle structure and the smooth lines.

All the while he kept his eyes fixed so firmly on me; it was as if he were a mannequin. I think he was testing himself as much as he was testing me.

"This is hard work," he finally said.

"You want to stop?"

"No. I can go a while longer. I can go as long as you can," he added.

My fingers began to tremble again as I moved down the drawing to the small of his stomach. Now, with every turn of the pencil, I felt I was actually running the tips of my fingers over his body, slowly working my way down until I had to draw his manliness. He knew I had reached that point, for his lips tightened into a sensuous smile.

"If you have to come closer, don't be afraid," he said in a loud whisper.

I dropped my eyes back to the easel and drew quickly, sketching so fast I must have looked like someone in a frenzy. I didn't have to look up at him again. The image of his body lingered on my eyes. I know I was flushed. My heart was pounding so hard, I don't know how I continued, but I did. And when I finally stepped back from the paper, I had drawn a rather detailed picture of him.

"Is it good?" he asked.

"I think so," I said, surprised at how really good it was. I couldn't remember drawing a single line. It was as though I had been possessed.

Suddenly, he rose and stepped up beside me to look at the drawing.

"It is good," he said.

"You can put on your clothes now, Beau," I said, without turning away from the drawing.

"Don't be so nervous," he said, putting his hand on my shoulder.

"Beau . . . "

"You've already seen all there is to see. No reason to be shy anymore," he whispered. When he put his arm around me, I tried to move away; I willed my feet to carry me off, but my command died somewhere on the way and I remained beside him, as pliable as soft clay, permitting him to turn me around so that I faced him and enabled him to kiss me. I felt his nakedness against me, his manliness harden.

"Beau, please . . . "

"Shh," he said, wiping my face softly with his palm. He kissed me tenderly on the lips and then he lifted me into his arms and carried me back to the lounge. As he lowered me onto it, he went to his knees and leaned over to kiss me again. His fingers moved quickly over my clothing, unbuttoning my blouse, unzipping my skirt. He undid my bra and peeled it away. My breasts shuddered, uncovered, but I didn't resist. I kept my eyes closed and only moaned as he kissed me on the neck, the shoulders, and then nibbled gently under and over my breasts. He lifted me gently and slipped my skirt down over my hips, quickly burying his face in the small of my stomach. His kisses were like fire now. Everywhere his lips touched me, I felt the heat build.

"You're wonderful, Ruby, wonderful. You're as pretty as Gisselle on the outside and far more beautiful and lovely on the inside," he said. "I can't help but love you. I can't think of anything else but you. I'm mad for you," he swore.

Wonder filled me. Did he truly love me with such passion? In a moment of exquisite silence, I heard the gentle tapping of the rain and felt a warm shudder pass through my body. His fingers continued to explore me, stir me. I seized his head in my hands, intending to stop him, but instead I kissed his forehead, his hair. I held him against my bosom tightly.

"Your heart's pounding and so is mine," he said. He looked into my eyes. I closed them and then, as in a dream, I felt his soft lips move over my cheek, in my hair, then lightly over my eyelids and finally my lips again. This time, as he kissed me, he slipped his fingers under the waist of my panties and drew them down.

I started to protest, but he quieted me with another kiss.

"It will be wonderful, Ruby," he whispered. "I promise. Besides, you should know what it's like. An artist should know," he said.

"Beau, I'm afraid. Please . . . don't . . . "

"It's all right." He smiled down at me. I was naked below him and his nakedness was against me. I felt him throbbing. It took my breath away, made it harder and harder to talk, to plead. "I want to be your first. I should be your first," he said. "Because I love you."

"Do you, Beau? Do you really?"

"Yes," he swore. Then he returned his lips to mine, slipping himself in between my legs at the same time. I tried to resist, keeping my legs tight, but as he prodded, he continued to kiss me and whisper and nudge me in places I had shown no boy nor man before. I felt like I was trying to hold back a deluge. Wave after wave of excitement washed over me until I was drowning in my own thundering flood of passion. I lost my final desire to resist and felt my thighs and my back relax as he moved with determination to enter me. I cried. I felt my head spin and a delightful dizziness send me reeling back into the echo of my own soft moans. The explosions within me, surprised, frightened, and then pleased me. Finally, his climax came fast, hot, and furious. I felt him shudder and then come to a peaceful stillness, his lips still pressed against my cheek, his breathing still heavy and hard.

"Oh, Ruby," he moaned, "Ruby, you're beautiful, wonderful."

The realization of what had happened, what I had permitted swept over me. I pushed on his shoulders.

"Let me up, Beau. Please," I cried. He sat back and I seized my garments and began putting them on quickly.

"You're not mad at me, are you?" he asked.

"I'm mad at myself," I said.

"Why? Wasn't it wonderful for you, too?"

I buried my face in my hands and began to cry. I couldn't help it. He tried to soothe me, comfort me.

"Ruby, it's all right. Really. Don't cry."

"It's not all right, Beau. It's not. I was hoping I was different," I said.

"Different? From what? From Gisselle?"

"No. From . . . " I couldn't say it. I couldn't tell him I was hoping I wasn't a Landry because he didn't know who my real mother was, but that's what I meant. The blood that ran through my veins was just as hot as the blood that had run

453

through my mother's and had gotten her in trouble with Paul's father and later, with Daddy.

"I don't understand," Beau said. He started to put on his clothes.

"It doesn't matter," I said, regaining control of myself. I turned to him. "I'm not blaming you for anything, Beau. You didn't make me do anything I didn't want to do myself in the end."

"I really care for you, Ruby," he said. "I think I care for you more than I've cared for any other girl."

"Do you, Beau? You didn't just say those things?"

"Of course not. I . . . "

We heard footsteps in the corridor outside my studio. I hurried to finish dressing and he stuffed his shirt into his pants just as someone tried the door. Instantly, there was a pounding. It was Daphne.

"Open this door immediately!" she cried.

I ran to it and unlocked it. She stood there, staring in at us, looking me over with so much disapproval, I couldn't help but tremble.

"What are you doing?" she demanded. "Why was this door locked?"

"We were just studying our play lines and didn't want to be disturbed," I said quickly. My heart was pounding. I was sure my hair was messed and my clothes looked hurriedly put on. She ran her eyes over me again as if I were a slave on an auction block in the antebellum South and then quickly shifted her gaze to Beau. His weak smile reinforced her suspicions.

"Where are your play scripts?" she demanded with a scowl.

"Right here," Beau said, and picked them up to show them to her.

"Hmm," she said, and then flicked her stony eyes at me. "I can't wait to see the result of all this dedicated rehearsal." She pulled herself up into an even straighter, firmer posture. "We're having some dinner guests tonight. Dress more formally," she ordered in a cold, commanding tone. "And fix your hair. Where's your sister?"

"I don't know," I said. "She left earlier and hasn't returned."

"Should she somehow get past me before dinner, inform her of my instructions," she said. She glanced at Beau again, her frown deepening, and then returned her gaze to me and fired her words like bullets. "I don't like locked doors in my house. When people lock doors, they usually have something to hide or they're doing something they don't want anyone else to know," she snapped, and then pivoted and left. It was as if a cold wind had just blown through the room. I let out a breath and so did Beau.

"You better be going, Beau," I said. He nodded.

"I'll pick you up for school tomorrow," he said. "Ruby . . ."

"I hope you really meant what you said, Beau. I hope you really do care for me."

"I do. I swear," he said, and kissed me. "I'll see you in the morning. Bye." He was eager to escape. Daphne's looks were like darts sticking into his facade of innocence.

After he left I sat down for a moment. The events of the last hour seemed more like a dream now. It wasn't until I got up and looked at the drawing I had done of him that I realized none of it was a dream. I covered the picture and hurried out, feeling so light, I thought I might just be carried out an open window by a passing breeze.

Gisselle didn't return home in time for dinner. She phoned to say she was eating with her friends. Daphne was very upset about it, but quickly hid her displeasure when our dinner guests, Monsieur Hamilton Davies and his wife, Beatrice, arrived. Monsieur Davies was a man in his late fifties or early sixties who owned a steamboat company that took tourists up and down the Mississippi River. Daphne had let me know that he was one of the wealthiest men in New Orleans, who they were trying to involve with some of my father's investments. She also let me know in no uncertain terms that it was very important I be on my best behavior and make a good impression.

"Don't speak unless spoken to and when someone does speak to you, answer promptly and briefly. They'll be watching the way you comport yourself so remember everything I taught you about dinner etiquette," she lectured.

"If you're worried about me embarrassing you, maybe I should eat earlier," I suggested.

"Nonsense," she said sharply. "The Davies are here because they want to see you. They're the first of our friends I've invited. They know it's an honor," she added in her most haughty, arrogant tone.

Was I some sort of trophy now, a curiosity she was using to enhance her own importance in the eyes of her friends? I wondered, but dared not ask. Instead, I dressed as she told me to dress and took my place at the table, concentrating on my posture and my manners.

The Davies were pleasant enough, but their interest in my story made me uncomfortable. Madame Davies, especially, asked many detailed questions about my life in the bayou with "those awful Cajuns," and I had to make up answers on the spot, glancing quickly at Daphne after each response to see if I had said the right things.

"Ruby's tolerance for these swamp people is understandable," she told the Davies when I didn't sound bitter enough. "For all of her life, she was led to believe she was one of them and they were her family."

"How tragic," Madame Davies said. "And yet, look at how nice she's turning out. You're doing a wonderful job with her, Daphne."

"Thank you," Daphne said, gloating.

"We oughta get her story into the newspapers, Pierre," Hamilton Davies suggested.

"That would only bring her notoriety, Hamilton dear," Daphne said quickly. "The truth is, we've shared these details solely with our dearest friends," she added. The way she smiled, batted her eyelashes, and turned her shoulders at him made his eyes twinkle with pleasure. "And we've asked everyone to be discreet. No sense in making life any more difficult for the poor child than it already has been," she added.

"Of course," Hamilton said. He smiled at me.

"That would be the least desirable thing to do. As usual, Daphne, you're a lot wiser and clearer thinkin' than us Creole men."

Daphne lowered and then raised her eyes flirtatiously. Watching her in action, I felt confident I was watching an expert when it came to manipulating men. All the while my father sat back, a smile of admiration, a look of idolization in his eyes. Even so, I was happy when dinner ended and I was excused.

A few hours later, I heard Gisselle return home and go to her room. I waited to see if she would knock on our adjoining door or try it, but she went right to her telephone. I couldn't hear what she was saying, but I heard her voice drone on well into the night. She seemed to have a slew of friends to call. Naturally, I was curious about what she gossiped, but I didn't want to give her the satisfaction of going to her. I was still very angry over the things she had done.

The next morning, she was all brightness and light, just bubbling over with pleasantness at the breakfast table. I was cordial to her in front of Daddy, but I was determined to see her apologize before I would be as friendly as I had been. To both Beau's and my surprise, she had Martin pick her up for school. Just before she skipped down the steps to get into his car, she turned to me and offered the closest thing to an apology.

"Don't blame me for what happened. Someone else told them we had gone to Storyville and I had to tell them about your friend," she said. "See you at school, sister dear," she added with a smile.

Before I could reply, she was rushing off. A

few moments later, I got into Beau's car and we followed. He was still worried about Daphne.

"Did she say or ask you anything else after I left?" he wanted to know.

"No. She was worried only about pleasing our dinner guests."

"Good," he said with visible relief. "My parents have been invited to dinner at your house next weekend. We'll just have to cool it a bit," he suggested.

But cooling things down was not to be my destiny. As soon as we entered the school, I sensed a different atmosphere about me. Beau thought I was imagining it, but it seemed to me that most of the students were looking my way and smiling. Some hid their smirks behind their hands when they whispered, but many didn't try to be discreet. It wasn't until the end of English class that I found out why.

As the class filed out, one of the boys came up beside me and bumped his shoulder against mine.

"Oh, sorry," he said.

"It's all right." I started away, but he seized my arm to pull me back beside him.

"Say, are you smiling in this?" he asked, holding out his hand and unclenching his fist to reveal a picture of me naked in his palm. It was one of the pictures that had been taken at Claudine's slumber party. In it, I had just turned back and wore a look of shock on my face, but most of my body was clearly exposed.

He laughed and hurried on to join a pack of students who had gathered to wait at the corner of the corridor. The collection of both girls and

459

boys gazed over his shoulder to look at the photograph. A kind of paralyzing numbness gripped me. I felt as if my legs had been nailed to the floor. Suddenly, Gisselle joined the group.

"Make sure you tell everyone it's my sister and not me," she quipped, and everyone laughed. She smiled at me and continued on, arm and arm with Martin.

My tears clouded my vision. Everything looked out of focus or hazy. Even Beau coming down the corridor toward me, a look of concern on his face, seemed distant and distorted. I felt something within me crack and suddenly, a shrill scream flowed out of my mouth. Every single person in the corridor, including some teachers, froze and looked my way.

"Ruby!" Beau called.

I shook my head, denying the reality of what was taking place before me. Some students were laughing; some were smiling. Few looked worried or unhappy.

"You . . . animals!" I cried. "You mean, cruel . . . animals!"

I turned and threw my books down and just lunged at the nearest exit.

"RUBY!" Beau cried after me, but I shot through the door and ran down the steps. He came after me, but I was running as hard and as fast as I had ever run. I nearly got hit by a car when I sprinted across the street. The driver put on his brakes and brought it to a screeching stop, but I didn't pause. I ran on and on, not even looking where I was going. I ran until I felt a dozen needles in my side and then, with my lungs bursting, I finally slowed down and collapsed behind an old, large oak tree on someone's front lawn. There, I sobbed and sobbed until my well of tears ran dry and my chest ached with the heaving and crying.

I closed my eyes and tried to imagine myself far away. I saw myself back in the bayou, floating in a pirogue through the canal on a warm, clear spring day.

The clouds above me now disappeared. The grayness of the New Orleans day was replaced by the sunshine in my memory. As my pirogue floated closer to the shore, I heard Grandmere Catherine singing behind the house. She was hanging up some clothes she had washed.

"Grandmere," I called. She leaned to the right and saw me. Her smile was so bright and alive. She looked so young and so beautiful to me.

"Grandmere," I muttered with my eyes still shut tight. "I want to go home. I want to be back in the bayou, living with you. I don't care how poor we were or how hard things were for us. I was still happier. Grandmere, please, make it all right again. Don't be dead and gone. Perform one of your rituals and erase time. Make all this just a nightmare. Let me open my eyes and be beside you in the loom room, working. I'll count to three and it will be true. One . . . two . . ."

"Hey, there," I heard a man call. I opened my eyes. "What do you think you're doing?" An elderly man with wild snow white hair stood in the doorway of the house in front of which I had collapsed. He waved a black cane toward me. "What do you want here?"

"I was just resting, sir," I said.

"This isn't a park, you know," he said. He looked at me more closely. "Shouldn't you be in school?" he demanded.

"Yes, sir," I said and got up. "I'm sorry," I said, and walked off quickly. When I reached the corner, I gathered my bearings and hurried up the next street. Realizing how close I was, I headed for home. When I arrived, Daddy and Daphne were already gone.

"Mademoiselle Ruby?" Edgar said, opening the door and looking out at me. This time I couldn't hide my tear-streaked face or pretend to be all right. He tightened his face into an expression of concern and anger. "Come along," he ordered. I followed him through the corridor to the kitchen. "Nina," he said as soon as we entered. Nina turned around and took one look at me and then at him. She nodded.

"She'll be fine with me," she said, and Edgar, looking satisfied, left. Nina drew closer.

"What happened?" she demanded.

"Oh, Nina," I cried. "No matter what I do, she finds a way to hurt me."

Nina nodded.

"No more. You come with Nina now. This will be stopped. Wait here," she commanded, and left me in the kitchen. I heard her go down the corridor to the stairway. After a minute or so, she returned and took my hand. I thought she was going to take me back to her room again for one of her voodoo rituals. But she surprised me. She threw off her apron and led me to the back door.

"Where are we going, Nina?" I asked as she hurried me through the yard to the street.

"To see Mama Dede. You need very strong gris-gris. Only Mama Dede can do it. Just one thing, child," she said, stopping at the corner and drawing her face closer to mine, her black eyes wide with excitement. "Do not tell Monsieur and Madame Dumas where I'm taking you, okay? This will be our secret only, okay?"

"Who is . . . ?"

"Mama Dede, voodoo queen of all New Orleans now."

"What is Mama Dede going to do?"

"Get your sister to stop hurting you. Drive Papa La Bas out of her heart. Make her be good. You want that?"

"Yes, Nina. I want that," I said.

"Then swear to keep the secret. Swear."

"I swear, Nina."

"Good. Come," she said, and started us down the walk again. I was just angry enough to go anywhere and do anything she wanted.

We took the streetcar and then got off and took a bus to a rundown section of the city in which I had never been, nor even seen. The buildings looked no better than shacks. Black children, most too young to go to school, played on the scarred and bald front yards. Broken-down cars and some that looked like they were about to break down were parked along the streets. The sidewalks were dirty, the gutters full of cans, bottles, and paper. Here and there a lone sycamore or magnolia tree struggled to battle the abused surroundings. To me this looked like a place where the sun itself hated to shine. No matter how bright the day, everything still looked tarnished, rusted, faded.

Nina hurried us along the sidewalk until we reached a shack house no better or no worse than any of the others. The windows all had dark shades drawn and the sidewalk, steps, and even the front door were chipped and cracked. Above the front door hung a string of bones and feathers.

"The queen lives here?" I asked, astounded. I had been expecting another mansion.

"She sure do," Nina said. We went down the narrow walk to the front door and Nina turned the bell key. After a moment a very old black woman, toothless, her hair so thin, I could see the shape and color of her scalp, opened the door and peered out. She wore what looked like a potato sack to me. Stooped, her shoulders turned in sharply, she lifted her tired eyes to gaze at Nina and me. I didn't think she was any more than four feet tall. She wore a pair of men's sneakers, stained, without laces, and no socks.

"Must see Mama Dede," Nina said. The old lady nodded and stepped back so we could enter the small house. The walls were cracked and peeling. The floor looked like it had once been covered with carpet that had just recently been ripped up. Here and there pieces of it remained glued or tacked to the slats. The aroma of something very sweet flowed from the rear of the house. The old lady gestured toward a room on the left and Nina took my hand and we entered.

A half-dozen large candles provided the light. The room looked like a store. It was that full of charms and bones, dolls, and bunches of feathers, hair, and snakeskins. One wall was covered with shelves and shelves of jars of powders. And there

464

were cartons of different color candles on the floor along the far wall.

In the midst of all this clutter were a small settee and two torn easy chairs, the springs popped out of the bottom of one. Between the chairs and the settee was a wooden box. Gold and silver shapes had been etched around it.

"Sit," the old lady commanded. Nina nodded at the easy chair on our left and I went to it. She went to the other.

"Nina . . . " I began.

"Shh," she said and closed her eyes. "Just wait." A moment later, from somewhere else in the house, I heard the sound of a drum. It was a low, steady beat. I couldn't help but become nervous and afraid. Why had I allowed myself to be brought here?

Suddenly, the blanket that hung in the doorway in front of us parted and a much younger looking black woman appeared. She had long, silky black hair gathered in thick ropelike strands around her head, over which she wore a red tignon with seven knots whose points all stuck straight up. She was tall and wore a black robe that flowed all the way down to her bare feet. I thought she had a pretty face, lean with high cheekbones and a nicely shaped mouth, but when she turned to me, I shuddered. Her eyes were as gray as granite.

She was blind.

"Mama Dede, I come for big help," Nina said. Mama Dede nodded and entered the room, moving as if she weren't blind, swiftly and gracefully sitting herself on the settee. She folded her hands in her lap and waited, those seemingly dead eyes turning toward me. I didn't move; I hardly breathed.

"Speak of it, sister," she said.

"This little girl here, she's got a twin sister, jealous and cruel, who does bad things to her causing much pain and grief."

"Give me your hand," Mama Dede said to me, and held hers out. I looked at Nina who nodded. Slowly, I put mine into Mama Dede's. She closed her fingers firmly over mine. They felt hot.

"Your sister," Mama Dede said to me. "You don't know her long and she don't know you long?"

"Yes, that's right," I said amazed.

"And your mother, she can't help you none?"

"No."

"She be dead and gone to the other side," she said, nodding and then she released my hand and turned to Nina.

"Papa La Bas, he eating on her sister's heart," Nina said. "Making her hateful, somethin' terrible. Now we got to protect this baby, Mama. She believes. Her grandmere was a Traiteur lady in the bayou."

Mama Dede nodded softly and then held out her hand again, this time palm up. Nina dug into her pocket and pulled out a silver dollar. She put it in Mama Dede's hand. Mama Dede closed her palm and then turned to the doorway where the old lady stood watching. She came forward and took the silver coin and dropped it in a pocket in her sack dress.

"Burn two yellow candles," she prescribed. The old lady moved to the cartons and plucked out two yellow candles. She set them in holders and then lit their wicks. I thought that might be all there was to it, but suddenly, Mama Dede reached out and seized the top of the ornate box. She lifted it gently and put it beside her on the settee. Nina looked very happy. I waited as Mama Dede concentrated and then dipped her hands into the box. When she brought them up, I nearly fainted.

She was clutching a young python snake. It seemed asleep, barely moving, its eyes just two slits. I gulped to keep down a scream as Mama Dede brought the snake to her face. Instantly, the snake's tongue jetted out and it licked her cheek. As soon as it had, Mama Dede returned it to the box and covered the box again.

"From the snake, Mama Dede gets the power and the vision," Nina whispered. "Old legend say, first man and first woman entered the world blind and were given sight by the snake."

"What's your sister's name, child?" Mama Dede asked. My tongue tightened. I was afraid to give it, afraid now that something terrible might occur.

"You must be the one to give the name," Nina instructed. "Give Mama Dede the name."

"Gisselle," I said. "But . . ."

Eh! Eh bomba hen hen!" Mama Dede began to chant. As she chanted, she turned and twisted her body under the robe, writhing to the sound of the drum and the rhythm of her own voice.

"Canga bafie te. Danga moune de te. Canga do ki Ii Gisselle!" she ended with a shout.

My heart was pounding so hard, I had to press the palm of my hand against my breast. Mama

Dede turned toward Nina again. She reached into her pocket and produced what I recognized as one of Gisselle's hair ribbons. That was why she had first gone upstairs before we left. I wanted to reach out and stop her before she put it into Mama Dede's hand, but I was too late. The voodoo queen clutched it tightly.

"Wait," I cried, but Mama Dede opened the box and dropped the ribbon into it.

Then she writhed again and began a new chant. *"L'appe vini, Le Grand Zombi. L'appe vini, pou fe gris-gris."*

"He is coming," Nina translated. "The Great Zombi, he is coming, to make gris-gris."

Mama Dede paused suddenly and screamed a piercing cry that made my heart stop for a moment. I thought it had risen into my throat. I couldn't swallow; I could barely breathe. She froze and then she fell back against the settee, dropping her head to the side, her eyes closed. For a moment no one moved, no one spoke. Then Nina tapped me on the knee and nodded toward the door. I rose quickly. The old lady moved ahead and opened the front door for us.

"Thank Mama, please, Grandmere," Nina said. The old lady nodded and we left.

My heart didn't stop racing until we reached home again. Nina was so confident everything would be all right now. I couldn't imagine what to expect. But when Gisselle returned from school, she wasn't a bit changed. In fact, she bawled me out for running away and blamed me for everything that happened as a result.

"Because you ran off like that, Beau got into a

fight with Billy and they were both taken to the principal," she said, stopping in the doorway of my room. "Beau's parents have to come to school before he can return.

"Everyone thinks you're crazy now. It was all just a joke. But I got called into the principal's office, too, and he's going to call Daddy and Mommy, thanks to you. Now we'll both be in trouble."

I turned to her slowly, my heart so full of anger, I didn't think I would be able to speak without screaming. But I surprised myself and frightened her with the control in my voice.

"I'm sorry Beau got into a fight and into trouble. He was only trying to protect me. But I'm not sorry about you.

"It's true, I lived in a world that most would consider quite backward compared to the one you've lived in, Gisselle. And it's true the people are simpler and things happen that city people think are terrible, crude, and even immoral.

"But the cruel things you've done to me and permitted others to do to me make anything I've seen in the bayou look like child's play. I thought we could be sisters, real sisters who looked out for each other and cared for each other, but you're determined to hurt me any way you can and whenever you can," I said. Tears were streaming down my cheeks now, despite my effort not to cry in front of her.

"Sure," she replied, moans in her voice, too. "You're making me out to be the bad one now. But you're the one who just appeared on our doorstep and turned our world topsy-turvy. You're the one who got everyone to like you more than they like me. You stole Beau, didn't you?"

"I didn't steal him. You told me you didn't care about him anymore anyway," I said.

"Well . . . I don't, but I don't like someone stealing him away," she added. She stood there, fuming for a few moments. "You better not get me in trouble when the principal calls," she warned and marched off.

Dr. Storm did call. After breaking up the fight between Beau and Billy, a teacher had taken the photograph and brought it to the principal. Dr. Storm told Daphne about the picture and she called Gisselle and me into the study just before dinner. She was so full of anger and embarrassment, her face looked distorted: her eyes large and furious, her mouth stretched into a grimace and her nostrils wide.

"Which one of you allowed such a picture to be taken?" she demanded. Gisselle looked down quickly.

"Neither of us allowed it, Mother," I said. "Some boys snuck into Claudine's house without any of us knowing and while I was changing into a costume for a game we were playing, they snapped the picture of me."

"We're the laughingstock of the school community by now, I'm sure," she said. "And the Andreas have to see the principal. I just got off the phone with Edith Andreas. She's beside herself. This is the first time Beau has gotten into serious trouble. And all because of you," she accused.

"But . . . "

"Did you do these sorts of things in the swamp?"

"No. Of course not," I replied quickly.

"I don't know how you get yourself involved in one terrible thing after another so quickly, but you apparently do. Until further notice, you are not to go anywhere, no parties, no dates, no expensive dinners, nothing. Is that understood?"

I choked back my tears. Defending myself was useless. All she could see was how she had been disgraced.

"Yes, Mother."

"Your father doesn't know about this yet. I will tell him calmly when he returns. Go upstairs and remain in your room until it's time to come down for dinner."

I left and went upstairs, feeling strangely numb. It was as if I didn't care anymore. She could do whatever she wanted to do to me. It didn't matter.

Gisselle paused in my doorway on the way back to her room. She flashed a smile of self-satisfaction, but I didn't say a word to her. That night, we had the quietest dinner since I had arrived. My father was subdued by his disappointment and by what I was sure was Daphne's rage. I avoided his eyes and was happy when Gisselle and I were excused. She couldn't wait to get to her telephone to spread the news of what had occurred.

I went to sleep that night, thinking about Mama Dede, the snake, and the ribbon. How I wished there was something to it all. My desire for vengeance was that strong.

But two days later, I regretted it.

19

Fate Keeps On Happening

The following morning I felt like a shadow of myself. With a heart that had a hollow thump, with legs that seemed to glide over the hallways and down the stairs, I went to breakfast. Martin came to take Gisselle to school, but she didn't ask me and I didn't want to go along with them. Beau had to go to school with his parents so I just walked to school, resembling someone in a trance—face forward, eyes moving neither left nor right.

When I arrived at school, I felt like a pariah. Even Mookie was afraid to associate with me and didn't, as usual, meet me at the locker before homeroom to chatter about homework or television shows. I was the victim in all this, the one who had been horribly embarrassed, but no one seemed to feel sorry for me. It was almost as if I had contracted some terrible, infectious disease and instead of people worrying about me, they were worried about themselves.

Later in the day, I ran into Beau rushing down the corridor to class. He and his parents had had their meeting with Dr. Storm.

"I'm on probation," he told me with a frown. "If I do anything else, break the slightest school rule, I'll be suspended and kicked off the baseball team."

"I'm sorry, Beau. I didn't mean for you to do something and get yourself in trouble."

"That's all right. I hated what they did to you," he said, and then he looked down and I knew what was coming. "I had to promise my parents I wouldn't see you for a while. But that's a promise I don't intend to keep," he added, his beautiful blue eyes blazing with defiance and anger.

"No, Beau. Do what they say. You'll only get yourself into more trouble and I'll be blamed for it. Let some time pass."

"It's not fair," he complained.

"What's fair and what isn't doesn't seem to matter, especially where rich Creole reputations are concerned," I told him bitterly. He nodded. The warning bell for the next period sounded.

"I'd better not be late for class," he said.

"Me neither." I started away.

"I'll call you," he cried, but I didn't turn back. I didn't want him to see the tears that had clouded my eyes. I choked them back, took a deep breath, and went on to my next class. In all my classes, I sat quietly, took notes, and answered questions only when I was asked directly. When the period ended and the class was dismissed, I always left the room alone, holding back until most of the students had gone.

The worst time was lunch. No one was eager to sit with me and when I took a seat at a table, the students who were already sitting there moved to another table. Beau sat with his baseball team-mates and Gisselle sat with her usual friends. I knew everyone was looking at me, but I didn't return their glances and stares.

Mookie finally had enough nerve to speak to

me, but I wished she hadn't, for she brought only bad news.

"Everyone thinks you deliberately did a striptease. Is it true you're good friends with a prostitute?" she asked quickly. A hot rush of blood heated my face.

"First, I didn't do any striptease, and no, I am not good friends with a prostitute. The girls and boys who pulled this horrible prank on me are just spreading stories to try to cover up their own guilt, Mookie. I thought you, of all people, would see that," I snapped.

"Oh, I believe you," she said. "But everyone's talking about you and when I tried to tell my mother you weren't as bad as people were saying, she got furious with me and forbid me to be friends with you. I'm sorry," she added. What she said to me made me stiffen.

"So am I," I replied, and gobbled down the rest of my lunch so I could leave quickly.

At the end of the school day, I went to see Mr. Saxon, the dramatics instructor, and told him I was resigning from the school play. It was obvious from the look on his face that he had heard all about the episode with the photograph.

"That's really not necessary, Ruby," he said, but he looked relieved that I had come forward with the idea. I could tell he had already anticipated my bringing an unwelcome notoriety to the cast which would take away from the performances. People would come just out of curiosity to see the wicked little Cajun girl.

"But if your mind is made up, I do appreciate

your doing this before it gets to be too late for me to replace you," he added.

Without saying another thing, I dropped the script on his desk and left to walk home.

Daddy didn't come to dinner that evening. When I came down I found Gisselle and Daphne sitting alone. With her eyes fixed angrily on me, Daphne quickly explained that he had fallen into one of his fits of melancholia.

"The combination of some unfortunate business ventures with the disastrous recent events have pushed him into a deep depression," she continued.

I gazed at Gisselle who continued eating as if she had heard this a hundred times before.

"Shouldn't we call a doctor, get him some medicine?" I asked.

"There is no medicine except filling his life with cheerful news," she replied pointedly. Gisselle jerked her head up.

"I got a ninety on a history test yesterday," she boasted.

"That's very nice, dear. I'll be sure to tell him," Daphne said.

I wanted to say that I had gotten a ninety-five on the same test, but I was sure Gisselle, and maybe even Daphne, would interpret it as my attempt to belittle Gisselle's accomplishment, so I remained silent.

Later that evening, Gisselle stopped by my room. As far as I could tell, even though poor Daddy was quite distraught over all that had occurred, she was completely without guilt or regrets. I had the urge to scream at her and see her poise collapse! I wanted her smiles to peel off like bark from a tree, but I remained silent, afraid of only causing more trouble.

"Deborah Tallant is having a party this weekend," she announced. "I'm going with Martin, and Beau's coming along with us," she added with sadistic pleasure. She looked like she was really enjoying pouring salt on my wounds. "I know he regrets giving me up so quickly now, but I'm not going to make things easy for him. I'm going to let him turn and turn out there like a ball on a string. You know how," she said with an oily, evil smile. "I'll kiss Martin passionately right in front of him, dance so closely with Martin that we look attached . . . that sort of thing."

"Why are you so cruel?" I asked her.

"I'm not so cruel. He deserves it. Anyway, I wish I could take you to the party, but I had to specifically promise Deborah I wouldn't. Her parents wouldn't like it," she said.

"I wouldn't go if she invited me," I replied. A cynical smile twisted her lips.

"Oh, yes you would," she said, laughing. "Yes, you would."

She left me, infuriated. I sat there steaming for a while and then felt myself calm down to a quiet indifference. I lay back in my bed reminiscing and finding some comfort in my beautiful memories living with Grandmere Catherine in the bayou. Paul came to mind and I suddenly felt terrible about the way I had left without saying good-bye to him, even though at the time, it seemed to be the best thing to do.

I sat up quickly and ripped a sheet of paper out

of my notebook. Then I went to my desk and began writing him a letter. As I wrote, the tears filled my eyes and my heart contracted into a tight lead fist in my chest.

Dear Paul,

It has been some time now since I left the bayou, but you haven't been out of my thoughts. First, I want to apologize for leaving without saying good bye to you. The reason why I didn't is simple—it would have been too painful for me, and I was afraid, too painful for you. I'm sure you were just as confused and disturbed about the events that occurred in our pasts as I was, and probably, you were just as angry about it. But fate is something we cannot change. It would be easier to hold back the tide.

Even so, I imagine you've spent a lot of time wondering why I just upped and left the bayou. The immediate reason was Grandpere Jack was arranging my marriage to Buster Trahaw and you know I'd rather be dead than married to him. But there were deeper, even more important reasons, the most important one being that I found out who my real father was and decided to do what Grandmere Catherine had asked as a dying wish-go to him and start a new life.

I have. I now live in an entirely different world in New Orleans. We're rich; we live in a grand house with maids and cooks and butlers. My father is very nice and very concerned about me. One of the first things he did when he discovered my artistic talent was to create a studio for me and hire a college art teacher to give me private lessons. However, the biggest surprise for you to learn is that I have a twin sister!

I wish I could tell you that all is wonderful, that being rich and having so many beautiful things has made my life better. But it hasn't.

My father's life has not been smooth either. The tragedies that befell his younger brother and some of the other things that happened to him have made him a deeply disturbed and sad man. I was hoping that I could change things for him and bring him enough happiness to cure his depression and sadness, but I haven't been successful yet and now I am not sure I can ever be.

In fact, at this very moment I wish I could return to the bayou, return to the time before you and I learned all the terrible things about our own pasts, return to the time before Grandmere Catherine died. But I can't. For better or for worse, as I said, this is my fate and I must learn how to deal with it.

Right now, all I want to do is ask you to forgive me for leaving without saying good-bye, and ask you when you have a chance, in a quiet moment, either in or out of church, to say a little prayer for me.

I do miss you.

God bless.

Love,
Ruby

I put the letter into an envelope and addressed it. The next morning, I mailed it on my way to school. The day wasn't much different from the one before, but I could see that as time went by, the excitement and interest other students had in me and what had occurred would wane. There was nothing as dead as old news. Not that those who had been friendly and interested in me started to be those things again. Oh, no. That would take much longer and only if I made a great effort. For the present, I was treated as if I were invisible.

I saw Beau a few times and every time, he looked at me, he had an expression of shame and regret on his face. I felt more sorry for him than he did for me and tried to avoid him as much as possible so things wouldn't be so hard for him. I knew there were girls and even boys who would rush home to tell their parents if Beau defiantly returned to my side. In a matter of hours, the phones at his house would ring off the hook and his parents would be enraged at him.

But on the way home from school that afternoon, I was surprised when Gisselle and Martin drove up to the curb and called to me. I paused and went over to Martin's car.

"What?" I asked.

"If you want, you can come with us," Gisselle offered, as if she were handing out charity. "Martin's got some good stuff and we're going over to his house. No one's home," she said. I could smell the aroma of the marijuana and knew that they had already started having their so-called good time.

"No, thanks," I said.

"I'm not going to invite you to do things if you keep saying no," Gisselle threatened. "And you'll never get back into the swing of things and have friends again."

"I'm tired and I want to begin my final term paper," I explained.

"What a drag," Gisselle moaned.

Martin puffed on his joint and smiled at me.

"Don't you want to laugh and cry again?" he asked. That set them both laughing and I pulled myself away from the window just as he accelerated and shot off, his tires squealing as he made the turn at the end of the block.

I walked home and went right to my room to do what I had said, begin my homework. But less than an hour later, I heard some shouting coming from downstairs. Curious, I walked out of my room and went to the head of the stairs. Below, in the entryway stood two city policemen, both with their hats off. A few moments later, Daphne came rushing forward, Wendy Williams hurrying with her coat. I took a few steps down.

"What's wrong?" I asked.

Daphne paused in front of the policemen.

"Your sister," she screamed. "She's been in a bad car accident with Martin. Your father's meeting me at the hospital."

"I'll come with you," I cried, and ran down the steps to join her.

"What happened?" I asked, getting into the car with her.

"The police said Martin was smoking that dirty . . . filthy . . . drug stuff. He crashed right into the back of a city bus."

480

"Oh no." My heart was pounding. I had seen only one car accident before in my life. A man in a pickup truck had gotten drunk and drove off an embankment. When I saw the accident, his bloodied body was still hanging out of the smashed front window, his head dangling.

"What's wrong with you young people today?" Daphne cried. "You have so much, and yet you do these stupid things. Why?" she shrilled. "Why?"

I wanted to say it was because some of us have too much, but I bit down on those thoughts, knowing she would take it as a criticism of her role as mother.

"Did the policemen say how bad they were hurt?" I asked instead.

"Bad," she replied. "Very bad . . . "

Daddy was already waiting for us in the hospital emergency room. He looked terribly distraught, aged and weakened by the events.

"What have you learned?" Daphne asked quickly. He shook his head.

"She's still unconscious. Apparently, she hit the windshield. There are broken bones. They're doing the X rays now."

"Oh, God," Daphne said. "This, on top of everything else."

"What about Martin?" I asked. Daddy lifted his shadowy, sad eyes to me and shook his head. "He's not . . . dead?"

Daddy nodded. My blood ran cold and drained down to my ankles, leaving a hollow ache in my stomach.

"Just a little while ago," he told Daphne. She turned white and clutched his arm.

"Oh, Pierre, how gruesome."

I backed up to a chair by the wall and let myself drop into it. Stunned, I could only sit and stare at the people who rushed to and fro. I waited and watched as Daddy and Daphne spoke with doctors.

When I was about nine, there was a four-year-old boy in the bayou, Dylan Fortier, who had fallen out of a pirogue and drowned. I remember Grandmere Catherine had been called to try to save him and I had gone along with her. The moment she looked at his little withered form on the bank of the canal, she knew it was too late and crossed herself.

At the age of nine, I thought death was something that happened only to old people. We young people were invulnerable, protected by the years we were promised at birth. We wore our youth like a shield. We could get sick, very sick; we could have accidents, even serious ones, or we could be bitten by poisonous things, but somehow, someway there was always something that would save us.

The sight of that little boy, pale and gray, his hair stuck on his forehead, his little fingers clenched into tiny fists, his eyes sewn shut, and his lips blue was a sight that haunted me for years afterward.

All I could think of now was Martin's impish smile when he had pulled away from the curb. What if I had gotten into the car with them, I wondered? Would I be in some hospital emergency room or would I have prevailed and gotten Martin to slow down and drive more carefully?

Fate . . . as I had told Paul in my letter . . . could not be defeated or denied.

Daphne returned first, her face full of agony and emotional fatigue.

"How is she?" I asked, my heart thumping.

"She's regained consciousness, but something is wrong with her spine," she said in a dead, dry tone. She was even palmer and held her right palm over her heart.

What do you mean?" I asked, my voice cracking.

"She can't move her legs," Daphne said. "We're going to have an invalid in the family. Wheelchairs and nurses," she said, grimacing. "Oh, I feel sick," she added quickly. "I'm going to the bathroom. See to your father," she commanded with a wave of her hand.

I looked across the hallway and saw him looking like someone who had been hit by a train. He was standing with the doctor. His back was against the wall and his head was down. The doctor patted him on the shoulder and then walked off, but Daddy didn't move. I rose slowly and started toward him. He raised his head as I approached, the tears streaming from his eyes, his lips quivering.

"My little girl," he said, "my princess . . . is probably going to be crippled for life."

"Oh, Daddy," I shook my head, my own tears rivaling his in quantity now. I rushed to him and embraced him and he buried his face in my hair and sobbed.

"It's my fault," he sobbed. "I'm still being punished for the things I've done."

"Oh, no, Daddy. It's not your fault."

"It is. It is," he insisted. "I'll never be forgiven, never. Everyone I love will suffer."

As we clung to each other tightly, all I could think was . . . this is definitely not his fault. It was my fault . . . my fault. I've got to get Nina to take me back to Mama Dede. I've got to undo the spell.

Daphne and I returned home first. By now, it seemed like half the city had heard of the accident. The phones were ringing off the hook. Daphne went directly up to her suite, telling Edgar to take down the names of those who called, explaining that she wasn't able to speak to anyone just yet. Daddy was even worse, immediately retreating to Uncle Jean's room the moment he stepped through the door. I had a message that Beau had called and I called him back before I went to see Nina.

"I can't believe it," he said, trying to hold back his tears. "I can't believe Martin's dead."

I told him what had happened earlier, how they had approached me on the way home.

"He knew better; he knew you couldn't drive and smoke that stuff or drink."

"Knowing is one thing. Listening to wisdom and obeying it is another," I said dryly.

"Things must be terrible at your house, huh?"

"Yes, Beau."

"My parents will be over to see Daphne and Pierre tonight, I'm sure. I might come along, if they let me," he said.

"I might not be here."

"Where are you going tonight?" he asked, astonished.

"There's someone I have to see."

"Oh."

"It's not another boy, Beau," I said quickly, hearing the disappointment in his voice.

"Well, they probably won't let me come anyway," he said. "I'm feeling sick to my stomach, myself. If I hadn't had baseball practice . . . I would probably have been in that car."

"Fate just didn't point its long, dark finger at you," I told him.

After we spoke I went to find Nina. She, Edgar, and Wendy were consoling each other in the kitchen. As soon as she lifted her eyes and met mine, she knew why I had come.

"This is not your fault, child," she said. "Those who welcome the devil man into their hearts invite the bad gris-gris themselves."

"I want to see Mama Dede, Nina. Right away," I added. She looked at Wendy and Edgar.

"She won't tell you any different," she said.

"I want to see her, Nina," I insisted. "Take me to her," I ordered. She sighed and nodded slowly.

"If the madame or monsieur want something, I'll get it to them," Wendy promised. Nina rose and got her pocketbook. Then we hurried out of the house and met the first streetcar. When we arrived at Mama Dede's, her mother seemed to know why. She and Nina exchanged knowing looks. Once again, we waited in the living room for the voodoo queen to enter. I couldn't take my eyes off the box I knew contained the snake and Gisselle's ribbon.

Mama Dede made her entrance as the drums began. As before, she went to the settee and turned her gray eyes toward me.

"Why you come back to Mama, child?" she asked.

"I didn't want anything this terrible to happen," I cried. "Martin's dead and Gisselle is crippled."

"What you want to happen and what you don't want to happen don't make no difference to the wind. Once you throw your anger in the air, it can't be pulled back."

"It's my fault," I moaned. "I shouldn't have come here. I shouldn't have asked you to do something."

"You came here because you were meant to come here. Zombi bring you to me to do what must be done. You didn't cast the first stone, child. Papa La Bas, he find an open door into your sister's heart and curled himself up comfortable. She let him cast the stones with her name on it, not you."

"Isn't there anything we can do to help her now?" I pleaded.

"When she drive Papa La Bas from her heart completely, you come back and Mama see what Zombi want to do. Not until then," she said with finality.

"I feel terrible," I said, lowering my head. "Please, find a way to help us."

"Give me your hand, child," Mama Dede said. I looked up and gave her my hand. She held it firmly, hers feeling warmer and warmer.

"This all is meant to be, child," she said. "You

486

were brought here by the wind Zombi sent. You want to help your sister now, make her a better person, drive the devil from her heart?"

"Yes," I said.

"Don't be afraid," she said, and pulled my hand slowly toward the box. I looked desperately at Nina who simply closed her eyes and began to rock, mumbling some chant under her breath. "Don't be afraid," Mama Dede repeated, and opened the top of the box. "Now you reach down and take out your sister's ribbon. Take it back and nothing more be happening than has."

I hesitated. Reach into a box that contained a snake? I knew pythons weren't poisonous, but still . . .

Mama Dede released me and sat back, waiting. I thought about Daddy, the sadness in his eyes, the weight on his shoulders and slowly, with my eyes closed, I lowered my hand into the box. My fingers nudged the cold, scaly skin of the sleeping serpent. It began to squirm, but I continued moving my fingers around frantically until I felt the ribbon. Quickly, I seized it and pulled my hand out.

"Be praised," Nina said.

"That ribbon," Mama Dede said. "Its been to the other world and back. You keep it precious, as precious as Rosary beads, and maybe someday, you'll make your sister better." She stood up and turned toward Nina. "Go light me a candle at Marie Laveau's grave."

Nina nodded.

"I'll do that, Mama."

"Child," she said, turning back to me, "the

487

good and the bad, they are sisters, too. Sometimes they twist around each other like strands of rope and make knots in our hearts. Unravel the knots in your own heart first; then help your sister unravel hers."

She turned and walked out through the curtain. The drums got louder.

"Let's go home," Nina said. "Now there's much to do."

When we returned, things hadn't changed very much, except that Edgar had added another dozen or so names to the list of those who had called. Daphne was still resting in her suite and Daddy was still in Uncle Jean's room. But suddenly, a little while later, Daphne emerged looking refreshed and elegant, ready to greet those good friends who were coming to console her and Daddy. She got him to come down to have a little dinner.

I sat quietly and listened while Daphne lectured him firmly about getting himself together.

"This isn't the time to fall apart, Pierre. We have some terrible burdens now and I don't intend to carry them on my shoulders alone the way I've been carrying so many other things," she said. He nodded obediently, looking like a little boy again. "Get a hold of yourself," she ordered. "We have people to greet later and I don't want to add anything to the embarrassment we already have to endure."

"Shouldn't we worry more about Gisselle's condition than how it's all embarrassing us?" I said sharply, unable to contain my anger. I hated the way she spoke down to Daddy, who was already weak and defeated.

"How dare you speak to me that way," she snapped, Pulling herself up in the chair.

"I don't mean to be insolent, but—"

"My advice to you, young lady, is to walk the straightest, most narrow line you can these next few weeks. Gisselle hasn't been the same since your arrival and I'm sure the bad things you've done and influenced her to do had something to do with what's happened now."

"That's not true! None of that is true!" I cried. I looked at Daddy.

"Let's not bicker amongst ourselves," he pleaded. He turned to me with his eyes bloodshot from hours and hours of sorrowful crying. "Not now. Please, Ruby. Just listen to your mother." He gazed at Daphne. "At times like this, she is the strongest member of our family. She's always been," he said in a tired, defeated voice.

Daphne beamed with pride and satisfaction. For the remainder of our short meal, we all ate in silence. Later that evening, the Andreas did arrive but without Beau. Other friends followed. I retreated to my room and prayed that God would forgive me for the vengeance I had sought. Then I went to sleep, but for endless hours, I dwelled fitfully on the rim of sleep, never finding the peaceful oblivion I desperately sought.

An odd thing happened to me at school the next day. The drama and impact of the horrible automobile accident put the entire student body into a state of mourning. Everyone was subdued.

Girls who knew Martin well were in tears, comforting each other in the hallways and bathrooms. Dr. Storm got on the public address system and offered prayers and condolences. Our teachers made us do busywork, many unable to carry on as usual and sensitive to the fact that the students weren't with it either.

But the odd thing was I became someone to console and not be ignored or despised. Student after student came up to me to talk and express his or her hope everything would turn out well for Gisselle. Even her good friends, Claudine and Antoinette especially, sought my company and seemed repentant for the pranks and the nasty things they had done and said about me.

Most of all, Beau was at my side. He was a great source of comfort. As one of Martin's best friends, he was the one the other boys came to when they wanted to express their sorrow. At lunch, most of the other students gathered around us, everyone speaking in soft, subdued voices.

After school, Beau and I went directly to the hospital and found Daddy having a cup of coffee in the lounge. He had just met with the specialists.

"Her spine was damaged. It's left her paralyzed from the waist down. All of the other injuries will heal well," he said.

"Is there any possibility she'll be able to walk again," Beau asked softly.

Daddy shook his head. "Most unlikely. She's going to need lots of therapy, and lots of tender loving care," he said. "I'm arranging for a live-in nurse for a while after she comes home."

"When can we see her, Daddy?" I asked.

490

"She's still in intensive care. Only immediate family can see her," he said, looking at Beau. Beau nodded.

I started for the intensive care room.

"Ruby," Daddy called. I turned. "She doesn't know about Martin," he said. "She thinks he's just badly injured. I didn't want to tell her yet. She's had enough bad news."

"Okay, Daddy," I said, and entered. The nurse showed me to Gisselle's bed. The sight of her lying there, her face all banged up and the IV tubes in her arm made my heart ache. I swallowed back my tears and approached. She opened her eyes and looked up at me.

"How are you, Gisselle?" I asked softly.

"How do I look?" She smirked and turned away. Then she turned back. "I guess you're happy you didn't get into the car with us. I guess you want to say, I told you so, huh?"

"No," I said. "I'm sorry this happened. I feel just terrible about it."

"Why? Now no one will wonder which one of us is you and which one is me. I'm the one who can't walk. That's easy to tell," she said. "I'm the one who can't walk." Her chin quivered.

"Oh, Gisselle, you'll walk again. I'll do everything I can to help you," I promised.

"What can you do . . . mumble some Cajun prayer over my legs? The doctors were here; they told me the ugly truth."

"You can't give up hope. Never give up hope. That's what . . . " I was going to say, that's what Grandmere Catherine taught me, but I hesitated.

"Easy for you to say. You walked in here and

491

you'll walk out," she moaned. Then she took a deep breath and sighed. "Have you seen Martin? How's he doing?"

"No, I haven't seen him. I came right to see you," I said and bit down on my lower lip.

"I remember telling him he was going too fast, but he thought it was funny. Just like you, he thought everything was funny all of a sudden. I bet he's not laughing now. You go see him," she said. "And be sure he knows what's happened to me. Will you go?"

I nodded.

"Good. I hope he feels terrible; I hope . . . oh, what's the difference what I hope?" She gazed up at me. "You're happy this happened to me, aren't you?"

"No. I never wanted this much. I . . . "

"What do you mean, 'this much'? You wanted something?" She studied my face a moment. "Well?"

"Yes," I said. "I admit it. You were so mean to me, got me into so much trouble and did so many bad things to me, I went to see a voodoo queen."

"What?"

"But she told me it wasn't my fault. It was yours because you had so much hate in your heart," I added quickly.

"I don't care what she said. I'll tell Daddy what you did and he'll hate you forever. Maybe now he'll send you back to the swamps."

"Is that what you want, Gisselle?"

She thought a moment and then smiled, but such a tight, small smile, it sent chills down my spine.

"No. I want you to make it up to me. From now on until I say, you make it up to me."

"What do you want me to do?"

"Anything I ask," she said. "You better."

"I already said I would help you, Gisselle. And I'm going to do it because I want to, not because you threaten me," I told her.

"You're making the pain come back into my head," she moaned.

"I'm sorry. I'll go."

"Not until I tell you to go," she said. I stood there, looking down at her. "All right. Go. But go to Martin and tell him what I told you to tell him and then come back later tonight and tell me what he said. Go on," she commanded, and grimaced with pain. I turned and started away. "Ruby!" she called.

"What?"

"You know the only way we can be twins again?" she asked. I shook my head. She smiled. "I'll tell you. Get crippled," she said, and closed her eyes.

I lowered my head and walked out. Mama Dede's prescription was going to be much more difficult than I could ever imagine. Unravel the sisters of hate and love in Gisselle's heart? I might as well try to hold back night, I thought, and went to join Daddy and Beau who waited in the lounge.

Two days later Gisselle was told about Martin. The news struck her dumb. It was as if she believed that all that had happened to her, the injuries, the paralysis was nothing more than a dream that would soon end. The doctors would give her some pills and send her home to resume her life, just the way she had been living it. But when she was told Martin was dead and in fact the funeral was being held that very day, she withered, grew pale and small, and sealed her lips. She didn't cry in front of Daphne or Daddy and when they left and I remained with her, she didn't cry in front of me either. But as soon as I started away to go with my parents to the funeral, I heard her first sob. I ran back to her.

"Gisselle," I said, stroking her hair. She spun around and looked up at me, but not with gratitude for my returning to comfort her, but with blazing, angry eyes.

"He liked you better, too. He did!" she whined. "Whenever we were together, he talked about you. He was the one who wanted you to come along with us. And now he's dead," she added, as if that were somehow my fault.

"I'm sorry. I wish there was something I could do to change it," I told her.

"Go back to your voodoo queen," she snapped, and turned away from me.

I stood there a moment and then hurried to catch up with Daddy and Daphne.

Martin's funeral was enormous. Many of the students attended. Beau and Martin's teammates were the pallbearers. I felt sick and horrible inside and was glad when Daddy took my hand and led us away.

It rained all that day and the next few. I thought the grayness would never leave our hearts and lives, but one morning I awoke to sunshine and when I arrived at school, I found the cloud of sorrow had moved off. Everyone was back into his or her niche. Claudine appeared to take over the leadership role Gisselle once enjoyed, but I didn't care, for I spent little time with Gisselle's friends. My interest was only in doing well in school and spending whatever time I could with Beau.

Finally, the day arrived when Gisselle could be brought home from the hospital. She had begun some therapy there, but, according to what Daphne said, she was still quite uncooperative. Daddy hired the private nurse, a Mrs. Warren, who had worked in veterans' hospitals and was very familiar with patients who had suffered paralyzing injuries. She was about fifty years old, tall with short dark brown hair and hard, almost manly features. I knew she had strong forearms, for I saw the way her veins bulged the first time she lifted Gisselle to make her more comfortable. She brought some of the military manner with her, barking orders at the servants and snapping at Gisselle as if she were a recruit and not an invalid. I was there when Gisselle complained, but Mrs. Warren wasn't one to tolerate it.

"The time for feeling sorry for yourself has passed," she declared. "Now's the time to work on getting yourself as self-sufficient as possible. You're not going to become a blob in that chair either, so get those thoughts out of your head. Before I'm finished, you'll learn how to do most everything for yourself and you will. Is that understood?"

Gisselle just stared at her a moment and then turned to me.

"Ruby, hand me my hand mirror," she said. "I

want to fix my hair. I'm sure some of the boys will be over to see me once they've learned I'm home."

"Get it yourself," Mrs. Warren snapped. "Just wheel yourself over and get it."

"Ruby will get it for me," Gisselle countered. "Won't you, Ruby?" She fixed her steely eyes on me.

I went for the mirror.

"You're not helping her by doing that," Mrs. Warren said.

"I know," I said. But I brought Gisselle the mirror anyway.

"She'll turn the lot of you into her slaves. I warn you."

"Ruby doesn't mind being my slave. We're sisters, right, Ruby?" Gisselle said. "Tell her," she commanded.

"I don't mind," I said.

"Well, I do. Now get out of here while I'm conducting the therapy," she snapped at me.

"I'll tell Ruby when to leave and when not to leave," Gisselle shouted. "Ruby, stay."

"But, Gisselle, if Mrs. Warren thinks it's better for me to go, I'd better go."

Gisselle folded her arms and peered at me with narrow slits. "Don't you move from that spot," she ordered.

"Now see here . . . " Mrs. Warren said.

"All right," Gisselle said, smiling. "You're excused now, Ruby. Oh, and please call Beau and tell him I'm expecting him in an hour."

"Make that two hours," Mrs. Warren advised. I nodded and left. For once I agreed wholeheartedly with Daphne: life was going to get far more complicated and unpleasant with Gisselle as an invalid. The accident, her horrible injury, and the aftermath had done nothing to change her personality. Just as before, she still thought everything was coming to her, even more so now. I realized I should never have confessed to her. She had only taken the opportunity to make me into her slave.

If I had any idea that Gisselle's condition would make her feel less secure about herself when it came to boys, that idea popped out of my head the moment I saw how she reacted when Beau and some of his teammates arrived to visit her. Like some empress who was too divine to have her feet touch the earth, she insisted Beau carry her from room to room, place to place rather than wheel her about. She gathered the young men around her, asking Todd Lambert to massage her feet as she spoke, mainly to complain about Mrs. Warren and the terrible ordeal everyone was putting her through.

"I swear," she said. "If you boys don't visit me every day, I'll go stark raving mad. Will you? Will you promise?" she asked, batting her eyelids at them. Of course, they did. While they were still there, she had to order me about, demanding glasses of water or a pillow for her back, snapping at me as though I really were her little slave.

Afterward, when Beau had carried her back upstairs to her room and each and every one of the boys had been given a kiss good-bye, he and I finally had a moment alone.

"I can see it's going to be particularly hard on you from now on," he said.

"I don't care."

"She doesn't deserve you," he said softly, and leaned toward me to kiss me good-bye. Just at that moment, we heard Daphne's footsteps clicking up the corridor. She marched out of the shadows firmly, but some of the darkness still hovered around her furious eyes. She paused a few feet away from us, her arms folded under her bosom, and glared.

"I want to see you this instant, Ruby," she said. "Beau, I'd like you to leave."

"Leave?"

"This instant," she said, her voice cracking like a bullwhip.

"Is there something wrong?" he asked softly.

"I'll discuss that with your parents," she said. He looked at me and then walked out quickly to join his waiting buddies.

"What's wrong?" I asked Daphne.

"Follow me," she ordered. She pivoted and marched back down the hallway. I tagged along, my heart thumping with anticipation. She paused at the doorway of my studio and turned to me.

"If Beau hadn't deserted Gisselle for you, she would never have been in that car with Martin," she declared. "Why did he leave a sophisticated young Creole girl for an unschooled Cajun so quickly, I've wondered. It came to me last night," she said. "Like divine inspiration. And sure enough, my heartfelt suspicions proved true." She threw the studio door open. "Inside."

"Why?" I asked, but did what she demanded. She stared furiously at me a moment and then followed me in and walked directly to my easel. There she threw back some of my current drawings until she came to the drawing I had done of Beau nude. I gasped.

"This is too good to come just from your sinful imagination," she declared. "Isn't it? Don't lie," she added quickly.

I took a deep breath.

"I've never lied to you, Daphne," I said. "And I won't lie to you now."

"He posed?"

"Yes," I confessed. She nodded. "But—"

"Get out and don't dare set foot in this studio again. The door will be locked forever, as far as I'm concerned. Go," she commanded, her arm extended, finger pointing.

I turned and hurried away. Who was the true invalid in this house, I wondered, Gisselle or me?

20

Bird in a Gilded Cage

Ever since the dreadful car accident, Daddy had been moping about like a man who had lost his desire to live. His shoulders drooped, his face was shadowed, his eyes dull. He ate poorly, grew paler and paler, and even took less care with his appearance. And he spent more and more time alone in Uncle Jean's room.

Daphne's tone was always critical and harsh. Instead of showing him compassion and understanding, she complained about her own new problems and insisted that he was only making things more difficult for her. Never did she first consider him and how he was suffering.

So it came as no surprise to me that she wouldn't waste a moment telling him about what she had found in my art studio and what it meant. I felt sorrier for him than I did for myself, for I knew how devastating this would be on top of what had already occurred. Whipped about by what he considered divine retribution for some past sins, he absorbed Daphne's revelations like a condemned man hearing that his final appeal for mercy had been denied. He offered no resistance to her decision to shut up my art studio and end my private art lessons, nor did he utter a single word of protest when she sentenced me to what amounted to practically house arrest.

Naturally, I was not to see or speak to Beau. In fact, I was forbidden to use the telephone. I was to return home directly from school each and every day and either assist Mrs. Warren with Gisselle's needs or do my homework. To reinforce her iron-clad hold over me and Daddy, Daphne called me into the study and cross-examined me in his presence, just to prove to him that beyond a doubt, I was as bad as she had predicted I would be.

"You have conducted yourself like a little tramp," she declared, "even using your art talents as a way to be sexually promiscuous. And in my house!

"Most embarrassing of all, you have corrupted the son of one of the most highly respected Creole families in New Orleans. They are beside themselves with grief over this.

"Have you anything to say in your own defense?" she asked like some high court judge.

I raised my eyes and gazed at Daddy who sat with his hands in his lap, his eyes glassy. The way he was, it made no sense for me to speak. I didn't think he would hear or understand a word and Daphne was sure to belittle and destroy anything I would offer as an excuse or justification. I shook my head and looked down again.

"Then go to your room and be sure you do exactly what I have told you to do," she ordered, and I left.

Beau was punished as well. His parents took away his car and restricted his social activities for a month. When I saw him in school, he looked broken and subdued. His friends had heard he had gotten in trouble, but they didn't know the details.

"I'm sorry," he told me. "This is all my fault. I got you and myself into a pot of boiling water."

"I didn't do anything I didn't want to do, Beau, and you and I do care for each other, don't we?"

"Yes," he said. "But there's not much I can do about it now. At least until everyone calms down, if they ever do. I never saw my father this angry. Daphne really got to him. She put most of the blame on you," he said, quickly adding, ". . . unfairly. But my father thinks you're some kind of seductress. He called you a femme fatale, whatever that means." He gazed about us nervously. "If he even hears I'm talking to you.

"I know," I said sadly, and described my punishments, too. He apologized again and hurried off.

501

Gisselle was ecstatic. When I saw her after Daphne had told her the details, she was positively buoyant with glee. Even Mrs. Warren said Gisselle was more exuberant and energetic than ever, performing her rituals of therapy without complaint.

"I begged Mother to let me see the drawing," she said. "But she told me she had already destroyed it. You sit right down here and tell me every detail," she ordered. "How did you get him to take off all his clothes? What position was he in when he posed? What did you draw . . . everything?"

"I don't want to talk about it, Gisselle," I said.

"Oh yes you do," she snapped. "I'm stuck in here doing stupid exercises with that grouchy nurse all day or doing the homework the tutor prescribes while you're out there having loads of fun. You have to tell me everything. When did this happen? Recently? After you drew him, what did you do? Did you take off your clothes, too? Answer me!" she screamed.

How I wished I could sit down and talk to her. How I wished I had a sister in whom I could confide, a sister who would give me loving advice and be compassionate and caring. But Gisselle just wanted to be titillated and relish my discomfort and pain.

"I can't talk about it," I insisted, and turned away.

"You'd better!" she screamed after me. "You'd better or I'll tell them about the voodoo queen. Ruby! Ruby, get back in here this instant!"

I knew she would go through with her threat,

and that on top of everything else at this point would surely drive poor Daddy into a depression from which he would never emerge. Trapped, chained by my own honest confessions to Gisselle, I returned and let her pump me for the details.

"I knew it," she said, smiling with satisfaction. "I knew he would seduce you some day."

"He didn't seduce me. We care about each other," I insisted, but she just laughed.

"Beau Andreas cares about Beau Andreas. You're a fool, a stupid little Cajun fool," she said. Then she smiled again. "Go get me my bedpan. I have to pee."

"Get it yourself," I retorted, and jumped up.

"Ruby!"

I didn't stop. I ran out of her room this time and into my own where I sprawled on my bed and buried my face in my pillow. Would I have been any more abused by Buster and Grandpere Jack? I wondered.

A few hours later, I was surprised by a knock on my door. I turned, ground away any lingering tears, and called out, "Come in." I was expecting Daddy, but it was Daphne. She stood there with her arms folded, but she didn't look angry this time.

"I've been thinking about you," she said in a calmer tone of voice. "I haven't changed my opinion of you and the things you have done, nor do I intend to lessen your punishments, but I have decided to give you an opportunity to repent for your evil ways and especially make things up to your father. Are you interested?"

"Yes," I said, and held my breath. "What do I have to do?"

"This Saturday is your uncle Jean's birthday. Normally, Pierre would go visit him, but Pierre is not in a state of mind to visit anyone, especially not his mentally handicapped younger brother," she said. "So, as usual, the difficult tasks fall to me. I will be going and I thought it might be decent of you to accompany me and represent your father.

"Of course, Jean won't understand who you really are, but—"

"Oh, yes," I said, hardly containing my excitement. "I've always wanted to do that anyway,"

"Have you?" She held me in her critical gaze for a moment, pressing her lips together. "Fine then. We'll leave early in the morning Saturday. Wear something appropriate. I expect you understand what I mean when I say that now," she added.

"Yes, Mother. Thank you."

"Oh, one more thing," she said before turning. "Don't mention this to Pierre. It will only make him feel worse. We'll tell him when we return. Do you understand?"

"Yes," I said.

"I hope I'm doing the right thing," she concluded, and left.

Right thing? Of course she was doing the right thing. Finally, I would be able to make a significant contribution toward my father's happiness. As soon as I returned from the institution, I would run right to him and describe every moment I had spent with Jean in detail. I went right to my closet to decide what would be appropriate to Daphne.

When I told Gisselle about my accompanying Daphne to visit Uncle Jean, she looked very surprised. "Uncle Jean's birthday? Only Mother would remember something like that."

"I think it's nice she asked me," I said.

"I'm glad she didn't ask me to go. I hate that place. It's so depressing. All those disturbed people and young people our age, too."

Nothing she could say would diminish my excitement. When Saturday morning finally arrived, I was dressed hours earlier than I had to be and took extra care with my hair, returning to the mirror a half-dozen times to be sure every strand was in place. I knew how critical Daphne could be.

I was disappointed to discover that Daddy hadn't come down to breakfast. Even though we weren't supposed to tell him where we were going, I wanted him to see how nice I looked.

"Where's Daddy?" I asked Daphne.

"He knows what day it is," she explained after looking me over from head to toe. "It's left him in one of his deeper melancholic states. Wendy will bring a tray up to him later."

We ate and then a short time afterward left for the institute. Daphne was quiet for most of the trip, except when I asked her questions.

"How old is Uncle Jean today?" I queried.

"He's thirty-six," she replied.

"Did you know him before?"

"Of course I knew him," she said. I thought I detected a slight smile on her lips. "I daresay there

505

wasn't an eligible young woman in New Orleans who didn't."

"How long has he been in the institution?"

"Almost fifteen years."

"What's he like? I mean, what's his condition like now?" I pursued. She looked like she wasn't going to reply.

Finally, she said, "Why don't you just wait and see. Save your questions for the doctors and nurses," she added, which I thought was a strange thing to say.

The institute was a good twenty miles out of the city. It was off the highway, up a long, winding driveway, but it had beautiful grounds with sprawling weeping willows, rock gardens, and fountains, as well as little walkways that had quaint little wooden benches all along the way. As we approached, I saw some older people being escorted by attendants.

After she pulled our car into a parking space and shut off the engine, Daphne turned to me.

"When we go in there, I don't want you to speak to anyone or ask anyone any questions. This is a mental institution, not a public school. Just follow alongside me and wait. Then do whatever you are told to do. Is that clear?" she demanded.

"Yes," I said. Something in her tone of voice and in her look made my heart race. The four-story, gray stucco structure now loomed above us ominously and cast a long dark shadow over us and our car. As we approached the front entrance, I saw that the windows had bars over them and many had their shades drawn down.

From the highway and even approaching it on

the driveway, the institution was very attractive and pleasant, but now, close up, it announced its true purpose and reminded visitors that the people housed within were here because they couldn't function properly in the outside world. The bars on the windows suggested some might even be dangerous to others. I swallowed hard and tracked after Daphne through the front entrance. She walked with her head high as usual, her posture regal stiff. Her heels clicked on the polished marble floor, echoing through the immaculate entryway. At a glass enclosure directly before us, a woman in a white uniform sat writing in charts. She looked up as we approached.

"I'm Daphne Dumas," Daphne declared with an authoritative air. "I'm here to see Dr. Cheryl."

"I'll inform him you've arrived, Madame Dumas," the receptionist said and lifted the receiver at her side immediately. "Take a seat if you like," she added, nodding toward the cushioned benches. Daphne turned and gestured for me to sit down. I hurriedly did so and waited with my hands in my lap, gazing around me. The walls were bare, not a picture, not a clock, nothing.

"Dr. Cheryl will see you now, madame," the receptionist said.

"Ruby," Daphne said, and I stood up and walked with her to the side door. The receptionist buzzed us in. We entered another corridor.

"Right this way," the receptionist said, and led us down the hall to a bank of offices. The first on the right was labeled, Dr. Edward Cheryl, Chief of Administration. The receptionist opened the door for us and we entered the office.

It was a large room with windows that had no bars over them. Right now, the drapes were half-drawn. To the right was a long, light brown leather sofa and to the left was a matching settee. The walls were covered with bookcases and here and there were Impressionistic paintings, mostly of rural scenes. One of a field in the bayou caught my interest.

Behind his desk, Dr. Cheryl had hung all of his diplomas and certificates. Dressed in a lab robe, he rose immediately to greet Daphne. He was a man no more than fifty, fifty-five, with bushy dark brown hair, small chestnut eyes, a small nose, and slight mouth. His chin was so round, it was as if his face had failed to form one. Standing a little under six feet tall, he had a slim build with long arms. His smile was tight and tentative like the smile of an insecure child. It seemed odd to think it, but he looked nervous in Daphne's presence.

"Madame Dumas," he said, extending his hand. When he lifted his arm, the sleeve of his robe slid more than halfway up to his elbow. Daphne took his fingers quickly as if she detested touching him or was afraid he could somehow contaminate her. She nodded and sat down in the bullet leather chair before his desk. I remained standing just behind her.

His attention immediately shifted to me. The intensity of his gaze made me feel self-conscious. Finally, after what seemed an interminable pause, he offered me a smile, too, but one just as tentative.

"And this is the young lady?" he asked, coming around his desk.

"Yes. Ruby," Daphne said, smirking as if my name was the most ridiculous thing she had ever heard. He nodded, but kept his eyes on me. Remembering Daphne's orders, I didn't speak until he spoke to me directly.

"And how are you today, Mademoiselle Ruby?" he asked.

"Fine."

He nodded and turned to Daphne.

"Physically, she is in good health?" he asked. What a strange thing to ask, I thought, knitting my eyebrows together with curiosity.

"Look at her. Does she look like anything's physically wrong with her?" she snapped. She spoke to him as sharply as she would speak to one of our servants, but he didn't seem to mind. He gazed at me again.

"Good. Well, let me begin by showing you around a bit," he said, stepping closer to me and farther away from Daphne. I looked at her, but she kept her gaze fixed ahead. "I'd like you to feel comfortable here," he added. "As comfortable as possible."

His smile widened, but there was still something false about it.

"Thank you," I replied. I didn't know what to say. I knew my father and Daphne made sizeable contributions to the institute, besides paying for Uncle Jean, but it still felt funny being treated like such VIPs.

"I understand you're almost sixteen?" he said.

"Yes, monsieur."

"Please . . . call me Dr. Cheryl. We should be

friends, good friends. If that's all right with you," he added.

"Of course, Dr. Cheryl." He nodded.

"Madame?" he said, turning back to Daphne.

"I'll wait right here," she said, without turning around. Why was she behaving so strangely? I wondered.

"Very good, madame. Mademoiselle," he said, indicating a side door to his office. I couldn't help my confusion.

"Where are we going?"

"As I said, I would like to show you around first, if that is all right with you, of course."

"Fine," I said, shrugging. I went to the door and he opened it and led me out through another corridor and then up a short stairway. This place was a maze, I thought as we made another turn and took another corridor in a different direction. We continued until we reached a large window and looked in on what was clearly a recreation room. Patients of all ages, from what looked like teenagers to elderly people played cards, board games, and dominoes. Some watched television, and some did some handicrafts like lanyards, needlework, and crocheting. Others were reading magazines. One boy with sweet potato red hair, who looked about seventeen or eighteen, sat staring at everyone and doing nothing. A half-dozen attendants wandered about the room overlooking all the activities, pausing occasionally to say a few words to one of the patients.

"As you see, this is our recreation area. Patients who are able to can come in here during their free time and do almost anything they like. They can even, as young Lyle Black there, sit and do nothing."

"Does my uncle come in here?" I asked.

"Oh, yes, but right now he's waiting in his room for Madame Dumas. He has a very nice room," Dr. Cheryl added. "Right this way," he indicated. We stopped at another door. It was obviously the library.

"We have over two thousand volumes and we get dozens and dozens of magazines," he explained.

"Very nice," I said.

We continued until we came to what looked like a small gymnasium.

"We don't neglect the patients physical well being. This is our exercise room. Every morning, we conduct calisthenics. Some of our patients are even able to swim in our pool, which is located in the rear of the building. Here," he said, taking a few steps and pointing down the corridor to the right, "are our treatment rooms. We have a dentist on a regular basis, as well as general medicine doctors on call. Why, we even have a beauty parlor here," he said, smiling.

"This way," he indicated, pointing down the opposite corridor.

I wondered about Daphne. It surprised me that she would sit back in his office and remain so patient. She had made it perfectly clear to me how much she hated coming here. I was sure she wanted to get in and get out as fast as she could. Now troubled as well as confused, I followed Dr. Cheryl. I didn't want to appear impolite or unappreciative, but I was eager to see my uncle.

We turned a corner and approached what looked like an entirely new administrative area. A nurse sat behind a desk. Two attendants, both big men in their late twenties at least, stood talking to her. They looked up as we approached.

"Morning, Mrs. McDonald," Dr. Cheryl said. The nurse at the desk looked up. She had a softer face than Mrs. Warren, but looked to be the same age with bluish gray hair cut at the nape of her neck.

"Good morning, Doctor."

"Boys," he said to the attendants. "Everything going all right this morning?" They nodded, their eyes fixed on me.

"Very well, Mrs. McDonald. As you know, Madame Dumas has brought her daughter here. This is Ruby," he said, turning to me.

I stared at him a moment. What did he mean, brought her daughter here? Why didn't he finish that and say, brought her daughter to see her uncle Jean?

"Ruby, Mrs. McDonald runs things down here and sees to everyone's needs. She's the finest head nurse on any psychiatric floor in the country. We're mighty proud to have her on our staff."

"I don't understand," I said. "Where's my uncle?"

"Oh, he's on another floor," Dr. Cheryl said, flashing that tight, small smile. "This floor is more or less for our temporaries. We don't expect you to remain here long."

"What?" I stepped back. "Remain here? What do you mean, remain here?"

Mrs. McDonald and Dr. Cheryl exchanged quick looks.

"I thought your mother had explained all of this to you, Ruby," he said.

"Explained? Explained what?"

"You're here for an evaluation, an observation. You didn't agree to it?"

"Are you crazy?" I cried. That brought a smile to the attendants, but Dr. Cheryl straightened up quickly.

"Oh, dear," he said. "I thought this was going to be one of our easier ones."

"I want to go back to my mother," I insisted. I looked back down the corridor, so confused and upset now, I wasn't sure which direction to take.

"Just relax," Dr. Cheryl said, stepping forward.

"Relax? You thought I was coming here to be a patient and you want me to relax?"

"You're not a patient as such," he said, closing and opening his eyes. "You're being evaluated."

"For what?"

"Why don't we just settle you in your room first and then we'll have a talk. If there is nothing to do, why you'll go right home," he said with that small smile again.

"There is nothing to do." I backed away. "I want to go to my mother. Right now. I came here to see my uncle. That's why I came."

Dr. Cheryl looked at Mrs. McDonald and she rose.

"You'll only make things harder for yourself if you become uncooperative, Ruby," she said, coming around her desk. The two attendants moved to follow. I continued to back away, shaking my head.

"This is a mistake. Take me back."

"Just relax," Dr. Cheryl said.

"No. I don't want to relax."

The attendant on my right moved quickly to block my retreat. He didn't touch me, but he stood behind me, intimidating me with his presence. I started to cry.

"Please," I said. "I want to go to my mother. This is a mistake. Just take me back."

"In due time, I promise to do just that," Dr. Cheryl said. "Can we show you your room? Once you see how comfortable it is . . . "

"No. I don't want to see any room."

I spun around and tried to get past the attendant, but he seized my arm and held me so tightly at the wrist, it hurt. I screamed and Mrs. McDonald moved in, too.

"Arnold," she called to the other attendant. He came forward to take my other arm.

"Don't hurt her," Dr. Cheryl said. "Careful now. Ruby, just let them show you your room. Go on, my dear."

I struggled in vain for a moment and then began to sob as they led me forward to another door. Mrs. McDonald pressed a buzzer and the door was opened. My legs didn't want to move, but they were practically carrying me along now. Dr. Cheryl followed right behind. They took me down the dormitory corridor and stopped at an opened door.

"See," Dr. Cheryl said, entering first. "This is one of our best rooms. You have windows facing the west, so you get all the afternoon sunlight and not the sunlight in the morning to wake you too early. And just look at this nice bed," he said, indicating the imitation wood frame bed. "Here's a dresser, a closet, and a private bathroom. This bathroom even has a shower. And you have this small desk and chair. Here is some stationery if you care to write a letter to someone," he added, smiling.

I gazed at the stark floors and walls. How could anyone think this was a nice room? It looked more like a glorified prison cell. The windows had bars, didn't they?

"You can't do this to me," I said. I embraced myself tightly. "Take me back immediately or I swear I'll go to the police the first chance I get."

"Your mother has asked us to evaluate you," he said firmly. "Parents have the right to do this if their children are still legally minors. Now if you cooperate, this will be short and sweet and not painful, but if you persist in fighting everything we do and everything we ask you to do, it will be most unpleasant for all of us, but mostly for you," he threatened. "Now, sit down," he ordered, pointing to the chair. I didn't move. He straightened up as if I had spit in his face.

"We've been told something of your background and know what sort of things you've done and how poorly you've been disciplined, young lady, but I assure you, none of that will be tolerated here. Now you will either listen and do what I tell you or I'll move you to the floor above where the patients are kept restrained in straight jackets a good deal of the time."

With a sinking heart, I moved obediently to the chair and sat down.

"That's better," he said. "I have to see to your mother and her visit and then I will send for you and begin our first interview. In the meantime, I want you to read this little booklet," he said, pulling a yellow, stapled booklet out of the desk drawer. "It explains our institution, our rules, and what we try to do here. We give this only to patients who understand, mostly patients who have committed themselves in fact. It even has a place in the back for you to write in your suggestions. See," he said, opening the booklet to show me. "We consider them, too. Some of our former patients have made excellent suggestions."

"I don't want to make any suggestions. I just want to go home."

"Then cooperate and you will," he said. He started out.

"Why would I be put here? Please, just answer that question before you leave me," I begged. He looked at the two attendants who retreated and then he closed the door and turned to me.

"You have a history of promiscuity, don't you, my dear?"

"What? What do you mean?"

"In psychology, we call it nymphomania. Have you ever heard that term?"

I gasped. "What are you saying about me?" I asked.

"You're having a problem controlling yourself when it comes to relationships with the opposite sex?"

"That's not true, Dr. Cheryl."

"Admitting to your problems is the first step, my dear. After that, it's all downhill. You'll see," he said, smiling.

"But I have no problem to admit to."

He stared at me a moment.

"Okay, we'll see," he said. "That's why you're here. To be evaluated. If you have no problem, I'll send you home directly. Does that sound fair?"

"No. None of this is fair. I'm being held prisoner."

"We are all prisoners of our ailments, Ruby dear. Especially, our mental infirmities. The purpose of this place and my purpose is to free you from the mental aberration that has chained you to this misbehavior and caused you even to hate yourself." He smiled. "We have a good cure rate here. Just give it a chance," he concluded.

"Please, my mother's lying. Daphne's lying! Please," I cried. He closed the door behind him. I knew there was no point in trying, but I did so anyway and discovered that it was locked. Frustrated and defeated, still in a state of utter shock, I sat down and waited. I felt sure Daddy knew nothing about this and wondered what sort of lies Daphne would concoct to explain my disappearance. I imagined, she would tell him I couldn't stand her discipline and decided to run away. Poor Daddy, he would believe it.

Nina Jackson shouldn't have gotten Gisselle's ribbon to throw into the box with the snake, I thought; she should have gotten one of Daphne's instead.

Finally, after what seemed like ages and ages to me, the door was unlocked and Mrs. McDonald appeared.

"Dr. Cheryl can see you now," she said. "If you will just follow me quietly, we can go to him without incident."

I got up quickly, thinking that the first chance I got, I would dart right out. But they anticipated that and one of the attendants was waiting outside to accompany us.

"You people are kidnapping me here," I moaned. "It's nothing less than that."

"Now, now, Ruby, you must not permit yourself to grow paranoid about this. People who care about you, love you, want to see what can be done to make you better, that's all," she said in such a sweet voice it was as if I were walking along with someone's nice old grandmother. "No one's going to do anything to hurt you."

"I'm already hurt beyond repair," I said, but that brought only a smile to her face.

"You young people today are so much more dramatic than we were," she commented. Then she inserted a key in the corridor door and unlocked it. "Right this way."

She led me back to the corridor Dr. Cheryl had described as the treatment area. I gazed down another hallway and considered running, but I remembered all the other doors that had to be buzzed to be opened and I was sure there were no windows without bars. The attendant moved up closer behind me anyway. Finally, we stopped at a door and Mrs. McDonald opened it to lead me into a room that contained only a sofa, two chairs, a table, and what looked like some kind of movie projector on a smaller table. There was a screen on the wall directly across from it. The room had no windows, but there was another door and a wall-size mirror on the right side.

"Just sit here," Mrs. McDonald instructed. I sat in one of the chairs. She went to the other door and knocked gently. Then she opened it and poked her head in to mumble, "She's here, Doctor."

"Very good," I heard Dr. Cheryl say. Mrs. McDonald turned back to me and smiled.

"Remember," she said. "If you're cooperative, everything moves faster." She nodded at the attendant and they started out. "Jack will be right outside should you need him," she said as a veiled threat. I looked at the attendant who returned my gaze with steely dark eyes. Thoroughly intimidated, I sat quietly and waited after they left. A few moments later, Dr. Cheryl appeared.

"Well," he said, beaming a wider smile, "how are we doing now? A little better, I hope?"

"No. Where's Daphne?"

"Your mother is visiting your uncle," he said. He went directly to the projector and put a file down beside it.

"She's not my mother," I declared firmly. If I ever wanted to deny her, I wanted to deny her now.

"I understand how you feel."

"No, you don't understand. She's not my real mother. My real mother is dead."

"However," he said, nodding, "she's trying to be a real mother to you, isn't she?"

"No. She's trying to be what she is . . . a witch," I retorted.

"This anger and aggression you now feel is understandable," he said. "I just want you to recognize it for what it is. You feel this way because you feel threatened. Whenever we try to get a patient to admit to errors or recognize weaknesses and illnesses, it's natural for him or her to first resent it. Believe it or not, many of the people here feel comfortable with their mental and behavioral problems because they've been a part of them so long."

"I don't belong here. I don't have any mental or behavioral problems," I insisted.

"Perhaps not. Let me try something with you to see how you view the world around you, okay? Maybe that's all we'll do today and give you a chance to acclimate yourself to your surroundings more. No rush."

"Yes, there is a rush. I've got to go home."

"All right. We'll begin. I'm going to flash some shapes on

the screen in front of you. I want you to tell me what comes to mind instantly when you see each one, okay? Don't think about them, just react as quickly as you can. That's easy, right?"

"I don't need to do this," I moaned.

"Just humor me then," he said, and snapped off the room light. He turned on the projector and put the first shape on the screen. "Please," he said. "The faster we do this, the faster you can relax."

Reluctantly, I responded.

"It looks like the head of an eel."

"An eel, good. And this?"

"Some kind of hose."

"Go on."

"A twisted sycamore limb . . . Spanish Moss . . . An alligator tail . . . A dead fish."

"Why dead?"

"It's not moving," I said.

He laughed. "Of course. And this?"

"A mother and a child."

"What's the child doing?"

"Breast-feeding."

"Yes."

He flashed a half-dozen more pictures and then put on the lights.

"Okay," he said, sitting across from me with his notebook. "I'm going to say a word and you respond immediately again, no thought. Just what comes first to mind, understand?" I just looked down. "Understand?" I nodded.

"Can't we just see Daphne and end this?"

"In due time," he said. "Lips."

"What?"

"What comes to mind first when I say, 'lips'?"

"A kiss."

"Hands."

"Work."

He recited a few dozen words at me, jotting down my reactions and then he sat back, nodding.

"Can I go home now?" I asked.

He smiled and stood up. "We have a few more tests to go through, some talking to do. It won't be too long, I promise. Since you have been cooperative, I'm going to permit you to go to the recreation area before lunch. Find something to read, something to do, and I'll see you again real soon, okay?"

"No, it's not okay," I said. "I want to call my daddy. Can I at least do that?"

"We don't permit patients to use the telephones."

"Will you call him, then? If you just call him, you'll see he doesn't want me to be here," I said.

"I'm sorry, Ruby, but he does," Doctor Cheryl said, and pulled a form out of the file. "See? Here is his signature," he said, and I looked at the line to which he pointed. Pierre Dumas was written there.

"She forged it, I'm sure," I said quickly. "She's going to tell him I ran away. Please, just call him. Will you do that?"

He stood up without replying.

"You've got a little time before lunch. Get acquainted with the facilities. Try to relax. It will help us when we meet again," he said, and opened the door. The attendant was waiting. "Take her to the recreation room," Doctor Cheryl told him. The attendant nodded and looked in at me. Slowly, I rose.

"When my father finds out what she did and what you're doing, you're going to be in a lot of trouble," I threatened. He didn't reply and I had no choice but to follow the attendant back down the corridor to the recreation room.

"Hello, I'm Mrs. Whidden," a woman attendant no more than forty said, greeting me at the door. "Welcome. I'm here to help you. Is there something in particular you would like to do . . . handicrafts, perhaps."

"No," I said.

"Well, why don't you just go about and look over everything until something strikes your fancy. Then I'll help you, okay?" she said. Seeing no point to my constantly protesting, I nodded and entered the room. I walked about, gazing at the patients, some of whom gazed at me with curiosity, some with what looked like anger, and some who didn't seem to see me. The redheaded boy who had been sitting doing nothing was still sitting that way. I noticed that his eyes followed me, however. I went to the window near him and gazed out, longing for my freedom.

"Hate being here?" I heard, and turned. It sounded like he had asked it, but he was still sitting stiffly, staring ahead.

"Did you ask me something?" I inquired. He didn't move, nor did he speak. I shrugged and looked out again, and again, I heard, "Hate being here?" I spun around.

"Pardon me?"

Still, without turning, he spoke again.

"I can tell you don't want to be here."

"I don't. I was kidnapped, locked up before I knew what was happening," I said. That animated his face to the point where he at least raised his eyebrows. He turned to me slowly, only his head moving, and he gazed at me with eyes that seemed as cold and as indifferent as eyes on a mannequin.

"What about your parents?" he asked.

"My father doesn't know what my stepmother has done. I'm sure," I said.

"What's the charge?"

"Pardon?"

"What's the reason you're supposedly here for? You know, your problem?"

"I'd rather not say. It's too embarrassing and ridiculous."

"Paranoia? Schizophrenia? Manic-depression? Am I getting warm?"

"No. Why are you here?" I demanded.

"Immobility," he declared. "I'm unable to make decisions, deal with responsibilities. When confronted with a problem, I simply become immobile. I can't even decide what I want to do in here," he added nonchalantly. "So I sit and wait for the recreation period to end."

"Why are you like this?" I asked. "I mean, you know what's wrong with you, apparently."

"Insecure." He smiled. "My mother, apparently like your stepmother, didn't want me. In her eighth month, she tried to abort me, but I only got born too soon instead. From then on, it was straight downhill: paranoia, autism, learning disabilities," he recited dryly.

"You don't seem like someone with learning disabilities," I said.

"I can't function in a normal school setting. I can't answer questions. I don't raise my hand, and when I'm given a test, I just stare at it. But I read," he added. "That's all I do. It's safe." He raised his eyes to me. "So why did they commit you? You don't have to be afraid of telling me. I won't tell anyone else. But I don't blame you if you don't trust me," he added quickly.

I sighed.

"I've been accused of being too loose with my sexual activities," I said.

"Nymphomania. Great. We don't have any of those."

I couldn't help but laugh.

"You still don't," I said. "It's a lie."

"That's all right. This place flourishes on lies. Patients lie to each other, to themselves, and to the doctors and the doctors lie because they claim they can help you, but they can't. All they can do is keep you comfortable," he said bitterly. He lifted his rust-colored eyes toward me again. "You can tell me your real name or you can lie, if you want."

"My name's Ruby, Ruby Dumas. I know your first name is Lyle, but I forgot your last name."

"Black. Like the bottom of an empty well. Dumas," he said. "Dumas. There's someone else here with that name."

"My uncle," I said. "Jean. I was brought here supposedly to visit him."

"Oh. You're Jean's niece?"

"But I never got to see him."

"I like Jean."

"Does he talk to you? What's he like? How is he?" I hurriedly asked.

"He doesn't talk to anyone, but that doesn't mean he can't. I know he can. He's . . . just very quiet, but as gentle as a little boy and as frightened sometimes. Sometimes, he cries for what seems to be no reason, but I know something's going on in his head to make him cry. Occasionally, I catch him laughing to himself. He won't tell anyone anything, especially the doctors and nurses."

525

"If I can only see him. At least that would be something good," I said.

"You can. I'm sure he'll be at lunch in the little cafeteria."

"I've never met him before," I said. "Will you point him out to me?"

"Not hard to do. He's the best-dressed and the best-looking guy here. Ruby, huh? Nice," he said, and then tightened his face as if he had said something terrible.

"Thank you." I paused and looked around. "I don't know what I'm going to do now. I've got to get out of here, but this place is worse than a prison-doors that have to be buzzed open, bars on the windows, attendants everywhere . . . "

"Oh, I can get you out," he said casually. "If that's what you really want."

"You can? How?"

"There's a room that has a window without bars on it, the laundry room."

"Really? But how can I get to it?"

"I'll show you . . . later. They let us go outside if we want after lunch and there's a way into the laundry room from the yard."

My heart lifted with hope.

"How do you know all this?"

"I know everything about this place," he replied.

"You do? How long have you been here?" I asked.

"Since I was seven," he said. "Ten years."

"Ten years! Don't you ever want to leave?" I asked. He stared ahead for a moment. A tear escaped his right eye and slid down his cheek.

"No," he said. He turned to me with the saddest eyes. "I belong here. I told you," he continued, "I can't make a decision. I told you I'd help you, but later, when it comes time to do it, I don't know if I can." He stared ahead. "I don't know if I can."

My brightened spirits darkened again when I realized he might just be doing what he said everyone did here—lying.

A bell was rung and Mrs. Whidden announced it was time to go to lunch. I brightened again. At least now, I would see Uncle Jean. Unless of course, that was a lie, too.

21

Betrayed Again

It wasn't a lie and I didn't need to have Uncle Jean pointed out to me. He hadn't changed very much from the young man in the photos, and he was, as Lyle had described, the best-dressed patient in the cafeteria, coming to lunch in a light blue seersucker sports jacket and matching slacks, a white shirt with a blue cravat, and spotless white deck shoes. His golden brown hair was neatly trimmed and brushed back on the sides. I could see that he still had his trim figure. He looked like someone on vacation who had stopped by to visit a sick relative. He ate mechanically and gazed around the cafeteria with little or no interest.

"There he is," Lyle said, nodding in Uncle Jean's direction.

"I know." My heart began to tap a rapid beat on the inside of my chest.

"As you see, despite his problem, whatever that may be," Lyle said dryly, "he remains very concerned about his appearance. You should see his room, how neatly he keeps everything, too. In the beginning, I thought he had a cleanliness fetish or something. If you touch anything in his room, he'll go to it and make sure you didn't smudge it or move it an iota of an inch out of place.

"I'm practically the only one he permits in his room," Lyle added proudly. "He doesn't talk to me as such. He doesn't speak to anyone, but he tolerates me at least. If someone else sits at that table, he'll create a stir."

"What will he do?" I asked.

"He might start beating a spoon on his plate or he might just scream this horrid, beastlike sound until one of the attendants comes over and moves him or the other person away," Lyle explained.

"Maybe I shouldn't go near him," I said fearfully.

"Maybe you shouldn't. Maybe you should. Don't ask me to decide for you, but if you want me to, I'll tell him who you are at least."

"He might recognize me," I said.

"I thought he never saw you."

"He saw my twin sister and will just think that's who I am."

"Really? You have a twin sister? Now that's interesting," Lyle replied.

"If you two want to eat, you had better get in line," an attendant advised us.

"I don't know if I want to eat," Lyle muttered.

"Now, Lyle," the attendant said, "you know you don't have all day to make this decision."

"I'm hungry," I said to help move him along. I went to the stack of trays and got one. Then I started down the line, gazing back once to see Lyle still considering. My action moved him finally and he joined me.

"Please, get two of whatever you choose," he said.

"What if you don't like it?"

"I don't know what I like anymore. It all tastes the same to me," he said.

I chose the stew and got us both some Jell-O for dessert. After we had our food, we turned to decide where to sit and I stared at Uncle Jean, wondering if I should approach him.

"Go on," Lyle said. "I'll sit wherever you want."

With my eyes glued to him, I walked directly toward Uncle Jean. He continued to eat mechanically and move his eyes from side to side, almost in synchronization with each forkful of food. He didn't appear to notice me until I was nearly upon him. Then his eyes stopped scanning the room and he paused, his hand holding the fork about midway between the plate and his mouth. Slowly, he scanned my face. He didn't smile, but it was apparent he recognized me as Gisselle.

"Hello, Uncle Jean," I said, my body trembling. "May I sit with you?"

He didn't respond.

"Tell him who you really are," Lyle coached.

"My name is Ruby. I am not Gisselle. I'm Gisselle's twin sister, someone you've never met."

His eyes blinked rapidly and then he brought the forkful of food to his mouth.

"He's interested or at least amused," Lyle whispered.

"How do you know?"

"If he wasn't, he would be smacking the plate with his fork or starting to scream," Lyle explained. Feeling like the blind led by the blind, I inched my way forward to the table and gently put my tray down. I paused a moment, but Uncle Jean just kept eating, his blue-green eyes fixed on me. Then I sat down.

"Hi, Jean," Lyle said. "The natives appear a bit restless today, huh?" he said, sitting down beside me. Uncle Jean gazed at him, but didn't respond. Then he turned his attention back to me.

"I really am Gisselle's twin sister, Uncle Jean. My parents have told everyone how I was stolen at birth and how I managed to return just recently."

"Is that true?" Lyle asked astonished.

"No. But that's what my parents are telling everyone," I said. Lyle started to eat.

"Why?"

"To cover up the truth," I said, and turned back to Uncle Jean who was blinking rapidly again. "My father, your brother, met my mother in the bayou. They fell in love and she became pregnant. Later, she was talked into giving up the baby, only no one knew there were twins. On the day Gisselle and I were born, my grandmere Catherine kept me when my grandpere Jack took the first baby, Gisselle, out to the limousine where your family was waiting."

530

"Great story," Lyle said with a wry smile on his face.

"It's true!" I snapped at him, and then turned back to Uncle Jean. "Daphne, Daddy's wife, resents me, Uncle Jean. She's been very cruel to me ever since I arrived. She told me she was bringing me here to see you but secretly she made arrangements with Dr. Cheryl and his staff to keep me here for observation and evaluation. She's doing everything she can to get rid of me. She's—"

"*Aaaaa,*" Uncle Jean cried. I stopped, my heart pounding. Was he about to scream and pound his dish?

"Easy," Lyle warned. "You're going too fast for him."

"I'm sorry, Uncle Jean," I said. "But I wanted to see you and tell you how much Daddy suffers because you're in here. He's so sick with grief, he cries in your room often and in fact, he's been so upset recently, he couldn't come to see you on your birthday."

"His birthday? This isn't his birthday," Lyle said. "They make a big deal over everyone's birthday here. His isn't for another month."

"It doesn't surprise me. Daphne simply lied to get me to come along with her. I would have anyway, Uncle Jean," I said, turning back to him. "I wanted to see you very much."

He stared at me, his mouth open, his eyes wide.

"Start eating," Lyle said. "Pretend it's business as usual."

I did as he advised and Uncle Jean did appear

to relax. He lifted his fork, but continued to stare at me instead of continuing to eat. I smiled at him.

"I lived with my grandmere Catherine all my life," I told him. "My mother died shortly after I was born. I never knew who my real father was until recently and I promised my grandmere Catherine I would go to him after she died.

"You can't imagine how surprised everyone was," I said. He started to smile.

"Terrific," Lyle whispered. "He likes you."

"Does he?"

"I can tell. Keep talking," he commanded in a whisper.

"I tried to adjust, to learn how to be a proper young Creole lady, but Gisselle was very jealous of me. She thought I stole her boyfriend and she plotted against me."

"Did you?" Lyle asked.

"Did I what?"

"Steal her boyfriend?"

"No. At least I didn't set out to do anything like that," I said.

"But he liked you more than he liked her?" Lyle pursued.

"It was her own fault. I don't know how anyone could like her. She lies; she likes to see people suffer, and she'll deceive anyone, even herself."

"She sounds like she's the one who belongs in here," he said.

I turned back to Uncle Jean.

"Gisselle wasn't happy unless I was in some sort of trouble," I continued.

Uncle Jean grimaced.

"Daphne always took her side and Daddy . . . Daddy's overwhelmed with problems."

Uncle Jean's grimace deepened. Suddenly, he began to turn angry. He lifted his upper lip and clenched his teeth.

"Uh-oh," Lyle said. "Maybe you'd better stop. It's upsetting him."

"No. He should hear all of it." I turned back to him. "I went to a voodoo queen and asked her to help me. She fixed Gisselle and shortly afterward, Gisselle and another one of her boyfriends got into a dreadful car accident, Uncle Jean. The boy was killed and Gisselle is crippled for life. I feel just terrible about it, and Daddy . . . Daddy's a shadow of himself."

Jean's anger seemed to subside.

"I wish you would say something to me, Uncle Jean. I wish you would tell me something I could tell Daddy when I do get out of here."

I waited, but he just stared at me.

"Don't feel bad. I told you, he doesn't talk to anyone. He—"

"I know, but I want my father to realize I've seen Uncle Jean," I insisted. "I want him to—"

"Ji-ji-ji—"

"What's he trying to say?"

"I don't know," Lyle said.

"Ji-b-b-jib-jib—"

"Jib? What's that mean? Jib?"

Lyle thought a moment.

"Jib? Jib!" His eyes brightened. "It's a sailing term. Is that what you mean, Jean?"

"Jib," Uncle Jean said, nodding. "Jib." He grimaced as if in great pain. Then he sat back,

533

brought his hands to his head, and screamed, "JIB!"

"Oh, no."

"Hey, Jean," the attendant closest to us cried, running over.

"JIB! JIB!"

Another attendant arrived and then another. They helped Uncle Jean to his feet. Around us, the other patients began to become unnerved. Some shouted, some laughed, a young girl, maybe five or six years older than I, began to cry.

Uncle Jean struggled against the attendants for a while and looked at me. Spittle moved down the corners of his mouth as his head shook with the effort to repeat, "Jib, jib." They led him away.

Nurses appeared and more attendants followed to help calm down the patients.

"I feel terrible," I said. "I should have stopped when you told me to."

"Don't blame yourself," Lyle said, "something like that usually happens."

Lyle continued to eat a little more of his stew, but I couldn't put anything in my mouth. I felt so sick inside, so empty and defeated. I had to get out of here; I just had to.

"What happens now?" I asked him. "What will they do to him?"

"Just take him to his room. He usually calms down after that."

"What happens with us after lunch?"

"They'll take us out for a while, but the area is fenced in, so don't think you can just run off."

"Will you show me how to escape then? Will you, Lyle? Please," I begged.

"I don't know. Yes," he said. Then a moment later he said, "I don't know. Don't keep asking me."

"All right, Lyle. I won't," I said quickly. He calmed down and started on his dessert.

Just as he had said, when the lunch hour ended, the attendants directed the patients to their outside time. On my way out with Lyle, the head nurse, Mrs. McDonald, approached me.

"Dr. Cheryl has you scheduled for another hour of evaluation late this afternoon," she said. "I will come for you when it's time. How are you getting along? Make any friends?" she asked, eying Lyle who walked a step or two behind me. I didn't respond. "Hello, Lyle. How are you today?"

"I don't know," he said quickly.

Mrs. McDonald smiled at me and walked on to speak to some other patients.

The yard didn't look much different from the grounds in front of the institution. Like the front, the back had walkways and benches, fountains and flower beds with sprawling magnolia and oak trees providing pools of shade. There was an actual pool for fish and frogs, too. The grounds were obviously well maintained. The rock gardens, blossoms, and polished benches glittered in the warm, afternoon sunlight.

"It's very nice out here," I reluctantly admitted to Lyle.

"They've got to keep it nice. Everyone here comes from a wealthy family. They want to be sure the money continues to flow into the institution. You should see this place when they schedule one of their fetes for the families of patients. Every

535

inch is spick-and-span, not a weed, not a speck of dust, and not a face without a smile," he said, smirking.

"You sound very critical of them, Lyle, yet you want to stay. Why don't you think about trying life on the outside again? You're much brighter than most boys I've met," I said. He blanched but looked away.

"I'm not ready yet," he replied. "But I can tell just from the short time I've been with you that you definitely don't belong here."

"I've got another session scheduled with Dr. Cheryl. He's going to find a way to keep me. I just know it," I moaned. "Daphne gives this place too much money for him not to do what she wants." I embraced myself and looked down as we walked along. Around us and even behind us, the attendants watched.

"You go ask to go to the bathroom," Lyle suddenly said. "It's right off the rear entrance. They won't bother you. To the left of the rest room is a short stairway which goes down to the basement. The second door on the right is the laundry room. They've already done their laundry work for today. They do it in the morning. So there won't be anyone there."

"Are you sure?"

"I told you, I've been here ten years. I know which clocks run slow and which run fast, what door hinges squeak, and where there are windows without bars on them," he added.

"Thank you, Lyle."

He shrugged.

"I haven't done anything yet," he said, as if he

wanted to convince himself more than me that he hadn't made a decision.

"You've given me hope, Lyle. That's doing a great deal." I smiled at him. He stared at me a moment, his rust-colored eyes blinking and then he turned away.

"Go on," he said. "Do what I told you."

I went to the female attendant and explained that I had to go to the bathroom.

"I'll show you where it is," she said when we returned to the door.

"I know where it is. Thank you," I replied quickly. She shrugged and left me. I did exactly what Lyle said and scurried down the short flight of steps. The laundry room was a large, long room with cement floors and cement walls lined with washing machines, dryers, and bins. Toward the rear were the windows Lyle had described, but they were high up.

"Quick," I heard him say as he entered behind me. We hurried to the back. "You just snap the hinge in the middle and slide the window to your left," he whispered. "It's not locked."

"How do you know that, Lyle?" I asked suspiciously. He looked down and then up at me quickly.

"I've been here a few times. I even went so far as to stick my foot out, but I . . . I'm not ready," he concluded.

"I hope you will be ready soon, Lyle."

"I'll give you a boost up. Come on, before we're missed," he said, cupping his hands together for my foot.

"I wish you would come with me, Lyle," I said,

and put my foot into his hands. He lifted and I clutched at the windowsill to pull myself up. Just as he described, the latch opened easily and I slid the window to the left. I looked down at him.

"Go on," he coached.

"Thank you, Lyle. I know how hard it was for you to do this."

"No it wasn't," he confessed. "I wanted to help you. Go on."

I started to crawl through the window, looking around as I did so to be sure no one was nearby. Across the lawn was a small patch of trees and beyond that, the main highway. Once I was out, I turned and looked back in at him.

"Do you know where to go from here?" he asked me.

"No, but I just want to get away."

"Go south. There's a bus stop there and the bus will take you back to New Orleans. Here," he said, digging into his pants pocket and coming up with a fistful of money. "I don't need this in here."

He handed me the bills.

"Thank you, Lyle."

"Be careful. Don't look suspicious. Smile at people. Act like you're just on an afternoon outing," he advised, telling me things I was sure he had recited to himself a hundred times in vain.

"I'll be back to visit you someday, Lyle. I promise. Unless you're out before then. If you are, call me."

"I haven't used a telephone since I was six years old," he admitted. Looking down at him in the laundry room, I felt so sorry for him. He seemed small and alone now, trapped by his own insecurities. "But," he added, smiling, "if I do get out, I'll call you."

"Good."

"Get going . . . quickly," he said. "Remember, look natural."

He turned and walked away. I stood up, took a deep breath, and started away from the building. When I was no more than a dozen or so feet from it, I looked back and caught sight of someone on the third floor standing in the window. A cloud moved over the sun and the subsequent shade made it possible for me to see beyond the glint of the glass.

It was Uncle Jean!

He looked down at me and then raised his hand slowly. I could just make out the smile on his face. I waved back and then I turned and ran as hard and as fast as I could for the trees, not looking back until I had arrived. The building and the grounds behind me remained calm. I heard no shouting, saw no one running after me. I had slipped away, thanks to Lyle. I focused one more time on the window of Uncle Jean's room, but I couldn't see him anymore. Then I turned and marched through the woods to the highway.

I went south as Lyle had directed and reached the bus station which was just a small quick stop with gas pumps, candies and cakes, homemade pralines and soda. Fortunately, I had to wait only twenty minutes for the next bus to New Orleans. I bought my ticket from the young lady behind the counter and waited inside the store, thumbing through magazines and finally buying one just so I wouldn't be visible outside in case the institute had discovered I was missing and had sent someone looking for me.

I breathed relief when the bus arrived on time. I got on quickly, but following Lyle's advice, I acted as calmly and innocently as I could. I took my seat and sat back with my magazine. Moments later, the bus continued on its journey to New Orleans. We went right past the main entrance of the institution. When it was well behind us, I let out a breath. I was so happy to be free, I couldn't help but cry. Afraid someone would notice, I wiped away my tears quickly and closed my eyes and suddenly thought about Uncle Jean stuttering, "Jib . . . jib . . . "

The rhythm of the tires on the macadam highway beat out the same chant: "Jib . . . jib . . . jib."

What was he trying to tell me? I wondered.

When the New Orleans' skyline came into view, I actually considered not returning to my home and instead returning to the bayou. I wasn't looking forward to the greeting I would receive from Daphne, but then some of Grandmere Catherine's Cajun pride found its way into my backbone and I sat up straight and determined. After all, my father did love me. I was a Dumas and I did belong with him, too. Daphne had no right to do the things she had done to me.

By the time I got on the right city bus and then changed for the streetcar and arrived at the house, I was sure Dr. Cheryl had called Daphne and informed her I was missing. That was confirmed for me the moment Edgar greeted me at the door and I took one look at his face.

"Madame Dumas is waiting for you," he said, shifting his eyes to indicate all was not well. "She's in the parlor."

"Where's my father, Edgar?" I demanded.

He shook his head first and then he replied in a softer voice, "Upstairs, mademoiselle."

"Inform Madame Dumas that I've gone up to see him first," I ordered. Edgar widened his eyes, surprised at my insubordination.

"No, you're not!" Daphne shouted from the parlor doorway the moment I stepped into the entryway. "You're marching yourself right in here first." She stood there, her arm extended, pointing to the room. Her voice was cold, commanding. Edgar quickly moved away and retreated through the door that would take him through the dining room and into the kitchen, where I was sure he would make a report to Nina.

I took a few steps toward Daphne. She kept her arm out, her finger toward the parlor.

"How dare you try to tell me what to do and what not to do after what you've done," I charged, walking toward her slowly, my head high.

"I did what I thought was necessary to protect this family," she replied coldly, lowering her arm slowly.

"No, you didn't. You did what you thought was necessary to get rid of me, to keep me away from my father," I accused, meeting her furious gaze with a furious gaze of my own. She faltered a bit at my aggressive stance, her eyes shifting. "You're jealous of his love for me. You've been jealous ever since I arrived and you hate me because I remind you that he was once more in love with someone else."

"That's ridiculous. That's just another ridiculous Cajun—"

"Stop it!" I shouted. "Stop talking about the Cajun people like that. You know the truth; you know I wasn't kidnapped and sold to any Cajun family. You have no right to act superior. Few Cajun people I've known would stoop to do the sort of deceitful, horrible thing you tried to do to me."

"How dare you shout at me like that?" she said, trying to recover her superior demeanor, but her lips quivered and her body began to tremble. "How dare you!"

"How dare you do what you did at the institution!" I retorted. "My father is going to hear all about it. He's going to know the truth and . . . "

She smiled.

"You little fool. Go on upstairs to him. Go on and gaze upon your savior, your father, who sits in his brother's shrine of a room and moans and groans. I'm thinking about having him committed soon, if you must know. I can't go on like this."

She stepped toward me with renewed confidence.

"Who do you think has been running things around here? Who do you think makes this all possible? Your weak father? Ha! What do you think happens when he falls into one of his melancholic states? Do you think Dumas Enterprises just sits around and waits for him to snap out of it?

"No," she cried, stabbing herself with her thumb so hard it made me wince, "it always falls to me to save the day. I've been conducting business for years. Why, Pierre doesn't even know how much money we have or where it's located."

"I don't believe you," I said, but not with as much confidence as I had at first. She laughed.

"Believe what you like. Go on." She stepped back. "Go up to him and tell him about the horrible thing I tried to do to you," she said, and then stepped toward me again, lowering her voice sharply and narrowing her eyes into hateful slits. "And I'll explain to him and to everyone who wants or has to know how you've been so disruptive since you arrived, you nearly caused a fatal family crisis. I'll force the Andreas boy to confess to your sexual games in the art studio and I'll have Gisselle testify to your friendship with that whore from Storyville." Her eyes widened and then hardened to rivet on me as she continued.

"I'll have people believing you were a teenage prostitute in the bayou. For all I know, you were."

"That's a lie, a dirty, horrible lie," I cried, but she didn't soften. Her face, the face with the alabaster complexion and those beautiful eyes, turned into the cold visage of a statue as she gazed down at me.

"Is it?" She smiled again, a small, tight smile that drew her lips into thin lines. "I already have Dr. Cheryl's preliminary findings. He thinks you're obsessed with sex and will so testify if I like. And now you've gone and run away from the institution, embarrassing us even further."

I shook my head, but there was no denying her vicious determination to overcome my defiance.

"I'm going to see Daddy," I said in almost a whisper. "I'm going to tell him everything."

"Go on." She lunged forward and grabbed my shoulders to turn me to the stairway. "Go on, you little Cajun fool. Go tell your Daddy." She pushed me toward the steps. I threw her an angry look and then charged up the stairs, my tears flying off my cheeks.

When I got to the upstairs landing, I saw the door to Uncle Jean's room was shut tight, but I had to get Daddy to see me; I had to get him to let me in. I approached slowly and knocked and then pressed my cheek to the door and sobbed.

"Daddy, please . . . please, open up and let me in. Please, let me talk to you and tell you what Daphne did to me. I saw Uncle Jean, Daddy. I was with him. Please," I begged. I continued to sob softly. Finally, when he didn't open the door, I sank to the floor and embraced myself, my shoulders heaving with my deeper sobs. After all that had been done to me and after my great effort to return, I was still shut out; Daphne was still victorious. I sucked in some air and let my head fall back against the door. Then I let it fall back again and again until finally the door was pulled open and I looked up at Daddy.

His eyes were bloodshot, his hair disheveled. His shirt was out of his pants and his tie was loose. He looked like he had slept in his clothes. He had an unshaven face.

I struggled to my feet and ground the tears out of my eyes quickly.

"Daddy, I must talk to you," I said. He threw me a quick glance of deepest despair. Then his shoulders slumped and he backed into the room to let me enter.

The candles were nearly burned out around Uncle Jean's pictures so the room was very dimly lit. Daddy retreated to a chair by the pictures and sat down. His face was shadowed and hidden in the deepening gloom.

"What is it, Ruby?" he said, speaking as though it took all of his strength to pronounce the four words. I rushed to him and seized his hand, falling to my knees at his feet.

"Daddy, she took me to the institution this morning, supposedly to see Uncle Jean for his birthday, but when we got there, she had them lock me up. She tried to have them keep me there. It was horrible, but a nice young man helped me escape."

He raised his head and gazed at me with his sad eyes showing just a hint of surprise. He shook his head in a bewildered fashion, the tears still eking from beneath his lids.

"Who did this?"

"Daphne," I said. "Daphne."

"Daphne?"

"But I got to see Uncle Jean, Daddy. I sat with him and spoke to him."

"You did?" he asked, his interest growing. "How is he?"

"He looks very good," I said, wiping the tears off my cheeks with the back of my hand. "But he's afraid of people and doesn't talk to anyone.

Daddy nodded and lowered his head again.

"Except, I got him to say something, Daddy."

"You did?" he replied, his interest quickly returning.

"Yes. I told him to tell me something I could bring back to you and he said 'jib.' What did he mean, Daddy?"

"Jib? He said that?"

I nodded. Then I had to tell him the rest.

"Afterward, he started to scream and held his head in his hands. They had to take him back to his room."

"Poor Jean," Daddy said. "My poor brother. What have I done?" he asked in a heavy, flat voice. One of the candles went out and a shadow came to darken his eyes even more.

"What do you mean, Daddy? Why did he say 'jib'? Is it what this young man sitting beside me thought . . . something to do with sailing?"

"Yes," Daddy said. He sat back, his gaze far-off now. He looked like he could see into the past. And then he began to speak like one in a trance. "It was a nice day when we started out. I wasn't anxious to go at first. Jean kept taunting me, making fun of me for being so unathletic. 'You're as pale as a bank teller,' he said. 'No wonder Daphne would rather spend her time with me. Come on, get yourself into the fresh air. Let's test those muscles and limbs.'

"Finally, I gave in and accompanied him to the lake. The sky had already begun to change. There were storm clouds hovering along the horizon. I warned him about it, but he laughed and said I was just trying to find another excuse. We started sailing. I wasn't as ignorant about it as I pretended and I didn't like my younger brother telling me to do this or that like some galley slave.

"He seemed particularly arrogant to me that day. How I hated his self-confidence. Why didn't he have any doubts about himself like I had? Why was he so secure in the presence of women, especially Daphne?

"The clouds mounted, expanding, mushrooming, darkening, and the wind grew fiercer. Our sailboat rose and fell as the water became rougher and rougher. Every time I urged Jean to turn us back to shore, he laughed at me for not being adventurous enough.

"'This is where we test our manhood,' he declared. 'We look Nature in the eye and we don't blink.'

"I pleaded with him to be more sensible and he continued to mock me for being too sensible. 'Women don't like men to be reasonable and sensible and logical all the time, Pierre,' he said. 'They want a little danger, a little insecurity. If you want to win Daphne, take her out here on a day like this and let her scream as the spray hits her face and the sailboat tips and totters like it's doing now,' he cried.

"But the storm grew worse than even he expected. I was angry at him for putting us in this unnecessary danger. I was angry and jealous and during our battle against the storm, when he was struggling with the sail . . . " He sighed, closed his eyes, and then concluded, "I sent the jib flying around and it struck him in the head. It wasn't an accident," he confessed, and lowered his head to his hands.

"Oh, Daddy." I reached up and took his hand as he sobbed. "I'm sure you didn't mean to hurt him so badly. I'm sure you regretted it the moment you did it."

"Yes," he said, lifting his face from his palms. "I did. But that didn't change things and look where he is and what he is now. Look at what he was," he said, lifting one of the silver framed photographs. "My beautiful brother." Tears of remembrance clouded his eyes as he gazed at him. Then he sighed so deeply, I thought his heart had given out, and lowered his chin to his chest.

"He's still your beautiful brother, Daddy. And I think that he could make enough progress to leave that place. I really do. When I spoke to him and told him things, I felt he really understood."

"Did you?" Daddy's eyes lit up as he raised his head again. "Oh, how I wish that were true. I'd give anything now . . . all my wealth, if that were true."

"It is, Daddy. You must go to him more often. Maybe you should get him better treatment, find another doctor, another place," I suggested. "They don't seem to be doing anything more than making him comfortable and taking your money," I said bitterly.

"Yes. Maybe." He paused and looked at me and smiled. "You are a very lovely young lady, Ruby. If I was to believe in any forgiveness, it would be that you were sent here to me as an indication of that. I don't deserve you."

"I was almost shut away, too, Daddy," I said, returning to my original theme.

"Yes," he said. "Tell me more about that."

I described how Daphne had tricked me into accompanying her to the institution and all that had followed afterward. He listened intently, growing more and more upset.

"You've got to get hold of yourself, Daddy," I said. "She just told me she might have you committed, too. Don't let her do these things to you and to me and even to Gisselle."

"Yes," he said. "You're right. I've wallowed in self-pity too long and let things get out of hand."

"We've got to end all the lying, Daddy. We've got to cast the lies off like too much weight on a boat or a canoe. The lies are sinking us," I told him. He nodded. I stood up.

"Gisselle has to know the truth, Daddy, the truth about our birth. Daphne shouldn't be afraid of the truth either. Let her be our mother because of her actions and not because of a mountain of lies."

Daddy sighed.

"You're right." He rose, brushed back his hair, and straightened his tie, tightening the knot. Then he stuffed his shirt into his pants neatly. "I'm going down to speak with Daphne. She won't do anything like this to you again, Ruby. I promise."

"And I'll go in to see Gisselle and tell her the truth, but she won't believe me, Daddy. You'll have to come up and speak with her, too," I told him. He nodded.

"I will." He kissed me and held me for a moment. "Gabrielle would be so proud of you, so proud."

He straightened up, pulled back his shoulders, and left. I gazed at Uncle Jean's photographs for a moment and then I went to tell my sister who her mother really was.

"Where have you been?" Gisselle demanded. "Mother's been home for hours and hours. I kept asking for you and they kept telling me you weren't here. Then Mother came by and told me you ran away. I knew you wouldn't stay away long," she added confidently. "Where would you go, back to the bayou and live with those dirty swamp people?"

Because I didn't say anything immediately, her smile of self-satisfaction evaporated.

"Why are you standing there like that? Where were you?" she wailed. "I needed you. I can't stand that nurse anymore."

"Mother lied to you, Gisselle," I said calmly.

"Lied?"

I walked over to her bed and sat on it to face her in her wheelchair.

"I didn't run away," I said. "Don't you remember? We were going to the institution to see Uncle Jean, only—"

"Only what?"

"She had other intentions. She brought me there to leave me there as a patient," I said. "I was tricked and locked up like some mentally disturbed person."

"You were?" Her eyes widened.

"A nice young man helped me escape. I've already told Daddy what she did."

Gisselle shook her head in disbelief.

"I can't believe she would do such a thing."

"I can," I replied quickly. "Because she's not really our mother."

"What?" Gisselle started to smile, but I stopped her and seized her full attention when I reached out to take her hand into mine.

"You and I were born in the bayou, Gisselle. Years ago, Daddy would go there with our grandfather Dumas to hunt. He saw and fell in love with our real mother, Gabrielle Landry, and he made her pregnant. Grandpere Dumas wanted a grandchild, and Daphne couldn't have any, so he made a bargain with our other grandfather, Grandpere Jack, to buy the child. Only, there were two of us. Grandmere Catherine kept me a secret and Grandpere Jack gave you to the Dumas family."

Gisselle said nothing for a moment and then pulled her hand from mine.

"You are crazy," she said, "if you think I'll ever believe such a story."

"It's true," I said calmly. "The story of the kidnapping was invented after I turned up here to keep people believing Daphne was our real mother."

Gisselle wheeled herself back, shaking her head.

"I'm not a Cajun, too. I'm not," she declared.

"Cajun, Creole, rich, poor, that's not important, Gisselle. The truth is important. It's time to face it and go on," I said dryly. I was very tired now, the heavy weight of one of the most emotional and difficult days of my life finally settling over my shoulders. "I never met our mother because she died right after we were born, but from everything Grandmere Catherine told me about her and from what Daddy told me, I know

551

we would have loved her dearly. She was very beautiful."

Gisselle shook her head, but my quiet revelation had begun to sink in and her lips trembled, too. I saw her eyes begin to cloud.

"Wait," I said, and opened our adjoining door. I went to the nightstand and found Mother's picture and brought it to her. "Her name was Gabrielle," I said, showing the picture to Gisselle. She glanced at it quickly and then turned away.

"I don't want to look at some Cajun woman you say is our mother."

"She is. And what's more . . . she had another child . . . we have a half brother . . . Paul."

"You're crazy. You ARE crazy. You do belong in the institution. I want Daddy. I want Daddy! Daddy! Daddy!" she screamed.

Mrs. Warren came running from her room.

"What's going on now?" she demanded.

"I want my father. Get my father."

"I'm not a maid around here. I'm—"

"GET HIM!" Gisselle cried. Her face turned as red as a beet as she struggled to shout with all her might. Mrs. Warren looked at me.

"I'll get him," I said, and left Gisselle with her nurse cajoling her to calm down.

Daddy and Daphne were down in the parlor. Daphne was sitting on the sofa, looking surprisingly subdued. Daddy stood in front of her, his hands on his hips, looking much stronger. I gazed from him to Daphne, who shifted her eyes from me guiltily.

"I told Gisselle the truth," I said.

"Are you satisfied now?" Daphne fired at

Daddy. "I warned you she would eventually destroy the tender fabric that held this family together. I warned you."

"I wanted her to tell Gisselle," he said.

"What?"

"It's time we all faced the truth, no matter how painful, Daphne. Ruby is right. We can't go on living in a world of lies. What you did to her was bad. But what I did to her was even worse. I should never have made her lie, too."

"That's easy for you to say, Pierre," Daphne retorted, her lips trembling and her eyes unexpectedly tearing. "In this society, you will be forgiven for your indiscretion. It's almost expected for you to have an affair, but what about me? How am I to face society now?" she moaned. She was crying. I never thought I'd see tears emerge from those stone cold eyes, but she was feeling so sorry for herself, she couldn't prevent it.

In a way, despite all she had done to me, I felt sorry for her, too. Her world, a world built on falsehoods, on deceits, and propped up with blocks and blocks of fabrications was crumbling right before her eyes and she couldn't stop it.

"We all have a lot of mending to do, Daphne. I, especially, have to find the strength to repair the damage I've done to people I love."

"Yes, you do," she wailed.

He nodded. "But so do you. You know, you're not totally innocent in all this."

She looked up at him sharply.

"We have to find ways to forgive each other if we're to go on," he said.

He pulled back his shoulders.

"I'd better go up to Gisselle," he said. "And then afterward, I'd better go see my brother. I'll go to him as many times as I have to until I've gotten him to forgive me and to start his real recovery."

Daphne looked away. Daddy smiled at me and then left to go up to my sister to confirm and confess the truth.

For a long moment I just stood there looking at my stepmother. Finally, she turned toward me slowly, her eyes no longer clouded with tears, her lips no longer trembling.

"You haven't destroyed me," she said firmly. "Don't think you have."

"I don't want to destroy you, Daphne. I just want you to stop trying to destroy me. I can't say I forgive you for the dreadful thing you tried to do to me, but I'm willing to start anew and try to get along with you. If for no other reason than to make my father happy," I said.

"And maybe someday," I added, although it seemed impossible to me at the moment, "I'll call you Mother and be able to mean it."

She turned back to me, her eyes narrow, her face taut.

"You've charmed everyone you've met. Would you try to charm me, even after today?"

"That's really up to you, isn't it . . . Mother?" I said, and turned away to leave her pondering the future of the Dumas.

Epilogue

Truth, like a foundation in the bayou, has to be driven deeply to take hold, especially in a world where lies could storm in and wash away the paper-thin walls of illusion any time. Grandmere Catherine used to say the strongest trees are the ones whose roots go the deepest. "Nature has a way of finding out which ones don't go deep enough and they get washed away in the floods and the winds. But that ain't all bad because it leaves us with a world in which we can feel more secure, a world on which we can depend. Drive your roots deep, child. Drive your roots deep."

For better or for worse, my roots were now set in the garden of the Dumas family, and I had come from the timid, insecure Cajun girl who trembled on the family doorstep to the girl who had begun to understand a little more about who she really was.

In the days that followed, Gisselle grew strangely weaker and far more dependent on me than ever. I found her crying often and consoled her. She resisted learning about our Cajun background at first, and then, slowly, she began to ask a question here and there that led to my describing places and people. Of course, she was uncomfortable with the truth and made me swear dozens of times in dozens of ways never to tell anyone until she was ready for it to be told. I swore.

And then, one afternoon while I was up in

Gisselle's room telling her about something that had happened during final exams at school, Edgar appeared.

"Pardon me, Mademoiselle Ruby," he said, after knocking on the doorjamb to get our attention, "but there is someone here to see you. A young man."

"A young man?" Gisselle quipped before I could respond. "What's his name, Edgar?"

"He says his name is Paul, Paul Tate."

The blood left my face for a moment and then rushed back in so quickly, I grew faint.

"Paul?"

"Who's Paul?" Gisselle demanded.

"Paul's our half brother," I told her. Her eyes widened.

"Bring him up here," she ordered.

I hurried down and found him standing in the entryway. He looked so much older to me and a good six inches taller, and far more handsome than I could recall.

"Hi, Ruby," he said, beaming a wide, happy smile.

"How did you find me?" I gasped. I hadn't left a return address on the letter I had written because I didn't want him to find me.

"It wasn't all that hard. After I got your letter and knew you were in New Orleans at least, I went to Grandpere Jack with a bottle of bourbon one night."

"You wicked boy," I chastised. "Taking advantage of a drunk like that."

"I would have drunk with the devil if it meant

I could find you, Ruby." We gazed at each other for a moment, our eyes locked.

"Can I give you a hello kiss?" he asked.

"Yes. Of course."

He kissed me on the cheek and then stepped back to look around.

"You weren't exaggerating, you are rich. Have things gotten any better for you here since you wrote me that letter?"

"Yes," I said. He looked disappointed.

"I was hoping you would say no and I'd talk you into returning to the bayou, but I don't blame you for not wanting to leave this."

"My family is here, too, Paul."

"Right. So. Where is this twin sister?" he asked. I quickly told him about the automobile accident. "Oh," he moaned. "I'm sorry. Is she still in the hospital?"

"No. She's upstairs, dying to meet you. I've told her all about you," I said.

"You have?"

"Come on. She's probably tearing up the room because I've taken so long."

I led him upstairs. On the way he told me that Grandpere Jack was the same.

"You wouldn't recognize the house, of course. He's made it into the same pigsty he had in the swamps. And the grounds are peppered with holes. He's still looking for the buried money.

"For a time, after you had left, the authorities thought he might have done something to you. It was something of a scandal, but when nothing to lead anyone to believe it was found, the police

557

stopped hounding him. Of course, some people still believe it."

"Oh. That's terrible. I'll have to write to Grandmere's friends and let them know where I am and that everything is fine."

He nodded and I showed him into Gisselle's room.

Nothing brought the tint back into Gisselle's cheeks and the glint back into her eyes as much as a handsome young man did. We weren't sitting and talking five minutes before she was flirting, batting her eyelashes, swinging her shoulders, and smiling at him. Paul was amused, maybe even a bit overwhelmed with such feminine attention.

Toward the end of the visit, Gisselle surprised me by suggesting that we go visit him in the bayou one of these days soon.

"Would you?" Paul beamed. "I'd show you around, show you things that would make your eyes pop. I've got my own boat and now I have horses and—"

"I don't know if I could sit on a horse," Gisselle moaned.

"Of course you can," Paul said. "And if you couldn't, I'd sit with you."

She liked that idea.

"Now that you know where we are, you don't be a stranger either," Gisselle told him. "We've got to get to know each other more and more."

"I will. I mean, thanks."

"Are you going to stay for dinner?" she asked.

"Oh, no. I got a ride in with someone and I've got to meet him real soon," he said. I could tell he was making that up, but I didn't say anything.

Gisselle was disappointed but she lit right up when he leaned over to kiss her good-bye.

"You come back real soon, hear?" she called as we started out.

"You could have stayed for dinner," I told him. "I'm sure Daddy would like to meet you. My stepmother Daphne is snobby, but she wouldn't be impolite."

"No. I really do have to get back. No one knows I came here," he confessed.

"Oh."

"But now that I know where you are and I've met my other half sister, I won't be a stranger. That is, if you don't want me to be."

"Of course I don't. And one day soon, I will bring Gisselle out to the bayou."

"That would be great," Paul said. He looked down for a moment and then looked up quickly. "There hasn't been anyone else for me since you," he confessed.

"That's not right, Paul."

"I just can't help it," he said.

"Try. Please," I begged him. He nodded. Then he leaned forward quickly and kissed me. A moment later, like some memory from the past that had flowed through my thoughts, he was gone.

Rather than go right back to Gisselle, I went out to the garden. It was still a very beautiful day with the azure sky looking like an artist's canvas, sprinkled here and there with dabs of puffy white clouds. I closed my eyes and I might have fallen asleep had I not heard Daddy's voice.

"Somehow I thought I would find you out

here," he declared. "I took one look at that blue sky and said to myself, Ruby's somewhere outside enjoying the late afternoon."

"It is a pretty day, Daddy. How was your day?"

"Good. Ruby," he said, sitting down across from me and looking very serious, "I've made a decision. I want you and Gisselle to attend a private school next year. She needs special attention and . . . frankly, she needs you. Although she'd never confess that."

"Private school?" I thought about it, thought about leaving the few friends I had made, and especially, thought about leaving Beau. Things were still difficult between us because of what Daphne had told his parents, but we were finding ways to see each other from time to time.

"It would be better for everyone if you two attended a live-in, private school," he added, his meaning quite clear. "I will miss you both terribly, but I'll try to be there often," he promised. "It won't be far from New Orleans. Will you do it?"

"A school full of snobby rich Creoles?" I asked.

"Probably," he admitted. "But somehow, I don't think you're afraid of that anymore. You'll change them before they change you," he predicted. "It's the kind of place where you'll have great balls and parties, travel excursions, the best teachers and facilities, and most importantly, you'll get back to your art. And Gisselle will have the special care she needs."

"All right, Daddy," I said. "If you think that would be best."

"I do. I knew I could count on you. So," he

said. "What's your sister doing? How come she let you get some free time?" he joked.

"She's probably brushing her hair and talking on the phone about our male visitor," I said.

"Male visitor?"

I had never told him about Paul, and when I began, he surprised me by telling me he already knew.

"Gabrielle wasn't one to hide such a thing," he said. "I'm sorry I missed him."

"He'll be back and we promised to visit someday," I said.

"I'd like that. I haven't been to the bayou ever since . . . ever since."

He got up.

"I'd better go see my other princess," he declared. "Coming?"

"I just want to sit here a while longer, Daddy."

"Sure," he said. He leaned over and kissed me and then he went back in to see my sister.

I sat back and looked over the grounds, but I didn't see the beautifully manicured flowers and trees. Instead, I saw the bayou. I saw Paul and I, the two of us, young and innocent, in a pirogue, Paul poling, me leaning back, the Gulf breeze flowing over my face and lifting strands of my hair. We turned a corner and the marsh hawk was there on a branch looking down at us. He lifted his wings as if to greet us and welcome us into the secret world that lay within our most cherished dreams and deep down in the softness of our hearts.

And then he dove off the branch and flew above the trees toward the blue sky and left us alone, drifting toward tomorrow.

IF YOU HAVE ENJOYED READING THIS LARGE PRINT BOOK AND YOU WOULD LIKE MORE INFORMATION ON HOW TO ORDER A WHEELER LARGE PRINT BOOK, PLEASE WRITE TO:

WHEELER PUBLISHING, INC.
P.O. BOX 531-ACCORD STATION
HINGHAM, MA 02018-0531